**THEIR FATE WILL BE BORN IN A CRADLE
AMONG THE BULLRUSHES . . .
THEIR PASSIONS WILL BE IGNITED BY
BURNING FAITH AND BLAZING LOVE . . .**

MOSES—Sent with his warriors out of Thebes, he is a proud, headstrong Egyptian Prince . . . until he discovers the truth of his birth. A murderer, a slave, a fugitive—this is his fate, until his shepherd's staff becomes a scepter for the Greatest King of all.

IRI—Last born son of the Lion Clan, his disfigured face has made him a freak among men . . . but his talents as an armorer will make him a hero to a rebel band.

NEFTIS—The most beautiful of all the Children of the Lion. Hers should have been a Queen's life, but an evil Magus made her his love slave . . . a woman willing to do anything, even betray her own kind.

KAMOSE—A puppet king the Egyptians called Pharaoh. Hate so controlled his heart that even his son's life could be forfeited in his thirst to destroy a people . . . and their Prince, Moses.

SETH—This Child of the Lion, most blessed and most cursed, would have all his powers tested by a cruel magician, as the powers of darkness gathered for one last battle . . . to decide the fate of all mankind.

Volume X

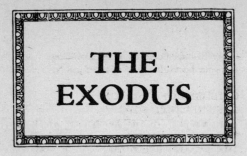

THE
EXODUS

PETER DANIELSON

Created by the producers of
Wagons West, San Francisco,
and **The First Americans.**

Book Creations Inc., Canaan, NY · Lyle Kenyon Engel, Founder

BANTAM BOOKS
NEW YORK · TORONTO · LONDON · SYDNEY · AUCKLAND

THE EXODUS

*A Bantam Book / published by arrangement with
Book Creations, Inc.*

Bantam edition / July 1989

Produced by Book Creations, Inc.
Lyle Kenyon Engel, Founder

ISBN 0-553-27999-8

Published simultaneously in the United States and Canada

PRINTED IN THE UNITED STATES OF AMERICA

O   0 9 8 7 6 5 4 3 2 1

Cast of Characters

Habiru

Moses—Prince of Egypt; leader of the Habiru
Aaron—Moses' older brother
Miriam—Moses and Aaron's sister
Jochebed—Moses, Aaron, and Miriam's mother
Joshua—Young boy who befriends Pepi

Children of the Lion

Seth—Moses' mentor; oldest and wisest of the clan
Demetrios—Mysterious owner of the largest fleet
             in the Great Sea
Iri—Chief Egyptian armorer
Neftis—Iri's unmarried older sister
Pepi—Neftis's son
Mai—Iri and Neftis's servant
Apedemek—Evil magus

Egyptians

Kamose—Drug-addicted king
Amasis—Regent; cult adept
Neb-mertef—Kamose's principal adviser
Set-Nakht—Neb-mertef's uncanny astrologer
Zoser—Wealthy merchant; friend to Iri and Neftis

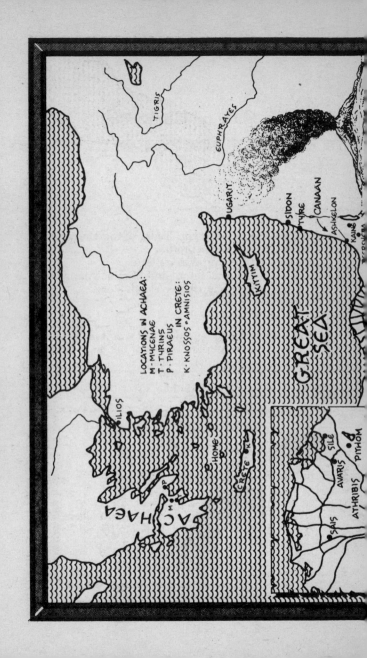

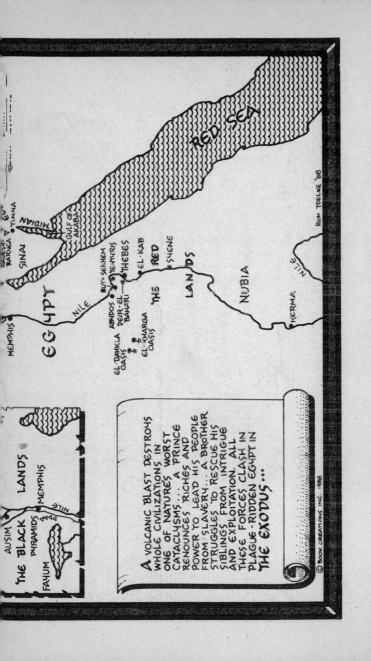

THE BLACK LANDS

AUSIM

PYRAMIDS

MEMPHIS

NILE

FAYUM

EGYPT

MEMPHIS

NILE

KADESH
BARNEA

TIMNA

SINAI

MIDIAN

GULF OF AKABA

RED SEA

BUTO
SEKHEM

ABYDOS

TENTYRIS

DEIR-EL
BAHARI

THEBES

EL-KAB

SYENE

EL-DAKHLA
OASIS

EL-KHARGA
OASIS

THE RED LANDS

NUBIA

KERMA

NILE

A VOLCANIC BLAST DESTROYS
WHOLE CIVILIZATIONS IN
ONE OF NATURE'S WORST
CATACLYSMS... A PRINCE
RENOUNCES RICHES AND
POWER TO LEAD HIS PEOPLE
FROM SLAVERY... A BROTHER
STRUGGLES TO RESCUE HIS
SIBLINGS FROM INTRIGUE
AND EXPLOITATION. ALL
THESE FORCES CLASH IN
PLAGUE-RIDDEN EGYPT IN
THE EXODUS...

RON TOELKE '86

© BOOK CREATIONS INC. 1986

Prologue

For the first time in many days, the caravan had camped within sight of water. Now, as they gathered around the guttering camp fire in the lee of the great rock that acted as a windbreak, they could see down the hill and beyond, to where the long finger of the Red Sea jutted deep into the cleft formed when the Great Rift had, countless centuries before, severed the land in two. As the evening waned, the full moon rose high and lay at just the point where its glaring orb was reflected in the water.

The chill circle of the moon, shimmering whitely in the faraway arm of the sea, was suddenly broken as a figure stepped between the seated crowd and the distant tableau. He stood tall and gaunt, and his long arms were raised high to draw the gathering's attention as the great voice boomed out.

"In the name of God, the merciful, the beneficent . . ."

The Teller of Tales! The focus of all eyes settled upon the speaker as he recited the familiar opening phrases of his eagerly awaited chant. "Hear now the tales of the Children of the Lion, the men and women of no tribe, and of their ceaseless wanderings through the nations beside the sea."

He turned and pointed to the scene behind him. "Yes, the sea—the unchanging and abiding sea. For long years the destinies of the Children of the Lion, the line of Belsunu and Ahuni and Kirta, had unfolded inland, on the shores of the great Nile, as they joined in the struggle against the marauding Hai Shepherd Kings, who had cut a bloody swath across the Valley of the Two Rivers, and Syria and Canaan, to settle in Egypt and usurp the mighty throne of the lords of the Two Lands.

"When at last the Shepherds had been driven from Egypt and destroyed, a new threat arose, one more deadly than any that had come before. After Amasis had brought the evil cult of the Great Mother of Egypt, there appeared in Nubia a magician named Apedemek, a member of a distant branch of the Children of the Lion, who had embraced the cause of evil, taking with him the wisdom and knowledge of his line and turning it to ends corrupt beyond all imagining."

His voice had a hard edge now, as the moon's reflection slid across the face of the waters behind him. "Apedemek confronted Seth, eldest and wisest Child of the Lion, in an epic struggle between two mighty minds. But Seth had met his match and was left broken and brain damaged. The evil Apedemek's Nubian army was then defeated by Egyptian troops under Prince Moses, the promised Deliverer both of Egypt and the enslaved Habiru, who bore him. While Seth withdrew to a quiet convalescence, Apedemek, exiled from Nubia, made his way northward, toward an Egypt unprepared for powers as great, as destructive, as his."

The sky was clear; the moon shone coldly. The Teller of Tales turned and lifted one long arm toward the bay below. "The sea . . ." he said. "Who could predict that this would be the tool God would use to work His will upon the earth? What mortal knows His unfathomable mind? Who could imagine that the thing that would at last cleanse Egypt would be the calm waters of the sea before us?

"The sea . . . the sea . . ." he intoned in a sighing voice that spoke of waves crashing against the distant shore. "Upon a different sea, to the faraway north, Seth was to find new life, new spirit, new hope. But upon this sea before us was to hinge the destinies of Egyptian and Habiru alike, as the time slowly came around for the great cataclysm that would change the face of the known world and leave no nation untouched!

"Hear now," he said, his voice sounding out over their heads, "of the calamity that shook the world! Hear of the *promised deliverance of the Habiru and of the miraculous working of the will of God! Hear of the cleansing of Egypt, and of the new and wondrous wanderings of the Children of the Lion in new lands! In new times! In a new world!"*

PART ONE

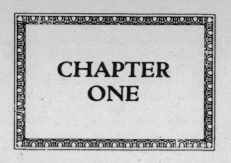

CHAPTER ONE

Crete

I

"That's the one," Heraclius of Tiryns said, shielding his mouth behind the cluster of grapes he held in his hand. "The one being shown to his couch."

Aias sneaked a furtive glance toward the tall, well-built young man being ushered into the great banquet hall of the palace of Minos. "Are you sure? He looks too young to be the man you described."

Heraclius motioned him to look away, lest their sudden interest in the most recent arrival draw attention from the merchants and nobles already assembled. "Don't look at him again until the banquet is well under way and everyone has had a bit to drink."

Aias turned back toward his mentor. The two half sat, half reclined on long, cushioned benches, awaiting the arrival of Minos, lord of Knossos and emperor of Crete. The big room with its patterned floor and colorful murals of bull dancers was better than half-full now, and the guests had already slipped off their sandals and pushed them under their couches. "Tell me more about him," Aias asked.

7

But a herald appeared at the door and announced, "Minos of Knossos, lord of the sea, emperor of Crete, servant of the goddess whose name be praised."

All scrambled to their feet and made obeisance as the king entered. The current Minos, heir to a name as well as a title, had taken office less than two years before. A young man, he nevertheless had resolution in his stance, and he gave a good impression; if not the man of affairs his recently deceased father had been, he seemed intelligent and assured. He gestured to the company to resume their places and took his own seat, while a boy, naked except for a wreath of flowers around his curly head, came forward to pour water over the king's hands and dry them with a patterned towel.

Heraclius looked around at the assembled nobles, traders, and shippers. The event was a dinner of state for Pronomus, Minos's envoy to mighty Egypt, and the guest was running late—disastrously so in terms of Knossos protocol, which required the king's entry to be the last. Such an affront would not be tolerated from any but the envoy to Egypt, a childhood friend of the king's. A messenger had come from the waterfront an hour ago telling of bad conditions for landing as the tide changed; Pronomus would be along anon. The king, keeping the spirit of the evening relaxed, had ordered the party to proceed without him.

"Tell me more about Demetrios," Aias asked again as the silence was broken by a dozen voices. "How did he become so rich and powerful at so young an age?"

Heraclius clapped his hands, and a slim youth came forward to serve him. "Wine and a mixing bowl." The custom was for the drinker himself to dilute wine with spring water at the table, a precaution against possible poisoning by someone seeking political gain. When the boy returned, Heraclius mixed wine from the tall jars and dipped first his own cup, then Aias's. "To your health," he toasted. "And success in the mission I shall propose to you."

Their heads almost touched as they leaned toward each other. Heraclius kept his voice quiet. "Nobody seems to know where Demetrios lives or where his offices are. He will sleep tonight aboard a boat of his fleet of merchant vessels, surrounded by a cadre of the finest bowmen on the shores of the Great Sea. When he is in his home territory, none enters his presence who has not been invited or who is not under constant surveillance by bodyguards."

"Then how do you expect me to—"

"Just listen, for now," Heraclius said. The two were virtually lips-to-ear. "Nobody knows where he comes from, but Demetrios could not have been his birth name. Look at that nose; it is not Achaean."

"Farther east, I'd say," Aias guessed. "Shinarian? Elamite? Damascene?"

Heraclius shrugged. "He's too light skinned to be Egyptian. And those eyes! Have you ever heard of a blue-eyed Egyptian? As for the riches—there's a mystery. It is possible to trace his fleet of ships to a cartel owned half a century ago by a black ex-slave named Akhilleus. But how this lad came by it, no one knows. One day the cartel was in charge; the next, he was the sole owner." He scowled. "Would that someone had drowned him a day before! He's been a thorn in my side ever since he assumed command."

"So there's more in this than a mere matter of commercial gain," Aias ventured. "You have an ulterior motive."

"I don't know the man at all," Heraclius denied. "But if he and his representatives have come between me and a lucrative deal with Minos once, they've done it fifty times. If it weren't for them, I'd be living in a house not much less opulent than this palace, and I'd be asking Minos to dinner rather than the other way round."

"Ah. And you want—?"

Heraclius kept a fake smile on his lips, but his eyes were as hard as the rock walls around them. "I want him out of my way. And I'll pay whatever it takes to get the job done. I want a clear road to Minos's ear. I want to be the merchant whose ships carry Minos's goods to market around the Great Sea. I want to be second only to Minos, and only this outlander's presence stands in my way."

Aias had half turned to get a better look at the subject of the conversation. Demetrios, across the room from them, reclined with a studied masculine grace. His bronzed limbs looked powerful, and he wore a chiton cut after the Minoan pattern but decorated with the unmistakable, fabulously expensive purple dyes of distant Tyre.

Aias looked back at Heraclius. "You're serious?"

"If I jest, may the gods strike me dead this moment," Heraclius replied. "Make me first in trade in the kingdom, and I will make you rich. And ever after, so long as I dwell in the king's favor, so shall you dwell there with me."

"Let me think on this," Aias said. "The evening will be a long one. When we are again out in the air, I will give you my answer."

It was odd that here, at a dinner party of state, not a single woman was present except among the entertainers. This was a society in which the principal god was female, and her priestesses were in charge of all celebrations having to do with childbirth, animal husbandry, agriculture, and the mysteries of the seasons. It was a sign of a changing world, with changing rules, that women might still control the mysteries, but men increasingly controlled the world of business.

Now the center of the floor was given to the musicians and dancers. One slim girl, wearing a long dress that bared her high and fetchingly pointed breasts and whose areolae had been enhanced with rouge, played the double flute while another, similarly adorned, strummed a kithara.

These girls had been trained but not chosen for the bull dance. They had the requisite grace and lovely, supple bodies but had had the misfortune to come up for the trials at a time when there were few vacancies and many qualified applicants. Generally the applicants' disappointment was easily solaced; dancers appearing before Minos made good money and were spared the dangers of the bullring. Many such had also found rich protectors in their audience.

Trained bull dancers were also acrobats of unparalleled skill. At one end of the hall a daredevil girl acrobat, having set razor-sharp swords point-up on the floor, leapt up and performed a backward flip, landing on her hands amid the blades, only to spring once more into the air and land outside the circle of weapons.

The guests paid little attention for the most part; their minds not yet addled by wine, they were absorbed in catching up with business or with the latest gossip from the exchange. Only Demetrios remained aloof. The merchant nearest Demetrios had spoken to him, and the polite, noncommittal reply had kept the questioner at arm's length.

Now, as the dancers and musicians retired, a new guest appeared at the door. As the king rose, all conversation ceased. Minos held his arms wide, welcoming the latecomer.

"My friends," he said in a strong, young voice, "let me present Pronomus, envoy to Egypt, returned from a month in Thebes." He silenced polite and premature applause with a wave of his royal hand. "Pronomus has earned my blessing and will be richly rewarded for initiating serious talks toward a trade agreement with Amasis, regent of Egypt. If brought to a successful conclusion, the agreement will be more favorable to us than any struck between his nation and ours."

There was a murmur of approval, and the king continued in an appreciative voice. "Come, take your seat beside me, Pronomus, and tell my distinguished guests how things fare in Egypt. If you and Amasis have restored the friendly relations that existed between Crete and Egypt before the Shepherd Kings' invasion of the Nile, we all stand to prosper from it."

Pronomus, smiling, bowed and stepped out of his sandals. Immediately one of the serving boys rushed to bathe his feet and hands in scented water. "My thanks to great Minos for his generous comments and for the undeserved benison of his gracious patronage. I hope some day I can come to earn such praise."

He waited for the polite applause to end before continuing. "As His Majesty suggests, there is reason for hope in Egypt. A rich and lucrative market will open, one that will make wealthy any who has the intelligence to exploit it and the resources to back up his ideas. Although our agreement is tentative, I have reason to think that on my next trip to the Egyptian capital—"

A rich and vibrant voice interrupted, and all eyes went to the speaker, Demetrios. "Your pardon, but could you tell us if there will be civil war?"

"War?" echoed Minos, incredulous. "Did you say war?"

II

Demetrios did not react immediately to the king's alarm. He remained in the same relaxed position on the couch and drank sparingly of his wine before speaking again. When he continued, the words had the ring of authority. "Your Majesty, of course, knows the thoroughly scandalous reputation of my . . . uh . . . network of spies."

Indeed, Demetrios had a reputation for omniscience, and it was rumored that he had an informant in every royal house in each major city of the Aegean.

Minos frowned, turning to glare at Pronomus. "It was my understanding that the regent had stabilized the country. At least that was the burden of the messages you sent me from Egypt."

Pronomus flushed with embarrassment. "Indeed, Majesty, there are rumors. I thought it best not to dignify them by giving them greater weight than they deserved."

Demetrios waved one bronzed hand, nonchalantly dismissing the subject. "I see I shall have to keep my own counsel. Of course, if a friend were to request advice . . . but no, the envoy is the expert here, and I would do best to keep silent."

Minos scowled. "Perhaps the noble Demetrios would share this advice with us? I am sure we all have urgent interests in Egypt, which would be materially affected by news of impending revolt."

All eyes went to the young man in the purple chiton. Pronomus's eyes blazed with anger and resentment.

"Very well, Majesty," Demetrios consented. He stood. "I have heard that King Kamose returned a broken man, world-weary, from his long expedition to destroy the Hai strongholds in Canaan and Syria. Amasis, who had reigned in Kamose's absence for nearly two decades, did not choose to relinquish the throne to a man in such a condition—king or no. Therefore, he quickly threw Kamose into prison and usurped power in Thebes—"

A dozen voices cried out at once. "What? What are you saying? Deposing the rightful king is treason!"

The king silenced the outburst. "These are serious charges,

Demetrios! It was my understanding the king was under medical care for his wounds."

Again Demetrios waved one well-manicured hand. "Please forgive me. I should not have interjected mere rumor into the conversation. I withdraw everything I have said."

This had the planned effect, which was to negate his own dissembling and give his statements immense authority. "No, no, Demetrios," the king said. "Please continue. We all want to hear what your sources have told you. Our questions can surely wait until after your recitation."

"I am honored by your exquisite courtesy, Majesty." Demetrios inclined his head. "As I understand it, the late vizier of Egypt, Baliniri, foreseeing an immediate takeover of the entire armed forces by Amasis, seized upon a pretext for ordering the Theban troops, under the nominal command of young Prince Moses, upriver to Nubia to deal with a minor insurrection." He reached for his wine cup and drank sparingly before continuing. He could see the puzzlement and chagrin in the faces around him; none of those present had heard this version of the events of the past year. "To resume: While Moses was away with the Theban garrison, Amasis attempted the murders of Queen Mara and Princess Thermutis, who were the only proper claimants to the throne if something untoward should happen to Kamose—or if Moses, the ranking member of the royal household, did not return from the border war."

Extreme concern darkened the king's expression. "Amasis ordered the assassinations of the reigning queen and a princess of the blood?"

"Yes, Majesty, but the attempt failed. The women escaped into exile in the western oases, where they now live under the protection of the Desert Legion, the two women's armies that control the trade routes between Egypt and Nubia. When Moses' forces defeated the Nubians and installed their own man on the Nubian throne after King Nehsi, whom we all mourn, died—"

"What? Nehsi dead?" someone erupted from across the room.

"Oh, yes," Demetrios confirmed. "I'm sorry. Didn't you know?" He turned to the king again. "Majesty! I'm shocked!"

"Go on," Minos said, lips pursed. It was obvious that he

was not well represented in the upper reaches of the Nile and that someone in the diplomatic service would pay dearly.

"Very well. While Moses was conquering Nubia—and, incidentally, completing his military education—two things happened: First, Baliniri was assassinated at Amasis' order, and second, Kamose escaped from Amasis' imprisonment and disappeared into the countryside. Even as I speak, he is gathering forces to topple Amasis and restore himself to power."

The king and the audience looked incredulous, much to Demetrios's enjoyment.

The young man went on: "The pivotal factor is the army that Moses took to Nubia. He is understandably reluctant to return to Thebes. If he merely returns the army to Thebes, Amasis will seize control of them and imprison Moses—perhaps assassinate him as a much-feared rival. The prince has been delaying the army's return, using as an excuse the injury suffered by his mentor and teacher, Seth of Thebes, during the crucial battle that won the Nubian war."

"You mean Seth, the Child of the Lion?" someone asked.

"The same," Demetrios verified. "Which brings up an interesting new element in the story—a mysterious magus of unparalleled might. He reportedly bested Seth of Thebes, damaging his brain."

"This magus is a man to be feared, I take it?" Minos said. "What is his name?"

"Apedemek," Demetrios answered. "He will be an unsettling and uncontrollable influence in political events. Given the description brought back to me, he will undoubtedly make his way downstream to infiltrate the volatile and unstable situation in Thebes."

"Apedemek. Apedemek. Have I heard that before?" Minos narrowed his eyes.

"Not many outside Nubia have, Majesty. If he ever had any intimates, they are now food for worms. Two things are certain: He has changed his name and has disguised his appearance. His only distinctive physical characteristic is that he is quite tall."

Minos frowned. "Then he could be here among us!"

"I highly doubt it." Demetrios's tone was somber. "I cannot reassure you totally, but the degree of probability is low."

"That is not enough to set my mind at ease. Please tell me more about him."

"He apparently functions best as a kingmaker and prefers not to rule directly. He has the ability to control strong minds as well as weak ones, and he can convince all with whom he comes into contact of virtually any illusion he wishes."

Around the room all the guests were sitting upright now. Demetrios found his sandals under the couch and put them on. "I have spoken out of turn, Majesty. I have meddled in the affairs of the noble and distinguished Pronomus and spoiled a triumphal homecoming that was richly merited. I can only beg your forgiveness." From the looks on everyone's face, no one believed these disclaimers. "Both your guests and I would profit, Majesty, if I were to take a breath of fresh air. By your leave? Majesty? My lords?" He bowed and, at a nod from the king, made his way out the door.

III

Outside the air was cool and the night clear. Demetrios strolled down the courtyard's long colonnade of painted columns, looking at the sky and at the towering, moonlit shape of Mount Ida. He whistled tunelessly and in a moment was joined by his companion Hieron, who had been lurking in the shadows.

The moon's bright rays fell on Hieron's broad smile. "I heard most of that," he said, chuckling heartily. "Poor Pronomus. He'll hate you forever."

Demetrios's smile was a wry one, and his voice had nothing of the idle-rich languor he had forced into it for the benefit of the gathering. "He has company—two men eyeing me all evening. Unless I miss my guess, one of them owes me an ill turn and won't wait long to deliver it."

"Heraclius?"

"The same. He was chatting in a very conspiratorial fashion with a big man named Aias. I bribed a servant to give me his name. I'll wager this Aias was being hired to do me ill."

"I'll notify—"

"Don't. I've handled worse. If he amounted to anything, he wouldn't pay attention to a disgruntled, out-of-favor merchant like Heraclius."

"In the end he may have his uses—for our side."

Demetrios nodded. "You're learning. As for that performance I gave in there: I didn't want Minos giving Pronomus authority to conclude an Egyptian trade agreement just yet. The best way to put a crimp in his plans was to tell the truth—as much as we know."

"Which isn't anywhere near enough," Hieron reminded him. "I must take a trip there myself, and soon."

"Indeed you must." He put a hand of friendship on Hieron's sturdy shoulder. Ten years older than his employer, Hieron was losing hair prematurely and as a result looked much older. Demetrios smiled affectionately. "Having you look into the matter is like having a second pair of eyes."

"I hope never to stop deserving your trust," Hieron said. "Do we sail in the morning?"

"The day after. I have business in port. A message came from Cadmus while you were in the city."

"I'll tag along, if you don't mind," Hieron said. "It will be nice to see old Cadmus again. He's been a wise and faithful associate."

"Quite true. No credit is due me: I merely inherited Cadmus's services from my predecessors. I suppose I could be commended for not being stupid enough to fire him." He paused. "You know, you couldn't fire anyone like Cadmus; you could only have him assassinated. He knows too much to be allowed to live except as a trusted associate."

"And his supposed profession is perfect, getting him into the innermost circles without exposing him to counter-surveillance."

Demetrios's face was a humorous mask of mock gravity. "Furthermore, he doesn't cost me a thing. He's grown rich at his job. If I could teach every spy on my payroll to be self-sustaining like that—"

Hieron put a warning hand on his arm. "Someone's coming. Let them see you go back inside the door at the other end of the portico. I'll stay behind this wall. I'll meet you at the ships in the morning and tell you what I've overheard."

Demetrios peeked around the corner at the approaching men. "They're the ones," he noted. "Keep your ears open." He moved out into the moonlight and made his way to the far door.

Heraclius and Aias had stopped between two tapered columns. Heraclius was about to speak, but he turned to see Pronomus bearing down on them.

"Greetings, noble Pronom—" Heraclius began.

"Did you see that?" he fumed impatiently. "That ill-born bastard ruined my homecoming! I'll be lucky if I'm not given a new assignment on some benighted island where you can't drink the water or eat the food and all the women have the pox!"

"Softer, my dear Pronomus," Heraclius urged. "The night air has ears." He beckoned Pronomus closer and steered the envoy and Aias into the center of the court, where eavesdroppers could be seen before they could come close enough to hear. "We will look like three friends enjoying the night air."

"I swear, I could kill him with my bare hands. . . ." Pronomus seethed.

Heraclius and Aias exchanged glances. "Patience," Heraclius soothed. "Chew bitter and spit sweet, I say. Act as though you hadn't a worry. Then, when your enemy least expects it—well, who knows what might happen?"

"The upstart! The nerve of him!"

"Patience, friend. He still has another day or so in port. One of my agents posed as a servant to Cadmus, the bull breeder, and brought Demetrios an invitation. He's going over tomorrow to Amnisios, on the coast, to see his old friend."

Pronomus's eyes widened. "Are you thinking what I'm thinking?"

"That Cadmus is his spy in Knossos? It seems beyond doubt!"

"Then we have him at last! For two years I've been trying to figure out who was Demetrios's man here." Pronomus smiled, his face craggy and ill-humored in the clear light of the moon.

"Not so fast," Heraclius counseled. "Cadmus is but the minnow with which we bait the hook. Tomorrow we catch bigger fish."

"Demetrios?"

Heraclius smiled humorlessly. "I know you have shipping interests that will prosper the moment he's out of the way, just as I—"

"Me? I assure you—"

"Come now. You're among friends. We both know about your partnership with Lukios. Relax. What Minos doesn't know won't hurt him. My good friend Aias here and I have already begun to devise a plan. You and I could become partners. Any way you look at the matter, the job would be worth whatever we pay Aias."

"When you put it that way . . ." Pronomus hedged.

"Then we are agreed. Here's my hand on the matter. Don't worry about the details."

Pronomus hesitated, then grasped Heraclius's hand. "I'm your man. And you, Aias? Have you done . . . comparable deeds before?"

Aias smiled. "I can do the job."

Heraclius's eyes glittered in the moonlight. "We might take two birds with one stone. Cadmus is old. At court he is well protected, but in Amnisios, he lives a simple life, with only one or two house servants."

Aias put up a cautionary hand. "I'll have to see what it's like when I get there, but if the opportunity presents itself, I'll try. I do guarantee to kill Demetrios." He paused. "Uh, Heraclius, you did promise half the money up front?"

"That I did, my friend. And a handsome bonus if no clues are left for the king's guards."

"And twice the sum if you murder Cadmus," Pronomus offered.

Heraclius smiled and took each man by the hand. "Here's a partnership sealed. Come with me to my villa."

"You go ahead," Pronomus said. "Minos wants to see me—I don't look forward to that. Heraclius, my trust in you is complete. Make a deal with Aias. Any amount you settle upon will be acceptable to me."

*   *   *

From the shadows behind the wall Hieron cursed silently as the threesome parted. He had not heard one word in three. He fretted, knowing that Demetrios would not allow himself to be escorted to Amnisios by a full complement of bodyguards; it was not his way to travel in that style on Crete. How could Demetrios's safety be assured, then? How does one protect a man who won't let himself be protected?

But his panic soon passed. He cursed aloud, spat in the dust, and straightened his back. He vowed to trust Demetrios's sixth sense for danger. Let trouble come! He would deal with it then, not beforehand!

IV

The morning fog had broken, and the sun shone bright and clear on the sea as Demetrios and Hieron wound their way down to the little port of Amnisios. Below, jutting out into the wine-dark sea, the tiny peninsula with its curving, graceful harbor sheltered a dozen fishing vessels, and the waterfront buildings gleamed whitely in the sunshine.

"It'll be good to see Cadmus again," Hieron remarked. "I suppose he'll be up and about already. He likes his work." He looked around. "So far, so good. No sign of anyone."

"We've been followed all the way," Demetrios corrected him. "It's Aias all right."

Hieron's hand went unconsciously to the ivory handle of the dagger at his belt. "I wish you'd let me bring a sword and a bow. And you! Not even a knife!"

"I am armed, in my way," Demetrios assured him. "You've never seen me in action, old friend." He smiled. "Now don't worry. Come along. That's Cadmus's villa on the promontory."

"It's quite a place! There are kings around the Aegean who have smaller estates."

"Cadmus has done well, no doubt about it." They walked along the gently curving path toward the village. "He not only has the exclusive contract to provide all the bulls used in the bull dance but recently has added a school for the bull dancers."

"A school?"

"Yes. The bull dance was traditionally performed by the sons and daughters of the poor because nobody else wanted to do it. But recently it's become the favored sport among the moneyed set, whose young ones are idle and bored. They bribe the Black Guard's officers to let them substitute for the regular dancers."

"But that's dangerous!"

"Of course it is. And if their incompetence betrays their impostor status, they not only risk death on the horns of the bulls, but—if they survive—being arrested for profaning the sacred ceremony. Minos will brook no sacrilege in his palace."

"Has anyone been caught at it?"

"Only one—by the bull."

Hieron lowered his voice. "I saw Aias duck behind a tree." They left the main road, avoiding the well-paved path down to the seaport, and took the rutted wagon road across the hills to Cadmus's villa. Hieron glanced back unhurriedly. "We've lost our shadow. But I'll bet he's still there somewhere."

"Let him come," said Demetrios. "I'm looking forward to the encounter."

The reunion with Cadmus was a warm one. Servants called the old man up from the bullring, and he met his visitors with open arms, calling for food and drink. "I knew you would not leave without coming to see me!"

Demetrios's face suddenly took on a somber cast. "Then you did not send a messenger to me? Saying you wished me to visit you?"

Cadmus rubbed his bald head. "Why, no, young master. I learned only last night that you were in port. Had I known earlier, I would have come to the palace to greet you."

Demetrios and Hieron exchanged surprised glances. Demetrios's eyes narrowed. "We have a problem."

"I don't understand," Hieron said.

"Don't you see? There's a good possibility that Heraclius has found Cadmus out. He's penetrated Cadmus's cover and now knows Cadmus is my spy inside Knossos."

"Then Pronomus and this lout who's been following us know, as well."

"Your pardon, my masters," said Cadmus. "But could someone please explain what is going on here?"

"Never mind," Demetrios told him. "I'll take care of it. Meanwhile, we can enjoy our visit. A sharp old fellow like you must have a few tidbits to pass along after this many months."

"Come," Cadmus said. "I told the servants to bring our provender to the shaded seats above the bull court. While we're talking, you can watch my pupils go about their lessons."

Demetrios put an affectionate hand on the old man's shoulder as they went out onto the terrace. The bull court below was an exact replica of the one in Minos's Labyrinth, where the bull dances took place before the assembled court and the priestesses of the goddess on festival days. "The renewed interest in your school among the idle sons and daughters of the rich is well-known. Are these"—he gestured at the slim youths in the court below, capering naked, doing cartwheels and flips—"perhaps some of them?"

Cadmus chuckled. "Yes. I work them from morning until night. There isn't an ounce of fat on any of them. Nor, I might add, is there any surplus left in their purses. They pay dearly for their revolt against boredom."

He sat and gestured to the others to join him on the long bench. "To answer your question, my master, there was something I wanted to bring to your attention. I visited the mainland recently, where my host took me to see the oracle at Delphi."

"What an adventure!" Demetrios enthused.

Cadmus nodded in agreement. "It was nothing like what I had been led to imagine. In the first place, the girl is mad, and to make her even more mad, she is given a drug that fires her up. It's supposed to be a solemn atmosphere, but it was all I could do not to burst out laughing when she started screeching like a hyena."

"Indeed. And what did she tell you?"

"Apparently the world as we know it is going to come to an end. Some time soon everything's going to be wiped away. Poseidon—he's one of their most powerful gods—is going to

destroy all the works of men. Funny . . . I almost believed it.
It sent chills up my spine, let me tell you!"

Cadmus looked Demetrios in the eyes. "I asked when
this was expected to occur. 'Not in your lifetime, old man.
But in the lifetime of the next generation.' " He looked at
Hieron and then back at Demetrios. "In *your* generation, my
masters."

Demetrios patted the old man's bony knee. "The prediction is not new to me. The seers and magi of the four corners
of the Great Sea have been hinting at just such weighty
matters for six months now. The wording in some cases is
amazingly similar to yours. I have a dozen astrologers at work
trying to pinpoint a date."

"Does this not frighten you?"

"Why should it?" Demetrios asked. "All things are in the
hands of the gods. If I panic, it is not for the gods to
propitiate me; it is for me to amend my attitude. We will
speak more of this later. Meanwhile, would you show Hieron
the indoor gardens? I know how proud you are of them—with
justification—and Hieron's many interests include the culti-
vation of rare medicinal herbs. I will take my ease out here."

"Very well, my master. Shall I dismiss the dancers?"

"Please. I would like to be alone to think. I will join you
when the sundial reaches the upright mark."

Cadmus reached overhead to ring a bell. The dancers
below scattered, leaving the bull court empty. Concerned,
Hieron looked back once at Demetrios, then let himself be
led away.

Demetrios moved down to the lip of the ring. He looked
up at the blue sky and smiled to himself.

"You can come out now," he called. "I know you're here."

V

Aias's first reaction was to shrink back behind the double
pillar that held up the far end of the portico. How had
Demetrios spotted him?

"Come on," Demetrios encouraged, his voice closer now. And all of a sudden there he was, peering around the edge of the pillar and looking at Aias with unreadable blue eyes. "It's all right. You're safe. Talk to me."

Aias's hand curved around the hilt of the dagger at his belt. *I could do it now! All I'd have to do is*— But then he let out a long breath, released his grip on the knife, and stepped into the warm sunshine. "How did you know you were being followed?"

"You're not very good at it," Demetrios said simply. He kept himself at rather more than arm's length, and he squinted against the sun's glare when he moved into the light. "I gather you haven't done anything like this before. Shadowing and eliminating a man for pay?"

Aias said nothing. His eyes remained glued to Demetrios, who was conspicuously unarmed. *Why do I not just strike him and get it over with? Why do I just stand here?* But the issue seemed less pressing now.

"Your reputation for omniscience is well earned," Aias said at last.

"Come," Demetrios urged. He turned his back casually, as if he had not just accused Aias of having been hired to murder him, and walked to the stairs that led down to the bullring. "I've never been down here. I've never even been to one of the bull dances at court during the festival season." He turned at the bottom and looked up. "Don't you want to satisfy your curiosity? Haven't you wondered what it's like to stand on the grass, waiting for the bull?"

Aias lumbered after him. But as he reached the bottom, there was a movement very close to him, almost too swift for the eye to follow. Suddenly there was a gleaming bronze sword, with a point as sharp as a housewife's needle, at his throat. He was backed against the wall, with Demetrios's icy blue eyes boring into his own and a humorless smile on the young man's lips. His own heart was pounding.

"There, now," Demetrios whispered. "That's one of a number of rules you've broken today: Never give your opponent the advantage. Otherwise—" The sword pulled back, still pointing at Aias's throat, and Demetrios's stance was as deadly as a snake about to strike. But instead he stepped back, saluted with the sword, and tossed it carelessly to the ground. He turned his back again and strode out onto the green grass.

Aias released a quivering breath and felt the perspiration run down his sides.

"It must cost Cadmus a fortune to keep this grass in such condition," Demetrios observed. "But if he's training dancers for the court ring, everything must be precisely as it is at court." He strode to the center of the ring and stood facing the bronze double doors at one end of the arena. "This is where the first dancer stands. The other dancers stand behind the barriers, watching the animal as it comes into the ring." He raised his arms. "As trumpets blow, the doors are flung wide open by the trainers. The bull enters! The crowd screams! The doors have all been closed. But now there is this one slim figure standing in the middle of the ring."

Aias stood in the sunshine, his hands on his hips. "Are you mad? There's no bull here. Why are you—?"

But Demetrios's enthusiasm—plus a certain theatrical quality—was affecting Aias. In his mind's eye he could almost see the crowds and the bewildered, angry animal in the center of the ring, its beady eyes darting back and forth, its great nostrils sniffing the wind, its head tossing, the gleaming tips of its horns glittering in the sunshine. He could see the sturdy hooves pawing the ground. He could see the huge hump of muscle atop the tall back. The bull charged, head down, horns aimed at Demetrios's belly!

Demetrios leapt into the air!

To Aias's amazement, the young man ran directly at the great animal, and at the last possible split second grasped it by the horns and executed a flawless flip, landing gracefully behind the bull.

The crowd cheered. The drums beat. The horns blew.

And now the bull stood looking at him, Aias! Flecks of foam hung from its bearded lips. The little eyes looked him up and down. Aias backed away. The animal pawed the ground once, twice, then charged.

He screamed, reaching for the dagger at his belt but dropping it! He ran, hearing the pounding hooves behind him! He turned, trapped in a corner, but saw Demetrios's bronzed body travel across the ring in a faultless series of cartwheels, ending in a flourish that brought him just under the bull's nose, where he reached out and tweaked the animal by the nostril, just as it tried to turn in midcharge. It brought itself instead to a clumsy halt, nearly dropping to its knees.

Demetrios danced around it, leapt into the air, bounced, and soared high above the bull's back to land on the far side of the huge animal.

The crowd went wild, screaming for more.

The bull's back was turned to Aias now, and he took the occasion to edge nervously toward the center of the ring, where his knife lay in the grass. He sidled closer, closer. But then the wind changed.

The bull sniffed, turning first its head, then the great, brutal body. It pointed the awesome, spreading horns at Aias. The hump on the bull's back stood higher than Aias's head, though Aias was much taller than an average man.

"Help me!" he cried. "Demetrios! Help me!"

The bull lowered its huge head, bringing the broad horns to gut level. Every motion spoke of limitless power.

"Help me!"

But there was no one in the ring. Aias ran for the barriers, but the doors had been shut and sealed.

With a terrible crash the heavy body slammed into the thick boards just to one side, and Aias saw the planks splinter. The bull had caught one horn in the wood. Aias moved away, heading for the center of the ring as the bull pulled free.

"Help!" Aias shrieked, looking around frantically. At the top of the stands sat Demetrios, looking slim and fit, his arms folded.

"Get me out of here!" Aias cried out.

Demetrios just sat looking at him.

The pounding of heavy hooves on the grass caused Aias to turn just in time to see the monster bearing down on him. He dived to one side, hit the ground, rolled, and felt the huge body thundering past, a razor-sharp horn just missing his face!

"Have you no mercy?" Aias screamed. "Open the gate!"

The bull turned, tossing its head. Aias knew it was all over for him. He could not escape. The knife he had dropped lay on the grass between the bull's forefeet. The animal's dark eyes blinked; the head lowered, and it charged. Aias closed his eyes and held his breath, knowing it would be his last.

But then there was nothing: no sound, no drums, no trumpets, no screaming crowd. He opened his eyes. The bull had vanished.

He turned. Demetrios stood five paces away, regarding him with serious eyes.

"We have some talking to do," he said. "I'll send to Cadmus for wine and olives. You and I have no quarrel, but I need to know some things. I pay generously—in coin other than money—for information."

"Lead," Aias said, wilting. "I will follow."

Demetrios went through the now open doorway and into the stands. His back was to Aias, but the hired assassin made no move to exploit the advantage. He followed the young man, feeling as if a great weight had been lifted from his shoulders.

Three days later Aias stood before the arched entrance of Heraclius's villa. He gazed at the friezes above the door, at the first-growth wood in the half-timbered walls, and smiled. He hit the bell to announce his presence once, twice.

To his surprise, Heraclius himself opened the door wide. "Aias! Why have I not heard from you? Where have you been? Come inside. Pronomus is here. You can report to both of us."

Aias bowed in respect to Heraclius's rank.

"Come inside. You don't expect to talk out here on the front steps, do you?" Heraclius's tone mixed impatience, petulance, and the contempt a man of his status never quite succeeded in suppressing when dealing with one so far beneath his esteem.

Aias looked at him, and saw him, and knew him for what he was.

He turned his head to the side. "This is the man. I bear formal witness."

Soldiers in the uniform of the royal bodyguard of Minos emerged from both sides of the doorway. Their leader managed to wedge a foot inside the door before Heraclius could close and bolt it.

Aias did not move as the soldiers swarmed into the

house. He knew it was not necessary to bear witness against Pronomus; all men in Knossos knew Pronomus, and Aias was certain that Heraclius would betray his coconspirator even before the torture began.

"You bastard!" Heraclius shrieked from inside the door. "I'll get you for this, Aias! He bought you out, didn't he? He offered you more money!" His voice grated, as if he were being restrained by force. "Curse you, Aias!"

His words stopped abruptly.

Aias reached inside his garment and pulled out the purse Heraclius had given him. He stepped inside and placed it, contents untouched, atop a table, next to the little niche where the goddess was honored.

How would he have been able to explain the currency with which Demetrios had paid him? How would one describe the absence of pain after a lifetime of mental anguish, of guilt, of anger, of hatred? His change of heart had nothing to do with gold or silver. He was Demetrios's man now and would follow him anywhere and obey any order. From now on he would act with a focused mind and a clear conscience.

He was at peace with himself at last! What else did a man need?

CHAPTER TWO

Thebes

I

The somber-faced slave, drably dressed, opened the door and bowed deeply to Neb-mertef. "My lord, His Excellency expects you. This way, please."

"Never mind," the adviser said. "I can find my way by now, thank you. I gather that my lord is on the roof?"

"Yes."

"Good. Please bring something for me to eat, and wine—the good vintage from the Fayum."

"Yes, my lord." The slave went away, and Neb-mertef turned toward the stairway to the roof garden. Amasis, as regent and highest ranking official in the Egyptian government, never presumed to occupy King Kamose's own lavishly appointed suite while the man still lived. The roof garden had been the vizier Baliniri's haunt before his untimely death.

Actually, Neb-mertef reflected as he went up the stairs, everyone in the palace knew that Baliniri's delightful rooftop hideout was the more pleasant of the two habitations. Here was a retreat fit for any king, where a man might look down unobserved on the entire city and the great Nile, where he might take his ease in the cool evening breezes that broke the dull, dry heat of a summer's day in Thebes.

He stopped at the top of the stairs and looked around. He did not see Amasis. Once again the unbidden thought came to him: *One of these days, all this will be mine.*

He shuddered and looked around him hastily, as though his thought had somehow been uttered aloud. *Have to watch that,* he thought. *Couldn't have something like that suddenly slip out.*

"I didn't hear you come up," said Amasis from the far corner of the rooftop, beyond the lattice. "Come over here. I'll send down for food and drink."

"I took the liberty of doing so on the way up, my lord," Neb-mertef said. "I know how you like taking afternoon refreshment up here."

"It's my favorite place," Amasis agreed. There was tension in his tone as well as in his face. "I was just wondering whether I'm going to be able to keep it."

"Oh, my lord! Surely—"

There was real fear in Amasis' voice. "He's hiding somewhere out there. Perhaps even here in Thebes. Or in El-Kab, where the damned nobles have never accepted me, curse them! Or in Edfu. You don't think Kamose is here in the city, do you?"

Neb-mertef fought off feelings of contempt before he answered: "I doubt it, my lord. If he is in Thebes, he has managed to elude patrols that sweep through virtually every neighborhood daily."

"It's not that simple. The patrols cannot ask openly about him. I certainly cannot offer a substantial reward for the head of the rightful king. And I can't just declare myself king while Kamose is alive."

"I know, my lord. It is indeed a vexing problem."

"If only I could catch him and kill him!" Amasis groaned.

Neb-mertef nodded gravely. From Amasis' point of view, that was the best solution. The fragile constitution of Egypt provided that the death of a reigning king must precede the assumption of power by a successor—any successor, whether a legitimate claimant with the proper bloodlines, like the still-absent Prince Moses, or an interloper like Amasis, with only the claims that raw power could assert.

And herein lay the rub. No one knew where Kamose was. The king had escaped from Amasis' thugs shortly after the bungled attempts on the lives of Queen Mara and the princess Thermutis.

Neb-mertef had his own suspicions about Kamose. The king could not surface now; he was pressured on all sides by Amasis' small but deadly security force. Kamose would wait until he had an army behind him, one capable of dealing with the foreign mercenaries Amasis had policing the capital.

But when *that* happened? Chaos! Civil war! Defeat! Surely the army would go over to the king! Then Moses would make contact with Kamose, and once he was satisfied with the king's health and mental stability, he would pass control of the Theban army over to the—

Suddenly the idea blazed forth in his mind. "My lord?" he ventured. "What if we were to spread the rumor that Kamose had died? He might be forced from hiding. Then we could have your men kill him."

"But wouldn't somebody rise to champion him?"

"Who? The queen? According to people from the caravans that have stopped at El-Kharga, she is living openly with one of those soldiers who helped her escape. If she were to come to Thebes, we would kill her. If she escaped us and testified on Kamose's behalf, she would have to return to his bed or face his official wrath. You know the law as it pertains to an unfaithful wife. She escapes justice now only because the oasis writes its own laws, favoring women."

A slow smile transformed Amasis' face. "That's brilliant. But there is another problem. If I assume the throne, Prince Moses won't just sail into Thebes and pass over control of his army to me—particularly if he's learned that Baliniri, his mentor, died at my orders. Furthermore, Thebes is ill defended, a poor place to fight in." He paused.

"Yes, my lord?"

A sly expression came over his features. "I could move the capital back to the delta, where the main body of my own command is. Little by little I've done away with the old army Kamose brought back from the North and revamped it with new mercenaries who answer only to my own command."

"I'm afraid I don't see where this is leading, my lord."

"*Let* Moses bring the army downriver to Thebes! He'll find nobody here but the ordinary citizens. We'll have moved!"

"Splendid, my lord! Why not rebuild Avaris? No one will be able to breach those Shepherd walls!"

Amasis' eyes glowed with a mad light. "Yes! Let him come! I'll put the slaves to work rebuilding the city. My friend, what would I do without you?"

Neb-mertef smiled. What indeed? But Amasis would have to cross that bridge when he came to it. First Kamose would fall, then Moses, then Amasis himself. And then he, Neb-mertef, would be king in Avaris, master of the Two Lands! King of Egypt! Master of the mightiest nation in the world!

II

In Neb-mertef's huge villa overlooking the Nile, an hour's ride upriver from Thebes, the astrologer Set-Nakht sat at a long table in his upstairs suite, staring at unrolled papyruses, frowning, and fretting.

He shook his head ruefully. "How stupid of me! How could I not have noticed it?" He sighed and went back to the first scroll, double-checking his figures. Then he went to the third, then back to the second. Next he compared the second with the first. All were in agreement.

"Curses!" he muttered angrily, wearily. "I've misread the whole chart."

One of the two tall Phrygian boys who had been sitting on the bed stood and padded over to Set-Nakht's table. He was stark naked except for gold jewelry gleaming here and there on his flawless body. He put a delicate hand on Set-Nakht's neck and caressed it.

"Poor master," the boy said. "You work so hard. Isn't it time to relax?"

"Go away," Set-Nakht said irritably without looking up. "I have work to do."

The Phrygian looked over at his friend on the bed and

pouted. "Come, master. I'll give you a nice, warm bath and rub you down with scented oils. Then we can play. You'll love it." Behind Set-Nakht's back, he made a mocking face for his friend's benefit. "Come now, master. You promised to take a break."

"Leave me," Set-Nakht ordered, his face tense. He picked up the second scroll and drew his finger down a long column of figures, then consulted the star charts on the third scroll. He looked up at last. "Neb-mertef will be home soon. What do you think will happen when I admit that I've misread the information?"

"I'm sure I don't know, master."

Set-Nakht ran his fingers through his disordered hair. "He'll have me beaten!"

"Beaten?" the Phrygian echoed, a faun's smile coming onto his epicene face. "How? You mean tied up, arms and legs, and lashed with a whip? How delightful! And you didn't tell us? Shame on you. Naughty master."

Set-Nakht scowled. "Don't you ever think of anything but that?"

He pouted again. "You weren't complaining about it last night." He moved closer, snaked a friendly arm around Set-Nakht's tense neck, and rubbed his front against Set-Nakht's shoulder.

The astrologer shoved the Phrygian roughly. The tall catamite fell on the floor. "Get away from me!" Set-Nakht snarled. "Go into the other room, both of you, and put something on!"

"*Well!*" The Phrygian got up and dusted himself off. "I like *that!*"

The other boy put a finger over his lips and shook his head violently. He got off the bed to hand his partner a long, modest linen loincloth. "There, now," he said. "Master must do important work to maintain his position in the world."

His voice was honeyed and sincere, but his eyes were rolling crazily around in his head, and his face mugged shamelessly. He did a quick acrobatic maneuver, which made an obscene pun on the word "position" and made bitter fun of Set-Nakht's sexual preferences. The other Phrygian smothered a giggle, then they went into the adjacent room.

Set-Nakht let out a long sigh and leaned back in his

chair. *I shouldn't let them get to me. They won't be around long anyway. Let them have their fun.*

He looked after them. They had lives hardly longer than those of the mayflies, he was thinking. Neb-mertef would buy him a new boy or two from the male brothels to reward him for doing something right, and there'd be a bit of novelty and variety for a few days. But then he himself would tire of them, or Neb-mertef would decide they knew too much, and the next thing he knew, they would be gone, with another boy or two in their place. He had no illusions about what had happened to all the boys who had disappeared. By now he also had little conscience about what Neb-mertef did to silence them forever. It was just the way of things.

They were his chains, his fetters. He was as much a slave here as they were. He closed his eyes and bitterly reflected on the shame of his self-inflicted servitude. He had been a free man once, a respected magus enjoying the esteem of his peers.

Then he had sought out Neb-mertef and offered his services to the powerful adviser. Neb-mertef, with his probing instinct for finding and exploiting a man's weakness, had seen who he was: a man simultaneously attracted to, and fearful of, the twilight world of the male brothels.

Wishing to gain exclusive access to his astrological insights, Neb-mertef had moved quickly to grant the wish he had hardly articulated, even to himself.

It was like feeding *shepenn* to an addict. He had taken to this steadily changing diet of increasingly shameless partners until he, too, had lost his sense of shame, his human dignity, his sense of identity.

If only he could just slip away! What if he were to get dressed, put on a dark cloak, slip out into the night, elude the guards, and make his way to the river? He could take a ferry to Deir el-Bahari and secretly book passage to some other part of the world.

But that would mean doing without the pleasures he had grown so used to. He blinked the tears of shame from his eyes. *Oh, how far I've fallen! Can't I go back to being the person I was before?*

He would have laid his head down on his forearms and wept like a baby had the door not opened suddenly to admit

Neb-mertef, all bustle and efficiency. The rich man looked around, disappointed not to find Set-Nakht deeply embroiled in some embarrassing orgy. "Have you finished the charts?"

Set-Nakht winced at the air of brutal authority. "Your pardon, my lord," he said in a weak and faltering voice. "I'm afraid I have bad news to report."

"What bad news?" The words came out violently. He winced once more. "That report you gave me isn't true? You've botched another reading? Speak up, man!"

"Misread, perhaps, my lord, but not b-botched. The charts are correct, and the calculations. I've checked them twenty times. But . . ."

"But what?"

"It's the interpretation. I . . . well, there's a major catastrophe coming—not immediately, perhaps not next year or the year after."

"What kind of catastrophe?"

Set-Nakht plunged onward. "Upheavals of the earth. Dark clouds that blot out the sun. Giant tidal waves that wipe out whole civilizations."

Neb-mertef stared with the unblinking eyes of a great hawk and sat down to listen. . . .

III

Unlike many of the other guests arriving at the party, Iri and Neftis came on foot, unescorted. Previous arrivals had been marked by conspicuous ostentation and squandered wealth; sedan chairs inlaid with gold and precious stones, borne by towering Nubian servants and accompanied by stout bodyguards, had been the rule.

Watching the latest of these, unpretentious Iri, a wealthy young man who earned his living in Thebes, had chuckled to himself. His older sister, Neftis, had hardly noticed at all, busy as she was with contemplating her reflection in her tiny bronze hand mirror.

Now Iri stood before Zoser's sprawling town house. He

looked at Neftis. "Shall I go up to knock, or do you want me to wait until you've finished primping?"

Neftis adjusted her wig and grimaced at her reflection. She was pretty enough to make huge, ugly faces and get away with it; there was a studied lack of feminine dissembling about her. At a similarly posh party, she had come without her wig, scandalizing everyone, and had passed the matter off airily with a joke about the artificiality of court manners.

The truth was, she appeared not to care what people thought of her. Neftis was devastatingly beautiful, rich—brother and sister, orphaned young, had inherited a sizable fortune, and Iri's wise investments had nearly doubled this in the past five years—and bored. She did not have to care about the impression she made; she did not have to hide her boredom; she did not have to have good manners.

Iri's hand unconsciously touched the huge, ugly red birthmark that disfigured his face and made strangers look away from him in sudden embarrassment. All the good looks nature had given her had been withheld from him, and while he shared some of her outsider's detachment when it came to court customs, the reason for his exclusion from the inner circles of society was that hideous deformity. Neftis had excluded herself—which only inspired people to seek her out.

He stifled the faint feelings of envy that remained after all these years despite his love and concern for his beautiful sister. "Let's just go in. You know you don't care what sort of impression you make here."

"Ah, but that's where you're wrong," she said, smudging the black kohl around her eyes. "I do care. I just don't care in the way they all want me to." She bared her teeth to inspect them. "They bore me, all of them. And the only thing duller than the old mossbacks is the young ones—so shallow and artificial. If only I could find a man with something to him! Who had a bit of dash or"—she turned to Iri, flashed that devastating smile of hers, and reached out one lovely hand to give his shoulder an affectionate squeeze—"maybe some of your good sense and understanding, dear Iri. He wouldn't have to be big and tall and strong and handsome. He'd just have to be different—unique. But most of these young eligibles would starve to death if they hadn't inherited money, and the rest are only interested in *my* money." The hardness

in her face broke, as it often did when she spoke to her
brother, her only real friend and confidant. "Oh, Iri! Why did
you have to be born my brother? If only I could find a man
with even half your good qualities!"

"You wouldn't give him a second look," Iri said sadly.
"Not if he looked like me."

She grabbed his hand and pulled it to her cheek impulsively. "Oh, darling, I know. I know. Poor dear. They don't
care how they hurt you. If only I'd been able to do something
to spare you that last hurt! She was cruel, wasn't she?"

"Think nothing of it," Iri replied, gently extricating his
hand. "I had a lesson to learn, and I learned it." He did not
like talking about that two-faced tavern girl who had milked
him for thousands. "Neftis, promise you won't do anything
scandalous in there. Every time you do, I have to patch
things up. You don't know how hard that can be."

"Then *don't*," she said stubbornly. "I don't want you to.
When I choose to scandalize these old frauds, I mean it to
stick. Why should I care what they think?"

"Please. For me."

She looked him in the eyes. "Oh, Iri, you know I wouldn't
do anything to hurt you. I know how awkward your relations
with these people are, and how you need the contacts if
you're ever going to give up being an armorer and build up a
jewelry business." She sighed. "It's just that . . . I hate
them so. They're such a lot of fakes and frauds."

"Promise?" he pleaded.

"Oh, all right. If I decide to pull someone's nose, I'll try
not to call attention to you." She gave him a quick kiss with
real sisterly affection.

Iri looked at her with resigned indulgence as he knocked
on the big door.

Circulating among the guests, Iri was more at ease than
he would be among fewer people. For one thing, the great
central hall of Zoser's huge house was so noisy that if anyone
were to make sport of his disfigurement, he could not have
heard it. For another, the bulk of these people knew his
exalted position in Thebes and thus did not give a fig how
ugly he was. Iri was the son of Sinuhe, grandson of Ketan, a

Child of the Lion, and was the finest armorer serving the government of Egypt, supervisor of the royal armsmakers.

This was a lofty status for a man his age, and the Children of the Lion were much revered in Egypt. The older people of the court showed him respect to his face, although they, like their juniors, did not allow their eyes to dwell on the red birthmark that disfigured him.

Iri, separated almost immediately from his sister by the crowd, strained to hear the conversation among several large landowners of Thebes. Behind him there was an opening in the crowd, and the musicians moved into this. "Pardon me, my lord," said one of them, brushing his arm.

He half turned to looked at her. "Here," he said politely, "I'll make room." He slipped to one side to let her move the gorgeous, ivory-inlaid lyre through, and she was quickly joined by the others.

He watched her setting up. Like the other women musicians, she wore a distinctive wig and translucent white robe, which bared small breasts and displayed the color of her flesh through its folds. Behind her the flutists and the kithara player moved into place. She smiled at Iri. "My lord, may we play a song of your choosing?"

He smiled happily. "Why, yes," he said. "Do you know 'The Land that Loves Silence'?"

"Oh, sir, that's a lovely one. I'll sing it for you myself. Not many people ask for the old songs, and they're still the best. There's a dance that goes with it."

He watched, still presenting her only his profile—in the crush he could not face her without poking one of the merchants in the ribs as the three dancers took their places. The lyre player whispered to them, then smiled at him, bowed, and settled her hands on the strings. But then someone jostled Iri, and he lurched to face the girl. He saw her shocked expression as she caught her first clear view of him. The moment was spoiled. He winced and closed his eyes. Awkwardly, with a false start, the music began, as he turned away to lose himself in the crowd.

"Did you hear?" Khenzer the wine importer was asking. "The local garrison was called out today, and all leaves were canceled. Something's up, I tell you."

Zau, who owned six quarries and two mines, frowned. "That isn't all. Amasis ordered inventories of all supplies owned by the city and the district. It's as though we were being put on wartime emergency alert. Do you suppose that someone has information about the army Baliniri sent to Nubia? Everyone has been waiting for them to come back, but nothing happens."

"Wouldn't General Khafre simply be ordered to pass control of the army to the regent?" someone asked.

"Perhaps not. The way I understand it, Baliniri sent them away to keep Amasis from asserting his authority over them. Mark my words: We could wind up with another insurrection on our hands."

"The gods spare me," Khenzer groaned. "Just when I thought things were going to settle down so I could make some money for a change. For the first time in years, trade is picking up."

"I don't think it will be an armed conflict," Iri said suddenly. He had kept silent so far, but this was a subject he knew about.

Several heads turned his way; as head armorer he would have very early information about any military moves.

"Indeed?" Khenzer asked, respectfully. Neither he nor anybody else looked at Iri directly. "If you've special information, Iri, it would be a great favor to us all if you were to share it."

Iri was about to answer when there was a soft touch on his arm. He half turned. One of the naked serving girls was at his elbow. "Olives, my lord? Nuts? Dates, anyone?"

He shook his head and turned away. "If Amasis were to see conflict coming, he'd send me an order to hire more help and call back my apprentices from their holiday. There's been no such order or news that Amasis is bringing up reinforcements from the delta. No—whatever it is, it's not that."

Somebody else jarred his arm: new guests arriving. Several women wore cones of perfumed fat atop their headdresses. These, as the day wore on, would melt in the warm air and create patterns down the sides of their black wigs.

The crowd shoved him away from the knot of businessmen to whom he had been speaking, and a wave of human flesh steadily moved him away from the musicians. He heard a phrase from the song he'd requested, sung in a clear and melodious voice: "Cast all evil behind you and think only of joy, till the day comes when you reach port in the land that loves silence. . . ."

He sighed and looked around him for familiar faces but saw none. This new crowd was younger, the last people in the world he wanted to see. They tended not to hide their disdain for the way he looked.

Again came the soft voice at his elbow: "Nuts, my lord? Dates? Figs? Olives?"

It was the same girl. He could feel her supple nakedness close to him. He shook his head, not wanting to look at her, to glance at her firm body, the delicious young breasts, flat belly, gorgeously graceful carriage of the shoulders. . . .

He looked into her eyes.

"Neft—!" he started to say, shocked.

But his sister put a hand on his lips and made a shushing sound, very low. She winked and smothered a wicked smile. "I bribed a slave to change places with me. I'm having the time of my life. Don't give me away."

IV

"What are you *doing*?" Iri demanded, enraged. "You get back out this minute and—"

"Quiet!" she said, replacing the conspiratorial grin with a neutral, servile look. "Don't give me *away*! I'll see you later."

She moved off, not looking back, offering her plate of refreshments to various guests. Iri tried to get his temper under control. This time she had gone too far. He wanted to stalk after her, grab her, *shake* her, and—

Oh, Neftis! What am I going to do with you? If only Mother and Father hadn't died so young! If only Khian were here!

Khian, whose grave dignity had always cowed his two younger siblings; Khian, who had been such a stern taskmaster before he had gone off to take his place in the world of commerce. Imagine their older brother hearing about any of her outrageous exploits! He *knew* what Khian would think, what Khian would do.

He shuddered and stole another look at Neftis. Oh, no! She was serving Zoser himself! Zoser must assuredly know all his slaves by sight and by name! Zoser would recognize her! Zoser could ruin her if he let word get around about the terrible prank.

Ah, but apparently Zoser had not noticed! Thank the gods! He had not taken his eyes off the delta businessman with whom he had been talking.

Oh, Neftis! What am I to do with you?

Afterward she went back through the elaborately decorated curtains to the kitchens and put down her empty platter. The slave whose place she had taken stared at her in disbelief.

"Well," Neftis said, "I've had my fun for the week. Here's your costume." She took the faience beads from around her hips and draped them about the naked girl's neck.

"Where's my dress? Oh, never mind, I see it." She slipped her dress on and stepped into her sandals. "Here's your wig. I'll take mine back. Actually, I like yours better, but you'd get in trouble if we swapped."

The girl said nothing. Her eyes were large and liquid. Nothing even remotely like this had ever happened to her before.

"Well, then," Neftis said brusquely, "you'd better fill the platter again and get back out there. They'll be yelling for you. I don't envy you having to work for Zoser. He's a real martinet to his servants. But then he owns you, doesn't he?"

It was a tactless and cruel thing to say, and Neftis realized it immediately. "Oh, I'm sorry. I didn't mean to say it like that—I mean rubbing it in and all."

The girl would not meet her eyes. "It's all right, my lady, I'm used to it."

Neftis gave her a long, wondering look, as if seeing her for the first time. "I've been callous, haven't I?" she asked softly. "I mean, doing something like this for a lark, when it could get you into terrible trouble if I was found out." She felt suddenly embarrassed. "I'm really sorry. Please let me give you some money."

"My lady, a slave can't own money."

"Oh, dear. Perhaps I could talk to your supervisor—"

"Oh, no, my lady! Please!"

"Quite right. That'd be stupid. I should have thought of you in the first place. I've put you in danger, and for nothing more than a silly whim, wanting to play a prank on these pompous frauds—"

"Oh, no, my lady! They're really very good to me. Especially my lord Zoser. He is allowing my daughter to be raised free. She won't ever be a slave. He's promised to feed her and house her until she's grown and he can find her a nice husband, a man with a trade."

"You've got a daughter?" It was as if she had never realized slaves had children.

"Yes, my lady. She's three now. I was really afraid for her when you were out there taking my place. If Zoser had found out and had chosen to—"

"To do what?" A new, deep, piercing voice broke into their conversation.

Neftis wheeled. *"Zoser!"* she said in horror.

The merchant, one of the wealthiest in the city and a civic leader just below Neb-mertef's exalted level, looked from one face to the other. "You, girl!" he barked at the slave. "Did you go along with this imposture?"

"Y-yes, my lord!" the girl said, blubbering. "I didn't mean any harm. I—I didn't know what to do when the lady—"

Neftis straightened her back and thrust out her perfect little chin. "My lord," she said, using the deferent form of address despite her near-equal rank, "the whole thing is my fault. The girl had no choice. I blackmailed her into doing it. I told her that if she didn't go along with my impersonation of her, I would make up a lie against her, and she'd get a beating."

"A gallant improvisation," Zoser said, his eyes burning, "but the girl knows I'd never have her beaten. We don't do that around my household."

"I tried to tell her!" the girl cried out in panic and fear.

"There, there, dear. Certainly you did." He reached out and patted the slave's head. "Now go out and serve our guests. Don't worry. Wipe your eyes and repair your makeup."

"Y-yes, my lord."

He shooed her away gently. Then he looked sternly at
Neftis. "And now *you*, young lady. I knew your father well. I
knew your older brother briefly, before he left Thebes. What
do you think either of them would say if they knew of your
escapades? Don't you think they'd be shocked? Angry?
Disappointed?"

She looked into his eyes, forcing herself not to look away
despite the fierce authority of his gaze.

He continued. "So far as I know, I am the only person to
have caught you at this little impersonation."

"My brother," she said in a voice that, to her chagrin,
had no assurance in it.

"Ah, Iri. And did he grow angry with you?"

"Very."

"You know that you're doing as much of a disservice to
him as you're doing to me. And to yourself and my guests."

The rebellion flared up. "Your guests are *asses*! They're
so *fake*."

"Ah. And you're real. A person of principle. Do I understand you correctly?"

She did not speak. She knew what he was going to say
next.

"Do you find my guests acting impulsively or scandalously to embarrass others? To scandalize strangers who have
done them no harm?"

She glared at him.

"How old are you now?" he asked.

She hesitated. "Twenty-two."

"That's a little old for childish pranks. Wouldn't you
agree?"

"Perhaps," she said grudgingly.

"Ah, me." The anger was gone from his voice and stance.
He looked weary instead. "If your father had only lived, to
find you a nice husband and settle you down! If your brother—"

"I don't want a husband!" she screeched defiantly. "Not
if it means winding up having brats by one of these dullards!
They're all so stupid, so hollow! I'd die of boredom! I'd rather
die a virgin! I'd rather drown in the Nile! I'd rather do
anything but wind up in subservience to one of these hinds!
There's nothing *to* them! Can't you see that?"

He looked at her, startled by her vehemence. "Perhaps I can. From time to time I find myself looking at the younger generation and wondering whether the bloodlines aren't getting a bit thin. They just don't seem, the youth of today, to have the fire, the drive, that my contemporaries had. Making it to the top of the pile when I was a boy was a bit of an accomplishment, if I do say so myself. The competition was tough. I fear I must agree with you. These boys today don't have much to them." He shrugged. "I don't agree with the ways in which you rebel against their dullness. But short of sending you to another country, what can we do? You'll have to find someone here you won't be bored with. If the young men lack your spirit and intelligence, well . . . I see we have a problem."

"We?" she echoed. "It isn't your problem."

"Ah. But you haven't any idea what to do about it, right?"

Her eyes blazed. "You know good and well I don't."

He looked her in the eyes. "You've got too much money and too much time on your hands, but neither of these is the problem. The problem is that you don't have anything in your life that means anything to you. That's very vexing."

She stared at him. *How did you know that? Nobody else seems to understand at all.*

V

Afterwards Iri met her at the door. "Come on," he said, expecting an argument. "Let's go."

"Gladly. I couldn't take a moment more."

A tall slave bowed them out the door. They stood on the front stairs, looking out at the slow traffic in the street.

"Really, Neftis!" Iri said, exasperated.

"Oh, don't chide me," she groaned. "I've already had my scolding for the day."

He took her arm and steered her down into the street. "Zoser?"

"Actually, Zoser was rather nice. I even found myself liking him. He understands me. If only I knew someone my own age who was as smart as you and he . . . someone I could respect and really care for. Oh, Iri, I do feel so lonely sometimes!"

"I'm being derelict in my fraternal duty," Iri declared. "I ought to be screening suitors. But I don't know anybody of marriageable age. And you know how hard it is for me to approach people I don't know. They all act as though I had some contagious disease."

"Oh, Iri, I wish I could do something to ease your pain. I do love you so." She squeezed his hand. "It could be worse, dear. You have your work, after all, and you're so good at it." She shook her head. "And no one teases you to your face anymore."

"Oh, I can take care of myself. People don't get into tests of strength with a metalworker, if they have their wits about them."

"I must be a terrible burden to you." Neftis hesitated, then giggled. "But it was such fun! It was as though I were invisible! I could walk around and see what asses they were, while nobody paid me the smallest bit of mind. Have you ever wanted to listen, unobserved, while people talk?"

"I get enough of the ugly side of people as it is. I don't need to seek it out."

"Well, it's different with me. They all want to impress me. They strut and puff themselves up. You know they'd beggar themselves to see me naked. And yet I moved among the lot of them wearing not a stitch, and they didn't even notice because they thought I was a slave."

Her face changed, sobered. "Oh, Iri, what a terrible life a slave must lead. Imagine nobody noticing you. Imagine being—oh, just a piece of furniture. Imagine everybody in the world walking right by and not noticing you unless they tripped over you and cursed you for being in the way." She stopped to face him, her face flushed with growing indignation. "You know the girl back there, the one I impersonated? I tried to give her money. But she said she couldn't own money, couldn't own anything. There was nothing I could do to make it up to her. I felt awful!" She shook her head sadly.

"Here was this poor girl with real problems, and I was toying with her. Playing with her life, like a little spoiled brat."

Iri smiled down at her. "So you've a real human streak in you, after all."

"I thought I was just having fun," she admitted. "But in the end I wound up really seeing things through a slave girl's eyes." She shuddered. "And it was horrible. It was the only time I ever felt ashamed of myself."

"You've learned something," Iri soothed. "And that's something you'll always have over the others: They never learn anything. They think they know it all already. Neftis, I know some slaves. I have *friends* who are slaves, and I feel so bad for them. There's a family over in Deir el-Bahari. They're foreigners, Habiru, from up in Canaan. The son of the family is named Aaron ben Amram. A rather impressive man, very intelligent and well-spoken. He could be a captain in the army or leader of a caravan. He's born to lead people. And what is he? Just another worker, cutting stone out of a quarry."

"How did you meet him?"

"I was supervising the loading of some ore there one day, and the guard called a number of the Habiru over to help out. I had to help too, and from time to time we'd talk. He knows several languages. His people value learning. Why, someone told me that Aaron was a distant relative of Joseph, the former vizier of Egypt under Salitis. Imagine! But his people were enslaved when Joseph died."

"What a sad story."

"It could happen to anyone. If some enemy nation were to conquer Egypt, it could happen to us. Our great-grand-father was a slave once, to the Shepherds, before he was blinded."

"Shobai? A slave? I'd never heard that."

"Mother and Father didn't tell us, or Khian either. As a descendant, I often learn the history of the Children of the Lion from strangers. We're a pretty famous lot. I knew about the birthmark our family members sometimes have on their backs. That much Khian did tell me before he left us in the care of our tutors."

"Tell me more," she asked as they turned down a side street.

"We have the line documented back to Belsunu. I saw

one of his swords; I didn't believe anyone could work metal that perfectly. I tried to match it but never succeeded."

"Don't undervalue yourself. You're the best around."

"I'm not running in a fast field here. Belsunu's son, Ahuni, never matched it, and neither did his son, Kirta. The same was true of Kirta's sons, Hadad and Shobai."

"You know, I've heard that name—Hadad. One of my suitors used to sing this terribly sad song about a cripple named Hadad, who saved his city from the Shepherd invaders. In the end the Hai killed him. What a sad song—I cried and cried."

"Every word is true. Hadad was Shobai's brother. He was our great-granduncle, one of the great heroes of the world."

"You're joking!"

"No. It's a wonderful story. The same man who killed Hadad blinded Shobai first. Shobai refused to make swords for the Hai, so this terrible person, Reshef the Snake, blinded him."

"Reshef the Snake? Tell me more."

"Hadad was a sweet little fellow, who'd never struck a blow in his life. He got into a sword fight with Reshef, the finest blade in the North, and in the end Reshef killed him. But he'd saved Haran, the town he lived in. He's almost a god there, they tell me."

"Oh, Iri, that's so *sad*. You're going to make me cry again. I don't mind being chided by Zoser or by you, but making my eye makeup run, that's another matter."

Iri laughed and squeezed her hand affectionately. "Here's the house," he said. "I'll leave you here, if you don't mind. I'm supposed to meet somebody. I'll be back later."

He gave her a quick kiss on the cheek. As he turned away, the image of Neftis, standing there not knowing whether to laugh or cry, remained fixed in his mind all the way down the street.

VI

Across the street, two men in shadow watched them separate and move away: Iri striding briskly down the street on short, slightly bowed legs; Neftis hesitating for a moment to look after him, then going through the door of the big house.

"So that's the man," Arsaphes said. "Gods, what a face! But if he's as good an armorer as you say, we'll need him."

Sata looked up at his towering companion. "The k—" he began, then corrected himself. "Our leader said that you have some background in that area. But your hands don't seem those of a smith."

Arsaphes held up his elegant, long-fingered hands and studied them. "I suppose not. It's been a long time. Other skills pay better in the long run and don't sear your lungs and burn white scars up and down your forearms. There's not much dignity in metalwork."

"And that would matter to you, I can imagine."

"You say he's a Child of the Lion?"

"Teti was his grandaunt."

"She trained him?"

"No. She died too soon. He finished the bulk of his training here in Thebes, under a couple of men who had been trained by Teti. He's pretty sharp in other ways—good investments and financial management."

"There's an older brother?"

Sata nodded. "But nobody knows much about him. He may be a scion or a wastrel—nobody seems to have any idea. He lives somewhere else. He doesn't figure in the lives of these two."

Arsaphes stroked his beardless chin. "Now tell me about the girl. Why isn't she married?"

"That's a puzzle. If her father were alive, there's no doubt someone would have arranged a very rich marriage for her. Heaven knows she's pretty enough."

"Pretty isn't the word."

Sata flashed a quick grin. "She'd bring a fine dowry too; but she's too high-spirited or too picky. And with no one to force her to accept a husband, she drifts. The young men of the city have courted her, but she's much too smart, shrewd, and observant for them. She sees through these young snips."

"So she needs an older man, a firmer hand," the tall foreigner observed.

"Perhaps. I prefer them soft-voiced and submissive, and this one makes you jump through the hoop and takes your skin off with her razor-sharp tongue."

"Yet . . . very attractive," Arsaphes said thoughtfully. "She reminds me of a wild, untamed young Moabite mare. One that's never been ridden."

"Well, I can't speak about that. She may well be a virgin."

"Hmmm. You say someone's meeting Iri about recruiting him? Where? When?"

Sata thought a moment. "Pebes, I think. At the inn at the Market of the West Wind. It's the only place where you can be sure of getting a private room this time of the evening. The Sign of the Dolphin."

"Good. I'll check with Pebes later. But the girl intrigues me. There's nobody but her brother to look out for her interests? They share the same house?"

"Some of the time. When there's a lot of work at the forge, he stays in that part of town. When he's there, she's alone—except for the servants you usually find with people of that class."

"Yes." Arsaphes' lips curled in a thin smile. "So if one wanted to move against her, one would have to make sure the brother was kept busy doing something else. Actually, he looks very strong. That comes with the trade; I was very strong in my youth—perhaps I still am."

"Don't go chasing her down, thinking you're going to put your mark on her. You may get more than you bargained for."

Arsaphes' eyes narrowed. "I don't chase women; they come to me. If I want her, she'll come to me and beg for it."

Sata snorted.

"I merely speak the truth," the tall man said. "I always get what I want . . . once I've figured out what it is that I want in the first place. Always."

"And you've decided you want her, eh?" He shuddered but kept his thoughts to himself. The foreigner was a braggart and a blusterer from time to time, but he did seem to get what he desired. And people did seem to follow him. Men, anyhow; previous to this he had shown little interest in women.

Sata frowned. Yes, in a fairly short time men seemed to fall into a servile attitude where Arsaphes was concerned. Well, that wasn't for him! He'd keep his independence, thank you. "Is there anything more?" he said. "I want to get home."

"That'll be enough for today," Arsaphes said. "I might wander down to the Market of the West Wind. Sign of the Dolphin, you said?"

At that precise moment Iri was walking under the dolphin sign and through the open door of the tavern. The place was almost empty. A disheveled man slumped in a far corner, and an off-duty soldier chatted quietly with a tavern dancer. She looked Iri's way and started to smile, then saw his face. She quickly turned back to the soldier, who suddenly found her more attentive.

Iri proudly straightened his back and walked up to the innkeeper, who was wiping off a table. "A man was supposed to meet me here."

"He's in that room over there, waiting for you. He left a description."

"Right." Iri slipped the man a small coin and strode past the dancer toward the half-open door the innkeeper had indicated. As he did, he self-consciously hardened his muscles to show them off. He knew that except for the red blotch on his plain face and the slight bow in his legs, he was a specimen any young woman might consider desirable.

He poked his head inside the door and saw Pebes sitting alone, a jar of wine and two bowls before him.

Pebes beckoned Iri inside. "Close the door. We won't be bothered. I have an understanding with the innkeeper."

Iri shut the door, then sat opposite Pebes.

"Have some wine," the man offered.

"No, thank you," Iri said. "I've been at a party. I've had a bit already."

"Have some anyhow," Pebes said roughly. "I don't like to have a man not drinking with me when I drink."

"I drink when I choose," Iri shot back, a sharp edge to his voice. "If you don't like it I can leave." He started to rise.

"Calm down," the other said quickly. "Suit yourself. I suppose you know why I asked you to come here. Our city and our country are deeply divided. A number of us would like a return to the old ways—the old religion, the old customs and festivals." He paused and looked Iri straight in the eye. "The *old* king."

"We still have a king. Which old king are you talking about?"

"Come on. Amasis is circulating rumors that King Kamose is dead and that it's time for *him* to be named king."

"Everyone knows that Prince Moses was being groomed to replace Kamose. The prince's bloodlines are better than Amasis' and Kamose's. I don't mean to take anything away from Kamose, mind you. What he did with the Hai was nothing short of heroic. Egypt owes him a lot."

"Forget Prince Moses," Pebes said. "If he's fool enough to come to Thebes and surrender the army Baliniri sent him southward to protect, he'll pay for it. Amasis will kill him."

Iri kept his eyes on Pebes'. "I think I will have that drink you offered me." He took the bowl and drank deeply.

Pebes leaned forward and spoke in a quiet voice. "Kamose escaped. He's alive and well in a place where Amasis can't find him. If Amasis can't find and kill him, he can't produce a body to show the priests of Amon. Without the body of the old king, there can't be a new one—not without a civil war Amasis would probably lose."

Iri's eyebrows shot up. "Let's get to the point. What do you people propose?"

Pebes grinned. "We propose to put Kamose back on the throne. And as for Amasis—" He made the sign of the fig: a clenched fist, with the thumb protruding between the first and second fingers. On one level it was a crude symbol of the male genitalia. On another it was a sign that meant impalement.

"Tell me how you intend to do it."

VII

Arsaphes sat next to the wall of the inn's private room, eavesdropping. He toyed with the bowl of wine before him but did not drink. Arsaphes did not like anything—drugs, wine, beer, or more potent fare—that caused him to surrender control of any situation.

He heard Pebes explain a highly watered-down version of their plan; it was the version they gave people whom they did not yet trust. It included very little in the way of damning information and no real names other than Kamose's.

He stopped paying active attention; it was obvious that Pebes could handle this one.

The organization of their conspiracy was a small masterpiece. Other than pivotal figures—himself, Kamose, and a couple of others—none of the members knew anyone by sight or by name outside of his own little cell. Meetings were conducted in secret, in disguise, and only the leader of each small group knew all his members. None of them knew anyone other than the sponsor who had brought him into the fold.

Thus, when Pebes brought Iri to his first meeting, he would know no one but Pebes. This would prevent a captured conspirator from implicating more than one fellow member, even under torture.

Odd, he thought, *how the coincidences multiply.* Just on a chance meeting, they had managed to snare a Child of the Lion!

He smiled. On the day when they could finally come out into the open, Iri would give them a legitimacy they could hardly achieve by other means. The Children of the Lion were well respected in Egypt. Having Iri in the movement was a real prize.

He smiled to himself, thinking of the armorer's sister. He had already begun to develop an interest in her, one that could only be satisfied by— His smile widened. His eyes narrowed.

Women were made to be tamed! To be dominated and brought low to the proper relationship with a man—which meant subordination, obedience, pliability! He longed to see her again, to tame her, to break her pride and spirit, to harness her passion, and to reduce her untrammeled sense of self to confusion and insecurity. He longed to hear her lovely lips plead for his orders, seek his will, beg for his attention.

His smile was now a demon's grimace.

Now that he thought of it, he had not had a woman in some time—not since the girl down south who— But that hardly counted. She had been taken by stealth. When he had raped her, she had hardly known it was he. It was no sport to have a woman this way. She had to be wide awake, aware. She had to know what was happening to her. She had to . . . she had to *want* it, want her own destruction, want to lose her pride, dignity, and autonomy. She had to be corrupted by her own wishes and be a participant in her own ruin.

How she would despise herself! How she would hate him! And how little she would be able to do about it!

Even as she hated him and loathed herself, she would beg him not to leave her.

He would build her seduction and her corruption as an architect might build a palace. One began with nothing, then would put the pieces together one at a time, solidly, confidently, always keeping the end result in mind.

He closed his eyes and brought her image to mind again: darkly intelligent eyes, haughty nose, graceful neck, proud posture, pert breasts thrust out, shoulders held back, slim, strong young legs astride.

An aristocrat. A princess, a potential queen. And, like her brother, a Child of the Lion, member of an ancient elite. This was what he had always wanted in a woman, and he had all too seldom found it. He needed a prize worthy of his conquering, of his despising! A citadel worth the wrecking and burning!

Bah! Sweep it all away! Throw it into the dust! Trample it underfoot! Leave it a thing unrecognizable!

Suddenly he was aware that he was breathing hard, that his heart was pounding fast, that he felt totally, vibrantly alive. His manhood had reasserted itself and in the fashion most dear to his heart. He wanted her now! Now!

But he opened his eyes and calmed himself. Patience! Patience! It would all come about soon enough!

VIII

When Iri came out of the back room of the Sign of the Dolphin, he used a separate exit from the one Pebes had taken and did not look back. Traversing the long common room, he noticed a tall man with piercing eyes staring at him. Iri scowled; people usually had the good manners to look away.

As he went into the twilight, he found himself not wanting to go home. He was agitated and upset by the things he had been told and needed to walk off his nervous energy.

He set out for the river. Whenever he was feeling disturbed like this, a walk along the quays, to watch the sailors and fishermen tying up for the night, calmed him.

He thought about what Pebes had said: *A revolution against Amasis! One with legitimacy, whose only agenda is to restore King Kamose—many times over a hero and the savior of Egypt these many years—to the throne!*

Imagine! Amasis had tried to kill the king after keeping him drugged for months, a prisoner in the house where, Amasis had solemnly assured the public, Kamose had been confined for medical reasons! This was treason!

So hot was his blood that he wanted to march on Amasis' palace right now, to confront him and demand that he step down. But of course Amasis was backed by an army of foreign mercenaries; to challenge him would be to challenge these. He wanted to participate actively in Kamose's behalf, but his natural conservatism made him cautious.

Of course, there was the army Moses had taken to Nubia. The prince was still at the helm, and the unit would be more than a match for the tough but ill-organized mercenaries.

The only hope for Egypt's salvation was if Kamose surfaced and reasserted his authority, ordering Moses to take Amasis and his cronies into custody. The city would unhesitatingly support him if he did this. Unfortunately, Kamose could not come out from hiding until his safety was assured; otherwise Amasis' thugs would kill him.

As Iri walked by the river, his attention was caught by a strange sight: Camped on the long waterfront was a huge crowd of people, surrounded by their sparse possessions.

Torches burned at the perimeters of their wretched waterside encampment, and mercenary guards, heavily armed, patrolled under the torchlight, making certain no one wandered away.

Curious, Iri approached one of the guardsmen.

"Be off with you!" the guard ordered harshly.

Iri bristled. "Wait a minute, my friend. Perhaps you don't know to whom you're—"

The soldier's hand grasped his sword. "I'm giving you to the count of three to move on or so help me—"

"What's your name, soldier?" Iri demanded.

"None of your damned business. One! Two!"

"Captain!" Iri shouted in the voice of command. "Captain of the guard!"

A broad-shouldered Greek walked briskly toward them. "Who calls? Oh! It's you, sir! What's the matter, sir?"

The guard stared first at the captain, then at Iri. "You mean this fellow—"

"This fellow, as you call him," the Greek cut in, "outranks both of us."

Iri, satisfied, commenced his inquiries. "What's going on here? These are the Habiru, aren't they? Weren't they assigned to the quarries in Deir el-Bahari?"

"New orders, sir. They're being shipped north to the delta. The way I understand it, sir, the entire court will follow. These here are being sent along before anyone else. They'll be unloaded at Athribis and marched over to Avaris."

"But Avaris is in ruins."

"Right you are, sir," the Greek confirmed. "But the regent wants these Habiru to rebuild it. The walls have still never been breached, and it's very sound as fortified cities go. The civic buildings and residential and business districts were damaged by the fires, though, and will need a lot of repair."

"But the court is moving to *Avaris*?"

"Yes. And I was told to yank up this bunch of weeds and plant 'em right here, preparatory to shipping out at dawn."

"Surely they can be treated better than this. There are women and children here."

"I have my orders, sir. Is there anything else I can do for you?"

A thought struck him. "Maybe there is. I'd like to go

into the encampment for a moment or two. I know one or two of the Habiru's elders. I'd like to talk to them."

"Very good, sir. Take my ring and show it to the underlings when you come out. They all will recognize it. It'll be taken as a badge of privilege and safe conduct."

"Thank you, Captain. I'll make sure it gets back to you." Iri walked under the first soldier's glaring gaze into the camp.

It took him a few minutes to locate Aaron. "Hello!" he said. "It's me, Iri. Remember?"

"Of course, my lord." The Habiru bowed slightly as a sign of personal respect; the Habiru, Iri had learned, were a proud lot. "I regret that I can't offer you the hospitality of my house. . . ." He gestured grimly at the quay, resignation on his face.

"I've just heard of Amasis' plans. This is an outrage, and I intend to do something about it."

"We're used to this, my lord. Besides, this will reunite us with the rest of our family, who are still in the delta. We haven't seen them in years."

"I don't have much time," Iri said, "but I have news that might cheer you. Prince Moses' army is upriver. The moment Amasis pulls the court out, Moses will be free to land here."

"That is good news. I fear it comes too late for us, though."

"Perhaps not. That's what I'm trying to tell you. There's a movement under way to restore the king."

"But Kamose hates us as much as Amasis does."

"But Prince Moses appears to be on your side. His will be a very powerful voice in a restored government."

Aaron nodded thoughtfully. "That's so," he agreed. "Things could improve, my lord. Please, look out for the prince, will you, my lord? He has enemies."

"I'll do what I can. Meanwhile, courage!"

From behind a tall pile of bundles, Dathan, Aaron's distant relative, eavesdropped on the conversation. Could these two actually believe the drivel they were speaking? he wondered. Egyptians would never help Habiru!

All this bleating about Moses! Why, Moses was a murderer! He, Dathan, had seen Moses kill an Egyptian guard and get away with it! The prince was no different.

In the middle of this outpouring of bile, however, Dathan's conscience reminded him that the killing had taken place in defense of a Habiru. Maybe Moses wasn't as bad as the rest.

But privilege was privilege, and Dathan, whose own family had produced Joseph, a slave who had become a grand vizier of Egypt, was painfully aware of the unfairness of the situation. Why should Moses have been raised in the lap of luxury while he, Dathan, was a slave condemned to back-breaking labor beneath the hot sun?

Moses be cursed! All of them be cursed! One Egyptian was as bad as another! If the opportunity ever arose for him to expose that murder he had seen Moses commit, he would do so in an instant!

IX

Mai, Neftis's personal maid and the head of their little household staff, met Iri at the door. "Welcome home, my lord," she said in her soft, melodious voice. "My mistress is waiting up for you in the south room."

Iri smiled tiredly. "Thank you, Mai. Go to bed now. Whatever possessed Neftis to stay up this late? She should have been asleep hours ago."

"So should you, my lord," the servant said, taking his cloak. "I know you don't like me to chide, but I'm only saying what your mother would have wanted me to say."

"I appreciate your concern. But go to bed now."

He watched her go as he kicked off his sandals and nudged them into the shoe niche beside the door. Mai had been with his family since before his birth. She was still attractive in her late forties, and he sometimes wondered if, free of encumbrances, she would have chosen marriage. He had suspected that some relationship had existed between her and the household scribe, who had taught him and Neftis to read. But that man had died years before, and Mai had since made the household her life. Her innate dignity prevented him from asking about her feelings.

Yawning, he padded into the south room. There Neftis sat cross-legged, her hair dressed for bed, her slim body covered by a soft robe. She smiled sleepily. "You're late. You've been up to something, haven't you?"

He did not answer for a moment. Mai had left out cheese and wine. He poured himself a bowl and sat on a matching couch opposite his sister. "Home feels good after a long day."

"You haven't answered my question. Now what's going on?" She joined him on the far end of his couch.

He stared at her. "You can always see through me."

Neftis wrinkled her little nose. "I just know you. You're a creature of habit. You don't disturb your schedule unless you're up to some mischief. Tell me."

He snorted, then drank more wine. "You remember those slaves I told you I met?"

"The Habiru?"

"Yes. I ran across them over on the waterfront all lined up like pieces in a board game."

"For what? They weren't going to drown them—"

"No. Amasis is going to have them taken downriver to work on the restoration of Avaris. He's moving the court there."

"That doesn't make sense."

"Maybe it does. Amasis has more soldiers in the delta. He can be well set up in Avaris and waiting for Moses when the prince returns."

"Would Moses declare himself king and defy Amasis?"

Iri hesitated, not sure how much to tell her. Finally their strong bond asserted itself. "No, but the king would."

Her eyes widened.

He took a deep breath and plunged on. "There's a movement to restore the king to the throne and depose Amasis."

"Iri! A conspiracy?"

"It's just in the beginning stages. It's a very secret, tightly woven group. Later on, after I've proven myself, they may let me meet some of the higher-ups. Maybe if I get to be trusted enough, they may let me meet the king. He's in hiding." He paused. "I wonder if it wouldn't be a good idea to tell them what I learned tonight at the docks."

"I suspect everybody will know by noon tomorrow."

"You're right. Where was I?"

"The cabal."

"Amasis' new plans will change everything. We could have a war between the rightful king and the regent. Amasis will have real problems then. The king is popular in the delta, and the priesthood of Amon will be behind him all the way."

"How exciting! What a wonderful cause to get involved in!" Her face fell. "If only I could do something important with my life, something I could really commit myself to."

"Neftis, you're not the type for this. People—including me—will be risking their lives on your ability to keep your own counsel."

"I'd be as quiet as a clam! Don't you trust me?"

What could he say? How could anyone trust her? On the other hand, how could he, her brother, exclude her? He sighed.

"You *are* going to tell me!" Her visage brightened.

"Against my better judgment. My next step is to attend a meeting the day after tomorrow. Everybody will be masked, so none of us can give any of the others away. They'll swear us in, and—"

"What's the matter, Iri?"

"I forgot. I have an important appointment that day—one I've been setting up for six months. I can't go. I'd have to sacrifice half a year's work to—"

"Let me go in your place, Iri!"

He stared at her. "*You?*"

X

The meeting had ended a half hour before, but only now was Neb-mertef able to get rid of the last of his subordinates. Finally, he bade farewell to the supervisor of his upriver properties, barred the door, and breathed a sigh of relief.

It had been a long, boring evening, but necessary. Now, after hours of discussion, the large details and the small, he had all his affairs set up for the future. Thanks to Set-Nakht's astrological predictions, he would be prepared when the great cataclysms befell them all.

Without letting any of his underlings know why, he was transferring his holdings from proven money-making ventures into abstract and speculative ones; selling properties that everyone was sure would only appreciate as time went by; diversifying his holdings.

On the short term he had already begun to anticipate the effect of tomorrow's shocking announcements concerning the move of the court to the delta. He had concluded several important sales that allowed him to pull out of Thebes. The buyers thought they had outsmarted him, but they would be ruined within the week, and he would be richer and more powerful.

He smiled; the smile became a chuckle; the chuckle became a savage and superior laugh. Fortune was favoring him these days!

It had been worth his every maneuver to move first into the inner circle surrounding Amasis, then to Amasis' side; joining the cult—despite his own privately held, unvoiced contempt for the goddess; bribing some officials and eliminating others; and, most importantly, taking the astrologer Set-Nakht into his service.

His smile was cruel as he thought of the matter. The astrologer was a broken man. He would never leave, and the only fetters that bound him were his own weaknesses.

Thinking of this, he decided to look in on Set-Nakht. With any luck he would catch the magus in some discreditable and humiliating activity. The two Phrygians were gone, delivered to an assassin. In their place was a single slave, purchased only the other day. With his latest slave, Neb-mertef hoped to seal the final bonds with Set-Nakht.

He tiptoed up the big staircase. The bolts to Set-Nakht's door had been removed so that he could have no privacy. To exacerbate the situation, the order had been given that a lamp was to be burning at all times in the astrologer's suite.

Neb-mertef put his ear to Set-Nakht's door but could hear nothing. He poised himself and pushed it open. To his surprise, there was no scene of licentious abandon. Instead, the new slave, fully dressed, lay unconscious, bleeding from a gash on his forehead, before the great bed. Clothing lay strewn all over the floor. The magus, whose predictions Nebmertef had claimed as his own to remain in power, was gone!

It was past midnight when Arsaphes strolled jauntily past the pitiful Habiru camp on the quay and made his way to the waterfront brothels and taverns. There was an extra bounce in the tall man's step, and he was doubly happy: First, he had met again with the king, who, unbeknownst to all but Arsaphes and Pebes, had slipped into the city at sundown and had met with both men at one of the cabal's many places of refuge. Second, Arsaphes had learned from an informant the good news that Amasis was moving the capital! That meant Moses could bring the army back to Thebes and pass it into the king's hands.

And—here Arsaphes smiled fiercely, clenching his fists as he walked—for all practical purposes the king would then pass it into his. A great victory!

As he congratulated himself, three men stepped out of the shadows and confronted him. "Who's there?" Arsaphes demanded. "What do you want?"

"There, now," said a rough voice. "He wants to know what we want. Him in his expensive robe and shoes. I'll bet he's got quite a purse in his pocket. The rich ones know they'll have to pay dearly for the kind of fun they're likely to want in this part of town." The ruffian chuckled. "What is it, Long Shanks? Boys? Girls? Whips and chains?"

Arsaphes' eyes narrowed. "Perhaps I came here looking for you. Maybe all three of you. But I can't see your faces. You might not be pretty enough for me. Show me your faces or you'll never see the color of my coin."

His voice subtly changed to a mocking tone. "Come now, boys. If you won't let me see your faces, I won't let you look at mine." He backed into the deep shadow, so they could see nothing but the glow of his eyes. "Come forth, boys. If you're as good company as I think you'll be, I'll give you the money freely." The voice was altering still. Subtly. Slowly.

"What kind of talk is this?" the first of the roughs said.

"You boys get on the left and right of him. He's probably got a knife. Watch his hands."

But then Arsaphes, or the thing that had been Arsaphes, moved back into the light. No longer was it the bony, hairless face of a tall, thin man. Now it had red, hateful eyes, a long, narrow, hairy snout, and a lipless mouth filled with sharp fangs. Covered with coarse hair, it was the face of a monster.

"*No!*" shrieked the first man who had spoken. He tried to move away, but it was as if his feet were rooted to the spot.

The paralyzed men stared in horror as the monster snarled, attacked, conquered, and, in the end, fed—horribly, disgustingly, and unhurriedly, leaving the carrion scattered in bloody pieces for the birds to peck at in the morning.

It fed on each in his turn, while the others had to watch in heart-stopping horror, unable to speak or move, each awaiting his own fearful, unspeakable end.

City guards found the remains at dawn. "It looks like they were attacked by some kind of animal!"

His mate shuddered. "But what would prowl this far into town, even at night? Look, they were armed! Gods! I know this one! He was a tough customer. Well, it looks like they met their match this time. Good riddance, I'd say."

"Let's leave this mess for the garbage boys. We'll make our report and let someone else shovel it all up. Nobody cares what happens to anybody who comes from this part of town. Come on, let's get out of here. The flies are beginning to gather."

XI

In the reception hall of the great house of Menkhuhor, the import-export tycoon, Iri fretted nervously. He had given up his whole day, including the important meeting with the cabal, for this appointment, and the merchant was late.

Perhaps he should have rescheduled. The word was that

someone really important was going to address the cabal, and now he was missing it. And all for the off chance that he might sell the merchant some jewelry.

Fat chance! Most likely the flunkies he'd left samples with had not even bothered to exhibit them to Menkhuhor. Most of his attempts to break into the really distinguished markets had failed.

A servant came from the back room, and Iri stood.

"The noble Menkhuhor has been unavoidably called away. He asked me to reschedule your appointment for next month, when he gets back from Corcyra."

Iri gritted his teeth. "If he'd seen my work, he'd have brought it along with him to sell in Corcyra!"

"That may be, but the noble Menkhuhor sends his regrets."

Iri, fuming, stifled an angry retort. It would only make this popinjay mad at him, with disastrous results for that rescheduled appointment. "All right," he said in a tight voice. "Thank you. When can we reschedule, now?"

Outside, Iri loosed a string of curses. Was he never going to break into the better markets? Was he stuck forever with making weapons?

Suddenly a voice hailed him from a doorway. "Psssst!"

He turned to see a haggard-looking man of medium height standing half-shaded in the opening to a shuttered warehouse. The man beckoned hastily with one finger.

Iri moved forward, feeling safe because of the man's expensive robes. "May I help you?"

"Yes, please," the man pleaded. "I'm running from a rich and powerful man." He wrung his hands. "I don't know how to explain it, but I am without money or resources, and I have to elude this person somehow."

"Who is after you?"

"This very highly placed person—"

"How highly placed? Amasis?"

The man sighed. "No, but it might as well be. His right-hand man."

"Neb-mertef?" Iri whistled. "What does he want to do with you?"

"I've been held prisoner for months. Months! Two nights

ago I managed to escape, but I've nowhere to go. Nothing's safe. He has people scouring the streets of the city for me."

"How can I help?"

"If you could hide me for a day or two? Until I can arrange passage out of town."

"Hmmm. Have you broken any laws? There's a stringent penalty against hiding a fugitive."

"Oh, no, nothing like that, although he's not above making up something if he has to."

"Could I hide you among my servants? Do you have any skills?"

"I'm a scribe and a magus."

"You don't look like a magus."

"How do they look?"

"Stuffy. Dignified."

"I have precious little dignity left, after all that time with him. If only I could find a place to lay my head for a few days—"

"All right," Iri gave in. "Go to the Street of the Well and turn right at the boulevard. My house is the big one three doors on the left—the house of Iri. My servant's name is Mai. Tell her I told you to await me there. Don't let anybody see you."

"Oh, thank you! Thank you so much!" Iri watched his mincing progress down the street.

Only then did he remember. *Gods! The meeting! It's all over now!*

From his invisible position behind the gauze screen, Arsaphes watched the masked figure at the end of the row. His mind was racing, and his heart was beating fast.

On the platform the king had taken off his mask to show himself to the people. He did not look like the idealistic young man the older people remembered going off to the Northland to destroy the Shepherd army. Unmasking was dangerous but necessary: The people needed confirmation of Kamose's identity and ability to govern.

Arsaphes had coached Kamose, virtually telling him word for word what to say. Thus, his attention was riveted on the slim figure at the end of the row. The girl of his fantasy, from two days before.

What a stroke of luck! What fate had favored him by delivering her into his hands? The dark gods were looking out for him. They *wanted* him to meet her. They approved of his plans for her.

He had recognized her before she had put on the mask. The attendees had entered the anteroom one by one and been given their masks by him, and he alone had seen the faces of all of them. And of course, since he had been wearing a mask, none had seen his face. He held the advantage over her already.

He smiled. He wanted her. He wanted her more than he had wanted a woman in years.

Set-Nakht, heart pounding, hands shaking, turned the corner off the Street of the Wall and stepped into the boulevard. He had not gone six steps down the street when two men blocked his path.

He wheeled. Two more were behind him.

"We've been looking for you," said one of them. "*He's* been looking for you. He wants you back. Surely you must know that."

As Set-Nakht shrank back, one of the men behind him grabbed his arm in an iron grip.

"Come along," said the man in a voice full of contempt. "There's a naughty fellow."

"No," he begged in a weak voice. "Please, no!"

At the meeting's end they filed into the cloakroom one at a time to doff the masks, then slip unobserved into the side alley. Neftis kept her eyes downcast, hoping no one would recognize her. But as she came out into the bright sunlight at the end of the alley, a tall man fell into step with her.

"Just keep walking," he said. "I have a message for you from your brother."

Nervously she increased her pace, not looking at him. "Pardon me. You must have me confused with someone else."

"I don't think so. Your brother is Iri, the armorer. You're Neftis, the daughter of Sinuhe."

She looked at him. He was unusually tall, and his face was thin and ascetic, but his eyes held her interest: They were intelligent, sensual, and intense. She stopped and stared up into those fascinating eyes. "You've got your facts right," she said, feeling strangely drawn to him. "What's the message?"

"It concerns the—the man who spoke to us. I don't want to blather on about it in the street."

"Where can we go?" she asked, feeling very adult, very involved, very much the dashing adventuress.

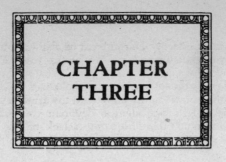

CHAPTER THREE

El-Kab

I

A week before, by stages and stealth, the army had been brought downriver from the Cataracts, anchoring first at Syene, then at Kheny, and finally disembarking to encamp on the legendary battlefield just south of the ancient city of El-Kab.

Prince Moses and General Khafre had decided on El-Kab as a base of operations for a number of reasons: It had been a major center for dissent, the only town of size and influence that had steadfastly rejected Amasis' cult of the goddess and sent its priests packing; it had remained politically loyal to Baliniri right up to the old vizier's death; and its leaders had helped Baliniri plan the maneuver by which the army had been saved, by sending it south to fight the Nubians.

Now, the commander and his general stood on a ridge overlooking the famous battlefield, waiting for Geb, Khafre's adjutant, to bring the latest reports from the downriver spies.

Khafre casually said, "Do you know about this promontory?"

"No," Moses replied, looking down at the troops engaged in weapons practice. He grinned. "I thought I knew something about history before I went on this expedition. But every step we take reminds you of a famous event I've never heard of."

Khafre pulled at his graying beard. "You'll have heard of this, I'll wager. From this very spot Teti the armoress watched the Battle of El-Kab. She saw the Egyptian army fall back in cowardly disarray before the fierce attack of the Nubians when Akhilleus asserted his claim on the Egyptian throne."

Moses whistled long and low. "Every schoolboy has heard of that. The great day the Nubian advance was stopped when the Egyptian line turned and came again and held at the second charge."

Khafre nodded in approval. "When the left flank of the Egyptian army bolted, only their young leader was left, surrounded by fierce Nubians. From a cowardly distance his men saw him face the entire Nubian unit and die, clutching his unit's flag, not having retreated so much as a step while his command crumbled around him."

"That was Netru, Teti's lover?"

"Yes. This field is named after him—not officially, perhaps, but go into the town and ask anyone where our army is billeted now. 'Netru's Field,' they'll say."

"That battle prompted Teti to move into the desert to live among the Black Wind's women and found the Desert Legion," Moses said. "Who initiated Teti into the Order of the Chalybes?"

The general was startled. "Here, now. Outsiders like us aren't supposed to know anything about all that. But it was Sado of Karkara." He waved a hand over the field. "Imagine her standing here, watching her lover die in combat. She'd never been in love before."

"She never had a man after Netru's death, did she? Not until General Riki."

"So they say. Which brings us to other famous military associations with this battlefield: El-Kab was the birthplace of Baba the Frog, the famous warrior and lover of Princess Ah-Hotep. They bore a son—"

Moses smiled. "Whom the army knew as Riki!"

"You learned your history well. It all comes alive, though, when you can stand in the place where it happened."

"I wonder," Moses said, "if we ourselves have not written history in the last few months . . . if perhaps we may not be about to write some more."

"We will if we win. If we lose, our faces will be chiseled off all the friezes, and our names erased off the papyruses. The history of a nation is the history of its winning side."

"I wonder if the losers don't also have something important to say—something more human, more moving. Was Netru a loser? He died defenseless and alone down there. And what about little Hadad the Cripple, up in the North?"

Khafre contemplated. "You do have a point."

"I've been thinking," Moses continued, "of what I learned back at Semna about my true parentage. Would I be celebrated as Moses of Egypt, remembered a century from now, while as Moses of the Habiru, a slave in a shepherd's cloak, I would be forgotten before the flowers fade on my grave?"

Khafre shrugged. "None of the prophecies we've heard about you seem to indicate that you're to be king." He shook his head. "Sounds like sheer madness to me, to be brutally honest. Prophecies can be wrong."

"And they can be right." He stopped, looking down the path. "Ah, here's Geb." The two returned the adjutant's salute as he joined them. "What news?"

"Seth is here!" Geb announced.

Moses grinned. "I don't believe it!"

"It's true," Geb said. "And with him a unit of the Desert Legion—and Weret and Tchabu!"

"Splendid!" Khafre said. "And not a moment too soon, with us poised on the edge of invading Thebes! Come on; let's go down and see them."

To the west of the Nile many paths cut across the desert: some were broad and well-worn, the highways of the desert for a thousand years; others were simple, one-man tracks known only to the most knowledgeable habitués of the desert. One of the most obscure wound through the hills and broke through the brush at a deserted spot right across the Nile from Edfu, just upriver from El-Kab. It was this track that Weret's patrol had traveled to bring Seth to his rendezvous with the army.

Now the aging general of the Desert Legion stood, lean and impressive in her statuesque nudity, the brown of her slim, rock-hard body accentuated by the gold ornaments Teti had made for her a generation before. Weret nodded at the prince and his companions; for her, a woman of few words, this was the equivalent of a speech of welcome.

The person Moses most wanted to see, however, was Seth. His mentor, best friend, and the wisest man he had ever met seemed a decade older, tired, and withdrawn—and the sight of him nearly broke Moses' heart.

The old man and young embraced. "Moses!" Seth said in a voice that was now slow and deliberate. "I have missed you more than words can describe."

"And I have felt like a man who has lost his heart and his good right arm," Moses responded. "Are you feeling better?"

"I will never be satisfied with my health," Seth said. "As I have never been satisfied with it. If I had waited any longer, who knows?"

"Tchabu tell Seth not go now," the dwarf beside him complained. "Seth not listen. Seth never listen to Tchabu."

Seth's hand rested affectionately on the little man's crooked shoulder. "That's not true. I always listen because you always speak the truth." He chuckled. "It *is* true that I sometimes listen to you and then do something else. A man has to follow his own instincts. Even," he said sadly, "if he knows into what folly they can sometimes lead him."

General Khafre clasped Seth's hand, then stepped back, looking around for Geb. "Is there news from Thebes?"

"Sorry, sir," the adjutant said. "I neglected to report in all the excitement. There's been a new development—maybe the breakthrough we've been waiting for. Amasis is moving the entire court—and the slaves from Deir el-Bahari—down-river to Avaris."

"No!" The single syllable came from a dozen throats at once.

"Apparently it's true. He must know that Thebes is indefensible and that if we were to face him there, he'd lose."

Khafre grunted. "A wise move. Avaris is well-nigh impregnable; that sloping Hai wall has never been breached. We would have to find someone inside the walls to betray it to us."

Moses was about to respond, but a sound caught his attention, and he turned. Little Tchabu, the dwarf, had pitched heavily to the ground, and his crooked little body was jerking and twitching wildly.

He fell to one knee beside the dwarf. "Quick! Somebody help! He's having a seizure!"

II

Seth wanted to stay by his fallen friend, but Geb touched his arm and whispered, "Weret is more experienced than any of us at handling Tchabu's attacks, and she doesn't like help. You know how she is."

"And you have some news for my ears alone," Seth guessed, letting himself be drawn aside. "All right, what's happening in Thebes?"

"You amaze me, sir. Well, Neb-mertef is now second in command in Thebes, and Amasis does little without consulting him."

"Strange!" Seth mused. "I was never impressed with Neb-mertef. He's a petty, backstairs intriguer."

"I agree, sir, but the word is—well, do you remember a magus named Set-Nakht?"

"I've heard of him," Seth said. "By reputation he's a good and respected astrologer."

"Our spy says he's being, uh, 'kept' by Neb-mertef, who evidently has some hold on the astrologer. He never comes out of Neb-mertef's house. And Neb-mertef's men comb the male brothels and buy a steady string of new boys. Nobody ever hears from them again."

"Buys them for Set-Nakht?"

"I think so, sir."

"This is most interesting. I'd guess that Set-Nakht is giving his predictions to his master, which are passed along to Amasis. That would make Neb-mertef look very good to Amasis."

"A lot of people have let Amasis down in recent months, and he's quietly had them killed, one by one," Geb remarked.

"Even cult devotees?"

"They have been the worst offenders. The cult is about worn out, while the old religion remains strong. Unfortunately there seems to be a new element within the priesthood of Amon—some hierarchic and doctrinal changes."

"Is Si-Ptah still head priest?"

"Yes, sir. That's the odd thing: Si-Ptah has always counted himself among our allies. But he has been making appointments that restructure everything below the level of the main temple."

"Could this be in response to pressure from Amasis' people? Have they infiltrated the temples of Amon?"

Geb frowned. "Could be."

Seth glanced back at where Weret had helped Tchabu to sit up. "Now what about the other matter?"

"Not a sign, sir, except for the odd things going on elsewhere. Considering all the changes, they don't make much sense unless——"

"Unless some new factor has entered the city and is causing them."

"Right, sir."

"You're as sharp as ever, Geb. Anything else I ought to know?"

"King Kamose, sir. He's reportedly in very good health but doesn't look like himself anymore. That will create a problem when he reasserts his claim in Egypt and takes the power back from Amasis. Kamose has organized an underground group, dedicated to putting him back on the throne. They're apparently growing in numbers by leaps and bounds, sir, mostly among the young."

"They never knew what he looked like when he was younger, so they have no preconceived notions. The cabal will help us legitimatize Kamose if we decide to hand the army over to him—"

"If, sir? But I thought it was all settled."

Seth put his hand on Geb's shoulder and began to steer the adjutant back toward Weret and Tchabu. "No. I want to talk to Kamose first, get to know the person he is right now. He's always been very unstable. Oh, I'm not condemning him; some of it is his blood. His father had an insane streak.

And Kamose's horrible childhood didn't help—seeing Apophis murder his mother."

"I understand, sir."

"And there's more." Seth's tone had become pensive. "I have a suspicion. . . ."

"Of what, sir?"

"Never mind—for now." He watched as the others helped Tchabu to his feet. "Tchabu!" he said sympathetically. "How are you, old fellow?"

Weret spoke up. "He's had an important vision, but we only heard a bit of it."

Tchabu stood blinking at them and shook his large, misshapen head.

Weret continued. "Some sort of great cataclysm: the oceans going mad, the earth opening up and swallowing people, great mountains exploding." Her eyes narrowed as she looked at Seth. "Do such things happen?"

"I have been in an earthquake, and the house around me fell, and when the roof caved in, it killed a man. I have never seen a mountain explode, but I once met an old man who said he had actually experienced this, down in the Mountains of Fire, far south even of the Sudd."

"Then Tchabu's vision might come to pass?"

"Not here, obviously. Perhaps he was dreaming of a place far away, whose misfortunes might still affect us. Such things are not impossible." He looked at Tchabu now. "Are you all right, old friend?"

"Tchabu . . . weak but good."

Seth thought for a moment. "Moses," he said at last, "come. I would speak with you." He turned to the rest. "Excuse us, please. My old pupil and I have some catching up to do."

They walked across Netru's Field and down to the Nile. "Seth," Moses said, "while I'm glad to see you, I was expecting you to take longer to recuperate. Are you quite sure you should be out in the world again?"

"I don't look it, do I?" Seth answered with a sigh. "I know. I've aged. But I couldn't sit around, just waiting for the boneyard. I'd rather die while tackling a problem."

"I understand. And the gods know I'm glad to see you! I

can use your advice. Tell me, old friend: What should I do now?"

"What do *you* think you should do?"

"Well, I have a strong desire to see Jochebed—I mean Mother—and Miriam. And to meet the rest of my family. As far as the army is concerned, I won't hand it over to Amasis—the gods forbid—or, without knowing more than I do now, to Kamose."

"I agree completely. I want to talk with Kamose."

"Seth! You're not thinking of going to Thebes?"

"Perhaps. Perhaps not. There's a part of me that's afraid. I keep asking myself, Am I finished? Is it all over for me?"

"Seth! No!"

"Moses, in that terrible confrontation with Apedemek, I was defeated by my superior, pure and simple. Even now there's something wrong with my mind, something I can't control, something I can't predict or guard against."

"All the more reason why you must stay away from Thebes! You know he *has* to be there!"

Seth's careworn face was as hard as stone. "I know. I know Apedemek's there."

"And you are willing to risk facing him?"

"If I don't, I'll never be a whole man again."

III

Back on the hill Weret met with General Khafre and Geb. "I would know your plans for the army," she said. "Everything you do in the matter of Amasis and the succession affects us at the oasis."

"No one plans anything rash," Khafre assured her. "Moses is a steady young man. He takes his obligation to Baliniri very seriously and plans to follow the instructions he received from the old man before he died."

"Good. Moses has changed, though."

"That's true," Geb confirmed. "Did you notice his weapons are gone? We made a fine swordsman of him, but he says his fighting days are over. He takes his new destiny as seriously as he ever took any previous duty. I consider it a terrible waste, but we might as well ask the Nile to change its course as try to influence him once his mind is made up."

"So he won't become king of Egypt," Weret said. "Where does that leave us if Kamose turns out to be unacceptable?"

Khafre frowned. "Good question. I've been putting off thinking about that, in the hope that Kamose is competent. I've also harbored the forlorn wish that Moses' sense of civic duty will dictate his actions. But he doesn't want to talk about that until he has seen his family."

Weret's eyes flashed. "Then don't let him see them," she said in a hard voice. "They'll only complicate matters."

"That may be an option," Geb ventured. "The Habiru may be in the delta already."

"And you want me to keep this fact from him?" Khafre asked, incredulous.

"Yes!" Weret urged. "For the time being, at least! When you send a party to Thebes to investigate the situation, his family won't be there to distract him."

Khafre pursed his lips and blew out a long sigh. "I don't like lying to him."

Weret snorted. "It'd be for his own good."

"That's true, sir," Geb added.

Khafre looked slowly from face to face. His emotions were violently at war. If Moses could be maneuvered into taking control of Egypt, they wouldn't have to deal with Kamose at all—a very attractive solution with no unknown quantities. Weigh that against the possibility of ruining Khafre's valued relationship with his young protégé. . . .

"Let me think about it," he decided.

The general fretted about the matter all afternoon, and only after the army had eaten and the camp fire was half burned down did he begin to have any idea what he was going to do. But in the end it was Moses who approached him, drawing him aside and sitting beside him before the glowing coals.

Khafre cleared his throat. "I was just going to—"

But Moses had things on his mind and hardly noticed his

words. "Khafre, I can't take the army into Thebes without some preliminary scouting."

"No, my lord. If you talk to the spies who came up today—"

"No," Moses interrupted. "I want to slip into the city myself, in disguise."

Khafre stared. "But my lord! Surely you realize how dangerous that would be!"

"I have to take the chance. I want to meet Kamose, and I want to see my family."

"Well, my lord, I can certainly understand that. And I suppose that with appropriate precautions, it could be arranged. I can send a squad of handpicked men with you."

"No," Moses said quietly but firmly. "Nobody at all. I'll borrow a fishing boat—"

"Fishermen are burnt black by the sun, my lord—all over."

"When Weret and the women were training me in the ways of the desert, I wore no clothes. I can pass for a fisherman."

Khafre scowled. "Too dangerous. I don't like it."

"I've already decided. You've no choice. I outrank you." Moses' grin was full of affection. "I know about the vow you made to Baliniri to keep me safe. But Baliniri's dead, and your loyalty is owed to me now."

Khafre snorted. "You've got an answer for everything, don't you?"

In the end they had an agreement of sorts, with a promise from Moses to take the greatest care and do nothing rash. And Khafre had committed himself: he had not told Moses about the Habiru being transported downriver. Khafre's conscience bothered him, but he clenched his teeth and forced himself to ignore it.

In the night Seth tossed and turned, bedeviled by nightmares. He dreamt he was back at Semna, alone in the anteroom of the fortress's dungeon. Suddenly, reaching through the stone wall as if it were as insubstantial as a fog, there came a giant hand, twenty times the size of a human hand. A sickly yellow, its knobby, clawlike fingers were tipped with cruel and ugly talons. It grasped Seth around the chest and squeezed hard.

He struggled in the viselike grip of the monstrous hand, unable to breathe. His hands tore at the huge hand but with no effect.

In his death throes, he had heard the tense voice of Princess Tharbis, as he heard it months before: "Stop it! You're murdering him!"

And now Apedemek's terrible voice, the voice he feared, boomed menacingly around the room. "*Not I, my little plaything. It is the lord of darkness, the prince of evil, whom I serve.*"

"Het!" the girl shrieked. "Try the door again!"

The disembodied voice cut through the air. "*Even now life seeps from him. Even now his mind fails. Even now his mental powers are being carved away, burned by the flames of hatred! Even now the lord of darkness is gutting his memories! Soon there will be nothing left of him. He will be an idiot, a broken hulk of a man. . . .*"

Seth struggled weakly, his vision blurred. There was no power in him. He was sinking, sinking. . . .

Abruptly he came awake, gasping for air and sitting bolt upright in his sweat-drenched bed. He was in the army of Egypt's encampment at El-Kab, in the midst of friends and comrades. He looked at the moonlit camp, the long rows of tents.

"I'm here, safe," he soothed himself in a broken whisper. "It's all right."

But even as he said it, he knew it for a lie. Most of him was here, but part of him was still in the dungeons of Semna, forever captive. The evil genius Apedemek had bested him, broken him, in the most desperate battle of his life.

He shuddered. The gigantic hand had, in reality, nearly killed him. Had it not been for the valiant efforts of his son, Het, and daughter-by-marriage, Tharbis, he assuredly would have died there, squeezed dry, mashed flat.

A part of him remained in thrall to that evil magus, and he would relive the horrible scene until he could relive it no more.

What can I do? he wondered in agony.

There was only one possible solution: He had to confront

Apedemek and defeat him—or die in the attempt. He shuddered again in recognition of his own weakness. Somehow he must find strength, then master the technique of controlling men's minds, which Apedemek had used upon him. He had no choice; he had to redeem himself.

The army did not need him anymore. In fact nobody needed him now that Moses was adult and independent.

He would go to Thebes. He would track Apedemek down, if it cost him his last breath!

IV

In the morning Seth told no one of his dream or his resolutions. And after a light breakfast Weret gathered up Tchabu and the patrol that had come with her and announced that they would return to the oasis.

Before leaving, however, she took Moses aside. "We must speak. I think I will not see you again."

Moses suddenly stopped. "What do you mean? Have you received some augury from Tchabu or Neku-re that says one of us is going to die?"

Weret's thin smile was appreciative. "You're as sharp as ever. The augury concerns the new life you are destined to lead and how it will turn your footsteps away from me and mine." She took his arms firmly. "Come. I want to talk with you, free from interference and other ears."

Moses fell in step with her. He and Weret were of a height, and her strides matched his, long and powerful. He was used to this brisk pace from the months he had spent in the desert with her and her private guard, learning the ways of the waterless land.

"Both Tchabu and Neku-re agree that our paths will not cross again. I will not worry about you. You are a good man and have been a good pupil. You will never get lost in the desert or starve or die of thirst."

"I trust what you have taught me," Moses responded. "I assume that I am somehow to free my people and lead them

across the Sinai to their ancestral homeland." He frowned.
"*My* ancestral homeland. I still haven't quite got used to the
idea."

"It does not matter. Destiny is destiny."

"True. I should let the auguries help me to understand
just when I am to make a move, and which move to make."
He sighed. "Still, how strange. I have a mother I did not
know was mine. A father and a brother—"

"A fine brother! You will like Aaron. He's strong and
upright and decent. And"—here she chuckled—"the best
hand with a slingshot you've ever seen. Who knows? That
may come in handy, particularly if you're serious about not
taking up any weapons." He nodded. "Ah, what a pity. I
remember our sword practice. I am not sure I could have
taken you even in the bloom of my youth. And that is a lot for
a proud woman to say."

"Oh, come now," Moses said. "Proud you may be, but
you are honest."

Weret turned away to hide her sudden shame over the
deception she and the others had agreed to. "Well, the world
will lose a great swordsman. What it will gain, I cannot
imagine, except that Neku-re assures me that your actions
will affect countless generations in all nations."

Moses, always a trifle embarrassed when discussing his
mysterious destiny, changed the subject. "About Tchabu's
last seizure . . . I need to know *everything*."

"You and the Habiru were mentioned," Weret admitted.

"Please, Weret!"

Her already thin lips became a straight, white line. "The
sea will rise and cover the path where you tread, and you will
never be seen again. Your name will be obliterated from all
the records of Egypt, and no man on the Nile will remember
you." She clenched her fists. "How can this be, given the
other prophecy? Yet Tchabu never errs."

"Is that all?" he asked, looking her in the eyes.

"He said you cannot escape. You must take the paths of
the sea. If you do otherwise, you will be cut to ribbons by the
enemy."

Moses thought about this and nodded. In the end he
walked more slowly with her down to the Nile. "I have

decided to go into Thebes, alone and disguised. I will find the Habiru first; then I will look up Kamose."

"And what if Kamose is unreliable?"

"I hope it does not come to that. If he has gone over to the side of evil, we cannot afford to have two such enemies. I have given my vow not to take up the sword, so I will kill him with my hands."

"Ah, the cub grows to full maturity. He takes responsibility. He acts first and works out a rationale later."

"He does what he has to do," Moses said flatly.

She sighed. "Never have I wished for the life of a conventional woman who walks behind a man and bears his children. But you have helped me to understand the love a woman may have for her son. You have become very dear to me."

"And I feel as though I have found an older sister to share the wisdom of a longer life with me. In the last months there has been something new and fine and strong in my life that I have never known before." He reached for her, and his eyes were damp. "Is it true, Weret? Will we never see each other again?"

She forced herself from his embrace and smiled her tight, rough-and-ready warrior's grin. "You will see with my eyes in the desert. You will sniff the wind with my nose. You will listen for telltale sounds with my ears. It will be my instincts that will guide you to water."

"Yes," he agreed. His eyes were streaming now, but the smile on his clean, young face was genuine. "And what do I leave with you, my dear friend?"

She firmed her jaw. "Memories and more. Through you I have discovered a side of myself that could love a man, even as a son. Through you I will achieve a kind of immortality, the kind a mother achieves through her child. Do not disparage this. It is a great thing to have given me. If I am remembered for a generation, I will be content. In Egypt there will be no friezes, no stored papyruses telling of the Desert Legion, the women of the oasis, Teti or Weret or Naldamak or—"

"But surely—"

"No. It is Tchabu's vision. He told me long ago. I will be wiped from this earth as surely as if I had never been."

Moses looked in her eyes and thought he saw the wet gleam of a stray tear. "Ah, Weret, Seth told me of the terrible sweetness of his days in the Land of the Two Rivers and of the people he came to love so there. 'The life of a love is as short as a mayfly's,' he told me. 'But it will have to do me. For the briefest time I have seen the sun break through clouds and warm the land and bring forth life where there was none. Could I have learned more in fifty years of it?' I saw the tears in his wise eyes, and I knew he meant it. At last I know why."

He felt her press her thin lips to his cheek.

"Go in peace, my dear. May your own people's God and mine protect you. May your days be long and happy." And then she turned on one hard, bare heel and strode away.

He smiled through his tears as she wiped her own cheek of the telltale sign. He swallowed hard. In the last year so many new people had come into his life: Seth, Khafre and Geb, Het and Tharbis, and the men of his army.

And now? Was the next part of his life to be all farewells? All losses? All poignant moments like this one? He who had been so rich in friends, was he to lose them one by one as the year progressed?

CHAPTER FOUR

Thebes

I

Amasis, having decided to relocate the court, had decreed that the whole working part of the city was to move with him. Little other than token markets, hostelries, and warehouses would be left behind—just enough to attend to the normal running of a town a fifth the size of imperial Thebes.

It had taken several days for advance notification to get to the delta, then for the flotilla that Amasis had ordered to make its way upriver. Now the quays at Thebes were totally occupied on both sides of the river with boats of every size and kind, and additional boats were anchored well out into the tide, awaiting their turn.

The streets, too, were clogged, with scores of wagons trying to get out of the squares and into the narrow thoroughfares or side alleys, which were blocked by men engaged in the frustrating task of moving large objects—furniture, crates of foodstuffs, and tall jars of wine or oil—into a position where the wagons could pick them up and cart them to the waterfront.

Amasis had tried to order the artisans of Deir el-Bahari downriver as well; but the art colony had defied him to remain near their building materials. What use would sculptors be so far from their quarries? Amasis had decided not to press the point, and the craft village had breathed a collective sigh of relief.

The rest of the city was plunged into a terrible bind: Few residents had learned about the relocation order early enough to dispose of property that would now be worthless. A precious few—chief among them Neb-mertef—had quickly unloaded their city property at bargain prices, but the investments had, by now, practically beggared the new owners.

Neb-mertef had managed to make a tidy bundle off the move and now had all his assets on deposit in gold with the bankers in Athribis. His agents in the delta were already evaluating possible new investments, to be reported to Neb-mertef and the thoroughly chastened and subdued Set-Nakht, who was casting horoscopes on the largest purchases.

The streets were full of soldiers—more than had been in Thebes since Baliniri had sent the Theban garrison to Nubia with Prince Moses. There were almost enough to make a stand if the Theban army was to come downriver from El-Kab. The citizens daily waited apprehensively for news that Moses' garrison might be spotted coming downstream.

But the army held its peace, while the citizenry trembled. It did not matter whether one supported Amasis or Prince Moses; the thought of civil war in the narrow valley that held Thebes and Deir el-Bahari was enough to scare anyone. If war was to come, better that it should come in the delta, where there were so many places for a peace-loving man to hide himself and his family.

Amasis had decided to stay in Thebes, supervising the move. He was still transacting business, holding daily but abbreviated divans, and receiving foreign emissaries and major merchants.

One of these was Demetrios's associate Hieron, who, at midday, had sat cooling his heels for far longer than he was used to. He glared at the closed door of Amasis' grand reception hall, growing more and more impatient. Finally he caught the eye of a functionary who had been scurrying to and fro, carrying messages. "You! Come here!"

The retainer looked at Hieron's fine purple robes and came forward. "Yes, sir?" he said in a tone equally lacking in contempt or deference.

"Is it Amasis' policy to keep guests waiting this long?"

The retainer raised a brow at Hieron's tone. "I beg your pardon, sir," he said cautiously, "but the regent is closeted with the ambassador from Punt."

"Indeed," Hieron said acidly. "And Punt does only a fraction of the business my master does with Egypt in an average year. What a wonderful reason to flatter Punt and snub me." He rose disgustedly.

This evoked the desired reaction. "Perhaps I could intercede for you, my lord," the retainer said quickly. "Whom shall I say is waiting?"

Hieron glared. "Tell him the trade representative of Demetrios the Magnificent."

The functionary swallowed hard and bowed. "A thousand pardons! I'll tell the regent myself, my lord. If you'd only be so kind as to wait—"

Hieron waved him away and watched him scuttle to the door, bowing and scraping every inch of the way until his hip banged against the door and rattled it.

Neb-mertef had been watching the exchange from cover. He frowned and quickly found his way to a side door that led into the inner conference room. He signaled to Amasis several times before Amasis noted him; then, scowling bad-temperedly, Amasis dismissed his visitor.

"What is the matter with you?" Amasis hissed.

"My lord, the representative from Demetrios the Magnificent is here. He demands an audience. But there is something of primal importance you must know before you speak to him. It affects what you dare say in front of him."

"*Dare* say?" Amasis sputtered.

The functionary from the anteroom was bearing down on them.

"My lord, a word with you."

Neb-mertef waved the lesser official away. "The regent will be with you in just a moment."

He led Amasis gently out of earshot.

"I have received a report from my spy in Crete. Our man Pronomus is no more."

"Pronomus? Dead? Why did you not tell me?"

"You have been extremely busy with the relocation, my lord. I didn't want to bother you. Frankly, I had been expecting trouble for some time. Pronomus was insecure, incompetent, and impulsive."

"Well, what did he do? Did he compromise us?"

"That, at least, he did not do, sir. When put to the torture, he died of heart failure. But he was foolish enough to engage in a conspiracy to assassinate Demetrios—"

"This same Demetrios? The merchant prince?"

"The very man. It seems that Demetrios humiliated Pronomus by giving King Minos an entirely different—and more realistic—account of the present state of affairs in Egypt than Pronomus had, and Pronomus let his anger get away with him."

"The fool! I should have dismissed him long ago! You can be right about such matters."

Neb-mertef let one eyebrow lift, then prudently brought it down again.

"They didn't get our other man there? Your man?"

"No, my lord. My man is still well placed. He spies for me not only on Crete, but upon Demetrios himself as well. He had been a spy for Demetrios, but I made him a better offer. He is now a double agent, working mainly for me."

"What would I do without you?"

"You flatter me, my lord. But Hieron is here—Demetrios's second in command and closest associate. He has been fretting over waiting so long."

"Should I see him?"

"Think, my lord. He works for the man who had Pronomus killed. I don't think you should see him at all. I think we ought to beg off, tell him you have come down with a sudden indisposition."

"Snub the richest trader in the world?"

"It's a risk, my lord. But we have other, equally good connections for all our essential imports, and our own ships are capable of moving all our exports. Demetrios will be angry for a time, but he is a man with a reputation for practicality, and such men seldom carry a grudge long."

"This is highly irregular!"

"I'll see him, my lord. Armed with what I know via my own network of spies—I mean *our* own network of spies, I can buy us some time for getting the economy safely restructured."

There was a cynical smile on Amasis' face now. "That means letting you consolidate the remaining half of the wealth of Egypt into your own capable—and, I might add, highly acquisitive—hands."

"All in the name of your own greater power and honor, my lord. Let me talk to Hieron. You can go out the back way."

Amasis hesitated, then he shrugged and smiled knowingly. "Do as you wish. Report to me the moment he's gone. I leave the matter in your hands."

"I shall endeavor, my lord, to be worthy of your trust." He bowed deeply. But when he returned to an erect stance, there was a chill smile on his face.

II

Most of Iri's forges and smelting furnaces had been closed down by now, and finished work and raw ore alike had been loaded on the ships bound for the delta. A single forge had been left in place, manned around the clock by two of his journeymen and their smoke-blackened, fire-scarred apprentices, in case emergency service was required. Only when Amasis and the last of the soldiers had embarked on the waiting vessels would Iri at last break up the forge, put out the fires, and move his men. Iri had elected to remain out of pride, making certain that everything produced by the forge and bearing his name met the highest standard.

Now he wondered if his decision had been wise. Across the square came his hated rival Khons, who had just received an order from Menkhuhor for fifty pieces of jewelry, and his already finished work had been thoroughly gossiped about in the marketplace.

"Hail, Iri!" As Khons's eyes lingered on Iri's birthmark, his lip curled in disdain. "I suppose you've heard about how my work has been accepted by Menkhuhor!"

"Why, no, Khons, I hadn't," he lied blandly. "Have you placed your little pieces? Congratulations. Have you deposited the money? I'd save it if I were you. You never know how long it's going to be before you make another sale."

"And you, Iri? Have you made any sales lately, or are you still supervising a bunch of itinerant tinkers, repairing scythes and chisels?"

Iri stifled the impulse to snarl. "My forges produce items that have real uses in the world, and as form follows function, there is a certain natural beauty about them. When I make a plowshare, it looks like a plowshare, and you can use it for one. But when you make a golden icon of Horus, it's more likely to resemble the dangling, uncircumcised yardarm of a Nubian whose pintle hangs all the way to his knees."

Khons's eyes had been widening and widening.

Iri waggled a finger. "Beware! One of these days the temple police may take a closer look at one of those lumpy *phalloi* of yours, and you're going to be in deep trouble." He snorted derisively. "No wonder Menkhuhor markets your work in Ashkelon. There's no law there against spoiling gold by making unintelligible lumps of excrement out of it."

Khons's mouth became a lipless line. "Very funny," he said. "Farewell, Iri. Oh, incidentally, have you seen your sister lately?"

"What do you mean? You'd better watch your filthy mouth, you son of a whore!"

"Oh . . . well, haven't you heard? That's funny. I always heard it was the husband who was the last to know. But then she doesn't have a husband, does she? And at her age! Perhaps she doesn't need a husband, just a man—"

Iri grabbed the closest thing to his hand, and it turned out to be a hook used to dig out the dried slag. He heaved it at Khons's head and barely missed as Khons scurried away behind one of the buildings fronting the square.

Iri stood watching his departed rival, heart pounding. Were people spreading filthy rumors about her? he wondered. He suddenly frowned more deeply. What if it was more serious? What if, in these last few days when he was breaking his back trying to get everything packed and moved, she had been— No! He pounded a fist into a palm.

"Something wrong, sir?" one of the journeymen ventured.

Iri let his tense shoulders droop. "No. Everything's fine." He spat into the dust.

"Yes, sir."

Iri looked at the journeyman. "Thanks for your support. I've just been tense lately, what with this move. I hate change." He grinned sheepishly. "Except, of course, for the changes I plan."

"I understand, sir. Is there anything we can do to make things easier for you?"

"How kind of you," Iri said, genuinely touched. "Just continue with the work. I think I'll go home."

"You're still in it, sir?"

"Yes. I sold it last week to a man who wanted it mainly for the marble. The buyer never intends to occupy my house; he wants to build a place in Avaris. He's allowing Neftis and me to stay there until we leave Thebes."

"Very well, sir. And—don't mind that fellow Khons. He'll never amount to anything. I've seen his work, and it doesn't have any soul to it."

"I appreciate that," Iri said, laughing. "You came on a month ago, didn't you? I regret to say I don't remember your name."

"It's Baufra, sir."

"I'll remember that. You've an interest in fine metalwork?"

"Yes, sir. I even do a bit of it myself, but it's not within a thousand leagues of yours."

"When we get downriver, I'll give you a tip or two about working with gold."

"It'd be a great honor, sir."

III

Iri walked unannounced into his sister's chambers. "Neftis! Where are you?"

Mai crossed the central hall toward him. "My lord, my lady asked me not to tell you, but—"

"What's going on? Her room looks as though she'd not been home in weeks!"

"It's not that way, my lord."

"Is she spending her nights away?"

"I'm sure that whatever she's up to—"

"Curse her! Sneaking around behind my back! How can I keep her name untarnished when she behaves like this?"

He let his arms fall to his sides. "Mai," he said plaintively, "what's going *on* here?"

"What can I say, my lord? She's a grown woman, no more under my influence than you are. She's long overdue to get married and start raising a family, my lord. If her brother had been here—"

"So Khian could handle her, and I can't?"

"You know he could, my lord. He always did. You too, sir. He always kept both of you in line. And you loved him for it, as I recall, my lord."

He smiled, albeit reluctantly. "Good old Mai. You always tell the truth, don't you? Well, tell me the truth about my sister. Has she taken a lover?"

"She hasn't seen fit to confide in me, my lord."

He sighed defeatedly. "Do you have any idea when she's due home?"

"I'm afraid not, my lord."

"When was she here last?"

"Three days ago, my lord."

"Three days! Three *days*!"

Four large, powerful male slaves bore Zoser's carrying chair through the thoroughfares and into the heart of Thebes. In the chaotic days preceding the move of the court from Thebes to Athribis, Zoser had added two burly freedmen to his entourage, who now cleared the way for his passage.

He spotted a familiar face in the Street of the Warehouses and signaled to the guard behind him.

"That girl," Zoser said. "Hail her for me."

Swiftly, efficiently, the freedman did as he had been told. The girl looked up at the portly figure on the chair, smiled nervously, and tried to get away. But the guard was persuasive, and at length the girl approached Zoser's chair.

"Greetings, Zoser," she said. "I'm honored to see you again."

He smiled down at her benignly, but the smile hid uncertainty and concern. "Greetings, Neftis. I have been thinking about our conversation. Have you been well? Have you given any thought to what we talked about?"

Neftis would not meet his eyes. "I've been well, thank you. I've been very busy. There's just so much to do."

"So much that you could not spare me an evening soon? As a good friend of your father's, I feel some responsibility for you. You would honor me by coming to my house for dinner."

She fidgeted, and he used the brief pause to look her over. The studied carelessness of her dress had been replaced by a genuine lack of interest in her appearance. This was not healthy in an unmarried woman of her age.

"I . . . I'm not sure," she faltered. "My schedule . . ." For just a moment, she did look at him, and there was a look of despair and utter vulnerability in her eyes, and she hovered precariously on the edge of accepting his offer of help and counsel.

"Yes?" he encouraged. He glanced at her hands and feet. The fingernails were broken and untended. Her ankles were dirty. "You wouldn't be imposing on me, you know. There have been no young people around my house for such a long time, and old people miss the freshness and honesty of the young."

"W-would Iri be invited, too?"

"If you wish." But he immediately noticed the hopeful light leaving her eyes and backtracked. "No," he corrected hastily. "No, just you, my dear. We'll get together with Iri on some other occasion." He paused, but her acceptance did not come. "Neftis, have I offended you in some way?"

She looked at him with eyes that held as much anger as desperation. "My schedule is so unsettled. I will send Mai over to confirm a date when I know a bit better what I'll be doing."

"Certainly, my dear. But don't wait too long. I'm not getting any younger. And if there are any problems in your life, perhaps I can lend a hand. I am not without resources."

"I will try, my lord." The utter longing and despair returned to her face—a silent plea for help. "Now, my lord, I really must beg my leave of you."

With a hasty curtsy she was gone, leaving Zoser feeling concerned and regretful. What could be wrong? What could have created this change for the worse? She had been impetuous, bored, and full of nervous energy; now, only a matter of days later, she seemed not to know who she was.

Zoser turned to the guard. "How long before our move to Athribis?"

"Three days, sir. On the morning tide."

Three days! Zoser thought. *So little time!* What could he do in three days? There would be no chance to find out what was bothering the girl. And if he waited until both of them were in Athribis, who knew how much mischief could be wrought with her life between now and then?

As soon as she had gone around the corner, Neftis ran until she could run no more and her breath came in terrible, hacking gasps. She stopped at last, to lean against a storehouse wall and to catch her breath. She had lost one sandal and had torn her dress.

She cursed her luck. Zoser was the last person in the world—other than Iri—she wanted to run into! She could fool virtually anybody else. She could usually look a man directly in the eyes while lying, and her conscience would not bother her—and a good thing, too, because she was doing a lot of lying lately. That and worse. In order to be true to *him*, she was finding it necessary to be false to everyone else in the world.

That usually wasn't so bad; but Zoser had been honest with her. He had looked into her heart and understood her. He had cared for her, in a kind and fatherly way.

Oh, it was horrible how, the moment you'd figured out a way not to *care* what anyone thought, somebody turned up whom you *did* care about. Somebody whose opinion *did* matter.

You must stop this, she told herself. *The only thing that will get you through is to abandon hope. It isn't going to get any better. You are what you are, and that's the beginning and the end of it.*

She shut her eyes and squeezed two large tears from under the lids. *And who are you? You are what he has shown you to be. All he did was hold a mirror that made you truly see yourself—a mirror that showed only ugliness.*

Sobs shook her, and she turned her face to the mudbrick wall. The rough surface tore at her skin, and she would not allow herself to shrink from the pain.

She had had such a superior image of herself; she had looked down on everybody. No matter how much she had despised the dull men around her, she had always reserved her worst criticism for their wives and mistresses. She had spoken of them as whores one and all, the wives having sold themselves for security, and the mistresses for money. She had called them stupid, vain, thoughtless sluts. And now she was one of the worst and the least of them, lying, cheating, doing whatever was required of her.

And for what? For pleasure that was also pain. For the regard of someone she despised and hated and feared. And needed! *Needed!*

Why had no one told her that love was worse than hate? That it made you feel less, not more; worse, not better; uglier, not more beautiful?

How could she have come this far without knowing what life was really like?

IV

Iri waited at the house for as long as he could, but by the time he had to leave for his appointment, Neftis had still not appeared. With a strangled curse he stalked out into the street, slamming the door behind him, and hurried through the chaotic traffic to the Market of the West Wind and the inn called the Sign of the Dolphin.

As always, the short-legged little dancer shot one quick

glance at him, recognized him, and turned her pretty, empty face away disdainfully. He ignored her and made his way across the dirty floor to where Pebes was waiting.

Pebes got up and signaled to Iri to follow, moving to a private room in the rear of the inn.

Once inside, Iri looked around: A burly man, grim-faced, gray-bearded, and powerfully built despite his middle years, sat behind a long table.

Pebes turned. "This is Iri, of whom I told you, Si—"

The stranger broke in. "No titles," he said brusquely. "You know the rule." His voice was a bitter rasp, and as Iri looked into his eyes, he was shocked by the hostility in them. "So this is the armorer. Child of the Lion, are you?"

Iri bristled. "Who wants to know?" He turned to Pebes. "I thought this meeting was just between you and me."

"Quiet!" Pebes warned. "Iri, this is the king. Kamose, lord of Two Lands."

Iri stared. "The king? I don't believe you."

Pebes needed more than a few minutes to establish Kamose's bona fides and mollify Iri while at the same time trying to keep Kamose's volatile temper from exploding. When everyone was convinced and calmed, Pebes said to Kamose, "Iri is moving his forges to the delta with the court, but he has sent his men ahead in two parties. One group will be working for Amasis; the other, the one judged most loyal, will be quietly arming our insurgents in another location. Sata will be our liaison, coordinating activities."

Kamose looked at Iri. "What happened to your face? Was it scarred in a fire? But no. It'd be part of that tendency your family has toward birthmarks, wouldn't it? You all have one right above your arses. Right?"

"Then I must be twice the man I claim to be," Iri said, "because I've got twice the birthmarks the rest of the family have. You don't beat around the bush, do you? Kings, I'm told, tend to be all full of themselves."

"Is that so?" Kamose said. "You've got a big mouth, friend."

Iri stood. "Pebes, if this is all you can give us for a king, we're in deep trouble. Arrogance isn't enough, frankly." His eyes were trained on Pebes. "Let's see, how much of my time have I wasted so far? Perhaps it's time to cut my losses. I don't mind taking chances, even risking the penalty for treason. But much depends on whom I'm taking the chances for. And when it turns out to be a brash, loudmouthed—"

Kamose sprang to his feet. "You insolent puppy! Arm yourself!"

Iri glared at him. "Kings duel with commoners?" he asked contemptuously. "Oh, but I forgot—you're not a king of the blood, are you? You're a bastard of a Shepherd."

Kamose's face was livid. His hand reached for his sword. Iri threw his head back and laughed heartily and long! "Very well," he told Pebes. "I'll accept him. Baliniri told me I'd know Kamose by his temper, as I'd know a good bell by its peal. And there's only one way to get a bell to peal, and that's to ring it madly."

He turned to Kamose. "You, sir," he said. "My apologies. I was testing you the only way I know how. I've had a trying day, and I'm hot and dusty and angry over something unconnected with all this. I probably need a drink worse than you do. I'm buying, king or no. Innkeeper! In here!"

After Iri had gone, Pebes turned to Kamose. "Well, what do you think?"

"There's mettle in him," Kamose said, satisfied. "He's quite a man, in spite of his youth and inexperience. We're lucky to have such a one on our side. He'll be very valuable."

Pebes looked sharply at the king. He looked terrible, like a man who had gone from being a *shepenn* addict to being a drunk. But he was no longer using the drug so then, what gave him the look of a man who was not in control of himself? Why did he give the impression that he was still the slave of something or . . . somebody, perhaps?

Was the king in some bondage to Arsaphes? There was something strange and powerful and frightening about the tall man. He was not a man to get close to—and yet Kamose hardly moved without consulting him.

If he, Pebes, were not sure that neither man was the boy-lover type, he would almost suspect . . . but no. Kamose was no pederast, although one could imagine Arsaphes indulging in any kind of perversity, as long as it inflicted pain, physical or mental. But there had been no sign of any leaning toward men.

Far from it! One of the cell leaders had said Arsaphes had taken up with a beautiful, aristocratic young woman in his unit whom Arsaphes had, within days, reduced to shameless and pathetic subjection. And now Arsaphes had started giving her assignments that he did not want to get his own hands filthy with.

Pebes shuddered. Imagine a woman with Arsaphes! How could she stand it? There was something loathsome about the man, something fearful and unclean.

But there you were. Women! Who understood them? He frowned. *Men like Arsaphes, that's who.* Men who shouldn't be allowed near a decent, honest girl. Men who ought to be locked up like animals in a cage.

He shuddered again. The poor girl!

His hunger sated for the time being, Arsaphes leaned back on the bed and watched the girl on the floor. Miserably naked, curled wretchedly into a tight ball, and hugging her knees to her chest, she was whimpering.

She was pretty enough, even now. Her narrow rump was pleasing to the eye, and the long, slim legs and delicate ankles were quite admirable. She was, however, merely a thing to pleasure his body. Of course, her beauty meant nothing to him now that he had destroyed her self-esteem.

He wondered if she was *really* broken. Could there be still some part of her she was withholding from him, some untouched and unsullied part that was still hers and not his? If there was, he would find it, rip it from her grasp, and wreck it before her despairing eyes.

He smiled and felt the flesh stirring once more. He would have her again, even after the four intense bouts that had already reduced her to a whimpering, defeated, exhausted mess. His heart beat faster; his eyes burned with a fierce inner light. The old lust was upon him again, savage and unforgiving.

"You. Come here. Now."

"No," she pleaded, hugging her knees all the tighter. "Please, no. You hurt me."

His fist clenched. He was breathing hard. "I said come here! You know you want it. You'll be begging for it in a moment. Get up here right now!"

V

Iri, full of nervous energy and suppressed anger, wandered the streets, elbowing people out of his way, fists clenched. Mothers, watching him pass like an avenging angel, hastily pulled their children out of his way and, seeing his terrible face with its hideous red birthmark, made the sign against the evil eye.

He emerged from a veritable thicket of twisting streets at the quays. Virtually all the long line of docks and loading platforms were occupied, full of hardworking laborers, loading the ships for the great move to Athribis.

As he scanned the waterfront, he spied a familiar face. "Baufra!"

His assistant turned, smiled delightedly, and came toward him. "Hello, sir! I had to come down to the boat to get something for the forge." Baufra held up a favorite bellows, which Iri had used since his own apprenticeship years before. "The other one never works quite as well. An apprentice can pump with this one for hours without tiring."

"Quite right," Iri agreed. "The design was better then. Could you duplicate this one? And make perhaps a half dozen more?"

"Nothing easier, sir. I'll just need a requisition for the materials."

"I'll leave word with the authorities that you speak in my name." He clapped Baufra on the arm. "Keep up the good work."

"Thank you, sir." Baufra smiled and bowed, then went away, the bellows under one arm.

Iri watched him, then sighed and turned back toward the water, his bad mood returning. *Baufra makes me feel better. I must spend more time with him.*

His eyes settled on a burly young fisherman who was tying up his boat. Its nets were hung to dry from the furled yard. Iri looked at the clean-featured young face, with its strong and un-Egyptian nose. *Where have I seen him before?*

The fisherman noticed his attention, hesitated, then stepped forward. "Pardon me, my lord." His speech was well modulated, soft voiced, and bore no trace of the coarse accent of the Thebes waterfront. "May I have a moment of your time?"

Iri shrugged. "How can I help you?" And all the time his mind was saying, *Where have I seen that face before?*

"I heard that the slaves from Deir el-Bahari—"

"Yes. The Habiru."

"Yes, sir. I heard that they had been brought over to this side of the river."

"That was a couple of days ago. They've all been moved downriver."

The fisherman's strong young face fell. "All?"

"So far as I know. I talked with one of them before they left, a friend of mine—"

"You have *friends* among these people?"

"Why, yes. A very decent fellow named Aaron ben Amram." He stopped. The fisherman's face held a strange expression. "Is there something wrong?"

"Oh, no. No, sir. I happen to know Aaron. Is he well?"

"He's as well as one can be in his unfortunate situation. He's as strong as a bullock. Anyhow, they were all shipped downriver to Avaris. The gods help them there. Amasis will work them to death."

"I see. Thank you, sir."

"Look, pardon me, but I have this strange feeling I've seen you before. Have you always been a fisherman?"

"Oh, yes, sir. Born and bred to it."

But the answer was too quick, and the cultured accent was of the court itself. Iri froze. "My lord!" he gasped. "Prince M—"

"Please," the fisherman said, looking right and left. "No one must know. You're Iri, the armsmaker, aren't you?"

"Yes. I made a sword for you at Baliniri's command."

"You did indeed. Come where we can speak without

someone overhearing. I'm here to look the situation over before I bring the army down."

"Don't my lord! Not now. Wait a bit. There's something wrong here."

Why? Why say this? He was betraying the very movement of which he was a part, but somehow it seemed the proper thing to say. Was it the meeting with Kamose? He had no idea.

"I see. I will investigate. May I call on a Child of the Lion for help if I need it?"

"Yes, my lord. You can find me at my house. Everyone knows the house of Iri. I'll be there until I move downriver three days from now."

"Then all the rumors about the move are true."

"Yes. Hold up the army until at least then."

Prince Moses put a hand on his shoulder. Iri liked the way Moses looked him in the eyes, as if the red blotch were not covering half his face and obliterating any good looks he might otherwise have boasted.

"I've got to go," Moses said. "Thank you. May you prosper and be happy."

He turned and walked away rapidly, carrying a cloth parcel under one brawny arm—a powerful young specimen of manhood.

Iri blinked after him. *A friend?* he wondered timidly. *At last a friend?*

At the far end of the quay Moses stopped as if transfixed to the spot. Two men in the travel garb of traders were coming off a larger boat. One noticed him and muttered to his companion, who then turned toward Moses and nodded.

Moses, his blood boiling with anger, made his way to the area above the docks called Sailortown. Once there, he turned and awaited the two men, his eyes blazing. When they drew near, he demanded in a loud whisper, "What are you doing here?"

Seth, his beard trimmed drastically and his head shaven, pulled the prince away from the stream of people in the narrow street. "The same thing you're doing—gathering facts. There are things I have to know here too. And when Khafre found out what I was up to, he told Geb to come with me."

"I'm sorry, sir," Geb added. "We'll try to steer clear, but we'll need to confer occasionally. If we learn something significant, you should know it too. And vice versa."

"That's true," Seth said. "Don't be angry. If we arrange a place to meet, and a time—" He stopped midthought as Moses nodded consent.

"I ran into someone just now who recognized me. A relative of yours, Seth. Iri, Ketan's grandson."

"He won't betray us?"

"I don't know. He suggested I not bring the army here yet. He said that something's wrong here, but he wasn't specific."

Seth and Geb looked at each other. "Very interesting," Seth said. "Anything else?"

"He said we could find him at his house if we needed him."

"I want to talk to him," Seth declared.

"If you don't know him already—you don't?—I think you will like him. He's devastatingly ugly, poor man. He has that birthmark on his face." Moses shook his head sadly.

"What else?" Seth asked.

Moses smiled tightly. "Iri knows Aaron, my brother, and speaks well of him. He says all the Habiru have been hauled off to Avaris. Seth, I don't want to wait. I want to see them now, before I do anything."

"But we need you here."

"Not if I delegate my authority—which I hereby do. I authorize you two—separately or together—to look into the situation and, if you think the coast is clear, to order the army down to Thebes."

"No, Moses!"

"I have to find out who I am! I've been waiting so long. You have taken away my old identity, and I need to replace it with the real one."

"If we've hurt you by this, I apologize," Seth said sincerely. "But you needed to know the truth."

"I did, and do. And now I have to know the rest of it. Don't try to hold me back. I have to go to them—and now!"

VI

Moses returned to his boat at dusk. He now wore a plain linen loincloth and a loose, short tunic. Topping all off was a shapeless cap he had found in the boat's chest when he had bought the boat.

He sat in the stern and unwrapped the parcel he had bought an hour before in the marketplace. Inside were bread and a handful of dates. He reached into the storage locker and drew out a skin of raw red wine.

As he prepared for dinner, he heard voices approaching and turned his head to hear better. One voice was aristocratic; the other that of a man of the working class.

"I don't see any sign of him. Are you certain he wanted to meet me here? Not at the brothel?"

"Oh, yes, my lord. My master was quite clear about that. He said his boys were getting suspicious and . . ."

Moses stole a look. The men were walking slowly. The aristocrat was an older man. The prince tried to get a better glimpse of the younger man, obviously a servant.

"I don't like this. Something is wrong. He never had problems finding boys for Set-Nahkt before. What are you leaving out?"

"I'm leaving out *this!*"

And with these words, the burly young man grabbed the aristocrat and grappled with him. The aristocrat, alert and agile, put up a struggle. They stumbled and toppled off the quay and into the Nile.

Moses was up in a moment and peered over the side. The older man came up, gasping for breath, but the younger man reached up from below, grasped him by the neck, and pulled him down.

Moses looked right and left. The boats and quay were deserted.

The older man and his attacker resurfaced. The younger man drew back and pounded the aristocrat in the face, and both sank beneath the surface once more.

Moses hesitated. If he was to intervene, it could ruin his cover. Guards would want to interrogate him. He cursed and went over the side in one easy motion.

He surfaced next to the two men and managed to pry the attacker's hands off the aristocrat. When the older man broke free, Moses gasped: "Get to shore! I'll deal with—"

But a big fist caught him in the mouth. Powerful fingers clutched at his throat, choking off breath. The prince tore at the fingers with his hands and went down. He pried one hand free, then the other; then his own fingers closed around his attacker's throat.

The two men came up under Moses' boat, banging their heads hard. Moses' mouth opened, and a string of bubbles shot upward. The other man struggled with superhuman strength, but Moses held fast, tightening his grip.

Slowly, gradually, he felt the strength leave his opponent. The huge body went limp.

Moses' head scraped on a barnacle, and he could feel a cut open. He let his man go and scrambled up around the boat to surface at last, gasping for air.

He wiped his eyes, treading water, expecting the other man to come up alongside him at any moment, fighting again, trying to kill him. But no attack came. He looked at the quay, where the aristocrat was holding out a boat hook.

"Here," he offered. "Grab this!"

Moses let himself be towed to shore. When his foot touched the first of the stone steps underwater, he climbed up wearily. He stood on the bank, swaying a bit, dizzy from the sudden and unexpected exertion. "Watch out," he advised. "Keep an eye out for him."

But as he scanned the dark waters, the other man did not come up.

Moses turned and looked at the man he had saved. Hastily, he turned his face away!

It was not fast enough. There had been the sudden light of recognition. The other man said, *"You!"*

Moses scowled. "Yes," he admitted. "You're second only to Amasis now, right?"

Neb-mertef looked frightened of Moses. "Yes. But I owe you my life. And there's something you ought to know: I'm in contact with the underground movement to restore Kamose to the throne. I was instrumental in the king's escape from Amasis' villa."

"I don't understand."

"I'm the movement's contact inside Amasis' court."

Moses stared at him, wondering if it was true. "Well, as you say, you're in my debt. You can pay it by forgetting you've seen me."

"Why?"

Moses sighed. "I have my reasons. Just honor my request."

Neb-mertef hesitated, then said, "All right: I haven't seen you since you left Thebes for Nubia."

"Good. Thank you."

"I have heard marvelous reports about what you did in Nubia. Accounts of your heroism."

"A leader does not win a war. An army wins a war."

"And a headless horse wins races." Neb-mertef snorted. "You are too modest."

Moses looked around uncomfortably. "I have a feeling that the fellow who attacked you will surface when we least expect it. I'm going to find someplace downstream to dock for the night, and you'd do best to get home before it's dark."

"No one would dare harm me."

"Someone just did."

"You're right. And his master is as good as dead. Well, thank you. And good luck."

Moses stepped on board his boat and cast off.

Seth and Geb sat on opposite sides of a long table in a dark tavern and finished their dinner.

"I don't like his leaving," Geb muttered. "There's too much danger in having him go down there alone."

"I couldn't have stopped him," Seth said.

Geb, disgusted, changed the subject. "What do you think we ought to do first?"

"I think I'll look up my kinsman Iri. Funny: I vaguely remember that Sinuhe had had a son named Khian, not Iri."

"I heard that Khian disappeared quite some time ago. There's a very beautiful girl named Neftis, too, if I remember. I haven't seen her since she was a child. All my dealings with Sinuhe were at the forge. I seldom saw his wife and laid eyes on only one of his children."

"Then I'll look the girl up too," Seth remarked. "And I'll ask about the older brother."

"And what do you want me to do?"

"Make contact with Kamose and the resistance movement. Talk to him. Sound him out. See what he's really like. Above all, take note of who is around him. Meet and, if possible, get to know all the people close to him."

"That sounds as though you have some suspicions. Whom are we looking for?"

"I don't really know. Call it a hunch. I think that if we dig far enough, we'll find something. And if it's what I think it is, I'm not sure how eager I am to find it."

" 'It'?"

"Perhaps I should say 'him.' "

"You mean—?"

"Yes. Apedemek. I can *feel* him somewhere around here. He's alive. I know it. Alive and strong."

Geb saw him shudder, then recover, stiffen his back, and set his jaw. But the old vulnerability was back in his eyes again. Vulnerability? Call it fear.

·VII

There was barely enough moon to sail by, but the helmsman knew the river well. Hieron had hired him for this ability back in Athribis after deciding to leave his own ship and go upstream in another, less vulnerable, vessel. The main thing was to get out of Thebes. Amasis' man Nebmertef had rudely destroyed any possibilities of trade agreements between Demetrios and Egypt and would not let Hieron meet with the regent.

They moved to the lee side of an island in midriver for the night, ten miles from Abydos, and dropped anchor in the shelter of the islet. Hieron had been below since his return to the boat, working by lamplight on his report. Now, as the oarsmen shipped their blades and climbed out of the cramped seats of the galley, he came topside and joined Yahadu of Mari at the rail.

Yahadu smiled in greeting. "As your nose will tell you,

the men brought a lamb aboard, and it's on the spit waiting for us. Are you hungry?"

"I'll settle for a plate of olives," Hieron replied. "And some wine."

"Very well, sir." Yahadu clapped his hands, and a sailor came running, took the order, then returned within moments with a tray.

"I sampled the wine an hour ago," the young man from Mari said. "I think you'll like it. These Egyptian chaps make good wine. There's a palm wine from Nubia—"

"I've tried it, Yahadu. Share a wineskin with a friend, and the next morning you're stiff as a deck plank."

"Try this then, sir."

"Not bad. Not good, but not bad. Don't ever try to tell a man from the Greek islands about wine, Yahadu. It's worse than telling a Hittite how to fan his forge."

"Or a Child of the Lion, sir? Your pardon, sir, but before we landed in Thebes, I saw you with your tunic off. I saw the birthmark. I didn't know you were one of—"

"Oh, yes. I'm a very distant relative of our employer's. We shared a great-great-grandfather, although my ancestor took off from the wrong side of the blanket. I even passed the apprenticeship as an armorer once, but Demetrios preferred having me away from the forge, and he pays well, as you probably know, to get what he wants."

"Quite so." Yahadu accepted the wineskin and drank deeply, then handed it back. "I did some asking around, as you told me, sir, about Demetrios's kin. I met a cocky fellow named Khons, an enemy of Iri's. I sometimes get better information from a rival than from a friend."

"What did he say? Khian will want to know."

"Khian, sir?"

"I mean Demetrios. Damnable slip of the tongue."

"Yes, sir. Khons thought Iri was involved in some illegalities. He acted as if he knew more but didn't want to get more specific."

"Anything about the girl?"

Yahadu looked grim in the torchlight. "Khons made like she was some sort of slut. I don't know if it's true, sir. He could have been a rejected suitor. There was real malice in his tone."

Hieron tried to accept this rationalization but found he could not—not entirely. "I have the feeling there's something to it. Anyway, Demetrios will want to look into the matter himself. He'll surely want to hear everything, including your own interview with Khons." He passed the wineskin to Yahadu. "You've impressed me during this trip, young man. You may wind up getting a promotion."

"I hope so, sir. I intend to wind up in the moneyed class. I gather that's a distinct possibility working with Khian."

"Not if you let him know that you've heard that name!"

"What name, sir?"

Hieron caught his meaning and smiled. "Very good. Now go below and get some sleep. We'll be sailing at dawn."

They stood in darkness at the unlit end of the main room of the Sign of the Dolphin. Arsaphes, sensing that Neftis would bolt and run if left to her own devices, grasped her bare arm so hard, the circulation was cut off.

"That's the fellow over there," he whispered. "He's a wealthy merchant. He has the assets to underwrite our whole program."

"You're hurting my arm," Neftis moaned in a small, woebegone voice. "There's going to be a bruise, a bad one. If you won't think of me, at least think of appearances."

"Speak when you're spoken to," he growled. "I asked around about him. He has a fatal attraction to young, pretty women half his age."

"No, please. Don't make me—"

"And he likes them submissive."

"Please. I can't do a thing like that."

"And wanton. Now's the time to show off some of those tricks I taught you."

"You can't really expect me to do this, not after we—"

He sneered down at her. She cringed, and he clutched her arm even more tightly. "Bring him to our room upstairs for privacy. The rest is up to you, right up to the moment I break in and surprise you two at it. Then I'll take over. But when I come through the door, I want him with his clothes off, so he'll be more vulnerable."

"I thought you l-loved me," she said between sobs.

"What has that got to do with business? This is business. We'll talk about love later. Now wipe your eyes."

"You don't," she wept brokenly. "You don't love me at all. You only s-said those things to get me to do what you wanted."

For a moment he thought he would have to go into her mind and control her that way. He had not wanted to; it was no victory when he did. It was better to take a woman by the sheer strength of his personality. So far she had come to him with only the few obligatory slaps and cuffs, and once her initial physical attraction to him wore off, she would be tied to him by her own guilt and sense of utter worthlessness.

"You'll do exactly what I say, or I'll put you out on the street, soliciting drunks in Sailortown. Do you hear me?" Carried away by the sheer violence of his savage mood, he slapped her once, twice. His hand came away from her wet cheek. "Now get him upstairs! Do whatever he says!"

VIII

Seth hesitated before knocking. Respectable people did not open their doors at this time of night to anyone, even those who claimed to be kin. Nevertheless he forced himself to knock. After a time a soft voice asked, "Who's there?"

Is this the girl, Sinuhe's daughter? But the door opened a crack, and the light of his torch fell on a sweet, round face that looked much older than the girl could possibly be: late forties or so, framed in hair that was showing traces of gray. Only then did he notice her garb: a servant's.

"What do you want?" she asked. There was mild apprehension in the soft voice, but no hostility.

"I beg your pardon, my dear," he said. "I'm looking for Iri the armorer." He displayed his empty hands, a sign that he bore no ill intent. "Actually I'm his kinsman. A cousin."

"Mai?" A male voice, irritated, strained, came from behind her. "Who is it? What does he want?"

"The gentleman says he's a kinsman of yours."

The opening suddenly widened, to reveal a burly fellow with the most off-putting visage Seth had seen in all his long life. Fully half his face was covered with an angry red blotch, one that destroyed all symmetry and distorted his facial expression. But out of the angry red birthmark looked eyes of extraordinary intelligence and vitality. "Yes? Can I help you?"

"My name is Seth. I knew your—"

The unreadable expression on the ruined face changed, and the eyes widened. "Seth! It *is* you, isn't it?"

Seth was ushered inside with enthusiasm, and the soft-eyed servant woman took his cloak.

"You'll stay the night here, of course," Iri said. "Mai! Bring refreshments!" He turned back to Seth. "You haven't eaten, I take it?"

Seth shook his head, smiling.

"To what do I owe this unexpected pleasure?" Iri offered his cousin a chair.

"My friends and I are quietly looking into the political situation here. I understand Kamose is here, and a scheme is under way to restore him to the throne."

"Yes," Iri confirmed. "I met Kamose very recently. I'd been toying with helping this conspiracy, but now I'm not so sure."

"Ah? Why?"

"There's something wrong. Call it a hunch."

"You find yourself with a man who trusts hunches. Tell me about it."

Geb, pleased with his success tonight, thought: *I wish Seth were here.*

But they had taken off in different directions at nightfall, each with a separate mission: Seth was to find Iri, and he, Geb, was to locate anyone connected with the cabal.

He had gone into a tavern and been recognized by a man who introduced himself as Pebes, a sutler to the army in Thebes before its expedition to Nubia. Pebes had then introduced him to a man claiming to be Kamose, true king of Egypt. They sat across the table from him now.

Geb waited while the innkeeper came forward, bearing the "jug of something better," that Kamose had ordered. The innkeeper poured, then Kamose raised his bowl and locked eyes with Geb. "Your health, my friend. And may our efforts create a better Egypt."

That was a wish they could all agree on, so Geb raised his bowl, tipped it toward the man who had saluted him, then drank.

Immediately he wished he had not. He swallowed a sizable portion of it, then spat the rest to the floor. "This is no good!" He scowled up at the innkeeper. "Bring us something decent!"

Only then did he notice that neither Kamose nor Pebes had tasted the wine. Kamose slowly put his cup down and looked at him, amused. "Something the matter?"

Geb tried to speak, but when he opened his mouth, nothing came out. He blinked at them. Only then did he see the tall man emerge from the shadows and make his way toward them.

The eyes! Nobody in the world had eyes like those! Eyes that held you fast and . . .

"That's about it," Iri said, standing and stretching.

Seth smiled fondly. "You're a fine young man. Moses spoke very well of you; he said you were very special."

To Seth's surprise Iri suddenly turned his face away. "What's wrong?" Seth asked, leaning forward.

Iri turned slowly and painfully back to him. "Yes, I'm special, all right," he said quietly, "I am a monster. Most people can't stand the sight of me."

"You're no monster," Seth said simply. "I happen to be very proud of you. And you've made a friend of Prince Moses."

"Yes," Iri said through unshed tears. "I have a few kind acquaintances who are not repulsed by my face. You, the prince, Aaron ben Amram . . . perhaps even my assistant, Baufra. What makes the lot of you so different?"

"Maybe we've all been lonely," Seth suggested. "Me, for instance—my father thought I was a bastard and wouldn't acknowledge me."

"Then you know something of . . . this. Aaron is a slave, so he'd understand. I don't know about my assistant; he may just be buttering me up. But Moses? He's never known anything but a life of ease."

"You mention Aaron ben Amram. You have friendships with slaves?"

"I don't approve of slavery. All my servants are free, even Mai—the woman who met you at the door. She was born free. She's like family."

"She's very lovely. What do you think of Aaron?"

"He's much like Moses. He has it in him to be a king."

Seth smiled. "Well said. Aaron is like Moses. What if I told you they were *exactly* alike? What if I told you they were brothers?"

The pause was long. Then Iri said hoarsely, "You're serious! You mean Aaron has royal blood?"

"No," Seth answered.

"You don't mean Moses is a slave?"

Seth nodded solemnly. "And on his way to assume his destiny as one. Voluntarily."

"How can you let him?"

"There is a prophecy, which says that only by giving up everything can Moses change the world. Forever."

Iri thought about this. "They'll crush him," he said finally. "When they find out who he is—"

"Yes. He'll need help. Friends. All he can get."

Iri let out a very long sigh. "He can count on me."

Seth smiled. "I know he can. Now tell me about your sister. Perhaps I can do something to help."

IX

Neftis awoke on the floor in the shabby rented room she shared with Arsaphes, her face in a pool of her own vomit. She lifted her head off the floor, gagged, and cringed against a stabbing headache. She got her elbows under her and pushed herself up. The room tilted wildly, and her headache became a red-hot knife stabbing through her skull. She put her palms to her temples and pushed hard.

Her eyelids were stuck together. She rubbed the lids, pried them apart and winced at the filth on her naked body.

When she tried to stand, the pain assaulted her in short, horrible bursts. She reeled, swayed, and staggered to the soiled bed. The movement disturbed her queasy stomach, and she bent forward just in time to vomit on the floor between her feet. The fit ended in dry heaves.

She looked around. Arsaphes was gone.

"Oh, *no*," she groaned. What if he was to come back and find her like this? And the room! He was so particular about cleanliness!

In a series of brutal, hammering shocks, she remembered how everything had got this way: She had gone through with it last night. She had actually had sex with a stranger. He had been old, ugly, and disgusting. His sexual demands had been as perverted as Arsaphes'. She had expected Arsaphes to break in the door before the deed was consummated, but he had not come.

And yet she had smiled all the while, letting him handle her body and strip off her clothes while she cooed and acted as if he were the most desirable of men.

She closed her eyes and shuddered against the memories. He had used her again and again. She had been there on her knees, gagging, the old merchant's filthy hands grasping her by the hair, when Arsaphes had finally entered and threatened the man, vowing to expose his philandering to his rich wife's influential and prudish brothers.

Her own humiliation had been as great as her victim's. She had cowered in the corner, naked, as the innkeeper, servants, dancers, and even some of the tavern's patrons came running upstairs, wondering at the ruckus. They had all seen her face. She'd been branded once and for all as a prostitute. And they were right.

She staggered toward the corner table, then managed somehow to wash. After half an hour of scrubbing she looked at her image in her bronze mirror. With the dark eye kohl washed off, she could see the bruises on her face clearly. Was there anywhere farther to fall? she wondered bitterly.

She looked around the room anxiously. The floor needed washing. She'd have to wash the filthy sheets and her own grimy clothes. Probably the fight Arsaphes had had with the old merchant had dirtied his own clothes, so she would have to wash his tunic and loincloth. It would all have to be done quickly, before he came back.

Neftis moved unsteadily to the chest where he stored his clothing. She opened the top. The chest was empty! She stood transfixed, her mouth open and her eyes uncomprehending.

No! He can't go! He can't run away! But it was all too obvious that he had. To her horror, the panic of losing him was greater than the guilt and degradation she felt.

Yes, there was farther for her to fall. And for all she knew, there were more levels, each worse than the last.

Seth sat on the rooftop of the inn called the Golden Crocodile in the cool morning air, eating raisins and puzzling over the note on the table before him.

He looked up and beheld the panorama of the great river before him: the nearby quays with swarms of workers loading boats and stacking household possessions; across the river, distant figures dismantling a bustling port; out on the river itself, sails large and small tacking in the light breeze.

The city would be relatively emptied within the week. He felt a terrible sense of loss, then realized that the mood had nothing to do with the abandonment of Thebes; it was Iri's story about his life—and about the problem with Neftis— that had saddened him beyond measure.

How could he help Iri? He could do nothing about the birthmark that set him irrevocably apart. But perhaps he could help the girl. He would look for her today. Maybe all she needed was a good talking to, from an older kinsman who cared about her.

He looked again at Geb's enigmatic note. The adjutant had not returned last night, but he had left the note under the door of the rooms they shared. When he, Seth, had returned from Iri's house, he had found Geb's bed unslept in, and this note on the floor: *Have found quarry. Everything in order. Suggest immediate implementation of plan.*

It was emphatic, direct, unequivocal. Then why did he distrust it? And where was Geb now? Where had he spent the night?

*   *   *

Ships going upriver habitually went under sail, pulling against the strong bore of the Nile; those heading downstream floated with the current, sails furled. Thus the hieroglyphic for "upriver" was the image of a boat under sail, while the symbol for "downriver" was a boat with the long yard shipped and the sail stowed out of sight.

But Hieron's boat, benefiting from the current, was in a hurry, so the crewmen were in the rowing seats, the hortator was pounding his drum, and they were passing boat after boat, making record time.

Hieron stood at the starboard rail, looking at the straggling traffic. Even near paupers had taken to boats to move their few, shabby household goods downriver.

He looked down, where a strapping young fisherman stood naked in the stern of his boat, leaning hard on the steering oar. The young man looked up and smiled. Hieron waved, thinking: *Fishermen eat better here than in the islands.*

Then he dismissed that thought, to wonder how simple a fisherman's life must be. Suddenly, impulsively, he leaned far over the rail. "Ahoy there! Where are you headed?"

The young man strained to hear, then grinned. "Avaris!" he said in a strong young voice. "And you?"

Hieron matched his grin. "Parts unknown. Far out across the Great Sea. To whom do I speak, fisherman?"

The young man sniffed the fresh air, and his huge chest filled. He looked proud, fearless, and confident of his identity and destiny. He did not say anything for a moment, and Hieron's long galley slipped past. But as the little boat fell behind, he cried out in a strong voice full of pride: "Moses ben Amram! Remember me!"

Hieron smiled indulgently. "Perhaps I will! Good fishing!" But now the young man could no longer hear him, and the galley swept past, sending broad ripples in its mighty wake.

X

Iri had arisen at dawn and had gone to court—what remained of it—to leave word that Baufra's requisitions were to be treated as orders coming from himself. After this he had disposed of errands and by noon had cleared his schedule without exhausting his enthusiasm or energy.

He did not remember when he had felt so good. There were still problems in his life—Neftis the most pressing. She still had not returned home after several days away. But new and positive aspects had entered his life.

Imagine! he thought, making his way through the Market of the Four Winds. *Several new friends! Moses! Baufra! Aaron! Seth! I have four friends! Four!*

After so many years of terrible, aching loneliness, perhaps the gods should have saved some happiness for later. Who knew when such bounty would come again in a life as lean as his?

He paused at the fruit stand, thinking to bring home some beautiful, fresh dates for Seth and Mai.

What a delight it was to have Seth visiting. The night's conversation had carried on into the late hours, when Mai, coming in to say good night, had commented that Seth seemed tired. Trust Mai to be so sensitive! He had seen the gratitude in Seth's eyes.

Their time together had been stimulating, exciting, and deeply satisfying. Iri could not recall when he had had such a good time just talking. Seth was so brilliant, so articulate, so witty!

Don't kid yourself! You would have been satisfied with a man less brilliant by many degrees. The main attraction was that Seth spoke to you as though your opinion was worth something; looked you in the eye as though you were normal.

Ah, how lonely he had been!

"Iri!" a voice said close behind him. He wheeled and saw Pebes, inclining his head as if to draw Iri aside.

Iri let himself be led past the fringes of the crowd, up a flight of stairs, and into an isolated patio.

"What is it?" Iri asked.

Pebes' eyes narrowed for a moment, then he blinked,

and the odd look went away. "Something *really* important has happened! Kamose wants me to bring you to him."

Iri looked at him sharply. "Now?"

"When you find out what it is," Pebes said, "you'll thank me for insisting."

But as Iri looked into Pebes' eyes, he realized that he did not trust the man. It was something in the way Pebes looked at him, as if he was forcing himself to conceal the contempt he felt. It was curious: A day ago he would have accepted the man's contempt as a matter of course.

"What's so important that it can't wait until evening?" He stopped. "It has to do with Kamose . . . and Prince Moses."

"How did you know? Who told you Moses was in Thebes?"

"I met him. I talked with him."

Now Pebes showed surprise. "What did he tell you? Is he going to bring the army to Thebes?"

"I don't know," Iri said. "At the time he hadn't made up his mind."

"Then you'll want to hear what Kamose has to say," Pebes told him.

"I'm sure I will," Iri said. "Lead on."

"You're sure you're not from the city guards?" the innkeeper asked.

"Not at all," Seth said benignly. "I understand your apprehension. I'd feel the same way myself. Rest assured: I'm a kinsman of the girl. She'll be glad to see me." He smiled conspiratorially. "Here, now. Tell me if this is the proper kind of poultice to put on your anxiety."

The innkeeper took the money. "This is very reassuring," he admitted, "but it will do me little good if the other fellow comes back and finds out I've gone and tipped off a stranger—"

Seth slipped another coin into the innkeeper's hand.

"Well, seeing as how you're related to the girl and all . . . but on the other hand, he's half again my size—"

"This will make you stand taller or run faster." Seth added another coin.

It was now evident that the cow had been milked dry:

The hard glint came into Seth's eyes, despite the smile on his face. "I don't know whether she's up there now or not."

"Never mind," Seth said. "I spotted someone of her description on the roof. It's a warm day, and she could be catching the breeze there. If I get no answer at the door, I'll go up and look around."

"Very good, sir." The innkeeper clinked the coins into his pouch. They made a satisfyingly substantial sound. He smiled and tucked his hands inside his robe.

The building that housed the inn towered four stories and looked down over the lip of a sunken passageway used for unloading the basement of one of the royal warehouses. As Neftis looked down, she felt giddy. The faraway ground seemed to swim before her eyes.

Her hands clutched the waist-high railing as she leaned far out over the precipitous drop, and all of a sudden she could imagine leaning too far and falling, seeing the earth rush up at her. It was too late to change her mind; she had made her choice and had opted for death, brutal and bloody, against the street far below.

Hastily she drew back and feared for a moment that she was going to be sick. But she held herself together by an act of will and forced herself to look over the edge once more. The ground was like a great invisible hand grabbing at her, pulling her over the edge, drawing her ever downward.

She knew she was at the end of her tether. The past brief span of days had ruined her life forever, teaching her enough to poison anything she could ever want to do. She had learned things about herself that no woman ought ever to know.

Her heart was pounding fast. She closed her eyes and put a hand on her chest to feel the frenzied beating.

A voice broke into her chaotic thoughts. "It's no good. You don't want to do that. Take it from me, who tried once." The voice was slow, gentle, deep, and as patient as the river itself.

She opened her eyes and stared.

The man was standing not three strides from her, at the edge of the staircase. His brows and beard were gray, and his eyes were set deep in his head. He could have been fifty—or seventy. There was still vigor in the powerful arms and authority in the broad shoulders, but all the compassion of the ages rested in the tired and sympathetic eyes.

"Who are you?" She drew away, moving slowly backward down the rail.

"A friend. And it may be that I am a kinsman. Would you perhaps be Neftis, daughter of Sinuhe? If so—"

"No!" she said. But her eyes told him yes. She looked away, then looked back. His robe was that of a man of the working class. "If it's money you want, go see Iri."

"I don't need money," the man said gently.

"Then what do you want? You have no business with me."

"My dear, I'm your cousin Seth of Thebes. I knew your father and your grandfather. And I'm rather good at getting people out of trouble."

The voice was calm, and the eyes were warm and forgiving. She blinked, and tears appeared on her cheeks. "Iri sent you," she said resentfully, her voice a strangled sob.

He smiled. "I've seen Iri. Do you think he's angry at you? Poor Neftis. Do you know how much he needs you and how lonely he is? Perhaps you don't. People tend not to know how it is with a man like Iri, sensitive and proud and achingly alone—"

"Bastard! You're trying to make me feel guilty. Don't try to manipulate me!"

"Where a kinswoman in trouble is concerned," he said slowly, gently, "I'll use whatever means I can to help you, my dear." He smiled. "You know I'm here to help, not hinder. I could manipulate you, I could bend your mind to do whatever I wished. But I choose not to."

Arsaphes had said that before! They were all the same, all of them! "Liar!" she shrieked. "Leave me alone! I don't want to talk to you!"

"But there's no one else you can talk to about this—not even Iri. You know how much it would hurt him to hear what you need so much to confess. You cannot hurt or shock me, or drive me away. I'll be here whenever you want me."

She buried her face in her hands. "Just go away!" she begged through tortured sobs.

But when she looked up, he was still waiting patiently, a placid smile on his lined face.

XI

"Who was that tall man I saw leaving just now?" Iri asked.

"Just one of the habitués of the Dolphin," Pebes said. "Don't worry about him. Just come along."

Iri scowled. He knew Pebes was lying, but why lie about something unimportant? He tried to adjust to the dark interior.

"Where is he? I can't see a thing."

Pebes led Iri to a corner table, where Iri finally focused on the dim figure. "Hail, Lord of Two Lands," he said sarcastically. He sat down. "I understand you've some sort of message for me, which Pebes here can't carry with both hands."

Kamose glared across the table at him. "We got some good news today. Word came from Moses that he's chosen to have the army sent to Thebes as soon as Amasis and the court have gone to Athribis." He waited for a reaction, got none, and went on sourly, "That's two days from now. Then our world changes drastically. We'll need the work from your forges almost immediately."

"Slow down," Iri advised. "I have to set up my 'official' forges in Athribis first, as a cover."

"You won't need a cover. Just arm our men with iron."

"I'm no ironmonger."

That was a lie; he could work iron, if at a much lower level both metallurgically and aesthetically than the masters of the craft. Seth could teach him more later; it was rumored that Seth had made the great Sword of Glory for Kamose, used in the fateful reckoning with the last of the Shepherds.

"Can't work iron?" Kamose sputtered. "What nonsense is this? Pebes, you told me he was fully qualified. Can't you get anything right?"

Iri snorted scornfully. "You know, Pebes, my faith is weakening. Any loudmouth can bluster and act insultingly. I always thought it took more than an overactive tongue to make a king."

Kamose reached for his sword, but before he could draw it, Iri's hand snaked across the table and grasped the king's wrist in a powerful grip. "Bad manners. We don't go pulling swords at the table around here—not unless we mean to use them."

"Get your hand off me, you ugly bastard!"

Iri's eyes widened in mock offense. "Why, King! That's no way to talk to a man you want to come out openly on your side. It's also a terrible way to treat a man you want to con into believing that Moses plans to deliver you an army, all wrapped up in a shiny package with a purple ribbon."

"Let me go!" Kamose said, struggling mightily but in vain.

"I met him myself yesterday," Iri continued. "He wasn't any more impressed with your group than I am."

"Pebes!" Kamose said, his voice strained and full of pain. "Make him stop!"

But Iri saw the movement of Pebes' hand. "Touch that sword hilt," he warned, "and you'll eat it for lunch, my friend." His cold glare rooted Pebes to the spot; then Pebes' hand drew back from his weapon. "That's better," Iri said. His grip on Kamose's arm had not relaxed, and he turned back to the man. "I don't like being called an ugly bastard. That may very well be what I am, but the wise man does not go out of his way to make me aware of the fact, nor does he get into tests of physical strength with a blacksmith. I'm a peaceful man, but when people press me too hard, I'm worse than the wrath of the whole pantheon. Understand?"

"Yes." The word was shoved between clenched teeth. "Yes, curse you!"

"And I hate being lied to. Moses didn't tell you anything about the army. Why did you lie to me?"

"You'll see. In three days I'll be in total command of the army that took Nubia. You'll talk out of the other side of your mouth th—"

"Ah! You'll threaten me still, will you?" He increased the pressure suddenly, enormously. Kamose howled and turned white.

But then, as quickly as it had begun, it was over. Iri released Kamose, flinging him back like a hated thing, and stepped back, his eyes on both men. "I don't like Amasis, and I'd do just about anything to get rid of him. But I have my limits, and perhaps you've found them today. Don't forget what you've learned."

The two stared back at him. They did not say anything.

Neftis sat on her neatly made bed. The floor was clean; everything in the room was immaculate, including herself. She looked straight ahead, musing. She did not know what to think about Seth. By all rights she should be happy, relieved to have a powerful protector who was willing to turn her life back around onto the proper path.

Instead she felt echoingly empty and terribly, crushingly alone. And worthless, utterly worthless.

Seth had told her, "Any time of the night or day, get a message to me at your house, and I'll come to you, whatever your problem. You've got a friend who will stick by you."

She had not just found a kinsman she had never known about; she had found a substitute for Father and for Khian. She had found a personage who would forgive her always, like some sort of expiatory and all-seeing god.

It ought to make her feel warm, safe, protected.

Then why did she feel so fearful?

She did not deserve Seth. She was worthless and did not deserve anything. Anything, that is, but the sort of punishment she had been getting.

Seth tried hard and meant well, but he could not understand her. Arsaphes—now *he* understood her.

The door burst open. She turned her head, startled. Arsaphes stood in the doorway, tall, rigid, unforgiving, his eyes like burning coals. He looked around the room, his face made of stone.

"You know you're supposed to be out of here, don't you? I checked out this morning. You've got a house to go back to, of course."

She stood up hastily. "Go back home?" she said, panic-stricken. "But—"

"You don't expect me to take you with me, do you? After that drunken exhibition you put on last night?"

"Please, Arsaphes! I won't drink anymore. It was because of—of that thing you made me do, with that stranger! I was so embarrassed when all those people rushed in! So humiliated!"

"Next time I'll find someone who hasn't such scruples," he said sarcastically, "acting as if it mattered who saw her do what—"

"It does matter! You know it matters!" She was in tears again, despite her resolutions.

"Why? The bastard isn't going to tell on you. I threatened to tell his wife's brothers about his little escapade." He laughed. "So he took out his purse and made a very generous contribution to our cause." He looked around the room casually. "I just dropped by to see if I'd left anything behind. I guess not."

"Arsaphes! Don't leave me! Not now!"

He moved into the hallway. "I'm going. This hasn't worked out. You've proved highly unsatisfactory."

"I'll do whatever you want! Just don't leave me!"

"What do you have to give me? Nothing."

"Arsaphes!" she cried out, desperate. "I—I do have something. Something you'll want to hear. Just promise me you won't go, and I'll tell you. Promise!"

"Tell me," he said.

"Seth. Seth's in town. You asked me about him, remember? You said to tell you if I ever heard the name. Well, I saw him. I talked to him. I know where he is. Please, Arsaphes! Don't leave me!"

CHAPTER FIVE

In the Delta

I

Athribis lay on the Damietta branch of the Nile and was poorly situated for defense. It would serve as a temporary relocation for the court, but the moment that enough of Avaris was rebuilt to serve as the seat of government, Athribis would be abandoned.

The great, sloping Avaris wall, with sides too steep to breach, was intact. Master craftsmen from all over Upper and Lower Egypt rebuilt the stout wooden gate from materials shipped from across the Great Sea. Meanwhile, the great gathering of the Habiru slaves, drawn from Thebes and the delta, were put to work clearing the rubble out of the streets.

Every day boats brought huge slabs of undressed limestone, which would be used in the rebuilding of the city, from the various quarries across the nation. Skilled craftsmen working double shifts would dress the stones according to a pattern established in the forgotten age of the building of the pyramids: one group rough-dressing the blocks with crude stone mauls, the other finishing the work with bronze implements.

120

Other craftsmen and their apprentices and journeymen were visible everywhere in the city streets. But whether the work being done was carpentry or stonework, the building materials—limestone blocks, heavy hardwood timbers—all had to be hauled in by hand. And this required the unceasing labors of the Habiru men, women, and children. Only the visibly ill and aged were spared, and the latter, unfed because unproductive, had to share the food of the able-bodied if they were to eat at all.

Their workday was from sunrise to sunset, and one of the jobs they dreaded the most—the restoration of the fire-damaged Temple of Amon—had fallen to their lot as well. This was the bitterest insult to the Habiru: A nation whose very lives were consecrated to the one God of their forefathers had to work themselves to death in the restoration of a temple dedicated to a native deity they considered false, reprehensible, and evil. Habiru singled out for this heinous task thought themselves scandalously ill-used, and their bitterness grew every day.

The presence of the standing army of the delta region, augmented by an ever-increasing number of mercenaries, exacerbated the tension. The standing army was arrogant and overbearing with the Habiru, but the foreigners were sadistic and heartless. Already two Habiru youths had been killed by mercenaries, and there had been several savage beatings.

Through all this, however, the Levite hierarchy, which had assumed internal command of the Habiru, maintained a rigid policy of nonretaliation, urging patience and caution upon the impulsive young as well as their more prudent elders. This, plus a developing Habiru capacity to endure, had spared them a bloodbath at the hands of the intolerant foreigners.

As the daily harassment continued, however, the tempers of the young were drawn tighter with every passing hour in the heat of the city. And nowhere was the tension felt more strongly than in the Habiru detail assigned to the Temple of Amon.

As the sun rose toward the zenith one warm morning, Dathan and his friend Mehir struggled to move a fallen limestone block from the wrecked temple courtyard. After much grunting and sweating, they had managed to move it onto the long track of heavy timber balks, which the young men had built.

A more arduous task remained: Somehow they had to get the stone up onto a stout stonerocker for repair and decoration by the master stoneworkers. The device would allow a stone placed atop it to be rocked, swung around, tilted to any angle, or—by means of hand wedges driven under the runners—raised vertically as much as thigh-high.

Once the stone was on the rocker, the mason's job would be much easier. Getting it there was, in Dathan's opinion, beyond realistic expectations for two strong young men. Through will and effort, he and Mehir managed to get one end of the block off the ground and up onto the edge of the deeply tilted rocker. Now, if they could slide it farther along the rocker, they might get the center of gravity of the stone even with that of the wooden platform.

This proved to be more of a job than it looked. Dathan strained, lifted, and finally turned around and got his back behind the stone, shoving hard.

"The cursed thing won't budge." He was panting and sweating profusely. "Isn't that just like a son of a bitch stone from this heathen temple?"

Mehir closed his eyes and breathed prayers against the protest. "Please, Dathan! Don't say things like that! One of the soldiers might hear you!"

"Let the bastards hear me," Dathan said defiantly. "I'm sick of pussyfooting around, worrying whether some pervert from Hellas hears me say an unkind word."

"Please! At least keep it down! You may want to get beaten, but I don't, and if you keep this up—"

Dathan snorted. He looked over at where the free masons were reshaping fallen stones. The apprentice shaped the stone roughly, then his master completed the job and checked the outcome with levels, plumbs, squares, and boning rods. "Look there! When we're done with the really hard work, they get all the credit. People compliment them and give them gifts. What do the slaves get? A beating if we talk too much—"

As if to illustrate, one of the guards—they were sun-blackened Greeks today, naked and dirty and sweaty—took note of them. "Hey! You two! Get to work!"

Dathan started to devise a sarcastic and insolent answer, but Mehir grabbed his arm. "*Please!*" he begged from between clenched teeth. "If we're beaten, we can't work. If we can't work, we don't eat—and neither will our grandparents. Is that what you want?"

Dathan shook off Mehir's hand. The Greek guard headed their way. Mehir glared at his friend. "Now see what you've done."

But as the guard raised his staff to aim a heavy blow at Mehir, a richly dressed courtier intervened. "Leave him alone. I'm sure he meant no harm. You boys were getting ready to get back to work, weren't you? There. You see?"

"Who the blazes are you?" the guard demanded. "If I want to beat these lazy Habiru swine, I'll—"

The rich man's eyes hardened, and his voice had a sharp edge. "Ask your supervisor," he advised. "He'll tell you who Neb-mertef of Thebes is." The name was sounded with such authority, the Greek lowered his staff, confused.

The rich man smiled smugly. "The name may not mean anything to you now, but I guarantee that by nightfall it will. Somebody will get in touch with you and cover that bare behind of yours with a nice suit of bandages, if you're lucky. If you're not, you'll find yourself sitting on that staff of yours, right up to the handle."

The guard, fear in his eyes, backed off. The man called Neb-mertef nodded at the two young men, smiled coldly, and walked away.

"Well," Mehir said quietly, "*that* was fortunate. If he hadn't happened along—"

"Rich bastard!" Dathan hissed. "Rich, privileged bastard! I hate them all!"

"How can you say that?" Mehir asked, incredulous. "He saved both of us from a terrible beating, perhaps even worse."

"Curse him! I'd kill him in a minute!"

Fifty paces down the street, Neb-mertef smiled to himself. *Well, there's one problem solved.* He had been wondering where he would get the new male toys required to keep Set-Nakht productive: the slaves! The Habiru! Obedience and compliance could be beaten into just about anyone—and it might just provide a certain pleasure for himself in the taming of the new recruits. And of course Set-Nakht would take to good-looking boys like these! He was sure of that!

II

When Dathan and Mehir returned to the Habiru tent city at the end of the day, Mehir insisted on describing the afternoon's adventure to Aaron ben Amram. Aaron was not a close relative but had begun, in recent days, to function as an arbiter and spokesman for the family interests. He not only had a certain reputation for wisdom, he had a talent for languages and could converse with all the groups put in charge of the Habiru since the move to the delta. His sister, Miriam, listened in.

"He looked at me like a butcher sizing up a piece of meat," Dathan said bitterly.

Aaron turned to Mehir. "And what do you think about the matter?"

"I was glad he didn't let us get beat up. But now that I've had time to think about it, I don't like the way he was looking at us; no, I don't."

Miriam broke in now. "Aaron," she said to her brother, "remember the rumors back in Thebes?"

"More to the point, in Deir el-Bahari," Aaron recalled. "About a rich man buying up young male prostitutes."

"What would he want with us?" Dathan asked. "Even if this was the same man, he couldn't have mistaken either of us for whores."

Aaron considered. "Young men were also disappearing from the streets. I talked to a woman whose son disappeared. He was only sixteen."

Dathan glared at him. "And the son? He wasn't a boy-lover?"

"No. His mother was sure he'd been kidnapped."

"And you think this Neb-mertef—"

"He's rich and powerful enough to do anything he wants."
Aaron looked Dathan in the eyes. "We've got a problem."

"But what can you do?" Miriam asked. "We can't just
hide them. The guards will tear the tents apart until—"

"There is one outside possibility. We could confuse the
issue. Tomorrow new guards from Crete take over in Avaris.
They won't know who was there yesterday. If we moved
someone into Dathan's and Mehir's place—"

"But Aaron! That would be sacrificing whomever we
substituted for them!"

"Not if the men we substitute for them are extremely
unattractive. I seem to recall a set of twins from the tribe of
Dan. . . ."

"Oh!" Miriam burst out laughing. "I know just the ones!
But where can we send Dathan and Mehir?"

"The dock crews in Athribis need some strong backs,
unloading the boats on the Nile." He turned to Dathan. "You
may like this work a bit better. The crew commander was
here today. His guards are all Egyptians. That isn't much,
but it's better than Greeks."

Dathan scowled. "Or Cretans, for that matter."

"Besides, there's not all that stonecutter dust to breathe
all the time. You ought to be safe there. I used to like the
work on the quays back in Thebes. You unload a boat, and
you're finished until the next boat docks. In Avaris, the work
is never done."

"Thanks," Dathan said. "I appreciate this." He didn't
sound grateful—but that was Dathan. At least the response
was polite, and Aaron settled for it. "When do we leave?"

"Immediately," Aaron said. "You have to be there in
time for the morning show-up the day after tomorrow. Nobody will be the wiser. The crew commander didn't care
whom I sent, so long as they have strong backs."

When they had gone, Aaron turned to Miriam. "We
never seem to run out of problems. Egypt grows more corrupt, so our life here grows more dangerous."

"Oh, Aaron," she said plaintively, "when will it ever
end? Will we ever see Canaan again?"

"Levi said we would," he answered, "and I am sure that
El-Shaddai spoke through him."

"But when? Everything seems so bleak."

"Perhaps we are enduring these hardships for a reason. We are being taught patience. And of course God wishes us always to turn to Him first—not just when our own feeble efforts have failed. Perhaps we are being forced to remember that. And in the long run, that might be a good thing."

"Ah, there you are," Amasis said irritably as Neb-mertef came in. "Where have you been? I needed you. This is Kara, the architect Zoser recommended. I'm putting him in charge of the renovation of the royal suite."

Neb-mertef exchanged bows with the sweating, obese architect. The two had met at a dozen official functions and parties and had immediately conceived a cordial and mutual detestation. He turned to Amasis. "You'll need temporary accommodations worthy of your rank while you're waiting for the renovation to be completed," Neb-mertef said impulsively. "Would you consider staying at my place here? I own a large house in Avaris."

Even as he said it, he recognized his mistake. He could not let the regent stay at his house! That would betray the existence of Set-Nakht, and Amasis would know that his supposed clairvoyance was in fact the gift of another! And once Amasis found out about Set-Nakht, he would want the man in his own service, and that would be the end of the influence Neb-mertef had over Amasis.

But the invitation could not be withdrawn. He waited with growing dread until Amasis responded. "Thank you. Your offer is most generous, and I accept."

Neb-mertef's heart sank, but he forced his face into a smile, one that—he hoped—betrayed none of the anguish and self-recrimination that was going on in his mind.

The huge house Neb-mertef had maintained in Avaris was one of the few fine residences that had not been destroyed when the city had fallen. It was operating on less than half a domestic staff now, and much of the edifice had not yet been reopened. Neb-mertef, his staff, and his slaves occupied no more than a third of the sprawling dwelling.

On the top floor of the central section Set-Nakht sat poring over his star charts. He wore a modest loincloth, and

Allat the Assyrian, the new slave Neb-mertef had bought for the astrologer, stood behind him, massaging his neck. Allat wore a plain robe; unlike so many of the other slaves who had paraded through Neb-mertef's apartments for the magus's amusement, Allat had little taste for bawdy behavior.

"You've found something," he said. "I can tell."

Set-Nakht reached back and affectionately covered Allat's hand with his own. "You always know my mind. Yes. I've found something that Neb-mertef would kill to get his hands on. See this configuration? Sometime in the very near future, something will occur to give Amasis additional power over his enemies."

"I see," said Allat. His hand brushed the hair off Set-Nakht's forehead and caressed his cheek. "You're brilliant. And kind, to share the information with me."

Allat's words disarmed him, unmanned him. He felt a sudden, powerful tug at his heart. He half turned in his chair and embraced the slave's waist, burying his face in the folds of the robe at Allat's belly. When he tried to speak, the words would not come; instead he let out something very like a sob.

"Why, what's the matter?" Allat asked, hugging his master's head to his body. "There, there, now. There, there."

Set-Nakht wailed all the more. Allat gently disengaged himself to sit next to the magus. "What's the matter? You act as though you'd just lost your dearest friend."

Set-Nakht forced himself to look at the slave. "I'm so weak. I haven't the guts to fight back. I've been trying to figure out how to conceal this configuration from Neb-mertef, but what I ought to be doing—"

"Why, nothing could be easier, dear. Just don't tell him." Again his hand stroked Set-Nakht's forehead; Set-Nakht, with a jerky motion, brushed it away.

"I won't tell him," Set-Nakht said. "Never fear about that. But that's not the half of it. There's something I have to tell you."

"Silly fellow," Allat crooned, smiling. "Tell Papa."

"Curse it," Set-Nakht said in a strangled voice. "You're in great danger. I have to do something about *you*. And right now."

"Danger? But you'll take care of me, won't you?"

"That's the worst part." He swallowed hard. "I'm a pris-

oner here. I know it doesn't look like it—there are no fetters,
no bars. But I've been held here by my own selfishness, my
own cowardice. And all the while, the stains on my conscience keep building, and growing."

"No! You're so good!"

"I'm not! Get that out of your head!" The anguish on his
face was heartrending. "Neb-mertef bought you for me, but
do you know how many slaves he's bought for me in the past
year? Or how long they have lived? Or what happened to
them as soon as he thought they knew too much about my
abilities?"

"Happened to them? What do you mean?"

"He had them killed, damn it! As he'll kill you, if I don't
do something about it! I've got to get you out of here, to
safety!"

Allat knew that Set-Nakht was telling the truth. "You
mean—?"

"I can't let that happen! You're not like the rest! The rest
were cheap whores! But you, I have feelings for you. I've got
to save you somehow!"

Allat's eyes filled with tears. The sight of him tore at
Set-Nakht's heart. But what could he do?

III

Just outside the mouth of the Nile, where the silt stain of
the great river still marked the blue waters of the Great Sea,
Hieron's boat crossed the path of a mighty bireme flying
familiar colors. Hieron, his heart pounding, ordered the same
colors run up the mainmast, and within hours both vessels
anchored together in calm water.

Hieron was carried in a coracle to the larger boat and
was helped up the side by sailors. On deck he saw a familiar
figure coming his way. "Demetrios! My greetings!"

The friends embraced, and without waiting Hieron gave
his report.

"You were wise to come away," Demetrios commended.

"I've received a report that Apedemek is loose in Egypt somewhere, as I had feared."

"Apedemek? The rogue Child of the Lion?"

"The same. The man whom the ranking body of the Chalybian Order has voted to ostracize." He paused. "I'd like you to return to Egypt and be my eyes there."

Hieron laughed ruefully. "I'm afraid I burned my bridges. Neb-mertef and I had words. I may well be arrested if I return."

Demetrios clapped his hands for wine and refreshments.

"That's why you'll go back in disguise, as an average trader."

"This is unavoidable?" Hieron asked unhappily.

"I'm afraid so. I don't fear Amasis. But imagine the worst that could happen there: Kamose becomes king; Apedemek controls Kamose and also the cult of the goddess and even the priesthood of Amon. He's quite capable of that, you know."

"Yes," Hieron agreed. "Apedemek came close to being the most powerful of us all—the more horrible that he should be the one to drag the sacred name of the Chalybians in the dirt."

"Quite so. Add to this the fact that Apedemek knows the secret of ironmongery and could arm Egypt with iron."

"Good heavens."

"Yes. And what if he got to my brother, Iri, and controlled him as well? Iri knows ironworking. Imagine Iri, controlled by Apedemek, running a string of a hundred forges, all turning out iron weapons to fight the rest of the world."

Hieron frowned. "You're right. I'd better get back there. What is my authority in this? If the job requires assassinating someone or subverting the country—"

"Do as you see fit. Just find a reliable way to keep me informed—and often."

"All right. There was some mention of your brother and sister. I didn't get it firsthand; there's a young man in my employ that I want you to meet—Yahadu of Mari. He spoke with a rival of Iri's and got the most scandalous reports. I didn't take the reports about Iri seriously; other people had good things to say about him. He's proud and strong and can whip anyone within reach. People make fun of him for his looks, but behind his back for the most part."

"Poor Iri," Demetrios said sadly. "If only I could do something for him. We do not all start the race at the same mark."

"True. This rival had ugly things to say about Neftis sleeping around, drinking, keeping bad company—that sort of thing. She's still unmarried—"

"At twenty-two? That's not good." Demetrios pursed his lips in thought. "Keep an eye on both of them, will you? If you can safely reveal yourself to Iri, enlist him in the cause. Someday I hope to bring him into the Chalybian Order."

"Good. I'd like to leave Yahadu with you. He could be trained into a worthwhile assistant."

"Good old Hieron. Always reaching down into the crowd and lifting somebody up."

"As you did with me. It's the only way I can pay back my good fortune. And you didn't even know I was a Child of the Lion." He laughed. "And neither did I. I'd never even heard of the order."

"It is the order's tradition to take care of its own. The common race of men have short lives and shorter memories. But the order is forever and never forgets. And it does not forget the bad any more than it forgets the good. That's why I want you to keep an eye on Apedemek for me. Find him, smoke him out, and stick to him like a barnacle to a boat. If he gets out of hand and there isn't time to call for me—"

"Yes. I must say, the kind of assignment you give isn't for the weak or the timid," Hieron said soberly. "Imagine! Apedemek!"

Demetrios looked with friendly esteem into his eyes. "I never give a man an assignment he can't handle," he said calmly. "Now let me meet Yahadu. I can use an assistant, now that I've just finished elevating you to an equal."

"Oh, no, my lord. Not an equal. Surely—"

"And to high degree in the order. You've earned it. It's long overdue."

"I don't know what to say!"

"Just say, 'Thank you, Demetrios. Now let's go meet your new assistant.' "

*　　*　　*

Many leagues back up the Nile, off the port of Athribis, Moses furled his sail and, manning the tiller, let the current guide him to shore a half league above the city docks. He beached the boat, then withdrew his hidden sack of clothing. He donned the loincloth, robe, sandals, and headdress of a young scribe of journeyman status, then tossed the empty sack into the water.

He stood for a long moment, looking at the boat. What could he do with it? Only then did he become aware of someone watching him from the rushes: a ten-year-old boy, big-eyed, underfed, his thin ribs showing.

"You, boy," Moses called. "Do you know what to do with a boat?"

"Yes, sir!" the ragamuffin said. "My father was a fisherman. He used to take me out. Amasis' soldiers killed him."

"Can you fish?"

"Yes, sir! Mother and I—"

A fisherman? he thought. *Well, why not? It doesn't require size or strength. Just endurance and resilience and an understanding of the water.* He grinned. "The boat's yours, boy. And God give you good fortune with it!"

"Thanks!" the boy said. "But which god do you mean?"

Moses looked at him pensively. "I'm not quite sure, but I haven't given up hope of finding out."

He watched the boy push the boat into the channel and climb aboard. The lad grabbed the steering oar and brought the vessel into the sluggish current. Athribis was not far away. The Nile seldom let a fisherman down; it was part of the endless bounty of Egypt that when all else failed, a man could still get a living out of the river. Thus the boy's future was secure—if he could hold on to his new acquisition. Plenty of people out there would try to take it away from him, but if he was resourceful, tough, and could learn quickly . . .

You speak of yourself every bit as much as the boy. Only where's the security in your life?

He had acquired a new identity, one whose nature and limitations he had yet to learn. But at least this identity was one based on truth. It would be a real life—the one he was meant to live. The challenge was to live up to it.

IV

To Dathan's disgust Aaron had decreed that he would be accompanied on his riverboat trip to Athribis not by his easygoing friend Mehir, but by his brother Abiram instead. Mehir would go on another, later, boat.

Abiram had been a thorn in Dathan's side for a long time, always taking the other side of every argument, often reporting on him to his elders. For the first ten leagues of their upriver journey, Dathan did not speak to Abiram, and this precipitated a protracted squabble. When they finally arrived at the Habiru camp in Athribis, Dathan was so angry with his brother that he could hardly sleep.

Thus, in the dawn hour when they turned out for the morning roll call, Dathan tried to draw apart from his brother, only to see Abiram push through the crowd to stand beside him.

"Get away from me!" Dathan hissed. "It's bad enough having you here to spy on me for Aaron. But during the work, I want to be on another crew."

"You there!" said one of the guards. "Shut up!"

Abiram's brows went heavenward. Dathan scowled at him. "Listen to that," he muttered, hardly moving his lips. "It's all your fault."

"You! I said quiet!" the guard bellowed.

Dathan glared silently at Abiram. Abiram looked straight ahead, his lips in a thin line.

"That's better!" said the guard. "Now, this first line, I want you to go to the big boat and fill the wagons with its cargo. That should take you until midday. Then I'll give you new work. The second rank will unload six smaller vessels due here in an hour. The wagons aren't here yet for that load. In the meantime, take those shovels. The big boat's latrine is full of night soil we've saved for fertilizer. I want you to haul it over to the new olive grove and spread it where the guards tell you to. Have you got that?"

"Ugh!" Dathan protested. "Hauling excrement! That wasn't what we were sent here for!"

"What was that?" the guard yelled. "You, over there!" There was no question whom he was addressing.

Dathan pointed at his chest and asked, "Who? Me?"

"Yes, you, curse it! You seem to have some comment about everything. Just for that, you're going to be shoveling with the boys in the second rank."

Abiram snickered.

The guard heard it. "All right!" he yelled. "You too! You right next to him! What are you waiting for? Draw your shovels!"

"You're sure?" Moses asked the clerk in charge of the slave records. "I was told I'd find them here in Athribis."

"No," the clerk said, rolling up the scrolls. "They were moved to Avaris, to rebuild the city. A bunch of them were brought back to unload the boats. If you want to take the chance that those you seek are among them, just follow this road here, turn left at the first crossing, then you'll pick them up right at the river."

"Thank you," said Moses, observing a scribe's punctilious courtesy by bowing unnecessarily. He sighed, thinking of the boat he had given away. Now he would have to book passage downriver to Avaris and waste money he would otherwise have been able to use helping his family.

He made his way down the road, excited to be at last in the vicinity of his kinsmen. He had been dreaming of this moment ever since he had first learned his true identity. He wondered how his mother had managed to keep his secret for so long. Only she and his sister, Miriam, had known the truth, that Jochebed had saved her infant son's life by substituting him for Princess Thermutis's dead child.

He had grown up thinking Jochebed and Miriam were his nurses. What would it be like to be with them now? And what would his brother, Aaron, whom he had never seen, be like? People who knew Aaron had spoken highly of him. *Will he like me? Will my people accept me?*

Abiram had fallen into the rhythm of the work, distasteful though it was, and had moved quite a large portion of the noxious substance from the barrow to the prepared patch of ground without complaint.

Dathan, however, had taken this assignment badly from the very first and had spent the entire time grousing resentfully, making faces, and abusing his brother. "Why did Aaron send you along? You won't ever let me be. All you think of is following me around."

Abiram smiled. "You don't want to carry on too loudly, Brother. The guard is looking at us again."

"That's your fault," Dathan complained. "Anyway, he's turning around and going back to the boat to talk to his friend. He'll leave us alone for a bit. Good. I was tired of having him hang around like that. Dirty bastard."

"You're making it harder for yourself by complaining," Abiram said. "Mother says you take everything too hard. She says you make everything into a major problem. Relax!"

"Don't tell me what to do. Who are you to give me advice?"

"You'd better ease off. A stranger is coming. He looks as if he could be somebody important."

"Curse him."

"Dathan. The man's coming closer."

"What do I care?"

"Please, Dathan! At least do some work! If the guard was to look this way—"

"Don't turn your back on me, you squirmy little worm!"

Abiram's patience was wearing thin. "Look, I don't care what you say about me, but—"

Dathan's frustration took over. Without thinking he let his fist lash out and strike his brother in the mouth. Caught by surprise, Abiram went down; then, blinking, he lay there, rubbing his jaw. "Dathan," he said in a hurt voice.

Dathan stepped forward, ready to deliver another blow, this time with his foot. But a hand on his arm restrained him. He turned to look into the eyes of a stranger. "Let go of me!" he snarled, "or I'll—"

"Hold," the other said. And, looking him up and down, Dathan thought twice about hitting him too. Unusually well-built and solid for a scribe, the man's shoulders under the white robe were broad and muscular. "Give up the violence. The guard over there hasn't seen you yet."

"Mind your own business—" Dathan began. But then something in the stranger's face jogged his memory. Who was he? When had he seen this man?

The scribe put powerful hands on Dathan's shoulders

and looked into his eyes. "I'm trying to save you from a beating. Help the other fellow up, now."

The memory came back. "Get your hands off me! Or are you going to kill me, the way I saw you kill the Egyptian?"

"What?" the scribe asked. "What Egyptian?" But then the two locked eyes, and he knew; they both knew. There was a stunned moment of silence.

"Are you going to give me away?" the scribe asked.

Dathan's ire was up, and he was in no mood to back off or to be quiet. "I know who you are. You should be punished for that. Why should you go around in fine clothing, answering to no man, when I have to work here like a herd ox, shoveling this—"

"Please, Dathan!" Abiram begged. He had stood up and was trying to restrain his brother. "If the guard hears—"

"I want him to hear! I want him to arrest this fraud here! I want him pulled down from that pedestal of his! He's nothing but a murderer! One who's wanted for murder by the guards back in Deir el-Bahari!"

"Please, Dathan! You, sir! Go! Before he turns you in!"

But now the guard had turned and had heard and was coming their way.

"Don't turn me in," the scribe said. "I only wanted to help you." He turned and moved hastily down the shore toward the docks at the next slip.

"What's going on over there?" the guard demanded, pulling the whip out of his belt.

Abiram pulled at Dathan's arm. He saw the scribe paying a boatman and climbing into a small sailboat.

"Dathan," he whispered. "Don't tell him anything." But Dathan was out of control. "That man down there! The one getting into the boat! Stop him! He's a murderer!"

The guard was hardly more than an arm's length away now. "He doesn't look like any murderer to me. Now you get back to work, or so help me I'll—"

Dathan was not to be stopped. "He murdered a guard in Deir el-Bahari! There is a reward on him! And you're letting him escape! Money! Lots of it! Just for turning him in or capturing him!"

For the first time the guardsman's eyes showed interest. "You say money?"

"Dathan!" Abiram cried out. "Don't! You can't!"

"Let go of my arm, you little bastard! I know what I'm doing! I saw him kill the guard."

"You saw it?" the guard said. "Well, a slave's word isn't worth much. But it might be worth my taking you to the captain of the guard and letting him question you for a few minutes."

"Dathan! Don't!" Abiram pleaded. For the first time Dathan began to realize what he had done. But it was too late—too late for both of them.

The guard grabbed his arm roughly. "Come along."

V

"What do you mean he's gone?" Neb-mertef demanded. There was already tension in his voice from having offered Amasis the run of his house. This new piece of news was enough to send him over the edge. "Answer me, curse you!"

"I don't know where he is," Set-Nakht said. "I finished the computations and lay down to take a short nap, figuring that I'd—"

"But how could he have got out? Weren't the guards on duty?"

"How would I know? I never venture far enough even to *see* the guards. Remember? You've ordered me to remain on the upper floors. For all I know he could still be in the house, hiding."

"You're right! I hadn't thought of that." Neb-mertef beckoned, and one of the guards approached. "Search the whole place—even the two unused wings." Then he turned back to the magus. "Weren't the two of you getting along? I thought—"

"Admirably. This one was special. I can't tell you how unhappy I am to see him gone. I hope you get him back."

"Oh, he won't be coming back here. If I find him, he'll pay dearly for this."

"Oh, don't say that! I couldn't bear it if something happened to him!"

"Who are you to—"

"I'd be so upset I just *know* I couldn't work."

Neb-mertef, knowing he was being manipulated, glared at him. But when the slave was recaptured and murdered, the magus simply would not be told. The first problem was to apprehend him. The slave now knew about the magus's specialty of divination and would undoubtedly let the cat out of the bag. There was no winning on this one! Unless . . .

I could move Set-Nakht to a new location, and keep him under heavy guard. If the slave does expose my secret, no one will be able to find the magus.

Set-Nakht noted the glint in his master's eyes. "What are you thinking of doing?" he asked suspiciously.

"None of your business," Neb-mertef barked. "I'm going now. Send a message to me if the fellow turns up."

Set-Nakht watched him go. His heart was still pounding; after his aborted escape attempt, he had tried to be submissive. But because his affection for Allat overrode his fear of reprisal from Neb-mertef, he had ripped apart spare sheets, made a rope, and eased Allat down from the second floor. Now he had no idea where Allat was. He would never see him again. How unfair it was! And yet how necessary.

A great sadness washed over him, but he felt proud to have acted responsibly for a change. It had taken courage, but he had reached inside himself and found it. This was, perhaps, how one went about putting one's life in order.

Little by little he was beginning to feel better about himself. He even hardened his resolve to keep from Neb-mertef the news about the planetary configurations he had discovered. He had virtually made Neb-mertef's political career. Now he would unmake it. What he had built, he could destroy.

Ah, but how it hurt, knowing he would never see Allat again! He closed his eyes, clenched his fists, and firmed his jaw. *Be strong! Be brave!* he told himself.

He opened his eyes and was the same weakling as before. But he had set his steps on the road to becoming something better. It wasn't much, but it was a beginning.

*   *   *

Dathan's friend Mehir and other workers for the docks had been sent back to Avaris from Athribis. Dathan had been left behind in Athribis, detained by the guards. Aaron paid a visit to their work detail on the Avaris quays, picking his way through the many guardsmen inspecting the credentials and the belongings of the new arrivals from Thebes.

When Aaron found Mehir, Mehir turned to the nearby guard supervising his work detail. "Is it all right for me to talk to my kinsman? I won't be long."

The guard nodded sourly.

Aaron led Mehir to a concealed space behind a tall pile of goods and asked about Dathan.

"Someone who's supposed to have killed a guardsman in Thebes a while back was spotted in Athribis yesterday," Mehir explained. "He seems to have escaped downriver. They're inspecting everyone who comes in here, just in case. Dathan was a witness to the crime."

A loud yell sounded from the crowd on the dock now, and Aaron looked that way. "Captain! Over here!" Two guardsmen took positions to either side of a sun-blackened boatman—a tall, sparely built man—and grasped him roughly by the arms.

Aaron turned back to Mehir. "Are they treating you all right?"

"It isn't too bad," Mehir said, smiling wryly. "I miss Dathan, for all his quarrelsome ways. Things are seldom dull around him."

"Yes," Aaron said thoughtfully. "He is impulsive, but he has a good heart. God knows he has a lot to be angry about. A slave's status does not sit lightly on our shoulders." He put a hand on Mehir's shoulder.

"No," Mehir agreed. "And losing his father didn't help matters for him."

He looked past Aaron toward the docks, and the next disturbance caused him to gasp. "Oh, no! Look! It's Dathan!"

Aaron wheeled. "Wait here!" he ordered Mehir, and moved quickly through the crowd.

"Captain," he said, "what's happening? This young man is my kinsman."

"I don't care who he is," the guard said gruffly. "He's

coming with us. He's witnessed a crime. Now get out of the way."

"Aaron!" Dathan cried out, raising his manacled hands. "Help me, Aaron!"

But the guard gave him a wicked cuff across the temple and drove him to his knees. "Shut up, you!" They yanked him to his feet and pushed him, lurching, down the path.

Aaron turned back to the scene before him after watching them go away. "What's happening?"

A soldier spat near Aaron's foot. "That one was witness to a murder. This one here"—he indicated the sparely built boatman, now trussed with his hands behind his back—"apparently gave the killer a ride down to Avaris. We'll need them both to identify the culprit, when we catch him. Now move along."

"But my kinsman "

"Apply to the captain of the guard. Just don't expect too much. Now move along!"

VI

Aaron walked away, perplexed. How had Dathan landed in this mess? When had he witnessed a murder, much less of a guardsman? How had the soldiers learned about it?

He stopped at the shack where the captain of the guard was usually to be found and bowed to the assistant at the door. "I beg your pardon. I am Aaron ben Amram—"

"I know who you are," the soldier said. "State your business."

"Thank you, sir. If it is possible I would like to see the captain of the guard. A young kinsman of mine was brought here to be interrogated."

"You might as well come back later. Midafternoon at the earliest."

Aaron blinked. "But what has he done? If he has done wrong, I will take full responsibility. If anyone is to be punished, it should be me, for having—"

The soldier's voice softened a bit. "Look, my friend, I know about you. You're their leader, aren't you? Those slaves over at the edge of the city?"

Aaron nodded.

"Well, I mean you people no harm, but the captain is hopping mad. This kinsman of yours spotted a killer, and nobody would listen to him until the culprit had already got away. It wasn't your kinsman's fault, but he won't be released until he's borne witness in this case."

"Then the lad won't be harmed? I saw someone deal him a terrible blow on the head as he was being brought ashore."

"Well, that's against regulations. He must have been talking or something."

Aaron sighed. "Yes, he was." He tossed his hands heavenward. It was a gesture of resignation, but one of such expressiveness that he would not have done it with a less sympathetic soldier looking on. "It is in God's hands," he said wearily. "There I will leave it, for now."

He bowed and moved away from the dock area, heading for the city proper. Suddenly a figure moved quietly out from behind one of the long line of trees that flanked the path and fell into step with him. Aaron turned his head, startled, and looked directly into the eyes of a man who was almost his height: a man powerfully built and tanned deep bronze by the sun but dressed in a scribe's robe and headdress.

"You're of the Habiru, aren't you?" the stranger asked.

"I am," Aaron confirmed. His mind was racing. He dared not look at the man; there was something strangely familiar about him, but Aaron could not pinpoint what it was.

"Good," the scribe said. "I need to make contact with them, and I don't even know where they're quartered."

The voice was cultured, confident, of the court. "Perhaps, sir, if I could know to whom you specifically wish to speak? There are many of us, and I can direct you to that person."

Aaron turned and looked at him again, at the proud northern nose, at the clear eyes. He stopped. His companion faced him, returned his gaze.

"Very well," the scribe said. "I seek the family of Levi of Canaan—his sons, grandsons, and their families."

"I am of the tribe of Levi."

The young man smiled. "Then you will know the woman Jochebed, wife of Amram, and her daughter, Miriam."

"Your pardon, sir," Aaron said cautiously. "If I might know for what reason you wish to find them?"

"Ah, commendable! I would protect my kin if I were you. I knew these people well when I was a child."

Aaron looked at his rich clothing again and remembered the years when Jochebed and Miriam had served in the palace. He said nothing.

The young man's face changed. "I promise I would have nothing bad happen to them."

"Were they your servants, sir?" What was it, he wondered, that was so unfathomably familiar about this man, yet so strange?

The man took in a deep breath and let it out, ready to dive into the unknown waters. "The women I seek are not former servants of mine."

"No?"

"No. They are . . . Jochebed is my mother."

The two locked eyes for a moment that seemed to last forever.

"Prince Moses," he whispered.

The other's eyes narrowed. "You—you *know*?"

Aaron said, "Yes. Few people have been told. But Jochebed is my mother, also. I am Aaron ben Amram. If you are the man you say you are, I am your brother."

The stranger's expression began to change. The eyes misted over and softened, and he blinked away tears, which ran freely down his cheeks. His lip trembled, and he tried to turn his expression into a smile. But it resisted and distorted into a mask of pain.

"Aaron," he said, embracing him with arms that felt stronger than ever before.

From an alley's shadows Allat the Assyrian watched the soldiers march in formation down the road, their spears held high. In the center, a young man staggered along, weeping uncontrollably, holding his hands crossed against his chest. The fingernails had been ripped out, and blood ran darkly down his forearms. As Allat watched, the young man tripped and fell to one knee but was jerked back to his feet before he could be trampled by the soldiers behind him.

What could he have done? Allat wondered. *And where are they going in such a hurry?*

He flattened himself against the building, panic-stricken; but they did not break ranks, and no one came his way. He breathed easier at last, listening to their retreating footfalls.

What madness this was! If he had any sense he would be far away from here by now. But even as he admonished himself, he knew that he could not, for the life of him, do anything other than what he was doing. He could not abandon Set-Nakht, who had saved his life, perhaps at the expense of his own.

How cruel that Set-Nakht should be a prisoner in another man's house! He could be a highly respected magus, living in modest but comfortable quarters of his own, beholden to nobody.

On the other hand, think of how many others he let go to their deaths before you!

True but irrelevant. The magus might have been weak when it came to the others, but he had mustered newfound strength for his, Allat's, sake. He would stay to help Set-Nakht, although the magus had expressly forbidden it. His loyalty, he knew, could cost him his freedom or even his life.

He stuck his head out from behind the wall and looked down the street at Neb-mertef's great house. One of the few residences not reduced to rubble in the neighborhood, it was crawling with servants and guards. One group of servants had come out an hour before, carrying baskets, boxes, and containers for dry goods. Someone was moving. And Allat thought he knew who, and why: It was not safe to have your private magus on the premises where the regent could bump into him unexpectedly. Set-Nakht had to be moved, concealed, guarded night and day, and visited only after dark to learn what new predictions Neb-mertef was going to claim for his own on the morrow.

This was why he, Allat, had to be here when the procession came out and follow them to wherever Set-Nakht was being taken. That was exactly what he intended to do! At all costs!

VII

They had passed a member of Aaron's family—Moses could not think of it as his own family yet—on the way to the tent city just outside the walls of Avaris. Aaron had quietly said a few words to their kinsman, in a voice so low, Moses could not hear. What he had said, Moses could not imagine; but by the time the brothers reached Aaron's tent, a roaring fire had been built, and people were coming from all sides of the encampment, bringing food, firewood, and even—nobody would say how this had come about—wine. The brothers had to shout to converse over the din.

Moses looked at the smiling faces and the intense activity and asked, "What's going on, Aaron? Am I interrupting a feast?"

Aaron smiled, and the edges of his eyes crinkled. "No, it's for you. A lost son of Israel has come home to his people."

"But where is all the food coming from? I understood the Habiru were living on the edge of starvation."

"So we are, as often as not. There has been a harvest recently, though, and the common people shared some of their produce with us in exchange for help in guarding their fields." He took Moses by the arm and guided him slowly through the crowd. "What you are seeing is characteristic of our people. We have a particular gift for festivals. We will put together a celebration on the smallest excuse. Our God approves, it appears, for He has scattered a growing number of sacred festivals throughout the year, to remind us that He is to be praised in all seasons. He is a God of joy."

"I have much to learn." The two finally broke through to the inner circle around the fire, where Aaron pulled himself up to his full, commanding height and waved his long arms for silence.

"Friends! Kinsmen!" he roared in a powerful voice. "A special moment has arrived! Allow me to introduce a distinguished member of our clan—one whose very existence was a secret to you until now! My brother and your cousin—Moses, prince of Egypt!"

The title caused some shock, but the assembled people were expecting a reason for cheering, so they cheered. Voices were raised at its conclusion, and one of them demanded, "Prince? How can a prince be one of us?"

"Our kinsman," Aaron called out, "was raised as the son of the princess Thermutis. It was the only way to save him at a time when the Egyptians were slaughtering the firstborn of all. Some of you remember this terrible time, the risks we all took. The opportunity was presented to my mother to save the life of her son. She took it."

"Does this mean the prince has come to save us?" someone asked.

"He has come to lend his strong arm to our fight for freedom," Aaron responded cautiously. "Now I want you all to welcome him. Let him see the warmth and love that a Habiru family festival can generate!"

At this there was another resounding cheer, and someone at the fringe of the crowd struck up a joyous song, which all sang. It was a song of Canaan, in a language Moses could not understand.

Aaron drew him apart and said in Egyptian, "I will begin your education in our language as soon as I can. But for now, let me do the talking. I'll convey your answers in such a way as to avoid misunderstandings."

"Good," Moses said. "What did that man ask?"

"If you had come to save us. I did not dare tell him yet that you do not come to us bringing power and wealth, but have set these things aside. Not everyone will understand."

Moses nodded. "I do not understand it myself. Although I know nothing of the God of our fathers, I can feel His hand upon me. Do you know Levi's prophecy about the Deliverer? Well, the seers of the south arrived at the same conclusions. I did not welcome this augury, but I have come to believe it."

Aaron's face took on a serious cast. "I know. I have heard of the words of Neku-re and Tchabu. The women of the oasis would come to me occasionally in Deir el-Bahari and keep me up-to-date on such matters. Although these seers are heathen and know nothing of El-Shaddai, there is but the one truth and no people hold it exclusively."

"Wisely put," Moses commended. "It took me some time to learn to accept the strange destiny God—El-Shaddai—planned for me. But now I am content to be in His hands."

"Brother," Aaron said, "if you can say that you abandon

yourself to His will, then you already know the most important thing about Him. This is the only way to approach Him."

He was about to say more, but several well-wishers pushed forward a small woman in a coarse brown robe and hair-covering. She looked tentatively at him before breaking into a tearful smile. "Moses!"

There was no mistaking who it was. "Mother!" he cried, and gathered her up into his arms.

Beyond the firelight of the Habiru's celebration, three robed and hooded men hurried unseen back through the city gates to the top of the Avaris wall. The two guards threw back their own cowls, then roughly tore the robe from Dathan. The captain of the guard joined them, grabbed Dathan by the nape of his neck, and pushed him against the wall.

"He was there, the one you fingered, wasn't he? Just try to tell me that he isn't the one, curse you! He exactly fits both your description and the one the boatman gave us!"

Dathan had cried his eyes dry. He felt totally drained, except for the sense of guilt that had come upon him when he realized he had betrayed a kinsman. "I didn't recognize anybody but my relatives," he said sullenly.

A guard who had taken Dathan to the slaves' encampment moved forward, his eyes glittering with anger. "Not them. The tall one we showed you. The one who looks like Aaron."

"I never saw him before."

The captain spun Dathan around to face him, then dealt the young man a stinging cuff from the back of his hand. He gestured to the guards to tie Dathan's wrists behind him. "You Habiru bastards, you stick together, don't you? He's one of you, isn't he?"

"I don't know. I couldn't say."

The empty, weary tone was not what the captain wanted to hear. In a rage he picked up Dathan, whose bloody, ruined hands were bound behind his back. The captain held him headfirst out over the twenty-foot drop to the ground. "You son of a bitch! If I let go of you, you'll land on your head, and the best thing you could hope for would be to die instantly. Otherwise it's a broken neck. Paralysis. The rest of your life spent sitting helplessly, having someone feed you and wipe your bum every third day. Is that what you want?"

Dathan, terrified, did not answer.

."Tell me! Is it he? If I get a positive identification from the boatman but not from you, I'll boil you in a pot of pig's blood."

"You w-won't harm me," Dathan said boldly. "It takes two identifications to get a conviction."

The captain hauled him back atop the wall. When Dathan was standing unsteadily on his feet, the captain slugged him in the face with his balled fist. The next blow was appreciably harder, and Dathan slumped to his knees. "Hold him up, curse you!" the captain said to the others. He slammed Dathan in the temple with the heel of his hand. "And you!" the captain snarled at the other men. "What are you standing there for? I want an arrest. Get him!"

Dathan started to speak, but the words were knocked right out of his mouth by the next blow.

And then there was dear Miriam to see, and Amram—his father, whom he had never met, a big forthright bear of a man—and a host of others. All gathered close, but few could communicate in Egyptian.

"Then you've come to stay?" Jochebed asked. "You'll be our protector? I prayed so for this—"

"No, Mother," Miriam said. "He's come to live with us, to share our life."

"Oh, Miriam," Jochebed said. "Have all my hopes and dreams come to this? That my son should become a slave like the rest of us? That his brilliant future should come to nothing? What curse has God put upon me that He should bring down such a judgment upon my son?"

"Mother! Please! Not now! I don't know how many people can understand what you're saying!"

"What does it matter?" Jochebed agonized. "Oh, Moses, Moses! Have I suffered for you and worried about you, that you should sink to this level once more?"

"Mother," Moses said patiently, "I am in the hands of God."

"Does God want you to be a slave? I have dreamed of seeing you king of Egypt! Baliniri promised me—"

"Mother!" Miriam said sharply. "Don't spoil his home-coming!"

This was enough to bring Jochebed back to reality. "I'm so ashamed," she said, and tried to wipe her still-streaming eyes. "Can you forgive me, Moses? I wanted this moment to be a happy one. And here I am berating you, and pulling everything down for you—"

He held her close, rocking her gently the way she had done for him when he had been a tiny child and she had been his wet nurse. "There, there," he whispered gently. "You haven't spoiled anything. This is the happiest day of my life. I promise you it is."

And then it was that they heard the rough voices of the soldiers, and the disturbance began.

Two guards dragged Dathan by the arms; he would not lift his feet or cooperate in any way. The pain in his legs and feet was as acute as the agony in his hands and shoulders. He could hear the commotion ahead. The happy family gathering was suddenly ringed by soldiers, each armed fearfully with gleaming bronze weapons. The spearheads pointed inward, forming a deadly fence that framed a few Habiru within the inner circle; those outside the soldiers' ring had scrambled to safety.

He heard the voice of the captain of the guard, loud, brash, insinuating. "You are Aaron ben Amram?"

Then Aaron's voice sounded out, strong and fearless. "Yes, I am. What brings armed soldiers to the camp of my people, who have done nothing to draw their wrath or, indeed, their attention?"

"Who is this man?" the guard demanded.

"A kinsman. We were welcoming him home to his fam—"

"You lie, Habiru! I'll tell you who he is: He murdered an Egyptian guardsman, a member of the Imperial Army, in the quarry areas behind Deir el-Bahari!"

"You are mistaken," Aaron responded calmly. "He is my—"

"Bring up the witness!" the captain ordered. And the guardsmen dragged Dathan forward.

Dathan closed his eyes. There were no tears left in him to express his shame.

"Is this the man?" the captain asked. "Speak up, curse you!"

VIII

Aaron stepped forward, reached down, and tilted Dathan's head up, examining the cuts and bruises. Dathan's eye was already beginning to swell shut. "What's this? I was given to believe that no harm would come to him. I would not have left him in your care if I had had any idea that you were going to—"

But now as he knelt beside the boy, he noticed the tethered hands and the dried blood. "You've torn out his fingernails!"

The captain of the guard roughly put his hand on Aaron's shoulder and would have yanked him to his feet, but the soldier caught the dangerous look in Aaron's eye. He pulled his hand back and watched as the big man stood.

"Baliniri gave specific orders," Aaron protested firmly, "that no torture was to be used in dealing with my people."

"Baliniri's dead," the captain of the guard retorted. "Who are you, a slave, to—"

"Baliniri is indeed dead," Moses interrupted, "and a sad day it was for Egypt when he passed to the Netherworld. But I am still alive, and I still outrank you."

"You? Who are you?"

Moses squared his shoulders. "Prince Moses. Commander of the Theban garrison. Shall I list my other titles? Sooner or later we will find one to strike fear into your soul, Captain. I guarantee it." His gaze was deadly. His tone was colder than the Nile at its source.

"How do I know you're any such thing?" the captain of the guard challenged. "This man here just called you his kinsman. Either he's a liar, in which case he gets the same thing this informer here—"

"No!" Dathan cried out. "Aaron, I didn't tell these people anything. Please believe me!"

"Release the boy," Moses ordered.

"By the gods, I will not!"

"Soldiers!" Moses said over the captain's head. "You have heard me, in my capacity as his superior officer, give him an order. I call you to witness that he refused the order in an insolent and insubordinate manner."

"Wait a minute there," the captain of the guard faltered. "Let's not be hasty."

"Hasty?" Moses echoed. "I have been patient beyond all reason. You have broken your word and tortured a Habiru youth."

"But he's a witness in a murder case!"

"And you torture witnesses? Has this young fellow been found guilty of any offense?"

"Look, Your Worship, if I—"

"Untie him this minute, or so help me, I'll see you impaled before the next phase of the moon."

The captain gritted his teeth. "Cut him loose."

"That's better," Moses said. "Now, as for the charges against me: If you insist on pressing them, I'll make you regret it."

The captain clenched his fists impotently. "All right, you win—for now. But I'm going back to find someone who can verify your credentials, or cancel them. I suppose I can find you down here, among your slave kinsmen, 'Prince' Moses?"

The irony in his voice was thick, and Moses looked at him with a basilisk's eye. "If you want me, you can find me here. Whatever your errand, you might inquire into the proper manner of address for a prince of the blood. You've exhausted my patience; I won't have any when you come back. If you come back."

The squad withdrew, the captain remaining quiet until they were out of earshot. Then he began cursing, first in Egyptian, then in several other languages.

"Sir," ventured one of his men, "are we going to come back for him tomorrow?"

The captain glared at him. "And go through all that again?"

"Sir, we got a positive identification from the boy today. I'll admit it was after the second hour of torture, but it was quite positive—and in front of witnesses."

"The boy will deny it."

"It doesn't matter, sir. If the boy should die, the testimony of the witnesses to his earlier identification—combined with the additional positive identification we got from the boatman—will be quite sufficient. And the boatman offered to testify anywhere, anytime."

The captain stared at him. "Tell me more. What if he is a prince, but one who broke the law? What if he did murder one of the guards?"

"And what if he was a fake, sir, and had done all of these things?"

The women of Dathan's family had come forward and helped him away, while Moses lingered with Aaron. "This is a problem, Brother."

"You don't think you've stopped them?"

"No. The truth is, they have more than one witness. A boatman who brought me here from Athribis saw Dathan denounce me as the man who murdered the guardsman."

"But even if that's true—"

Moses put a hand on his arm. "Aaron, I *did* kill the guardsman."

Aaron's eyes widened.

"And would do it again. The man was harassing a slave. I saw oppression and acted before I thought. But it was the right thing to do; he was a bad man who would have killed more people."

"Curse Dathan for turning you in!"

"Aaron, don't blame the boy. You saw to what lengths they went—and he seems not to have cooperated even under torture."

Aaron blew out, his face softening.

"And they're not finished with him," Moses predicted. "They'll be back. Aaron, watch over the boy. I wouldn't put it past him to try to take his own life."

"But he is a witness against you. What if he isn't strong enough to withstand the next session?"

"He may not be. Which is why I have decided to turn myself in."

"What? You can't be serious!"

"Let them try to bring me to justice for killing a guardsman! The man disobeyed a direct order. I had the rank of general in the army, so I was his superior officer, even if I wasn't in uniform at the time."

Aaron's eyes darkened with concern. "But is it safe to deliver yourself into Amasis' hands? If he ever stuffed you away in some prison, you wouldn't last the week."

"That might be true," Moses agreed, "if I didn't take some pains to enlist public opinion on my side. Amasis will attend the Feast of Hathor tomorrow and will preside over the opening of the festival. Everyone in the delta will be there."

"So?"

"I will turn myself in at that time and announce the formal dedication of a large parcel of food-producing land in the twentieth nome to the people of that district."

"How?"

"Princess Thermutis settled on me all her agricultural lands before I left for Nubia. I am going to buy the people's goodwill by giving this particular parcel away."

"And as publicly as possible, during the festival, with everyone watching." Aaron chewed on his lower lip. "It might work. If Amasis arrests you, it'll provoke controversy—something he doesn't want while he's trying to win the throne permanently from Kamose."

Moses nodded. "I stayed in Thebes long enough to convince myself that there's something wrong with Kamose's campaign. I warned Seth and Geb to investigate Kamose carefully—including the people around him—before delivering the army into his hands."

"A wise move. Kamose is unstable."

"There's more to it than that. I must tell you about Apedemek."

"Apedemek? I don't know the name."

"I'll tell you about him as we walk. But now let's go look in on Dathan. We have to help him to forgive himself."

"I have passed for a wise man among our people," Aaron said, "but I think I am going to learn much from you, my brother."

IX

It was well after dark before they finally came out, but when they did, Allat the Assyrian knew very well what was happening. Two men bearing torches came before and after, to light the way through the streets of Avaris. Between them two burly servants carried a huge woven basket suspended from stout poles on their shoulders—a basket that obviously bore a very heavy load.

Allat let them move well past, so he would not be within the circle of light cast by their torches when he followed them. He had already removed his sandals and stuffed them into his robe, the better to move silently. This was no easy task; staying out of the light meant forgoing a clear view of the uneven ground, and the streets of Avaris had not been resurfaced in nearly two decades.

Allat stumbled more than once. Cursing silently at his own clumsiness and at the damage the Nile's spring flooding had wrought on the street, he kept pace until the bearers came to a turn and disappeared from view. He jogged forward, reached the cross street, then managed to catch a fleeting glimpse of the servants as they turned onto the Street of Sobek.

Where were they going? he wondered, peering through the dark at a long row of abandoned warehouses. But of course. By commandeering a warehouse—probably one of Neb-mertef's own; he virtually controlled the street—he could control access to it. The men would deliver Set-Nakht there, then provide food, drink, and the materials an astrologer would need to get his work done. But at the same time they would keep him well guarded.

He caught sight of them as they stopped before the fifth warehouse. *The fifth,* he told himself. *Remember that!*

Imagine Neb-mertef holding Set-Nakht prisoner like this. Why, he was a freeman! A professional man!

Allat knew he had to free Set-Nakht, as Set-Nakht had freed him. Somehow they would escape to the countryside and make their way to freedom and safety, beyond the borders of this wretched dictatorial Egypt, with its hideous plots and counterplots and contention and war.

* * *

The removal of the magus had come not a moment too soon: Within an hour of Set-Nakht's relocation, Amasis arrived without warning, with bodyguards, litter bearers, serving girls, musicians, dancers, masseurs, maids, and food tasters.

Neb-mertef, his staff already reduced by the relocation of Set-Nakht, was a nervous wreck as the long line of royal retainers and servants filed through the not-yet-immaculate rooms of his impressive town house. If only there had been time to clean the place thoroughly! How could he have been so foolish as to issue an invitation to the regent on such short notice? And how could Amasis have been so improvident as to arrive without warning?

There was only one thing to do. "I'll give orders, my lord, that you be moved into my own suite. It's the best in the house, and you may even find it marginally comfortable until your own rooms are ready in the palace."

"And where will you live in the meantime?" Amasis asked.

Neb-mertef was so flustered that he almost spoke the magus's name, indicating whose rooms he would occupy. "There's space on the next floor. It was occupied earlier by one of my business representatives. I've ordered him to another part of the delta." There: That sounded plausible.

"Very well. I assume there's enough space for all the people I brought? If you could find accommodations for them, I'll go to bed. It's been a tiring day, and I have to be up early tomorrow to supervise—"

There was a sudden, insistent pounding on the door. Neb-mertef's heart almost stopped. Who could it be? Those damned guards, coming back to report some new disaster? Could the magus have got free? No, that was impossible. He had doped the man's drink with enough *shepenn* to keep him comatose for hours.

"Well?" Amasis asked impatiently. "Answer the damned thing!"

Still he hesitated, until he saw the look on Amasis' face. Then, heart thudding, he gestured to a servant to draw back the bolt.

A sweating, angry, thoroughly unraveled-looking captain

of the guard stalked in, followed by a half-dozen men. "I was told the regent is here."

"I'm here, blast it!" Amasis grumbled. He strode across the room to confront the man. "What are you doing, barging in at this time of night and demanding to see me? What's your name and rank, soldier?"

The answer, coming in great, lurching blocks of words, told of the arrival of Prince Moses in Avaris, and of the many strange and unusual occurrences that had accompanied his arrival. . . .

Unable to sleep, Moses had taken his bedroll out of the tent assigned to him and spread it under the starlit sky. He had come to enjoy sleeping outdoors during the Nubian campaign and had found that his dreams on those nights spent under the stars were better than those that came to him under a roof.

But now dreams would not come. Instead he was plagued by doubts: *Am I doing the right thing? Will my actions lead to the events the prophecy spoke about?*

The worrying had begun long before his arrival in the delta, but once he was here and committed, the doubts had multiplied and increased in intensity.

Now, too, there were problems he had not envisioned, which complicated everything beyond measure. What bitter fate had prompted the boy Dathan, full of unfocused anger and resentment, to denounce him as the man who had killed the guardsman a year before?

Now the deed was done, and the Egyptians would not leave it alone. But exactly what they would do was an open question.

He sighed and looked at the stars. *You out there,* he thought, *whoever You are—help me, please. Tell me what to do. These people, who believe in You and depend on You . . . they need my help now, as well as Yours. But I haven't any idea what to do. If You could give me some sign . . .*

"Well, now," Amasis drawled when the captain had finished. "This *is* interesting! It would appear that Prince Moses—if prince he is—has fallen helpless and unarmed into our hands. Whatever shall we do with him?" He turned on

Neb-mertef suddenly. "And why is it that my peerless predictor of the future has said nothing to me of this development? Did you not see it coming? Are you losing your touch?"

"My lord," Neb-mertef sputtered, "my mind has been preoccupied with the move to the delta. I have been working well into the night every day since—"

"Never mind. You can explain later. Don't you see what this means? We have a charge of murder against the prince, although we may not be able to execute him without risking a charge of regicide."

Neb-mertef's mind raced. "What if it could be proved that Moses is an impostor, substituted in infancy for the real royal child?"

"And how are we going to prove that?" Amasis asked caustically. "The whole thing would depend on getting testimony from Princess Thermutis, and she's beyond our reach—not that she would help us by telling the truth."

Neb-mertef pressed forward feverishly. "My lord, there would have been several people involved in the switch—servants, slaves, even Baliniri."

"Baliniri's dead. I don't think there's a single servant left from that period. Several personal attendants of Queen Mara and Princess Thermutis were sent elsewhere or put to death, you'll remember. Maybe they knew too much."

"But, my lord," Neb-mertef said, improvising wildly. "There must be others!" His eyes widened. "The real mother!"

Amasis stared.

"Moses' real mother! They wouldn't have had her killed to silence her. Their minds didn't work that way."

"Wait. Wait! There were two Habiru women who were kept around to look after the child for quite a number of years. Whatever happened to them?"

"Yes!" Neb-mertef erupted. "One of them was the wet nurse!"

"Ah! And a wet nurse is commonly a woman who has just lost a child of her own—"

"—in this case, a child who was being restored to her. She was nursing her own child!"

Amasis' face became distorted with hatred. "Find the women. The wet nurse and the other one. Send a raiding party into the Habiru camp at dawn tomorrow! If he's a fake, he has no defense. He's just a guard killer—and a slave masquerading as a free citizen."

The venom in his triumphant smile sent chills down Neb-mertef's spine. *Have I redeemed myself?* he wondered anxiously. *Or will he lose confidence in me for not predicting this occurrence, when I have been so accurate in the past?*

And this gave rise to another thought: Set-Nakht had failed him in this matter. Why?

CHAPTER SIX

Thebes

I

Among the last of the proud galleys lined up along the quay, the small boat that was to take Iri's remaining assistants and apprentices downriver to the delta looked like a mouse moving among hippopotamuses. Iri looked around, uncaring. One of the big boats bore some of his possessions in Thebes, but they were afterthoughts, left behind when the first boats had been loaded with his household goods.

"Are you sorry you're not coming, sir?" Baufra asked.

"In a way," Iri admitted. "For one thing, I'll miss you and our conversations; I've enjoyed working with you."

"But I expect you to come downriver within the week, sir. A month at most. You'll find it boring here now that everyone is gone."

"I have no choice," Iri said sourly. "There's the problem of my sister." He had grown comfortable with Baufra and trusted him. "She still hasn't come home. I have people combing the city for her, but you know what it's like now—there's nobody dependable left."

"Is Seth looking for her?"

"No. And that's the oddest thing. I suspect that Seth knows something he isn't telling me. When I bring up her name in conversation, he changes the subject as soon as he can politely do so."

"Ah. You think he knows where she is."

"That's part of it. If it weren't for that, I'd give up and go downriver, figuring that if she's to be found, she's to be found there. On the other hand, I think I saw her a couple of days ago."

"You saw her, sir?"

"I think so. From a great distance. When I called out, she didn't hear me. Or perhaps she did, and didn't want to see me. By the time I got there, she was gone and I could find no trace of her."

"Did she look all right, sir?"

Iri frowned. "I couldn't tell, I was so far away. But the thing that made me wonder if I might have been mistaken—"

"Yes, sir?"

"She didn't *move* right."

"Did she limp or look as if she'd hurt herself?"

"No, nothing like that. Neftis was a proud girl, very conscious of her beauty and superiority. She expressed this awareness in the way she walked—very erect, with the head held high, chin out. And *this* girl . . . her shoulders drooped. She looked beaten down by life. But I still think in my heart of hearts that it was she. I guess I just want so much to believe that Neftis is still alive."

"I do hope you're right, sir. But I assume there'll come a time when you'll have to abandon the search."

"I hope it won't come to that. But I can't go to the delta not knowing what has happened. And there's Seth—frankly, I'm as worried about him as I am about Neftis."

"Why?"

"His nightmares. I hear him screaming almost every night. They must be quite horrible. I had to awaken him last night. I had the feeling that he could have died from fright."

"Die? From a dream?"

"I told you he had a confrontation in Nubia with this Apedemek fellow, didn't I? Well, both men are able to control people's minds. Seth showed me once. Very harmless, but when he told me to count to ten, I couldn't say the number 'seven,' no matter how hard I tried—well, I didn't believe him at first, but I do now."

Baufra raised an eyebrow. "A party trick."

"Not as these people use it. For example, one man can will his enemy to believe he's being strangled by a great snake."

Baufra's incredulity showed. "Do you really believe that, sir?"

"What's wrong with your hand, Baufra? The right one? It's turning blue. Gods! It's turning black!"

"Sir! Help me!"

But the illusion went away as quickly as it had begun. "Everything's all right," Iri assured him, grinning. "Seth showed me the method and promised to teach me more."

"Sir! I really believed—I thought that—" He held up his hand, wiggling the fingers.

"I know. Now imagine if I'd said there was a giant hand clutching your heart."

"Oh, sir! Don't even say it in jest!"

"Very well. But something like that happened to Seth. And it haunts him. I don't know how he has the courage to go to sleep at night, knowing something like that could come again." Iri shook his head sadly. "If one could spare one's friends the suffering they have to go through . . ."

Yes, Baufra thought, watching the proud and lonely face mirror all the hurt and confusion in him, *if only one could spare them their suffering!*

Seth came out of his room looking pale and tired. It was a full hour after dawn, much later than he usually arose. Mai met him in his sitting room with a tray of food.

"No, no," he said, waving it away. "Thank you, Mai, but I couldn't eat just now. Where's Iri?"

The soft-eyed woman smiled. "He left to see Baufra and the ships off. It was so early, he didn't have the heart to wake you, sir."

"Please don't call me 'sir.' Just plain 'Seth' will be quite enough, thank you." He looked at her now—the lovely round face, still unlined, with the dark hair, streaked with gray, softly framing it, and the large, expressive brown eyes. "What do you mean, he didn't have the heart to wake me? Why is today any different from any other?"

"You had another of those dreams last night. We were all frightened half to death."

"Don't be." He paused. "Why didn't you go north to the delta? It's safer there. I worry about you. The streets are full of hoodlums now."

"You worry about me, Seth?"

"You know I do. I'd rather you had gone down with Baufra. He's young and strong and can guard you against harm."

"He asked me to go with him. Right after Master Iri did."

"Hah! But of course you decided to stay."

"You and Iri need taking care of, Seth. Without me, there'd never be any peace and quiet in your lives."

Seth stared at her. "That's a rather presumptuous evaluation." He stroked his beard and smiled. "But quite true. Do you come out with enlightening observations often? If you do, I'll have to pay more attention to what you say."

The light danced in her eyes. "I'm not telling. The only way to find out whether I'm worth listening to is to listen to me."

Seth's eyes narrowed, and his expression conveyed both annoyance and newfound respect. He winked at her. "You win. I'll listen. That doesn't mean that I'll do everything you say, mind you. If you're counting on anything like that—"

"I'm not counting on anything, Seth. Now will you kindly eat your breakfast, or do you want me to stand here holding it all day?"

Seth snorted but accepted the tray. "I'll take it up to the roof. I want to think, and I can do that better in the open air."

"As you wish. Since it's still early, I won't tell you to put something on your head against the heatstroke."

"Hah!" He laughed appreciatively, then slowly made his way up the stairs to the roof garden.

He set the tray on a table and went in search of a chair. As he did, he happened to glance toward the river.

"By the gods!" he sputtered, stopped in his tracks. "He's done it! But why? *Why?*"

He went back down the stairs, almost falling in his haste.

"Seth!" Mai said. "What's the matter?"

"It's Khafre! He's brought the army downriver!"

"How could he do that? Doesn't he know——? He must have got your letter to hold off until further instructions!"

"I don't know. I gave the letter to——" Again he stood rooted to the spot. "I gave the letter to Geb to send off. And Geb's been acting very odd lately. Ever since he had that meeting with Kamose, he's been——"

"Yes?"

Seth pressed his fingertips to his temples and looked at Mai in horror. "Someone else has control of his mind. Somehow, at Kamose's, he's run into Apedemek. That has to be it! Oh, my stars, if that's true, then Kamose is under Apedemek's control, too. This is terrible. What am I going to do?"

Mai reached out timidly to touch his arm. "Seth, don't do anything hasty."

"Hasty? Anything I could possibly do would be too late."

There was a knock on the door. Mai went to answer it. Seth returned to his room and opened the chest to get his outer robe, while muttering under his breath.

Mai came back into his room. "Seth, you'd better come to the door. There's a man with a message for you." She paused, frowning. "He claims to come from Neftis."

Seth blanched, and he put a hand on Mai's shoulder. "Mai, I—found her a while back. She's in bad shape, involved with some brute who mistreats her."

"Not my baby!"

"Listen: I'm going to Neftis. You find Iri and bring him to us. Here's where we'll be. . . ."

II

Iri, having seen Baufra off, was striding briskly up the hill toward the city when someone nearby spotted the sails. "Sail ho!" the fellow sang out. "It's the fleet! It's the army, returned from Nubia!"

Iri turned and stared, unable to believe what he was seeing. What were they doing in Thebes? Surely they'd got Seth's instructions to hold off until they received further notification!

As the boats continued coming—over a dozen already in view, and others undoubtedly to come—he remembered watching Seth hand the missive to Geb, whom Seth had introduced as the "best underofficer in the army."

Could Geb have sold them out? Could the courier have been kidnapped, his message intercepted and rewritten?

Iri hurried down toward the Nile, where the first boat was now alongside the dock. A man in the uniform of the Second Troop jumped ashore with the forward lines in hand, ready to tie up. Iri recognized him as Anti, a soldier who, a year before, had often visited his forges. Iri broke into a lope and was at the soldier's side in a moment.

"Anti," he said, "what is happening here?"

Anti grinned and clapped Iri on the back when the lines were secured. "Sorry, old fellow. Orders from on high. Not supposed to talk to anyone. Now if you'll excuse me . . ."

Iri let him go. He stood watching the rest of the ships steer to shore and disgorge squad after squad of battle-hardened young soldiers, their muscular bodies burnt dark by the Nubian sun, their weapons gleaming in the morning sun.

Orders? he thought. *Orders from whom? Certainly not from Seth or Moses!*

What was going on here?

Hieron, sailing his little one-man boat, had been among the first to spot the fleet coming into Thebes. He had steered to shore immediately and docked at the northernmost slip, and by the time the first soldier debarked, Hieron was ashore.

From well out in the current he had spotted Iri and recognized him. Now, watching the powerfully built young smith look over the landing, his stance speaking eloquently of his incredulity, Hieron strode toward Iri and in a moment had reached him.

"Excuse me," he said. "You are Iri of Thebes?"

But the young man was so absorbed by the fleet's arrival, he could not give his attention to Hieron. "Will you look at that? For a year taking the greatest pains to keep the army out of the clutches of the son of a bitch, and now they come ashore and prepare to hand the whole thing over to him."

"Excuse me—"

Iri shook his head unbelievingly, then turned to look at the stranger. "I beg your pardon," he said. "Were you addressing me?"

Iri looked him in the eyes; Hieron met his gaze without flinching from the birthmark. "I have business with you, but it might be better discussed away from the ears of the entire army."

Iri scowled. "Look at them! They've just lost us the war!"

"Have they, now?" Hieron asked. Then: "When I've talked to you for one minute, you'll agree that I'm worth your time."

"I can spare that, I suppose. But before I go with you, I have to know who you are."

Hieron spoke in a subdued voice. "I am Hieron of Crete, an associate of your brother, Khian. I come in his name. Like you and Khian, I am a Child of the Lion."

Iri looked at the man in amazement. "You're right, we need privacy for this." He steered Hieron toward the far end of the quays. "We can talk at my place without fear of interruption or of being overheard."

The two set off at a robust clip down the street that led to Iri's house.

Seth's progress down the street was not as rapid as he wished it to be. But it had allowed him time to think.

It had to be something Geb had done, he decided. Somehow Geb had altered the written message he had been given to send upriver.

But why? It was not the sort of thing Geb would have done if he had had his wits about him. He had to be under the control of someone like Apedemek, whose mind was so powerful that he was Seth's superior.

But now; that was defeatist talk. He had been defeated only once. In the time since that confrontation at Semna, he had rested and recuperated, with both Tchabu and Neku-re helping him, healing him, teaching him.

Whom am I trying to fool? he thought despairingly. *I'm*

*less than I was when Apedemek first met me. I'm over the
hill. Past my peak. Worn out.*

His slow steps were those of a man thirty years older
than he. His hands shook, and his strength ebbed with every
passing moment.

"What's this?" Iri said, stopping. "Mai? Is that you?
Haven't I told you not to go out into the street alone?"

"Iri!" his nurse gasped, out of breath from hurrying
down toward the waterfront. "Seth's gone! He got a message
from Neftis, and—"

"From Neftis?"

"She sent a man to fetch Seth! She's in trouble! I think
Seth is walking into terrible danger! He does, too! Something
he's very afraid of! I saw it in his face as he prepared to go!"

"Danger? What kind of danger?"

"He didn't say. Maybe it has something to do with the
dream he had last night."

"Apedemek!" Iri moaned. "He's found Apedemek!"

"What did you say?" Hieron demanded.

On the docks the soldiers formed ranks, and their officers inspected them. General Khafre strode down the lines,
pronounced himself satisfied, then turned to Geb. "Where is
Kamose? I expected to have seen him here by now."

"He'll be here any moment," Geb reported. "I have his
promise on that. He's probably assembling a proper bodyguard. While the king is afraid of nothing, his aides won't let
him go out alone."

Khafre looked sharply at his old assistant. "Is there something wrong? There's something different about you."

"Nothing's wrong with me, sir."

Khafre scowled. "I know you better than you know yourself, and you're not yourself, curse it. Is it that desert fever
again? I've half a mind to order you to bed for a day or two."

"I'm quite all right, sir. Don't give it another thought.
Look, here he comes."

"Call the men to attention," Khafre instructed his adjutant. "Have them present arms."

*   *   *

She had done what she could to cover the most livid bruises, but no cosmetics could mask the puffiness and the half-closed eye. When she opened the door, she could see the horror in Seth's face.

"Gods above!" he erupted, pushing his way gently inside and closing the door behind him. "What's happened to you, girl?"

It was here that she faltered in her resolve. She hadn't been expecting a man who showed no concern at all for himself but thought only of *her* pain, *her* bruises. She firmed her jaw and balled her fists. Arsaphes had told her that every man thought only of himself, as he did. He had said that her impression of Seth as a caring and selfless man was a cruel and bitter illusion.

But look at him! He was exhausted. He was old. He was frightened. Yet he had come, as he had promised, in spite of the potential danger.

Suddenly the cold, heart-stopping panic overtook her.

"Seth, you've got to get out of here. He'll be back any moment, and he'll hurt you. I'll be all right. I shouldn't have called for you. I didn't know what I was doing. I—I hope someday you can forgive me, Seth, but now, please go."

"I'm not going without you," he said in a voice drained of strength. "Get your things. We're leaving here forever. It won't be hard. You just put one foot in front of the other."

What is he drawing on? she wondered. *He looks so old, so lost.* She grabbed his arm. "Seth, please."

But it was too late. The door opened, and *he* stood there, tall, commanding, powerful, and smiling triumphantly.

"You!" Seth rasped.

III

"Arsaphes!" Neftis pleaded. "Let him go! Don't hurt him! I'll do whatever you want. Just let him go." She moved to shield Seth.

Arsaphes' smile had no humor. His eyes bored into

Seth's soul. "Listen to her," he said in a deceptively soft voice. "Begging for your safety—pleading for your soul, Seth. Your soul! You'd never know, listening to her, that the bitch was just pleading with me not to abandon her, and selling you out to keep me here." He snorted. "She sounds all innocence now, though, doesn't she?"

He laughed sourly. "They're all that way. There isn't a one of them that's worth a damn, and this one is no exception. They'll happily sell a man to his worst enemy—" He chuckled. "Wouldn't you describe me that way, Seth? The man who broke that fine mind of yours? The man who broke your pride with it?"

"Don't listen to him, Seth!" the girl shrieked, sobbing as she spread her arms wide to interpose her slim body between the younger, powerful man and the older, faded one. "It's true! I admit it! I was weak! But I won't let him do this to you."

"Stand aside," Arsaphes ordered. "I'm warning you."

"No, Arsaphes!"

"His name isn't Arsaphes," Seth said quietly. "It's Apedemek."

She whirled to look into his eyes with horror.

"Yes, the one I told you about," he confirmed. "We've known each other for some time."

His calm confused her. She was tempted to feel relief: He wasn't frightened, so no harm must be coming to him.

But then the truth occurred to her; this was the quiet acceptance of a doomed man. He knew he would not last the hour. From the moment he had made his promise to her, he had expected this betrayal. And yet he had still come for her, like the all-forgiving father she had always dreamed of.

"Indeed," Seth continued softly, "it almost seems Apedemek and I have always known each other—as if I split apart in my youth, and one half placed his steps firmly in the path of evil, for power and riches, and the other chose the path of normal human uncertainty, where every step could bring great harm."

Apedemek sneered. "And look where your precious 'uncertainty' led you! Your self-absorption brought about the deaths of everyone you've ever loved!" He threw his head back and laughed loudly. "This!" he said to Neftis, throwing his arms wide. "*This* is the paragon you don't want me to harm! This contemptible worm who groveled before me in Semna and begged me to leave him alone!"

Neftis looked at Seth, appalled.

Seth put a hand on her shoulder. "I was defeated in Semna," he whispered. "This much is true." His fingers closed on her shoulder, and the touch brought a fleeting comfort. "As for groveling, Apedemek has a vivid imagination; otherwise, he could not get such effects when he tampers with people's minds."

Neftis cringed slightly, and Seth looked into her eyes. "Has he tampered with yours, my dear? I think not yet—not in the way he tampered with mine, or Princess Tharbis's, or the others'. He preferred in your case, I would guess, to trap you into trapping yourself, innocent and inexperienced as you were. With his greater knowledge of the world, he knew he could manipulate you. It was the greater sport to trap the prey without the hidden snare."

Apedemek gave him a sardonic salute. "My compliments. You're more perceptive than I had thought. But that's because you and I are alike—deep inside, the same person."

"The rule in such matters," Seth said calmly, addressing Neftis, "is never to let the demon engage you in conversation. Either he will force you to lie as he does, in which case you forfeit your self-respect, or he will lie and you will be forced to tell the truth, placing you at a disadvantage. It is best not to hear what he says.

"But this time I have to listen," he continued, "because I want *you* to hear it, my dear. You must learn to recognize the lies. Oh, Neftis, you think you have spoiled your life, because he's guided you into making the wrong choices. But you can turn your life around at any moment; indeed, you already have. When you moved between us and tried to protect me from him, that was lovely. Never forget that you did that. But this fight is between Apedemek and me. Move to one side, my dear. Please, do it now."

But when Apedemek began to raise his hand, she flew at him, hands flailing. "No! You can't! I won't let you!"

The blow came from nowhere, and it was harder than he had ever hit her before. It caught her off balance and knocked her against the wall, where she hit her head hard and slid to the floor. When she looked up at him, she saw double and felt blood running down the side of her face.

She blinked to focus. She tried to rise, but something happened: She could see his lips moving, but she could not hear what he was saying. As Apedemek waved his hand, she found herself unable to move, unable to speak, unable to do anything but watch.

And then Seth came alive. It was like watching the years fall away from him. His eyes blazed and made contact with Apedemek's. Suddenly Apedemek's body began to glow, first red, then white. Apedemek screamed as his clothing burst into flames.

But it was over almost before it had begun. Apedemek shook off the spell and seemed to grow a handspan in height. The mad, horrible laughter burst from him.

"Is that the best you can do, old man? Old! Old! That's what you are! The dotard managed to make one last, pitiful show of strength, but then the power leaves him a burnt-out shell!"

Seth raised his hands, and bolts of light shot from them, blasting Apedemek back against the wall and holding him there, his eyes glazed and his face twisted in pain.

Neftis looked at Seth, and her heart sank. Although Apedemek was held fast, the power was draining from Seth rapidly. His lips were white; his hands trembled.

At last Apedemek broke free, but it was not his own strength that accomplished it; there seemed to be something wrong with Seth.

"No," he moaned brokenly. "Don't fail me now. My mind . . . nothing there . . ."

Seth! her mind called out. *Fight back! Pull yourself together, or he'll kill you!*

But her words found no voice. She watched him crumple to the ground, his hands holding his head. What tragedy had resulted from her folly!

"There now," Apedemek said. "Watch the death of a fool dedicated to ideals!" His eyes went to her. "There is only power! There is only the strength of one's own mind and body! There is only the self! Remember that, while you look at this broken weakling on the floor who has given his life for nothing! Nothing at all!"

No! she wanted to say. *He is giving his life for me! Don't you dare say that his bravery is wasted!* But her lips would not move.

"Now," he continued, "I will show you how the weak can destroy themselves on command. I am going to order his mind to wipe itself clean by stages, until he is more alone than any man has ever been! And when there is nothing left, I will command his heart to fail. His death will be like that of no other man's since the world began."

Seth! she thought, her eyes full of unshed tears. *Forgive me!*

IV

Because Mai's legs were short, she had to take two steps to the men's one, but she did keep pace. She had listened to their talk for some blocks—talk of sorcerers and wizards and suchlike—but now she had to interrupt for the sake of her own curiosity. "Pardon me, sir," she asked Hieron. "Did you say that you came from dear Khian?"

"Yes," he confirmed. "As soon as we've time, I'll tell you all about him. You're one of his favorite people, and he sends you his best wishes."

"Thank you, sir. He's become a great man?"

"Greater than many kings. In their councils he is called Demetrios the Magnificent. Of course, they have no idea that he's Egyptian, and few connect him with the Children of the Lion. He administers an empire built a century ago by a man all Egyptians know—Akhilleus, once the king of Nubia."

"Akhilleus?" Iri said. "How did Khian—"

"Akhilleus left his shipping empire in the hands of trusted subordinates but retained control. Upon Akhilleus's death, his son, Nehsi, found it impossible to serve as king of Nubia and heir to the greatest shipping organization in the world. He put out feelers for bright young men to train for the job, and in all the lands there was none brighter than Khian.

Keeping Akhilleus's tradition alive, Khian took a Greek name when he assumed control. There's no time for further explanations now. Seth may be in grave danger."

"I'll be still, sir. Who would want to harm a sweet, gentle man like Seth?"

"Seth has himself proved dangerous to some people—most of all to the man I think he's with now. Iri, is that the address up ahead?"

"I think so," Iri said. "Gods! I was a fool for coming out unarmed like this!"

"The threat to Seth comes not from conventional weapons. What he faces is much worse!"

Seth knelt on the floor, his head in his hands. His upper body swayed unsteadily.

Apedemek leaned against the wall, an expression of feverish anticipation on his long, bony face. "The child, the boy, and the young man who were Seth are gone—all the things learned, all the memories. And now we come to the middle years. Fading away are Criton of Hellas, your first friend. And the princess Shala, your beautiful wife, who loved you as no other woman ever had. They are fading from your memory, and with them you yourself are fading. The great loneliness will soon be more than you can bear."

Neftis watched impotently. She wanted to say: *Apedemek! Take me instead!* But her thoughts were walled up by the spell he had cast upon her.

But while her other physical faculties had been paralyzed, her sight and hearing were unaffected. And now she heard footfalls on the stairs. Neftis looked at Apedemek, but his intense eyes gave no sign that his concentration had been disturbed.

Suddenly the door burst open, and in the doorway stood Iri, with him a man she had never seen.

The stranger roared, and his anger cut through the close atmosphere. *"Apedemek!"*

As Apedemek turned, startled, the spell on Seth was broken, and he lay gasping, while the damage came undone.

"Apedemek, hear your destiny! Receive the judgment of the gathered masters of the Order of Chalybia!"

Apedemek's face turned white. He backed against the wall, his hands outspread behind him. "W-who are you?"

"I am Hieron of Crete, assistant to Demetrios the Magnificent, called Khian among the Egyptians!"

"Khian!" Neftis uttered, and found she could also move her limbs. She crawled to where Seth lay, to cradle him in her arms.

"Who are you to tell me that I—" Apedemek began in a voice much altered.

"Know," Hieron said, "that the high council of the thirty-third degree has met and considered your case. A master of the order may not use its secrets and wisdom in the cause of evil."

"They have no jurisdiction here!" Apedemek sneered. "That bunch of old—"

"Silence!" Hieron thundered.

Apedemek cringed.

Hieron continued: *"Know now that the full powers of the order have been arrayed against you—save only the killing of you. You will die, your power gone, your triumphs forgotten, a man grown suddenly small and alone."*

Apedemek stared Hieron in the eyes and stood tall. "You people have underestimated my powers. When I've accomplished what I came to Egypt to do, I'm coming after all of you! I'll crush you as I've crushed this fool at our feet!"

"Demonstrate your power," Hieron challenged. "You will find it does not work in this room."

There was a flash of panic in Apedemek's eyes, and then he recovered. "I acknowledge myself temporarily outflanked. But heed my warning. You and all those of the order will suffer! I'll pick you off one by one!"

As Hieron responded, Iri crossed to join Neftis and Seth, and Mai edged her way around the wall, entering the room. "You have heard the judgment of the order rendered. There will be no place you can hide, no solace you can turn to. Now go!"

Apedemek's bony fist clenched and relaxed. It was a surprisingly ineffectual gesture for a man who had been in the seat of power only moments before. He paused at the door, pointing a skinny finger at Hieron. "You in particular will hear from me. I give my oath to see you dead!"

And then he was gone.

*   *   *

Iri and the two women helped Seth to his feet. "Are you all right?" Mai asked. "Can you stand alone? Here, lean on me, my dear. There. You're safe now."

Seth looked at them in utter desolation. "I was witnessing my own extinction, destroyed moment by moment, and I could do nothing about it. I've failed. Failed!"

Neftis, weeping, buried her face in his chest. "Oh, no, Seth! You saved me! I'm alive because of you!"

Seth almost fell, so they helped him to a chair. When they did, Hieron knelt on one knee, the better to look directly into his eyes. "Seth, your part in this is done. You have fought a brave battle and carried a burden better suited to a younger man. The time has come for you to relinquish the standard."

Seth's eyes went to the ground, and a tear hung on his lashes.

Hieron put a hand under the older man's chin to tilt his head up. "Seth, I'm sending you to safety. Younger men, whose strength has not been sapped in a long and punishing battle, will carry on the fight." He looked up at Mai. "You must take Neftis and him to Nubia, where they can be cared for by Seth's son, King Het. Stop first at the oasis, for whatever help you may need."

Neftis found it hard to speak. "I—I don't know if you'll all want me, when you learn what I've done."

"You will learn to forgive yourself," Hieron told her. "When the troubles are over, I will come for you and Iri and take you to your brother, Khian." He looked at Seth now. "Khian will carry the fight to Apedemek, in the name of the order. Khian is of the thirty-second degree."

"Khian?" Seth asked. "Sinuhe's son? But why have I never heard of him before? My kinsman a Chalybian, and more advanced in the craft than myself?"

"Yes," Hieron verified. "I am your kinsman as well. I will explain later. The order is large, and the Children of the Lion are many, my friend. And they take care of their own. If you ever have need of Khian, who commands the loyalty of many, get a message to any port on the shores of the Great Sea that you want to reach Demetrios. He can always be reached by a fellow Child of the Lion."

Hieron looked at Neftis again and saw self-loathing in her eyes. He reached out and touched her forehead, and she instantly fell into a deep sleep; Iri had to catch her in his arms.

"Care for her in particular," he advised. "In some ways her hurt is greater than Seth's."

"We will do as you say," Mai promised. "You sound like a man who is leaving us."

Hieron nodded. "I have some messages to get to Demetrios and to other members of the order. Iri, you have business in the delta, I believe. Khian ordered me to bring you into the order; it's long overdue, and it's a shame to put it off, but I suppose we must."

"We will never forget you," Mai assured Hieron. She sent a protective glance first at Neftis, then at Seth. Her gaze lingered a bit over the latter.

"Go along. I'll join you in a moment," Iri said.

As she guided Seth out of the room, Iri scooped up Neftis as if she were a small child. He looked at Hieron. "I have seen great work here today. We are well met. Take my love and blessing to my brother. And find time, one of these days, to tell me more about this order of yours, will you?"

V

Mai put a comforting arm around Seth's back. "There, now, dear, we're going to take care of you. Don't worry."

"I'm finished," he said. "I'd thought I might rise to the occasion, but it was a vain dream."

"Look, Seth, as we age, there's no use trying to fight the process. Why, if I had gotten disturbed when my looks started to fade . . ."

For a moment the misery in his eyes lifted. "Nothing has faded, Mai. You are a beautiful woman."

Startled, she smiled. This was the thing to do. Get his mind away from himself. "You're just saying that to make me feel better. I'm an old frump, past my best years."

Seth realized what she was doing. He smiled. "Well, it appears we need each other, if only to shore up our fading self-esteem." He patted her hand. "Could I lean on you as we walk? Who knows? Maybe I will recover my strength someday and will be able to repay the favor."

"Oh, Seth. The world has leaned on you for so long. It's time we all tried to give you back the strength you have squandered on others." She looked him in the eyes. "Why, Seth! What's the matter?"

"Gods! I almost forgot. Kamose! He's got the army now. We've lost! The whole thing's in the hands of Kamose and Apedemek!"

Iri came up behind them, carrying his sister. "We've still got Moses. He's a powerful man." He looked at Mai. "We'd better get going. They could decide to close the port, and then we'd be trapped."

Iri, with his sister, and Mai, leading Seth, quickened their pace. Looking down the side streets, Mai could see soldiers, armed to the teeth, marching down the parallel main thoroughfares.

"I wonder where Apedemek went," Iri said. "I'm surprised Hieron let him go like that. Do you think Hieron could have killed him, Seth?"

"I'm not sure," Seth replied. "There was no test of powers, only a test of wills. Apedemek chose to avoid a confrontation and beat a strategic retreat. Hieron didn't say what level he was; he did say that Khian was at the thirty-second degree. There's only one higher rank that I know of."

"Do you think he'll actually let me in?" Iri asked.

"You're a Child of the Lion," Seth answered. "Yes, I think you can count on it, unless something drastic happens. If you are reunited with Hieron, he'll read you into the order. I could do so myself if you came upriver with us now."

They turned a corner and wandered through an alley to avoid the patrols of soldiers. "I have to go to the delta," Iri said regretfully. "If Apedemek doesn't denounce me, I'm halfway accepted by both Kamose's camp and Amasis' while being tied to neither. And no one knows of my ties to Moses and Aaron."

"What are your plans?" Seth wanted to know.

"Play both sides against each other," Iri admitted. "They both need a good armorer."

"Beware," Seth cautioned. "Kamose's side doesn't need one. It has Apedemek. Like all Children of the Lion, he knows the art. I even heard a rumor that he is certified in the making of iron."

Iri stopped and stared. "You're right. I'll watch myself. As it stands, I am officially working for Amasis as his armorer, and unofficially I'm supposed to be working for Kamose as a double agent, spying on Amasis. But he doesn't trust me, and I don't trust him."

"Don't start trusting him," Seth advised. "And make sure that Moses doesn't, either."

Hieron stepped back into the shadow of an abandoned warehouse and let the patrol pass. They were clear-eyed, sober looking, tough, and seasoned—unlike the dissolute foreigners who fleshed out Amasis' army in the delta. The story was, they had defeated the Nubians at Semna and pacified the border almost without losses.

A pity they had to fall into the hands of Kamose—which was to say, into the hands of Apedemek. Things were bad in Egypt now. He would have a very pessimistic report for Khian when they met, in a week or two. The only good thing he would be able to report would concern the fate of Khian's siblings. The girl would recover, particularly if the stories of Tchabu and Neku-re, the seers of the El-Kharga oasis, were true.

He stepped out into the sunlight and made his way slowly along the deserted alley, keeping an eye out for soldiers. *Iri, now,* he thought, *is quite another matter.* Iri was impressive, in spite of the handicap he carried through life so uncomplainingly. It would be a pleasure initiating the young man into the secrets of the craft.

Hieron's reverie set him too much at ease. His eyes were on the opening of the street far ahead, and his mind was on the future. He did not perceive the presence that moved behind him. He did not hear the soft footfalls. With no clairvoyant gift, he did not sense the shadow that moved slowly along the bleached wall at his back.

He heard the last step behind him as his follower's foot

kicked a stone down the alley. He half turned, and the long knife slipped into his back and buried itself to the hilt, hard enough to push him a step forward. He looked down and saw the blade protruding from his belly.

"W-wha—?" he began.

His attacker pulled the knife out and struck again. This time the blow caught him in the upper back. He tried to turn, but his legs were growing weak and his robe was a wall of blood. He caught a quick glimpse of the man who had stabbed him, was stabbing him again, and all of a sudden his legs gave way, and he fell to the ground.

The breath was knocked out of him, and he was unable to catch his breath. He looked up with blurred eyes.

Apedemek stood over him, his face a mask of hatred, his hands and forearms stained with blood.

"Well!" the tall man said. "Where are all those brave words now? For all your vaunted powers it would appear you don't have eyes in the back of your head."

Hieron tried to speak, but the words did not come.

"You humiliated me!" Apedemek scolded. "And fool that I was, I let your reputation frighten me. I could have taken you! I know I could!"

Hieron closed his eyes, and the world spun beneath him. When he reopened them, Apedemek's image was still blurred.

Think! he urged himself. *You can still defeat him before you die if you can remember what to do.*

Apedemek waved the bloody knife crazily. "I've beat you now." He was exhilarated. "And before you could get a message to Demetrios! He'll assume that everything is all right. By the time his suspicion is aroused and he comes here to check up on you, I'll be too powerful for him to do anything!"

Hieron closed his eyes, and as his powers faded, he concentrated and grabbed hold of them. Up from his mind rose demons, harpies, monsters, and dragons: disembodied horrors that rose to twice Apedemek's height and reared their gory heads high, while howls of rage issued from their gaping jaws.

Apedemek shrank back.

One by one they began to fade.

No! Hieron thought. *Please! Stay just long enough to destroy him!*

But the grotesque menagerie vanished.

"I've beaten you!" Apedemek howled. "If I can defeat you, I can defeat Demetrios! I'll have no master in the world!"

The last thing Hieron saw was the blurred and hateful grin of victory on Apedemek's face.

VI

"What's going on here?" Khafre demanded. "What do you mean, 'General' Geb? Geb's no general."

"Are you questioning my authority?" Kamose asked coldly. "And so soon after delivering my army over to me?"

"Well, no, Sire," Khafre said in a tight voice. "Not your authority. It's just that—"

"Then perhaps my judgment?"

"No, Sire. Geb is a solid underofficer but is not the type to be named—it's just that this seems so sudden." He looked over to where Geb was reviewing the assembled Third Troop, as confidently as if he had been doing this for years. "A jump of that many ranks at one time tends to undermine discipline in the army, Sire."

"Aha. Then you question my understanding of military discipline, hierarchy—"

Khafre bit off a sharp retort, determined to avoid a fight. "Sire, you know as well as I do that—"

Kamose's lip curled. "Well," he said sarcastically, "I'm glad you grant me *that*: I know something as well as you do." His face hardened. "You've been testy ever since you landed in Thebes, General."

Khafre's eyes narrowed. "Now that you mention it, Sire, I have. Something odd is going on, and I intend to get to the bottom of it. Moses was supposed to be here. The order to come to Thebes was supposed to have come from him. Instead, there's no evidence that he was even in the area when

the order was sent upriver to me. I can't find any trace of
Seth. I'll willingly obey any order from Prince Moses, and I'll
consider one from Seth. But an order from Geb? If I had
known Moses had nothing to do with it, I wouldn't have
come."

"The order came from me," Kamose said. "I gave it to
General Geb to transmit to you."

Khafre's hands were shaking with rage. "He misrepre-
sented it. The papyrus said it came with Moses' authority,
and—"

"And Moses' authority is greater than mine?"

"Sire, for quite a long time you weren't yourself. I was
ordered by Baliniri not to hand the army over to you unless it
was proved to me or to Prince Moses that you were all right
again."

"And I tell you I am. Do you question that?"

The rage began to build in the old general. "Frankly,
Sire, yes. The old Kamose wouldn't have allowed Geb to
mislead me. And the Geb I've served with for years would
never have gone along with anything as roundabout as this."

"I see. We're all a nest of liars, is that it, General?"

"I don't know. And who is Arsaphes? How does he draw
so much water around here? Geb kept mouthing off about
how everything had to be referred to Arsaphes. I've never
heard the name. Has some smooth-talking transient sold you
all a bill of goods?"

Kamose's face was solid granite. "I will overlook your
insolence because of your long service. But I'll remind you,
General, to moderate your tone when speaking to your king."
Kamose looked past him and nodded.

Khafre wheeled and looked into the wrathful eyes of
Apedemek. The general's hand, driven by pure instinct, flew
to his sword hilt, but Kamose's powerful hands grasped his
wrists from behind and yanked them both behind his back.
He struggled, cursing, and looked once more into the magus's eyes. Suddenly the strength left him.

Apedemek, his power over Khafre complete, looked at
Kamose. "I could control him, but what would be the use?
We'll want our own men in charge. Kill him."

Khafre listened helplessly, unable to move or to speak.

"Where have you been?" Kamose asked. "You're up to your elbows in blood."

"I was eliminating a problem," Apedemek answered. "One that promised to be very vexing." Savage triumph lit the mad eyes. "I feel good. I know how strong I am. No enemy can stand in our way. You'll be the undisputed Lord of Two Lands before the year's out."

Kamose smiled. "Good. And to celebrate, we'll get rid of this fellow here."

And so saying, he moved to stand in front of Khafre. "Good-bye, General," he said, drawing his sword. With a terrible smile, he lunged as unconcernedly as if the object of his thrust were a target of straw.

Zazamankh, adjutant of the Fourth Troop, had been supervising a loading detail on the docks, but he handed the job over to a subordinate when he spotted a familiar face. He made his way briskly to the little group at dockside. "Pardon me," he said to their clustered backs. "Aren't you Seth of Thebes?"

The older man turned toward him, and the young officer, seeing the devastation that the day's activities had wrought, winced at the sight. "I know you, don't I?" Seth said. "You were with me in Nubia."

"Yes, sir. Zazamankh's my name. I was with the Third Troop but was promoted in El-Kab after you came downriver. If you don't mind some advice, I don't think you ought to be around the waterfront just now."

Iri stepped forward. "Do you know me?"

"Yes, sir. Iri the armorer. Sir, you'd better get these folks to safety across the river. Seth's name has been mentioned as an enemy of the state, and if you're with him, you may wind up with trouble you didn't bargain for. There are some very strange things going on; an hour ago I was ordered to arrest the brother of an old friend of mine on charges I couldn't have justified in a lifetime."

"I understand," Iri sympathized. "If you'd be so kind as to protect my companions for a few minutes, I'll hire a boatman to ferry us across the river."

"Right you are, sir." Zazamankh watched Iri stride briskly

to the water's edge, then he turned to Seth. "Sir, I wish we'd never come downriver. I don't like what's happening."

"Nor do we," Seth said. "I had hopes of making it to Nubia, with the women, where my son—"

"A good thought, sir. But Nubia's a long way, and we left pickets to keep an eye on all boats sailing upriver from here."

Seth frowned. "Then what can we—"

"If you can make your way to Deir el-Bahari, sir, the craftsmen remain there. They were very loyal to Baliniri and, I suppose, to you by extension."

Seth's eyes lit up for the first time. "That's good news indeed!"

"Look up a woman named Ti, in the artisans' village. She has a kinsman named Nemti. . . ." He let the sentence hang.

Seth's face came alive. "So Nemti comes to town from time to time, eh? Perhaps to spy for Weret?"

"Yes, sir, taking his life in his hands every time he does."

Seth nodded knowingly. "Is he still Queen Mara's lover?"

Zazamankh nodded. "You can imagine how the king would react to that, sir. She's sworn never to return to Kamose."

"Yes."

Iri returned then, and Seth hurriedly explained the situation.

"This sounds like the answer to your problem," Iri remarked. "You'll go to the oasis first and spend time with the dwarf once more. My thanks, Zazamankh. I'll not forget the favor. Perhaps I can return it; I'm staying here in Thebes while my friends make a dash for it."

Zazamankh raised one brow. "Are you sure that's what you want, sir? If I weren't married to the army, I'd give serious thought to escaping with Seth and these ladies. We've a bad situation, one that promises only to get worse."

"Thanks for the warning, but my place is in the middle of things. Good fortune to you." He smiled and led his companions toward the waiting boat.

As the boatman poled the little vessel away, Iri tried not to feel so disconsolate. *What am I doing?* he wondered. *Here*

I've just bade farewell to the only people who care about me, while I'm left in this hornets' nest.

That was not the worst of it. In order to rejoin Moses, Aaron, and Baufra, he would have to leave Thebes and seek out an even more dangerous life in the delta among Amasis' minions.

What kind of idiot would seek out certain danger? The answer came quickly enough: *a lonely one.* He had been spoiled by having real friends who accepted him and dealt honestly with him—like his assistant Baufra, who was loyal and wanted to learn from him; like Moses and Aaron, brave and true and intelligent.

He had never had friends like these before. And he could not wait to see them again. Curse the danger anyway!

CHAPTER SEVEN

Avaris

I

In the morning Aaron came to visit Dathan, who lay in the tent, staring miserably at nothing. Aaron sat cross-legged beside the young man.

After a few minutes, Dathan rolled over to look at him. "Aaron," he whispered, his voice cracking.

Aaron put a comforting hand on the young man's forehead. "Don't think about it just now. You've been through a lot and can't be expected to sort things out so quickly."

"But Moses!" Dathan said, trying to sit up. Gently Aaron eased him down again. It did not take much strength to do so; Dathan was greatly weakened by his ordeal. "Aaron, where is he? I want to talk to him."

"He awoke before dawn and left camp almost immediately."

"Gone!" Dathan cried out. "Oh, no! Where?"

"To Amasis' court to turn himself in," Aaron answered. "Don't worry. I'm sure he knows what he's doing."

"To the court! But they'll—"

"He has a plan for enlisting the support of the people against Amasis. It's brilliant . . . if he can make it work."

182

Dathan shook his head. "You've no idea how they hate him! How badly they want him! He's been a thorn in Amasis' side ever since—"

"—he was born." Aaron's voice was mild. "As long as Moses is alive, neither Kamose nor Amasis can sleep soundly as regent or king of Egypt."

Dathan put his bandaged hands to his temples. "You've got to stop him!"

"Too late," Aaron said. "I sent Ezbon after him, but he spotted Moses going into Neb-mertef's town house. He was flanked by soldiers."

Dathan's face was tense, and although he lay flat and unmoving, an anguished energy exuded from him, as if he were about to erupt with violent emotion. Then, suddenly, he went limp, and the effect was even more alarming than the tension had been.

"Then I can do nothing to prevent his death, nothing to expiate my own guilt."

"I told you not to think about that," Aaron protested. "It wasn't your f—"

"Don't tell me it wasn't my fault!" the boy shouted. "I betrayed him! He'd be safe if it hadn't been for me!"

"Hush, now," Aaron soothed, taking one of Dathan's bandaged hands gently in his, carefully avoiding the fingertips. "It is all in God's hands. We must trust in Him, as my brother has chosen to do." He sighed. "It is curious, Dathan. Moses knows nothing of our customs or rituals, but I believe that he has found the heart of God anyway. His faith is already greater than mine. What a priest of El-Shaddai will he be when he has lived among us for a time!"

"If he lives among us," Dathan moaned. "They'll show him no mercy."

"God will not abandon him," Aaron pointed out. "To be sure, I do not know the will of God, but I have learned to trust."

Dathan sighed deeply. "Then where was He when I needed Him? When they were torturing me? Why did He not stop them? Why does He enslave us, beaten, starved, wretched—"

"Dathan! Have patience!"

"This is the sort of talk that has kept us slaves."

Aaron put up a cautionary hand. "It is the first day of the Feast of Hathor, and—"

"Heathen observances!"

Aaron smiled. "Rest assured that Amasis probably looks on the observance every bit as skeptically as we do, if for different reasons. The cult he tried to introduce here has slowly dissolved. The Egyptians have stuck with their old ways, and the priesthood of Amon remains very powerful."

"I hardly see how that benefits us!"

"With Amasis and the priests of Amon locked in a struggle for power, neither has the time to do a proper job of oppressing us." He chuckled and patted Dathan's shoulder. "Today even slaves like us have the day off to celebrate the feast of—"

"Of the sacred cow!" Dathan snorted.

"Think of it as a day off, and forget where it comes from. There'll be food and drink. Come, get dressed. You may even see my brother make fools out of Amasis and his lackeys."

"There's no talking sense to you!"

Aaron smiled. "Moses can take care of himself. He is a general and has fought in a war. He had the reputation of being the finest man with a sword in the entire command."

Dathan scowled. "He's given up the sword! Everyone knows that! He's declared himself a man of peace! Is this the Deliverer promised us? A man who knows how to fight but won't?"

Aaron looked serious. This had not occurred to him. If Moses was indeed their promised savior, would he not come as a warrior? The Egyptians would never let the Habiru out of Egypt without a fight, and even if they managed to survive the grueling journey across Sinai, they would undoubtedly have to fight their way back into Canaan—they had been gone too long, and the land had been taken over by people of different blood and different customs, who would regard the land as their own. How could the Habiru reestablish themselves if their leader would no longer wield a weapon or strike a blow in anger?

"I see you do understand the problem," Dathan said bitterly. "I was afraid you wouldn't."

Aaron forced himself to face Dathan optimistically. "Enough of this. You're coming with me to the festival."

Dathan struggled slowly to his feet. "You're right," he allowed. "The least we can do for these Egyptian bastards is eat up as much of their food as we can."

Aaron grinned. "You sound like your old self again—bitter and sarcastic."

Dathan brushed himself off with his bandaged hands. "Well, I'm not. I'll never be the same again."

"You must learn to forgive yourself. God chooses the ways for us to learn and grow."

"Don't blame it on God!" Dathan said bitterly. "It wasn't His fault. It was mine!"

Aaron put a comforting hand on Dathan's shoulder as the two went out into the morning sunshine. "Spoken like a man. I think this experience will make a better man of you."

Dathan spat into the dust. "I hope so. It couldn't make me any worse."

The provender for the great feast was being brought in when Aaron and Dathan approached the vast clearing before Avaris. Wagons drawn by great oxen rumbled down the long road, loaded with sacks of bread, jugs of wine and beer, and stacked cakes of various descriptions.

The animals to be slaughtered for the feast were herded by their keepers to the butchering place. Birds were borne by servants of the temple. At any other festival, cows would be slaughtered, but this custom was understandably set aside on a feast day dedicated to the cow goddess. This suited Habiru ways; their preference for mutton over beef was well-known but was never considered.

Aaron could see his kinsmen joining the procession that was wending its way toward the long row of tables on which the food would first be offered to the greater glory of Hathor, then dedicated by Amasis and the high priest of Amon, and finally offered to the gathered thousands to eat, drink, and make merry.

He wondered at what point Moses would appear and announce his bequest to the citizens of the district. He also wondered if Moses would be allowed to court the people in so direct a fashion. He closed his eyes and breathed a silent prayer: *God keep him safe! God protect him! God return him unharmed to his kin!*

II

An hour passed, and still the provender for the great feast came, along high road and beaten path, in ox cart and on the backs of donkeys and onagers. The food came from all parts of the district and from neighboring nomes; the onlookers gathered before the walls of Avaris admired varieties of regional dress not seen in that city since the Shepherds had left many years before. Peasants in ankle-length wraparound skirts of brightly colored cloth that left both breasts fetchingly bare undulated down the road, balancing baskets of fruits and vegetables on their heads. Beside them Bedouin women in heavy robes, faces veiled, led stout-legged, barely tamed onagers bearing heavy loads of dates. There were even soldiers of the Theban elite guard, their only garment consisting of a narrow belt around their waist and an all-purpose blanket, tightly folded and positioned diagonally across their chest; these men, on leave today from their duties guarding the Athribis waterfront, carried stout sticks.

Behind these came the priests of Amon in their stately white robes, tall and dignified, and behind them the entertainers: musicians, dancers, and acrobats, wrestlers, jugglers, and magicians of every description. At the end of the procession came attendants leading racing hounds and carrying fighting cocks.

All these passed between the long lines of spectators on the high road, who were held back by tall guardsmen. Soldiers were everywhere: The people were made constantly aware that the religious observance took place by special dispensation of the secular authority.

Aaron pushed his way through the crowd, looking back often to make certain Dathan was behind him, until he had made his way to the front. Looking down the lines he spotted what he had been looking for: the massed formation of guards, marching four abreast. This meant that the officials in charge—Amasis, Neb-mertef, and their subordinates—were coming.

He bent his head to Dathan's ear. "If Moses is coming, he'll be in that last group."

Dathan squinted. "I can make out Neb-mertef. I can't see Amasis yet. Wait—there he is! The damned foreign—"

"Hush!" Aaron hissed, digging an elbow into his ribs.

"I wish I could see Moses. He doesn't seem to be—" Dathan's face filled with tension. "Oh, Aaron. Oh, no."

Aaron looked where the young man was numbly pointing. The soldiers were dragging a prisoner behind them by jerking roughly on a rope around his neck. He wore only a torn loincloth, and his wrists were bound behind his back. They had spared him the humiliating complete nudity of a slave captured in war; they had spared him nothing else. He had been beaten, and his back was crisscrossed with the red weals of a leather whip tipped with knots. A filthy gag was jammed in his mouth.

"M-Moses," Aaron said in a strangled voice. "They're not going to let him speak. They're going to kill him right before our eyes!" He closed his eyes. In his mouth was the taste of bitter bile. *God of Jacob, where are You now? Could You not have spared us this?*

A stout beam of wood brought all the way from the northern forests projected from the front of the warehouse, above the second story. The pulleys and ropes of a crude hoist dangled from it, for hauling items from the ground to the upper level.

Allat, an agile and strong-fingered climber, tested the rope by pulling hard on it, to see if it would hold his weight. Satisfied, he shinnied to the top, where he transferred his grasp to the beam and hung for a moment before hand-over-handing his way to the opening.

Once inside, he whispered: "Set-Nakht! Are you there?"

There was no answer at first, then he heard a rustle in the darkened corner.

"Allat! Is that you?"

"Shhh!" Allat said. "Come here in the light where I can look at you! And for goodness' sake, please keep quiet about it!"

The next moment he was being given a bear hug by his friend. "Thank heaven you've come!" the magus breathed. "Quickly! Somehow we have to get down. There's a guard still downstairs, but the other two are gone."

"We're going out that opening," Allat told him. "Right down that rope. The guard's on the other side."

"No," Set-Nakht quavered. "I'm terrified of heights."

"That's no problem," Allat said, looking around. "Bring me that basket over there."

"All right. But what are you doing?"

"Watch." He reached down out of the opening and pulled the long rope into the room. He tied the end to the tightly woven basket, using the secure knots of a man born on the banks of the Tigris.

"All you have to do is stand in the basket, close your eyes, and hold tightly to the rope. I'll let you down a hand span at a time."

"Oh, I couldn't!"

"Think of how much fun we're going to have when we've escaped. Can you swim?"

"Yes, but—"

"Good. I was afraid I'd have to carry you across the river. We will get to the island first, and when it's dark we'll cross the other channel and head west. I have relatives in Saïs."

"Saïs! But that's many days' journey!"

"The more the better! I hope we never hear the word *Avaris* again. You've no idea how wonderful it'll be."

"But who would take me in? I can't farm or fish. My hands are the soft hands of a scribe."

"You can tell the future, my silly fellow. You can tell fortunes in the marketplace. There's more money in that than there is in farming since Joseph nationalized the growing of food. We'll dress you up like a Chaldean and you'll make us a little fortune. Just wait and see."

Set-Nakht stared at him through eyes misted over with tears. A master magus telling fortunes like a fake in the public square? And then his face relaxed. "You're right. I can live with that. I can do it easily. Yes, I'll do what you say. But—"

"But what?"

"Never leave me. Please. Otherwise I don't think I could—"

"Silly fellow. Of course I won't! Why do you think I'm here? Now come on. There's no time to lose!"

*   *   *

Workers had raised a dais before the altar, to which Amasis now mounted, his eyes blazing, his face taut. He stood looking around him, flanked by two burly guards, his powerful arms folded across his chest.

After a time he held up his hands for silence. The noise was instantly reduced by half; the guards, bellowing into the crowd menacingly, finally brought the gathering under control. Amasis turned to the men behind him. "Bring him up."

Then he turned to face the huge crowd. His voice boomed out. "Citizens of the Twentieth Nome! In a moment the priests of Amon will open the great Feast of Hathor. Until then the altar is unconsecrated, so now is the time to speak of secular matters. I have uncovered a great conspiracy involving fraud, deceit, sacrilege, and the attempted pollution of the royal bloodlines!" He waited for this to have its effect on the masses, then he went on. "Shall I tell you of this treason? Shall I recount the crimes planned—and in some cases already executed—against the Throne of the Two Lands, against the laws of Egypt, and against you, the people?"

The spectators cried out, "Yes! Tell us! Tell us!"

Amasis stifled a victorious smile. Swiftly he recounted a highly colored biography of Thermutis's child and of how, at Baliniri's urging, the child of a slave had been substituted for the rightful heir to the throne.

"Who was it?" the gathering demanded. "Who was the impostor? Where is he?"

"Here he is!" Amasis cried out.

The guards dragged the prisoner into view. There was a great expression of shock and distress as the crowd recognized him.

"Yes!" Amasis thundered. "You all knew him as Prince Moses, the grandson of King Sekenenre. The great general who won the war in Nubia. The protégé of the traitor Baliniri. Behold now the fraud! The slave who dared to masquerade as a prince of the blood! The slave who murdered a member of the royal guard in cold blood!"

A voice spoke up from the rear, loud and assertive: "Let the prisoner speak for himself! Let him confirm or deny this!"

Aaron wheeled to see guards pushing through the crowd toward Dathan, who suddenly ducked into the masses to disappear. And now others in the gathering demanded that the prisoner be allowed to speak.

"All right!" Amasis said. "Let the prisoner convict himself!" The guards removed the gag. Moses was weaving dizzily, and Aaron could see the red skin around his neck where the rope had rubbed it raw.

"Fellow citizens—" Moses began hoarsely.

"Silence!" Amasis bellowed. "Slaves speak when they are spoken to! Just answer my questions!"

Moses looked at him, and Aaron could see in his eyes a trace of the suffering he had endured. Moses closed his eyes and took a deep breath.

"Are you or are you not a slave? A member of the wretched subject race of the Habiru, from Canaan? The son of slaves and the grandson of slaves? Have you been living a lie, posing as a prince of the blood? Speak up! Are all these things true?"

Moses blinked, looked around, and found Aaron. His back straightened, and he almost managed to smile at Aaron. *No!* Aaron told him silently with his eyes. *Deny it! Save yourself!*

Moses, head held high, looked around the crowd. When at last he spoke, it was as a general addressing his troops, his words loud and clear. "Yes!" he said. "A Habiru, and proud of the fact!"

"You hear?" Amasis screamed at the crowd. He turned back to the prisoner. "And did you or did you not kill an Egyptian guard in Deir el-Bahari?"

"He was oppressing my people!" Moses shouted. "I would kill another such in a moment!"

Aaron's heart sank as the crowd roared!

Amasis' voice boomed out. "And what is the penalty for these crimes?"

And the crowd cried out as with a single voice: "Death!"

III

Moses raised his head and would have spoken. "Citizens of Egypt! Hear me! I—"

But one of the guards jerked so powerfully on the rope still around his neck that he fell to his knees. The other guard raised a pike and slammed Moses in the head with the blunt end; this time he fell heavily on his face, insensible.

Only now, amid the general din, did Aaron hear protests. One—Dathan's again!—called, "Let him alone! Get your filthy hands off him!"

But it was too late. Moses' limp body was dragged to a half-erect position, and one of the guards stooped to get his shoulder under the body of the unconscious man. He hefted Moses and turned to Amasis for instructions.

"To the dungeon!" Amasis snarled.

Aaron, however, noticed the guard's hesitation and edged closer, hoping to read the guard's lips.

"My lord, the workers haven't finished the restoration. The dungeon won't be finished for another week."

Neb-mertef moved to the edge of the dais. "That's right, my lord. But there's an old barracks just outside the city, which survived the burning of Avaris. We could keep him there, under guard."

"Right," Amasis agreed. "He won't be there long. Take him there and post guards around the place. I don't want any of these louts trying to break him out."

Neb-mertef nodded to the guardsman who stood holding the unconscious prisoner. "You heard him. And you men, go with him. Make sure nothing goes wrong."

Amasis watched with satisfaction as the guards moved away; then he turned back to the crowd and raised his hands for silence. Several tall guardsmen from a Shairetana unit had to push their way into the crowd and silence some of the angry spectators.

At last Amasis spoke. "The traitor shall pay for his treason. The lawbreaker shall be punished for his offenses. In the meantime, this day remains sacred to the goddess Hathor, and we are commanded to make merry and be joyful in her honor."

Aaron heard the cynicism in his tone. It was no secret that Amasis still harbored resentment over his failure to establish a new religion on Egyptian soil. Despite this the regent turned to the waiting priests who moved ponderously up onto the dais, welcomed them with elaborate graciousness, and bowed deeply.

"Let the ceremony begin," he intoned piously, unctuously.

Dathan saw Aaron's tall form moving slowly through the masses and took note of his despair and anger. He pushed his way to rendezvous with Aaron.

"Did you hear the son of a whore?" Dathan hissed.

"Don't let anyone hear you," Aaron said. "Come with me. We've got until tomorrow at dawn to save him. We have to think this out."

The hotheaded young man looked incredulous. "Think it out? We can't sit around and muddle over this."

"I want to call a council of the elders. Call them together as quickly as you can. We'll meet beside my tent. I want everyone else to stay at the festival and look as if they're enjoying themselves."

"Do you honestly believe that anyone can have fun while Moses—"

"Of course not. But I want them to steal as much food as possible. Whatever we do tonight, it'll earn us the Egyptians' enmity. They'll try to starve us, and a few of us will be beaten. We may even lose a man or two."

Dathan stopped. "Are we going to fight them this time?"

"Only if we have to," Aaron answered. "I doubt we'll be able to avoid it. But this much I can tell you, Dathan: They're not going to kill him tomorrow morning. Not without killing me first."

Dathan's eyes shone. "And me as well!"

The barracks to which the soldiers took Moses had at one time housed the elite guard of the Avaris court; ordinary soldiers slept in tents. The building had rapidly undergone a drastic loss of status as the unit it had been built to house had been found to include spies. The elite guards were dispersed among other units, and when a young Kamose had come downriver with his army and begun the long siege of Avaris, the building, filthy, its paint peeling, had become a brothel for the enlisted soldiers.

In recent years it had been used without permission by the homeless of Avaris, who climbed through its narrow windows to sleep indoors. They had left their garbage and refuse behind them, so the place had an awful stench when Amasis' guards forced the rusty hinges of the oak door and pushed their way inside.

"Ugh!" said the man carrying the prisoner. "Someone light a torch so I can put this son of a bitch down. Gods! What a stink! I'm glad I wore my parade boots—I wouldn't want to walk around here in my bare feet."

A subordinate came in carrying a hastily improvised torch made of dry reeds. "Let's have a look around. You over there! What's in the next room?"

"Forget the other rooms," the other man advised. "They're worse than this one."

"All right. Seal off the other rooms. We'll keep him in here. And break open that window over there. I want our men to be able to look in on him. Go ahead, kick it open. He's not going to escape—his shoulders are too broad to squeeze through. I'll say one thing, he's in good shape for a man they've just damn near beat to death."

"He was a soldier," his partner put in.

The guard stooped and let Moses sink gently to the floor. "Glad you told me. I've got a soft spot for a fellow trooper, even if he is an impostor and a Habiru. How do you suppose they're going to kill him? The proper execution for a soldier would be to stand him up before a squad of archers."

"No such luck for this fellow," his partner said. "They're going to impale him and leave him for the crows."

"Poor bastard. That's an ugly death. Just between us, our glorious leader strikes me as having a crazy streak a couple of hand spans wide."

"Come on. We'll leave him for the rats. I wonder if the others brought any wine. But no, there wouldn't have been time. Well, we can send somebody after food and drink. No use in our being the only people in the whole delta going hungry and thirsty today."

He gave the unconscious prisoner one last look before backing out the door and closing it behind him.

IV

"I see most of you are here," Aaron said to the gathering. "Some of the tribal elders are too ill to come, but they would not be involved in today's activities anyway. I'm glad to see their younger brothers or their sons here. All the tribes should have a hand in this."

"Aaron," a voice said from the rear. "Why did Moses not deny us? If he had, Amasis would never have been able to find him guilty."

Aaron shook his head. "My brother is a man of principle. He understood fully the consequences of his actions when he chose publicly to throw in his lot with us and forsake his status as a prince. But Moses has abandoned himself to the will and mercy of El-Shaddai."

Privately, however, Aaron asked himself the same question. Now that Moses was in prison and sentenced to death, was he having second thoughts? Not that it mattered. Amasis wanted Moses' death, and no recantation would stop him from carrying out the sentence.

He wished he could speak to Moses now. He frowned and pushed on, desperate to ignore his own apprehension. "The deed is done. Unless we act swiftly and decisively, Moses will pay a terrible price for identifying himself as a Habiru."

Another voice called out. "But what can unarmed slaves do against the might of the Egyptian army? Do you know how many soldiers are here today?"

"As it happens, I do," Aaron replied. "But remember, it is a festival day. The new barley beer has been brought in from the breweries, and it is more potent now than at any other time of the year. Furthermore, Amasis has made generous gifts of provender and wine to the priests of Amon —especially wine: good, strong vintages. The soldiers are being allowed to participate in the festival in shifts, so we can halve the number of men normally on duty at any given time. The rest will be getting drunk and won't be available in any emergency . . . until long after we've finished our work. They'll be passed out behind a tent or lying with the foreign whores Amasis brought in for the festival."

"But Aaron!" said Imnah, of the tribe of Asher. "That's still half a garrison to contend with. How are we to deal with so many men?"

"Think," Aaron exhorted. "The only soldiers we really have to deal with are the men guarding Moses. As for the rest, we must only direct their attention elsewhere so we might complete our mission without interference."

Ezbon, of the tribe of Gad, was the next to speak. "How will we remove the soldiers without calling attention to ourselves?"

"I'll get to that in a moment," Aaron answered. "We will be freeing Moses and putting him on the road to freedom. The women are preparing food for him and skins full of water, enough to allow him to make his way into the desert."

"The desert?" Ezbon sputtered. "He'll never survive. Get him to the Great Sea."

"All direct routes to the sea are closely guarded. When his escape is discovered, the authorities will be expecting him to try to get to the sea. What they—and you—don't know is that Moses is superbly qualified to find his way across the desert in safety. He was trained in desert skills and crafts by the best teachers in the world, the women of the western oasis, Weret and Naldamak."

This prompted a murmur of appreciation. Both warrior-women were much respected among the Habiru, especially because food had been smuggled to the Habiru at Deir el-Bahari by women of the western patrols, at Weret's orders.

"Amasis doesn't know this," Aaron continued, "so the last place the soldiers will search for Moses will be along the overland route to the Red Sea."

Zohar, of the tribe of Simeon, spoke up. "I see the logic! You are directing Moses to Midian!" His guess was confirmed when Aaron nodded. "An excellent choice. There are people of our blood there who will hide him from the Egyptian patrols and from the slavers who look for men to send to the mines at Timna."

"Exactly," Aaron verified. "If Moses can reach Midian, he will be safe until it is time to return."

"Why should he want to return?"

Aaron looked into the faces before him. When he had their undivided attention, he went on. "You all must remember the prophecy Levi gave us, of a Deliverer who would lead us out of bondage in Egypt and back to our homeland."

"But, Aaron," Imnah said, "what has this to do—"

Aaron held up one hand. "God spoke to me last night."

There was a great sigh from the crowd.

"And He said that the promised Deliverer was finally among us."

For a moment there was no sound. Then someone spoke up from the rear. "How can that be? Would God allow the Deliverer to become a captive of the Egyptians?"

"I cannot know the will of God," Aaron replied solemnly. "We can only accept His will, if we are wise. If Moses escapes from Egypt with our help and finds his way to safety, then obviously it is God's will that this take place. I am convinced that by God's will was Moses trained by Weret and Naldamak in the desert skills, so he might lead us, his kinsmen, across Sinai to Canaan. And when our time comes, we will benefit from this."

He raised himself to his full height and let his piercing gaze move from face to face. "Kinsmen, think about it: If God wills him away from us now, may it not be that there are yet things He wants our Deliverer to learn before he leads us back to Canaan? Things that must be learned in the solitude of the desert, to assure our arriving safely in our homeland instead of dying horribly of thirst and starvation?"

Aaron saw the understanding dawning in the eyes of one man after another. "We must help our kinsman pass safely from this terrible land, to learn the things God wishes him to learn, so he may come back to carry us to freedom."

There was a fervent expression of assent from all sides.

"You mentioned some kind of diversion," said Ezbon. "Shall we have some of our young men get into a fight with the villagers? That would certainly bring the soldiers a-running."

"Yes," Aaron said. "What sort of problem might draw the attention—and perhaps the en masse participation—of all the thousands of people, soldiers and civilians, gathered here outside the walls of Avaris?"

"I don't know," Ezbon confessed.

"I do!" shouted Dathan, pushing through the elders to the front line. "The most important thing to Amasis just now.

The most visible thing we could destroy. Something that would throw panic into Amasis' black heart when he saw it going up in flames right before his eyes."

There was a pause, then someone from the rear called out. "Avaris! Avaris itself!"

V

The numbness in Moses' hands persisted long after he had managed to untie the knots binding his wrists. He rubbed them together now, to stimulate sensation. The late afternoon sun slanted in sharply through the single window, and he stood in a pool of light.

Where am I? Where have they taken me? But looking out the window, he recognized nothing.

In the distance he could hear the drone of men's voices but nothing of what they were saying. "Guard!" His voice was raw and husky from his having been dragged about with a rope around his neck. No one responded, and he assumed no one had heard.

Well, now, you've finally done it, haven't you?

He knew what they were going to do to him. Before they had knocked him senseless, he had heard the crowd calling for his execution, just as Amasis had instructed them, sealing his fate. The question was how, and when.

"Guard!" he shouted, then cursed the soreness in his throat.

It was curious, he thought. He should be angry with himself. A simple lie would have kept his status in doubt. Instead he had blurted out the one thing that would doom him to death.

Then why did he feel that he had done the right thing and the only possible thing? He shivered suddenly, avoiding the thought. Then he closed his eyes, sighed, and allowed the thought to come: He had been in the grip of God.

On the surface it sounded like a foolish notion. Would God make him do the thing for which others would kill him?

Now the realization came to him: Before the unknown hour of his execution, God would deliver him from death.

He leaned forward against the wall, thinking.

There was a pattern to his life that he had yet to discover. His task was to find it and be true to it. His steps had been guided toward Seth, toward Weret and Naldamak, toward the seers Neku-re and Tchabu, and eventually toward the reunion with his people.

He pressed his forehead against the cool stone. *I must not forget this moment of insight!* He sighed, straightened his back, and gazed out the window at the setting sun.

He could hear the distant strains of music, of merriment, of a great multitude enjoying the Feast of Hathor. From this and the sun's position he surmised that he was west of the city, but not far west.

The sun was a flattened ball, and the sky mad with color. With dramatic suddenness, the sun disappeared from view, and there was a long, lingering moment of afterglow. And then darkness came on with startling swiftness.

In the morning, if Amasis had his way, he, Moses, would die. Would Amasis have his way, or would God intervene?

There was a rustle in the grass outside.

"Who's there?" Moses whispered hoarsely.

He saw a face just outside the window.

"Hush!" a voice said softly. "It's a friend."

"Who?"

"Dathan. We're going to get you out tonight. Don't be frightened when the time comes."

"I understand. But how—?"

"Don't worry about it. By dawn you'll be out of town. Are you all right? Have they hurt you?"

"I'm fine. It would take more than what they did to me to put me out of action."

"Good. Good. Uh, Moses?"

"Yes, Dathan?"

"I . . . I know I can't ask you to forgive what I did, but—"

"Think no more about it."

"I—"

"Now go, before the guards hear us. I'll see you again before I leave, won't I?"

"No. I'm part of the diversion."

"Yes, I can see where that would be necessary. Aaron thought all this up. Right?"

"Yes."

Moses' hand squeezed through the window bars and touched Dathan's briefly. "Good-bye," Dathan said.

"Go with God," Moses replied. But he knew as he said it that the young man had already slipped away into the darkness.

The dais area had been tripled to accommodate the regent's party, and Amasis, guarded by burly soldiers, sat with his closest advisers, enjoying the feast. It was important, he had decided, that as regent, soon to be declared king, he should publicly observe all the festival customs he would soon reign over.

His mood was more elated than usual because one of his most feared enemies had been delivered into his hands and was in custody at this very moment—to die with the dawn. Under the circumstances, he had decided to relax and had consumed more wine than was his wont.

Now, feeling almost mellow, he watched as two huge wrestlers—one white, one black—battled, sweating and naked and dusty, before the leaping fire. His eyes lingered on the taut bodies with their bulging muscles, and he waved a fist, egging them on. "Now!" he shouted. "You've got him! Don't lose the advantage!"

Neb-mertef sat beside Amasis, looking at his master with increasingly jaundiced eyes. The strain of being Amasis' host was beginning to show. Amasis was a demanding guest, and the household routine had been badly disrupted by the introduction not just of the regent, but of his entire retinue. They had taken over his house, and there was no place for him—the owner of the house. He was, he admitted to himself, beginning to hate Amasis.

He sat up and stared as Amasis encouraged the wrestlers. But of course! How could he have missed it? There was no mistaking the gleam in those ugly little eyes. They roamed over the athletes' sweaty bodies. Lust! Lust for male bodies!

Neb-mertef's mind went to the magus Set-Nakht. He had not visited the seer since his hurried relocation from the town house. There had been no opportunity; Amasis had demanded his presence everywhere, at all times.

Yet he desperately wanted to see the magus again. There were things he had to know, horoscopes he wanted drawn, future events he wanted described. More than that, he had an investment in the magus, and he was beginning to worry about that investment. Perhaps it was time to slip away, go back to the city, and look in on Set-Nakht.

He stood. "My lord," he said, looking at Amasis and wanting to vomit at what he saw. "I am feeling indisposed. With your permission I would like to retire." Amasis ignored him, his eyes on the forms of the grunting wrestlers. "My lord!" he reported, raising his voice.

"What?" said Amasis, not looking up. "Yes. Go. I'll see you at the house."

Neb-mertef backed away, watching first the regent, then the wrestlers. He had never been so disgusted. How could he have missed it? Come to think of it, Amasis had taken one of his hulking, private guards into the bedroom with him in recent days. Everyone had thought him fearful of assassins and spies; no one had even speculated about other motives.

He turned, spat contemptuously on the ground beside the dais, and signaled to his own guards. "Come," he said. "We're going back to the city."

VI

The drums beat madly: large drums, small drums, earthen drums, and side drums. The clash of great gongs and the jingle of finger cymbals punctuated the dull drumbeat with a brazen counterpoint. The shrill howl of the shawms wailed above these, drowning out the flutes. Voices were raised in song, and everywhere there was dancing by the capering light of the great fires dotting the plain.

By midevening the goddess Hathor, in whom the sun rose and set, was honored as also being the goddess of happiness and dance. As the wine flowed ever more copiously and the inhibitions of the worshipers were shed, the dance became unashamedly sexual. Several girls danced seductively before the fires, wearing nothing but a thin film of sweat. Young men, also naked, came from the crowd to dance beside them with no thought of the onlookers. The whirling, heaving bodies touched now and then, then retreated provocatively. One by one, the couples, hand in hand, slipped into the night, to be replaced by other dancers. The music played louder, the drums beat faster, and the songs grew bawdier. The Egyptian goddess Hathor was quite forgotten. The spirit in the great gathering was more like that of the pagan goddess Amasis had sought to introduce to Egypt—the carnal and lusty goddess whose favors were granted only to a man marked for death as a human sacrifice.

Amid all this, Aaron's men had begun to move off into the darkness. Now they gathered just south of the barracks where Moses was being held, and waited, screened from the firelit feast by a hedge of ornamental trees.

After an interval there was the agreed-upon signal, and the scout returned, moving silently into their midst. "The guard is at half strength, Aaron, as you expected," he reported. "They've had a bit to drink. Has the horse been brought up?"

"It's hobbled by the trees just to the northeast of the barracks, where the desert road begins. The women have packed his provisions, and we've stolen a sword for him, in case he—"

Ezbon spoke up. "Forget the sword. He's vowed not to use one. But he's made no vow against the quarterstaff. For a true son of Jacob, that's a better weapon anyway. Would he know how to use it?"

"He knows all the weapons—although I might still have something to teach him about the sling. He'll need every defense to make his way across the desert, then up the Arabah to Midian. The Ishmaelites are still in the area, and they don't like strangers."

As Neb-mertef and his men entered the city, a feeling of foreboding came over him. He looked around. By the light of his guards' torches the city seemed deserted, and only the faraway sounds of the feast were audible.

"Guard," he said, "do you see or hear anything unusual?"

The nearest guard responded. "No, my lord. Everything seems in order."

"I don't feel right. There's something odd here." He sniffed the wind. What was it in the air?

"If I were you, sir, I'd follow my instincts. Everyone knows about your prophetic gifts."

Neb-mertef scowled. "Come this way," he said. "We're going to one of my warehouses. I want to check on something."

But as he spoke, he experienced the same strange feeling. His skin crawled, reacting to it. And what was that smell in the air? No, he was imagining things, surely.

Dathan's first stop had been in the commercial quarter. He and his men broke into a warehouse where lamp oil was stored in amphorae. "We're going to fan out," he told the others. "Each of you take a jar." He indicated the man closest to him. "You: Douse the first three warehouses you come to. Make certain they're in a row, without breaks. I want the whole block to go up in flames. There's a westerly breeze, so set the fire on the east end of the street. When you've used up your oil, start the fire."

"Right." The man took down an amphora and ran down the street.

Dathan turned to the next man. "You do the same at that big civic building being renovated at the end of this street. I particularly want that one burned. I worked on it, and what I put up against my will, I definitely want to see taken down. When his city is burned and his prisoner is set free, Amasis will know it was the sons of Israel. We might as well give him something big to retaliate for. He's going to hurt us anyway."

"What are *you* going to set on fire?" one of his youngest helpers wanted to know.

Dathan's foxlike smile was visible in the moonlight. "I'm going to burn down the house Amasis is staying in. I'm going to torch Neb-mertef's town house."

"He's gone!" Neb-mertef shrieked at the astonished guard. "There's not a sign of him anywhere! How could you let this happen?"

"My lord, I—"

"Hold that torch down here! Look! Look, in the dust! A second set of footprints. He had help. But from whom?"

"I'm sure I don't know, my lord. I know I deserve your anger, sir, but I'll make it up to you. I'll find him myself. I'll bring him back."

"Bring him back? You'll never find him."

There was a sudden call from down the alley. "My lord! Look!"

Neb-mertef's eyes went to the end of the street. He gasped. The warehouse on the end of the row had burst into flames, and the fire was spreading rapidly.

"Fire!" he cried. "The city's on fire!"

Traversing the last stretch of the river, Set-Nakht was horribly aware of creatures in the water with him. Already beset with misgivings and fright, he conjured up images of crocodiles, their hard, horny bodies almost brushing against his skin. Panic-stricken, he flailed helplessly and almost went under; but at the last moment he touched the far bank, and strong hands grabbed him and pulled him to shore.

"There!" Allat said cheerfully. "Safe and sound! And none the worse for wear, I'll wager. Don't get up just yet. Rest a moment and get your breath back."

"I . . . I thought the crocodiles . . ."

"Oh, don't bother about them. They seldom feed at night. You have to stir them up a lot worse than the two of us did. You're on your way to freedom!"

But then he looked up, as did Set-Nakht, and both of them saw it.

For a long moment neither spoke. Then Allat whispered in an awestruck voice: "Well, by the gods!"

Avaris was on fire! The flames, leaping high above the city walls, were visible all the way from here! And now they could hear the sound of the crowd.

VII

At the end of the street Neb-mertef's heart sank. *No*, he thought. *Not my house. They wouldn't dare.*

"My lord!" said the towering guard beside him. "Isn't that—?"

"I think it is," Neb-mertef seethed. "And if it is, someone's going to pay." He set out at a brisk walk, suppressing the impulse to break into an undignified run.

It had been too late to save the warehouses. He had sent one of the guards to Amasis with the news—as if anyone could remain unaware of what was going on, with the flames leaping higher than the walls—and taken another guard with him. Above the rooftops of the city, he could see the red glow of new fires scattered throughout the quarters. The foreboding he had felt upon entering the city now drew him to his own mansion.

Yes! There it was! Someone had taken pains to make sure that all the wings had been set on fire. Approaching the front door—it was open, and flames were leaping out toward the street—he could see pieces of a broken amphora. He stooped and picked one up to smell it. Lamp oil! The same lamp oil he had spent so much money importing from Crete, which made the purest oil in the world!

He was going to lose hundreds of thousands of *outnou*— more, if he bothered to build a comparable mansion here. Figures swam before his eyes; he felt sick. If the whole of Avaris was to be rebuilt, Amasis would have to double the tax on the rich. The regent would have to double the tax on the temples, which would cost him dearly in terms of support. All this would hurt him, Neb-mertef, terribly.

Then why did he suddenly find the whole thing so funny? Why did he want to laugh and laugh? He was ruined: the loss of a house, possessions, a warehouse of lamp oil, and worst of all, Set-Nakht.

The astrologer's escape was the problem. The talents that had brought him this far into Amasis' confidence had belonged to another, and he had been claiming them as his own. Now the bird had flown, and he was about to be exposed as the fake he was.

He threw his head back and laughed as if it were the funniest thing he had ever heard. He was still laughing when the first emergency crews came running down the street toward the burning house.

The guards assigned to the abandoned barracks posed no great problem; as Aaron and his men approached, they were standing together, looking with astonishment at the huge flames leaping high over the walls of Avaris. They did not even hear the Habiru approaching, and Aaron, coming up swiftly behind his man, clamped a forearm of iron around his quarry's throat and rendered him unconscious without making a sound.

The other two were not so easily removed. One guard managed to draw his sword and wound one of the rescuers before Aaron's sling, as accurate as ever, felled him with a rock the size of a child's fist. In a few moments the improvised prison was undefended. Aaron called for the horse and provisions, then went to the door and slid the bolt. "Moses? Are you here?"

There was a pause, then Moses called out. "Aaron! What's happening?"

"Quickly, now. There's no time to explain. Put on this dark robe; it'll make you harder to see."

"Aaron," Moses said, "they'll see your hand in this. I can't just go off, knowing that you'll be here paying for my escape, perhaps with your life."

"Don't worry. We're virtually the only labor force Amasis has to rebuild the city—and now it'll *really* need rebuilding. And he also knows that he can't control my people without me. Just go. The best thing you can do for us is make the thing we've done tonight a success."

Moses clasped Aaron's arm warmly, then the brothers went outside.

"I've given your route a lot of thought. There is only one road they won't be patrolling: the route into the desert. We'll steer you in that direction and get you started. Meanwhile, we'll send another man off in another direction to mislead them."

Someone put the reins of a dark horse into Moses' hand as Aaron continued. "When you get to the end of the road, where it joins the overland caravan trails, the route you'll take will be due south, toward the Red Sea. When you reach the sea, you'll be able to find passage with a fisherman. In these sacks there's a bit of money stolen this afternoon at the festival. It should get you where you're going."

"Thank you." They had reached the high road, and the others were loading skins full of water and sacks of provender onto the animal's back.

"Find someone who's willing to take you up into the Gulf of Akaba, to Ezion-geber. But don't stop; you're going north of there."

Moses chuckled. "To Sodom? Gomorrah? A splendid idea."

"Don't jest with me. And don't feel too confident. There are Egyptian patrols all the way up and down the rift. Our kinsmen the Midianites are there. Look for a man named Jethro—or perhaps Reuel. He sometimes uses that name. He has the reputation of being a sly old fox. If anyone can hide you, he can. He controls an oasis up one of the side valleys, off the beaten track, where the Egyptians seldom go."

Moses smiled at his brother and embraced him. "How have I got along without you all these years? I can't wait until I see you again. Give my love to Mother, Father, Miriam, and the others."

"I shall. Now go!"

"How will I know when it is safe to return?"

"It will never be safe to return. But if God wants you to return, then He will tell you when the time comes. I leave you in His hands."

Moses climbed onto the horse, waved once, and kicked the mount into a gallop down the road and into the darkness.

The fire was out of control in all quarters. The breeze had whipped into a steady wind, and the entire city would probably be lost.

Neb-mertef had remained before the ruin that had been his town house. Now the laughter was no more. He looked broken, defeated, and dejected. His mind was wandering when Amasis joined him. He had come in a chariot, with his personal driver, and had already visited other sections of the city.

He stared balefully at Neb-mertef. "Well?"

It took Neb-mertef a moment to realize he was being spoken to. Then he turned his head and looked at the regent with dull, expressionless eyes.

"Well?" repeated Amasis, his voice dripping with malice. "What have you got to say for yourself? Do you realize that all the court records we brought down from Thebes were in your house? All the plans for the rebuilding of Avaris will have to be redrawn. The contracts. The financial arrangements. The tax records. Everything."

"I suppose they will." The toneless voice did not sound like his.

"You don't sound very sympathetic. People will have to work long hours to replace these scrolls. You yourself have a lot of work to duplicate."

"I don't understand. What have I to do with all this?"

"You idiot! You've lost all your own papyruses! Your calculations! The predictions! The horoscopes! All in that inimitable style of yours! You realize, of course, that I expect them all recast and redrawn? And quickly, too. I'll expect them waiting for me when I get back from Athribis in seven days."

Neb-mertef closed his eyes.

"How is it," Amasis went on in the same bullying tone, "that you never predicted this? Are you losing your touch? You haven't been attending to your duties, that much seems clear. I've heard reports about you, about your raiding the male brothels and—"

Neb-mertef sighed. He shook his head, and shoulders drooping, he walked slowly away, not hearing the furious tirade. Behind him, ahead of him, to all sides, the great flames leaped heavenward, as Avaris, once dead and half-resurrected, died once more.

VIII

After a while of watching the city burn, Amasis could stand no more. He jumped back into the chariot and ordered his driver to take him to the festival grounds. But the streets were full of people, hastily organized by the guardsmen into bumbling and inept fire-fighting squads. Containers of water passed from hand to hand, connecting the few city wells with the fires; in the act half the water was spilled.

Finally the regent snatched the whip from his driver. "Get out of the way, you fools!" he bellowed, using the lash on the people blocking his way. Then, as a hole opened, he used it on the horse. "Go!" he shouted. "Go, curse you."

The driver, alarmed, hopped out of the way as Amasis took the reins, bulling his way through the multitudes. The driver even considered jumping down into the crowd to escape Amasis' mood. But in the chaos outside the walls, he reflected, the regent might need protection. Thus he hastily fingered the sword at his belt and decided to stay with his master.

Once through the gate they went at a breakneck rate. Only when they approached a squad of guardsmen did Amasis slow to a stop. "You! Captain!"

The officer stepped forward and saluted smartly. "Yes, my lord?"

"Have you found out who is responsible for this?"

"Yes, my lord. The Habiru slaves seem to have used it to mask an attempt to free the impostor."

"Eh? An attempt? So it was not successful?"

"I regret to say it was successful, my lord. There were tracks of two horses, hoofprints going in two directions—one toward the desert, one toward Sile. We think the right one, the one bearing the prisoner, has headed toward Sile. We think they wanted to trick us into sending a squad into the desert, where the soldiers would be imperiled by the elements. Surely one man on horseback could never survive."

"Sile! Quick, take a message to—"

"My lord, I have already sent messengers in that direction, both by horse and by the sea."

"Very good. And the perpetrators? Do you have them in custody?"

"Just their leader, my lord, the one called Aaron ben Amram. He readily admitted his guilt."

"Where is he? I want to see him."

The captain motioned to two subordinates, who left on the run and returned with the Habiru leader within minutes.

"Here he comes now, sir." The guardsman pointed to a tall young man in the robes of a slave.

Amasis started to climb down, but after realizing that the slave would then tower over him, he remained on the high platform of his chariot and stared balefully down at the prisoner. "Well?" he said acidly. "What have you to say for yourself?"

The prisoner looked up at him calmly and spoke in a well-modulated voice. "You knew I wouldn't let you kill him. He's beyond your grasp, and you'll never catch him now. But he'll be back to haunt you. Mark my words."

Amasis sneered. "He'll be back before a day has passed. All the routes to Sile are carefully guarded. If we don't catch up with him from the rear, the guards along the way will hold him for us." He spat the next words out. "And this time the execution will be in public, and no one will be allowed to miss it."

Aaron shrugged.

"Least of all you. You'll be on the stand next to him! You'll have the pleasure of watching him die slowly, painfully, then you'll be next!"

But he could see that his words were not having the desired effect. Aaron calmly waited out the tirade, his eyes expressing amused detachment. "You try my patience unduly," Amasis seethed. "I may not wait until then to have you cut to pieces in front of your assembled kin!"

"You won't kill any Habiru," Aaron said calmly. "And you'll give up your attempts to find Moses' old wet nurse. You need to rebuild the city. Soon you'll also need us as farming crews; if you can't bring in the harvest before the food rots, Egyptians will starve."

Amasis looked on, slack-jawed, mute.

"You can't use the army for the harvest because they'll be needed to deal with Kamose. You do know, of course, that he has formally assumed command of the army my brother brought back from Nubia? He vows to have your head on a pike before the year is out. Do you really think your ragtag mercenary army can handle a superb fighting unit trained by a man like General Khafre?"

Amasis' lips moved, but he said nothing.

Aaron paused, and the pity in his voice was more insulting than any overt scorn could be. "Now Kamose is coming downriver to kill you, and you'll need every man who can bear arms to flesh out your inadequate army. That leaves the Habiru. Some of us can help out with the harvest, which would free able-bodied Egyptians for the army. The rest can rebuild the city. But nobody can control my people the way I can. That's why you won't kill me—at least not until the city is rebuilt, Kamose is repelled, and the harvest is gathered."

Amasis' eyes blazed. "None of that will save your brother."

"My brother is already saved. He's flown by your nets." He smiled victoriously. "You'll never find him, but he'll find you. And when that happens . . ."

He let the sentence hang in the smoky evening air.

The moon's cool light shone on the pile of rubble up ahead. Moses reined the horse to a stop. This, then, was where the road ended. From here he must make his way southward across uncharted desert, all the way to the Red Sea. He hesitated as, for the hundredth time, doubts gathered in his mind.

He had thought he would be sent to the delta to free his kinsmen. Instead, they had freed him, and now he was slinking away into the desert to hide. This was the will of God? He closed his eyes. *I need to know. I am new to this. I have no background of faith. If You could speak to me . . .*

There was no answer. He opened his eyes and looked up at the countless stars, recognizing the familiar patterns the women at the oasis had taught him. *You, Who control the paths of the stars, give me a sign. Let me know that this is the destiny that You have picked out for me, and I will follow it blindly.*

But there was no answer. He would have to follow blindly without any reassurance. Perhaps, he thought, that was the nature of faith.

He turned the animal's head sharply to his right and set out along the unmarked trail.

CHAPTER EIGHT

El-Kharga Oasis

Weret stood flanked by two of her superbly trained young warrior-women. Her brown, bare body was spare and powerful looking and, despite her years, hardly suffered by comparison to theirs. "You're sure this is what you want to do? You'll always have a home here with us."

Seth's smile did not hide the suffering on his drawn face. "I feel reassured in hearing that, my dear. I can't imagine a truer friend. Nevertheless, I find myself wanting to be with my son and daughter-in-law, especially since they are soon expecting their first child." He tightened the bellyband around the pack animal, then looked with affection at Mai, who stood with her slender arms loaded down with provender ready to be loaded on the onager. "I've never had a grandchild. I think it will be good for my state of mind to be there when Princess Tharbis presents Het with a son and heir."

"Or a daughter," Weret pointed out.

"Men like to spoil their granddaughters even more than their grandsons," Seth said. "I thank you from the bottom of my heart, but I think we will be going. And thanks also for the honor guard you're sending with us."

"It is no more than you deserve," Weret replied. Then, as if uncomfortable with this display of sentiment, she said,

"Tchabu and Neku-re send their best from El-Dakhla. They wish you would let them work on you longer."

Seth waved away the request. "I know what is wrong with me. The problem is my learning to live with it. I think I will do that more gracefully among my kin."

"By the way," Weret said, "word came from the delta that Prince Moses is safe." She recounted the report she had received.

"So where is Moses now?" Seth asked.

"The desert—into the Sinai. He'll be safe there for as long as he needs to hide."

"Thanks to you," Seth commended. "Well, I won't keep you. I have this other animal to load. If you see Neftis, could you send her here?"

"Yes. I know where she is," Weret responded. "Seth, she really ought to stay with us. I could find a place for her among my women. Neftis has been harmed by a man, and women can best heal the hurt."

"If you can talk her into it, you'd have my blessing. But she seemed to want to put as much distance between her and Apedemek as possible. And that means Nubia."

"With your leave I will talk to her," Weret said.

Seth bowed his permission and an elegant farewell. As Weret and her young warriors strode away, Seth's gaze lingered on the slim bodies of the two girls, and a smile flickered on his lips.

Mai did not miss this. "You've still an eye for the young ones, have you?"

Seth put an arm around Mai's soft waist. "My eyes are for all women," he intoned. "The rest of me is yours, my dear. They only pique my interest and feed my fantasies. Then I bring the fantasies to you, so we can work them out together."

She snuggled against him. "I like that. I can accommodate all the fantasies you wish to bring me." She rested her warm face against his chest. "Tell me: Would it please you if I went around as they do?"

He hugged her close. "Only in the privacy of our own home. A large house has been prepared for us by Het and Tharbis, and we can dismiss the servants at night, and I'll chase you around the place."

"Or I'll chase you!" she teased. "Oh, Seth, I'm so happy! I keep telling myself that all this horror and suffering can't have been all bad if it brought us together!"

Seth hugged her closer, and when she put her much-beloved face up for his kiss, he sought her lips as hungrily as if the two of them had been in the first bloom of youth.

Weret found Neftis tying on her robe. "That's good," she approved. "With your fair skin you'll have to get used to the sun a little at a time."

"What does it matter," Neftis asked bitterly, "if I cover up or go naked? If I stay here or go away? If I live or die?"

Weret's eyes narrowed. "If you feel that way, you should stay here. My women can look after you. We understand the hurt men can bring."

"Here? No, thank you! I'm going upriver, where nobody has heard of me."

Weret was taken aback by Neftis's vehemence. "Of course. I just thought that—"

But now Neftis turned on her, a savage expression on her taut face, a touch of madness in her eyes. "I thought I'd reached rock bottom. I thought I'd reached the lowest level of degradation."

"I don't understand," Weret said. "If you have a problem, tell me about it. Perhaps I can help."

"I doubt that," she said bitterly. "Now if you'll excuse me—"

But Weret could not restrain the impulse to reach out and hold her back. "Please," she said earnestly. "Tell me. What's the matter? What could possibly be wrong that a friend could not help with it? If I—"

Neftis shook herself loose. Her face was contorted with pain and self-loathing. "Apedemek. I'm carrying his child."

CHAPTER
NINE

Thebes

The tall, stately, high-sterned ships, swift and deadly, were lined up at the quays, ready to be manned by thirty-two oarsmen each, sixteen on a side. Their great masts and broad yards were shipped and braced amidships and forward in huge Y-shaped cleats that stood higher than a tall man's head, and the bulk of their great weight rested atop the deckhouse, aft.

One by one, the grim-faced men of the Nubian expedition filed aboard as their officers supervised.

Standing a bit apart and watching officers and men alike, King Kamose, commander of the army after Khafre's death, stood, burly arms crossed over his chest. He frowned as General Geb, who had been made Kamose's personal assistant, joined him at dockside.

"Everything's ready, sir, and as soon as everyone's aboard, we can sail. But I thought you'd be interested in hearing a message one of our spies just brought upriver."

Kamose motioned to Geb to get on with it.

"Iri has landed and sends his greetings. He reports that Moses, under sentence of death, has escaped into the desert. It appears Moses revealed that he was actually a slave's get and not the child of Princess Thermutis."

"Eh? Well, that's interesting! A slave's child, eh?"

"Yes. Thermutis bore a deformed infant who died shortly after birth. Baliniri was grooming a replacement for you, my lord."

"Hah! And he was always so polite to my face. You can't trust anyone, can you? Well, that removes one obstacle from my return to power."

"Iri says that most of Avaris burned to the ground and that Amasis' position has never been weaker. He thinks Amasis knows it, too. There's a good chance we won't even have to fight, that we'll be able just to move in and take over. Amasis will try to negotiate a settlement."

Kamose's eyes narrowed. "We'll see about that. He thinks I'm going to share power with him, after what he did to me?" He laughed mirthlessly.

"So what are you going to do, my lord? Kill him?"

"Oh, no," Kamose said. "There's still sport to be had from him. No, I'll make him a lapdog—a servant, without power. A jester, if you will."

But now, as the two of them watched, the tall, solitary figure of Apedemek came striding majestically toward the ships. Kamose shook his head. "Look at him! He waves his arms, and the sunlight seems to go away. He's a great sorcerer, he is."

On the quay the tall scarecrow's arms went heavenward, as if to grasp the very sky itself in those long fingers. There was a savage grin of triumph on his face. The hands became fists, and he shook them defiantly at the skies. It was a threat—but what kind, and to whom, no one could say. Men made the sign against evil, as if a demon among demons was loose—a monster at whose scalding touch the harvest would fail, the good earth would go barren, life would sicken and die, and the very stars themselves would wink out one by one. A new age had dawned. And it was to be feared by one and all.

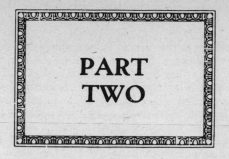

PART TWO

Ten Years Later

CHAPTER TEN

In the Greek Isles

I

The runner came for Yahadu of Mari shortly before noon, as he was supervising the olive harvest. Slender, sun-bronzed, as innocent of clothing as the hard-muscled young men in the upper branches of the trees, the runner pulled up beside Yahadu, little fatigued after his hard run through the valley. "Sir, Demetrios sends his compliments and asks if you would join him in the city."

"Tell him I'll come, of course. If you'll wait until I've changed into a clean mantle, you can go back with me in my chariot. No use making you run all that way again."

"Thank you, sir," the runner said. He looked around. Half the harvest force seemed to be up in the trees, knocking the ripe olives down with long poles; the other half was on the ground, collecting the olives in reed baskets. Nearby, two young men in the cap and loincloth of the grower caste operated an olive press; sweating and straining, they added their own heft to that of a large bag full of stones, which weighed down the business end of a huge lever that pushed the press downward and

219

forced the oil out of the mash, where it collected in large pots.

Yahadu sighed happily. He was glad the harvest would be a good one, since it would be the last he would see on the island. "I shall miss this place," he told the runner.

"Demetrios will find us a better one," the runner said. "Likely he's already picked it out and purchased it."

Yahadu's eyes went to the southern horizon, where the ever-present plume of smoke could be seen above the hills. The smoke masked a mountain of fire, one that had recently begun to belch clouds of smoke and ash and to rumble underfoot.

The island, oddly enough, had no popularly accepted name, although passing fisherman called it The Smoker or The Shaker. But none showed enough interest in the islet with its half-dozen volcanic cones, to sail in and investigate. This was all well and good, for no visitors were wanted, and none who entered without the permission of the lord of this isle off the Achaean mainland would ever sail back out again.

To the inhabitants it was simply Home. This was the name also used by the men of the ships of Demetrios's huge fleet of merchant vessels—those few, at least, who were allowed to approach Home and dock there. Not all of Demetrios's fleet were given this honor: Most of his captains did not even know Home's location and communicated with his representatives only in prominent seaports around the Great Sea. To these, folklore had Demetrios living on board his flagship, with no more permanent domicile than the deckhouse of a merchant vessel.

In reality, as Yahadu had witnessed over the ten years he had been in Demetrios's employ, the man was a landlubber. His business kept him at sea much of the year, but he had always spent some months in his sprawling villa nestled warmly in the friendly hills of Home, resting from his labors as absolute ruler of the mightiest merchant fleet the world had ever known.

This custom was about to end, however, because Home itself was about to be destroyed. The fire cones around the island now produced dark smoke plumes year round, and the earth shook at irregular intervals. Furthermore, for a decade

Demetrios's astrologers had been in agreement: A great cataclysm was to occur.

Demetrios had been planning to leave Home for a year now, and his scouts had combed all lands bordering the Great Sea, seeking out a new site for a new secret hideaway.

Yahadu looked around. He had come to love this place, and his place in it. Through the good offices of his sponsor, Hieron—may the gods protect his soul!—he, Yahadu, a nobody, had been given as high a rank in Demetrios's organization as any man could get who was not born a Child of the Lion.

Since Hieron's mysterious disappearance a decade before, Demetrios had placed more and more confidence in Yahadu. Currently an overseer of domestic affairs, he had recently been led to believe that his status was about to be upgraded again, but to what level he could not say.

Demetrios had just returned from a tour of the major Greek and Cretan ports, renewing important trade contacts and communicating with his most reliable colleagues. Always heavily guarded and with his itinerary carefully prepared by his subordinates, Demetrios visited the great ports like Knossos-Amnisios, Piraeus, Tiryns, and mighty Ilios. What information would he have about the relocation? What news would he have for Yahadu of Mari, his faithful servant and protégé?

Suddenly full of urgency, he turned to the runner. "Come, my friend. Let's go see what Demetrios has to say."

Home's main port was bustling with activity. Galleys lined all the docks, and numerous smaller fishing vessels dotted the waters. By brute strength sailors had dragged a galley on long rollers onto the beach and were now scraping her bottom. It was painted a dull blue-black, with a jaunty red trim above the tarred decks. As with all Demetrios's vessels, there were aspects that made the craft a hybrid of Egyptian and Greek influences.

Because merchant ships were customarily sailing craft, Demetrios's oared merchantmen were considered rare. Although his ships required a larger crew, they were never becalmed at sea, thus carving many days from their schedules.

The additional crew had another function: An attacking privateer soon had a lusty fight on his hands, and at one point a full quarter of Demetrios's fleet had been composed of captured pirate vessels.

When Yahadu and the runner pulled up at dockside, Demetrios appeared on the deck of a galley. "Yahadu!" called the entrepreneur. "Over here!"

As Yahadu stepped down from the chariot, the runner took the animal's reins and led the vehicle away.

"Welcome home!" Yahadu responded cheerfully.

He was about to board when Demetrios, trim and muscular looking in a white tunic, leapt ashore. "I've found a new home. I want you to look at it with me."

Yahadu could not believe his ears. This was a great honor. "Anything that pleases you, my lord, will please me."

Demetrios reached out and clapped him on the shoulder. "I want your opinion. After all, you're to be chief administrator of our new home."

Yahadu's eyes widened. "My lord!"

"I like surprises, don't you?" said Demetrios amiably. "Come along to the inn. I'll tell you about the new place."

II

At the end of Home's brief main street, an extended ropewalk radiated paths in all directions before ending with great suddenness at a low promontory. On this was the town's only inn, a refuge for those of Demetrios's captains who were allowed to visit the secret stronghold but did not have their own houses here. Atop the inn was a roof garden, one of Demetrios's favorite vantage points on the island. It commanded a view from the bay to the smoldering volcanic cones.

To this place Demetrios and his new administrator now repaired. As they climbed the stone steps, the earth shook and Demetrios almost fell. Yahadu reached out and steadied him, but Demetrios disengaged himself once the aftershocks had ended.

They took seats on opposite sides of a table at the garden's edge. "That was an unusually violent one, wasn't it?" Demetrios remarked.

"I'm sorry to say, sir, that this has become more common in recent days. I'm afraid you'll find some damage to the retaining wall of your villa. The workmen have been repairing it."

Demetrios waved to the innkeeper for refreshments. "Why repair something that'll be buried under volcanic ash in six months?"

Yahadu frowned. "So soon, sir?"

"The Mesopotamian school says we have half a year; the Egyptian soothsayers say it could happen any day now, even as we sit here."

Yahadu shuddered. The innkeeper, bowing low, put a plate of fruit and cheese on the table, then poured wine for both men and quietly left.

"Imagine," Demetrios said. "One of these cones is going to give birth to a monster. With little warning it will shake the teeth out of the heads of anyone injudicious enough to be here when it happens."

"I hope we're out to sea before the eruption." Then he thought of something. "But, sir, won't tidal waves swamp any ship that's—?"

"Not ships well out to sea, in deep water," Demetrios replied. "If we're ten leagues out when catastrophe strikes, in water many fathoms deep, we probably won't even be aware that anything has happened. The peculiarity of these waves can allow for some village on the shore of an island halfway across the Great Sea to get the brunt of the wave in a matter of minutes. A wave four times the height of this inn will suddenly appear offshore, building and building, and when it breaks, it will tear trees up by the roots, toss boulders heavier than my house about, and will leave not a structure standing." He shook his head in wonderment. "I talked to a man who had seen such a wave from a height, in his youth. He said that the ocean drew back from the shore—like a man drawing back his fist before dealing a deadly blow—leaving the offshore shelf high and dry for nearly as far as the eye could see. When the water came back it was in a huge, crushing, frightening wave."

Yahadu shuddered again.

"Our new home is as exposed to tidal waves as this place," Demetrios continued, "but it's in the wrong direction to be buried under ash. We won't move into the new site until the explosion has come and gone, and the great wave with it."

Yahadu paused with his wine bowl halfway to his lips. "Sir?"

"We're going to live on shipboard—all of us, until it's safe to build the new estate on dry land."

"Sir! From time to time I'm simply staggered at the scale on which you do things."

"When we build the new village, it will be from scratch. No human has ever lived there. You'll be earning your pay, that I promise you." Demetrios grinned. "That's why I'm doubling your salary as of today."

"Why, sir! Thank you, sir. The new site—what does it look like?"

"Much like this. A semicircular bay, a protected harbor that used to be a haven for pirates. I'll have to find us an architect to build houses for us." His expression turned thoughtful. "I had hoped to employ my distant kinsman Seth of Thebes. But he seems to have disappeared. If only I could find him . . ."

"Sir, if I might ask: Kamose has ruled Egypt for a decade, and Amasis, who prompted your withdrawal of our vessels, has been degraded. Do you intend to reopen trade with Egypt?"

"A good question, and one you yourself might answer."

Yahadu looked startled.

"I want you to go to Egypt. I'll arrange a false identity for you. Look into the situation and find out whether it's worth our getting reinvolved with them."

"Yes, sir!"

"And while you're at it, look around. Find out how my brother and sister are doing. See if you can find any trace of Seth. If you can find him, there'll be a generous bonus for you."

Yahadu was grinning like a boy now, and the air fairly crackled with his enthusiasm. "Sir! If he's alive, I'll find him. If he's dead, I'll dig him up and bring him back to life again. Count on it, sir! I'm your man!"

CHAPTER ELEVEN

The Hills of Midian

I

Bata, eldest son of the trader Sekhti of Bast, turned his horse and rode back past the caravan to where his father, comfortably sitting his mount, plodded his way slowly up the path. "Father! The point men say we're to leave the road here! Is that true?"

Sekhti smiled placidly. His son was still an emotional lad who had not learned self-control. "Patience. They do this on my order."

"But to lead the animals off the main track in this waterless land—"

"Patience, I say," Sekhti advised again. "I plan to stop at Selah, to see an old friend. Trust me, my son. I know what I'm doing. The side trip is not long, and it's quite beautiful. And there's water there, if you know where to look."

"Very well," the young man agreed.

"You will see that things are not always what they seem. Up that path lies not just an oasis but a whole valley, one settled over a hundred years ago by distant relatives of the Habiru."

Bata scowled. "Those slaves in Avaris? The ones who have been rebuilding the city all this time?"

"That's correct," Sekhti responded. "The Habiru were a great people once—and they may be again. When you meet my friend, I don't want to hear you say anything derogatory of the Habiru. I wouldn't want his feelings hurt; he's been a true friend and a good trading partner."

Bata looked at the forbidding cliffs above them. "What could he have to trade from a place like this?"

"You'll see. You may be interested that our destination is probably the only truly impregnable hideout you'll ever lay eyes on."

"You mean it's fortified?" Bata calmed his skittish horse and fell into the same unhurried pace his father's mount had been maintaining.

"No, it's naturally impregnable. It has quite an interesting history."

"Tell me."

"The patriarch Jacob was the junior of identical twins and a bit of a trickster in his youth. When it came time for his father, Isaac, to divide his property among his sons, the elder twin, Esau, learned that Jacob had stolen his birthright."

"And this was the patriarch?"

"Hear me out. It was done with the connivance of the boys' mother. She knew that Jacob, the wiser, was the proper one to rule. Esau went into a rage and ran his brother out of the country for twenty years. They became reconciled only when the Shepherds passed through Canaan. While Jacob negotiated with the Shepherds in Canaan, Esau brought his family down here, to the mountains of Edom. He wasn't sure that Jacob could negotiate a truce with the Shepherds, so he went in search of a place to hide—and he found one. Selah."

"That's the name of where we're going?" Bata asked.

"Yes. Of course it had no name then. Esau stumbled across it and quickly understood what a wonder he'd discovered: Half a dozen men and enough arrows could hold off an army."

"Father! You're joking!"

"Not at all. It's really a most amazing place. We'll enter the valley through a cleft in the hills that goes on for leagues and is so narrow that we'll have to ride through it single file."

"And at the end of this long cleft?"

"A hidden valley with tall, towering sandstone walls of bright red. It's as if nature had gone mad. There are springs some distance up the valley, but the well provides enough water for a whole society. Esau saw this and settled there, and it is his progeny who live there now. They call themselves the Kenites, and they've inherited the occasional prickliness of Esau himself. Like many of the Habiru they run to red hair and hot tempers, but they're a decent lot, and my friend Jethro—he's the leader and high priest—is as good a fellow as you'd want to meet."

"What does Jethro have to trade?"

"His people have a name as weavers. You'll be impressed by the quality of their work. I stop there on the way north and sell all I buy there up in Damascus."

"I see. So this side trip is business?"

"In part. I would not pass through here without a visit to Jethro. Now keep your eyes and ears open while we're in Selah. Jethro is a wise and knowledgeable man, and much is to be learned from him."

"Do you have an exclusive franchise on Kenite woven goods?"

"I'm working on it. It will require patience, delicate maneuvering, and some tough bargaining. Keep this in mind, my son: It is often wise to seem less than wise. If you get your associates relaxed, you can do a lot of good business."

The path turned and headed straight for a rock wall. "Where are we going, Father? We've reached a dead end."

Sekhti smiled. "You've a surprise ahead of you, my son."

Sekhti was as good as his word. The trail threaded into a cleft in the hills that was wide enough for several pack animals to enter at the same time; but soon it narrowed, making a single file necessary. They passed guards to right and left, but Sekhti knew them all by name and was welcomed.

Rounding a corner, they went from the sunless shade of the cleft to bright sunshine on towering sandstone cliffs, as red as the rose!

"Father! I thought you were exaggerating!" Bata marveled.

Sekhti beamed. "I wasn't exaggerating about anything, my son," he said. "Least of all about how much you can learn if you keep your mouth closed for the next few days!"

*   *   *

The lessons began almost immediately. "That's Jethro," Sekhti said, spotting a robed man approaching. "Now don't smile. Accepting an invitation is a serious matter here, and the smallest offense against protocol can destroy a friendship it's taken years to build."

The Kenite approached, bowed, and spoke at length in his own tongue. Then, apparently for Bata's benefit, he and Sekhti switched to Egyptian.

"Ennoble me, my lord, with your presence at my house."

"I am honored beyond measure, my lord, but I cannot accept your gracious hospitality."

"Surely that cannot be."

"It is with the most exquisite pain that I must decline, although the bread and salt of your house are bywords through all the known world."

At this juncture Jethro seized Sekhti by the arm and virtually began to drag him down the street toward a great canopied cave carved directly into the rock—evidently his home. Sekhti half turned to wink at his son. And Bata, suppressing a smile, followed in their wake.

So this was the way a man went about doing business in Midian! Bata shook his head in astonishment. Would wonders never cease?

II

Once inside the patriarch's unusual dwelling, his behavior—and Sekhti's—reverted to something a bit more conventional. His father introduced him with pride. "My son has not yet learned about your tribal customs," he said. "We will have to complete his education while we are here."

"Well!" Jethro said, beaming. "He looks to be a bright lad. We'll teach him all a man needs to know. Really, my boy, if you're puzzled by our methods of welcoming a guest from afar, you'll be astonished by our methods of saying good-bye!"

Sekhti grinned and turned to his son. "It's very hard to get a Kenite to let you go, once you've stayed at his house. Under no circumstances will he allow you to leave on the first day."

"Or the second," Jethro put in. "So I'm afraid you're stuck with my company for a while, young Bata. Welcome to my poor abode. What is mine is yours."

"Poor!" Bata sputtered. "I've never seen anything like it. Do others live in the caves?"

"Just the richest. Mostly we stick with our old customs, from Canaan; only recently have we begun to add other means of attracting the gold of traders."

"My father," Bata said, "has told me of your people's skills at weaving, and of the popularity of your products in the markets of the North." From the severe expression on Sekhti's face, the boy knew immediately that he had spoken out of turn and quickly stopped there.

It was too late. Jethro's brow raised. "Ah? Seems to me that you were complaining about how poor sales were, and how I should lower my prices."

"My son has a talent for exaggeration," Sekhti explained.

But the sardonic gleam remained in Jethro's eye as he changed the subject. "I will call for food and drink. And I will send one of my daughters to stable your horses and tend to the pack animals of your caravan."

"Oh, no, sir!" Bata said. "That's my job. I'll get to work right now. You and Father will want to talk about old times without me. Besides, I'd like to look around a bit if I might."

"With my blessing," Jethro said, waving one hand in courteous dismissal. He watched the boy go, then turned back to Sekhti. "Perhaps he will take a fancy to one of my daughters? Perhaps you and I could arrange a marriage, eh, old friend? Kenite wives are highly prized. I have so many daughters, and no son, except—"

He stopped here so quickly that Sekhti shot a sharp glance at him. "Except whom? It was my impression that all your daughters were unmarried."

Jethro winced. "How can I fault your son speaking too quickly when I am guilty of the same sin? Forget what I said."

Sekhti pressed on, though. "Come, now. What kind of

friendship do we have, after all these years, if it does not invite confidences?"

Jethro sighed. He clapped his hands, and from the darkness behind them came a comely young woman bearing fruit and wine on a platter. He let her serve them silently, nodded, and watched her leave. "Daughter Number Three. And Daughter Number Two is still without a husband. I despair of seeing the younger ones ever finding a man. I tell you, I have been happy here in Selah, but there are times . . ."

"Has the eldest found a man, then?"

"Yes. Zipporah did. Ten years ago. They have a son of nine."

"Ten years ago?" Sekhti sat up suddenly and spilled his wine.

"I know, I know. My apologies. But it would be most dangerous if it was to become known in Egypt who my son-by-marriage is."

"Why should anyone in Egypt care whom your daughters marry? He's not a criminal, is he?"

"It depends on what you call a crime."

"You'll have to explain more clearly."

"The worst crime in Egypt would be plotting the overthrow of the Crown. But there's been so much plotting in recent years that when Kamose became Lord of Two Lands once more and deposed Amasis, he didn't even have Amasis impaled for plotting against him."

"Because Amasis was never a serious threat. He could never have reigned in Egypt—he hasn't a drop of Egyptian blood. Am I correct?"

"Yes, but what about a pretender to the throne of Egypt?"

"You don't mean it. Moses! Prince Moses! *Here?*"

"Yes. I implore you, don't tell anyone—not even your son. I'll let you talk to Moses later. He wants to hear the latest news from Egypt."

"Gods! Moses! And here, in—" He stopped himself.

But Jethro smiled ruefully. "You were about to say, 'in the middle of nowhere,' I believe? Oh, don't deny it. I sometimes think like that myself, when I'm really tired of this place's insularity. I should get away for a bit, and go up to Damascus and see for myself how well my people's weaving is doing in the markets."

"Hah! You mock me."

"Not at all! I flatter you, letting you think you have fooled me all these years."

Sekhti shrugged good-naturedly. "You can't fault a trader for trying to get the best crafts for the least money." He paused. "I have an offer: I'll trade Moses everything I know about Egypt for the true story of what happened to him."

"There has been no official explanation for his escape, after all these years?"

"None. Of course, that all happened just before Kamose regained power, and as the sailors say, when the anchor lifts, all debts are paid. Let me tell it when Moses is here. No use telling it all twice." He selected a dried date. "I can't get over it. All these years, and only now do you tell me—and reluctantly, at that."

"My primary responsibility is to my people," Jethro explained. "How long do you think we'd last if the Egyptian garrison at Timna was to learn that I have been hiding Moses here, right under their noses, for ten years?"

"But I thought you could hold off a whole army."

Jethro shook his head vigorously. "Oh, no. There's a back way into here. You have to go around the whole mountain chain, but it's there—and not defensible at all. The garrison at Timna is the meanest in the northern command. When Kamose conquered the area, he slaughtered the Hai defenders to the last man. That left no one in charge of protecting the mines. So he freed the mine slaves and put them in charge—just up and swore them in as soldiers. He asked who was the toughest man there, and of course they pointed at some ugly bastard with scars all over his face. Kamose pointed at him and said, 'Very well. There's your new officer.' "

"That's the old Kamose," he said with a shudder. "He's changed now."

"For the better?"

"Call Moses. Then I'll tell you everything."

Jethro clapped his hands, and the girl appeared again at the door. "Bring Moses, will you, my dear?"

III

A decade before, the face of Prince Moses had been well-known to all men of Sekhti's standing in the Egyptian community. Yet when the girl returned with a burly, broad-shouldered man of about thirty years, Sekhti looked closely but did not see any resemblance to the prince he had last seen as a youth. The newcomer was no longer the half man, half boy whom Sekhti remembered from the days before the Nubian expedition. He had the air of concentrated, controlled force that came only with maturity. His hair was long, after the northern fashion, his beard was black and full, and the garment he wore was a shepherd's: coarse white cloth with a woven pattern, little more than knee length and leaving one powerful, well-muscled shoulder bare. The bare arms were deeply tanned and hard.

Only the eyes betrayed him. Sekhti had met Moses twice, at official functions in Thebes, and he remembered the eyes: clear and intelligent and direct. He rose and bowed deeply. "Your Highness," he said.

Moses returned the bow, but in the fashion of the North. He shot a look at Jethro. "He knows, then? Very well. I know you would not tell anyone who could not be trusted. Please, sit."

Moses turned to Sekhti. "I must insist on one thing: We are equals here; you must not treat me as if I were a prince. Prince Moses is dead. He began to die little by little on the way to Nubia, when Seth of Thebes told him who he truly was. I am not a pretender to the throne of Egypt. That was Baliniri's hope, but not my destiny."

"I see," Sekhti said respectfully. "And that is . . . ?"

For the first time a flicker of doubt crossed Moses' face. "That has yet to be revealed. It has been said that I am the promised Deliverer of my people, who would lead them out of bondage to Canaan."

"I see. Your God, then, has notched an arrow for you and has bent your bow. All that remains is for the arrow to be loosed."

"And therein lies the great puzzle," Moses said. "When I escaped from Egypt and found my way here to Jethro"—he bowed his head in deference to his father-by-marriage and smiled affectionately—"I knew that I came here to complete my education and to await the voice of God."

"And?" Sekhti asked, leaning forward.

Moses sighed. "For ten years God has been silent. I do not know why."

"There is the possibility that the education you spoke of is still going on," Sckhti suggested. "There is much to be learned from a man like Jethro."

"Agreed," Moses said earnestly. "I suspect that one of the things I came here to learn is patience. When I left Egypt I was young, impulsive, and unattached—a man with no responsibilities except those he chose. I am now a husband and father and the loving servant of my wife's father, and I see that I have learned the natural rhythms of time itself, which I did not know when I slipped out of Egypt."

Sekhti said affably, "I told your esteemed father-by-marriage that if you would tell me the details of your escape from Egypt, I would tell you all the news from Avaris and Athribis."

"Then the capital has not returned to Thebes?" Moses said.

"No. That in itself will tell you something."

"I agree to your bargain," Moses responded.

Swiftly he sketched in an account of his last days in Egypt and his perilous trip through the desert to find refuge with Jethro in Selah.

"I've been happy here," he concluded. "As happy as a man can be who knows it can all end in a moment." He smiled. "Now tell me of Egypt."

Sekhti pursed his lips in thought for a moment. "To begin with, things aren't as they seem. After Kamose vanquished Amasis' mercenaries with the army you'd commanded in Nubia, the king made Amasis his lackey. It *looks* as though a decade of peace has come and gone, with Kamose reigning wisely and with an even hand. There is order in Egypt, but of a particularly sinister kind. Amasis is now little more than a bitter, powerless functionary. The rebuilding of Avaris has been the saving of your people. The freemen want nothing to do with it."

"Why should they? It's a living symbol of Shepherd

might! Why should any loyal Egyptian wish to be reminded that a bunch of the Hai came to Egypt, conquered it, and ruled over it for generations?"

"To be sure. Furthermore, Kamose grows daily more garrison minded. He is fearful of being assassinated. The astrologers predict both a great cataclysm in which multitudes will die and Kamose's own violent death. He wants a fortress-city in which he can hide from trouble."

"Who is really the power in Egypt now?"

"Apedemek, for all that he prefers to rule through Kamose. He has even corrupted the priests of Amon. No one knows how he does it."

"He has the ability to control people's minds. Which reminds me: Is Seth still in Thebes?"

"My sources tell me that Seth had a confrontation with Apedemek—"

"Oh, no!"

"I'm afraid so. Seth was vanquished and left the city a broken man. He made his way to Nubia, where he is being cared for by his son."

"Ah! That's a comfort. Het will take good care of him. And perhaps they can bring some friends up from the oasis. There are a couple of people there who have the healing touch." He cut off abruptly, as if he had said too much, but then relaxed. "Speaking of the oasis, what is happening there?"

"The women and the desert trade routes are safe. My own caravans pass through El-Kharga now and then, you know. Now I will tell you of your family if you'd like."

It became very quiet. Sekhti looked from face to face. "The news is not good. Apedemek hates the Habiru even more than Kamose or Amasis ever did. When the restoration of Avaris is complete, I expect a terrible slaughter. I don't think they've got much time."

Moses' fists clenched. "Why does God not speak to me? The time is getting near, and here I sit."

"There, now," Jethro soothed. "This is something over which you have no control."

Moses looked miserable. "How is my brother, Aaron?"

"He continues to be a tower of strength, but his lot is a hard one. He deliberately places himself between his people and the authorities and accepts the blame for anything that goes wrong. He recently took a terrible beating at Kamose's own hands. And for nothing! Nothing!"

Moses' face was contorted with anguish. "What can I do?" he groaned. "What can I do?"

IV

Neither of the older men said anything for a moment. Then, after glancing at Jethro, Sekhti said, "I apologize for causing you anguish, young man. But if you would permit me one last observation . . ."

Moses nodded.

Sekhti put a comforting hand on Moses' hard forearm. "Let me speak by way of analogy: I count myself a loving father, but often I am preoccupied with business. When I inadvertently neglect my son, it may sometimes be up to him to remind me of what I have forgotten to give him."

Moses looked at him solemnly. "But I pray to Him often."

Now it was Jethro's turn to offer a suggestion. "In the old days, one sought God on the heights, far from the haunts of men. This is what the patriarch Abraham used to do when he had a problem."

Moses looked grateful. When he spoke, his voice was calmer, lower. "I will follow your wise advice. Thank you." He got up. "I'm going to talk to Zipporah now. And I think I'll take a long walk. I am pleased to have made your acquaintance, sir," he said to Sekhti. He bowed and went out into the sunlight, his back straight, his head held high, a fine figure of a man.

"Quite a remarkable fellow you have here," Sekhti said thoughtfully. "I can well believe he's been singled out for great things."

"Yes," Jethro agreed, "although I sometimes find myself doubting that our people have been set apart, destined for greatness and God's favor. After all, who are we that God should choose us from among others? A backwater people, better than half of whom are slaves in your country."

"Who is any man that he should give himself airs? Your son-by-marriage amazes me: Imagine, a man of his background speaking so humbly! What do you think he will do now?"

"I think he will pray. He will most likely wander among my flocks, on the slopes of nearby Mount Horeb."

"I wish him good fortune and the favor of his God."

Jethro smiled. "Come, my friend, let us do business. In my present mellow mood you will find me a poor bargainer, ill able to defend myself against your assaults. You will probably get the exclusive franchise on my people's crafts for a fraction of what I was going to ask."

Moses found Zipporah in her little herb garden, speaking with a young man in Egyptian garb. He watched her, unnoticed, as she identified the plants: "This one is cumin, and that's mint over there. And here's coriander, and mustard, and garlic. Our garlic is not very good; according to my husband it hasn't the pungency of the garlic grown in Egypt."

"Our good Egyptian garlic is famous among all the nations," the young man said. "Will it grow here?"

"My husband thinks it might. But we haven't any samples to try it."

"It so happens that our caravan carries a supply," he said. "I'll have some brought to you."

"That would be kind of you!" She turned and saw Moses. "Ah! Here's my husband! Moses, this is Bata, our guest."

"Ah, yes. Son of Sekhti, whom I just met. Greetings, young man. I have just been the recipient of your father's wise counsel."

"And I of your wife's excellent hospitality."

Moses bowed slightly. "Would you be so kind as to excuse us for a moment?"

Bata bowed in assent, then Moses drew Zipporah aside. "I'm going out with the flocks. I need to be alone, to think."

Zipporah's lovely face became tense. "Is there anything I can do to—?"

"No, no," he said, embracing her.

"Bata's father and Jethro gave me the idea. I must seek

God's advice in solitude. I thought I'd go to that old altar on the side of the mountain. Abraham, Isaac, and Jacob used to make sacrifices on such an altar when they needed the answer to a vexing question."

"How long will you be?"

"A couple of days," he replied. "Don't worry; I'll be all right."

"I'll pack some food for you."

"Good. And tell Gershom I love him. You know what to tell yourself from me."

She smiled, and her face lit up. "I do," she agreed, "but I wouldn't mind hearing you say it."

"I love you." He kissed her, then reluctantly moved away. "If I don't go now, I won't go at all."

Gershom came down from the higher pastures a little after Moses had left. He was a bright boy with his mother's green eyes. "I was looking for Father," he said to her, "but I couldn't find him."

"He had to leave for a couple of days, dear," she said. "He was sorry to have missed you and asked me to give you his love."

There was a quizzical look on his young face. "Is Father going to leave us?"

"I hope not, sweetheart. But your father must do whatever God tells him. You know that."

"Mother, I had a dream that he had to go far away, into terrible danger."

"It was just a dream, dear."

"But it seemed so real, and I remembered it so clearly after I awoke. We went to Egypt, and we had to run away. People were chasing us, wanting to kill us."

"Now, darling, nobody wants to kill us."

"And we were traveling with a lot of people, and all of a sudden the sea towered over our heads, and—"

"The sea doesn't do that, darling. The waves are gentle, little things that splash over the rocks and can wet you a bit, but nothing to be afraid of. The next time you have a nightmare, come to Mother as soon as you wake up. Promise?"

He looked at her with fear and disbelief.

She forced a smile. "Now go and wash up, dear. We have some guests all the way from Egypt for dinner."

He went away unconvinced, uncomforted. She watched him, frowning. It was hard to lie to a child as bright and sensitive as Gershom. He could tell when the adults were telling him the truth and when they were hedging. And by telling him there was nothing to his fears, she was lying. He would not have missed that.

Lately she, too, had been having nightmares, the desperate trip across the desert, the brutal pursuers breathing hot on their necks. And the sea rising above them, to crash down on their unprotected heads and obliterate them!

V

After two hours his path had left the valley, and he was winding his way slowly into the high hills around Selah. Now he was above the sandstone layer and was climbing along the limestone plateau. Almost immediately the surroundings changed: Various small springs came to the surface, and what had been waterless desert began to sprout little flecks of green.

Still he climbed and in the wadis passed bushes, plants, and even trees. The higher he climbed, the greener things became. Honeysuckle, caper, and flowering aloe displayed themselves, their creepers clinging tightly to the rocks. He would have to come this way in spring. The desert flowers would be breathtakingly beautiful, the white blossoms of the broom set off by purple irises, crimson anemones, and golden buttercups. Yes, he would bring Zipporah and the boy here.

A great and sudden wave of sadness passed over him. No! He would never see another spring here. The time was soon coming for him to leave Selah.

But he was as rooted to this land as the creepers were rooted to the rocks. He had come to Selah a stranger, a man whose blood belonged here but whose mind was Egyptian. He had even named his son Gershom, "the exiled," in remembrance of his own early feelings as a foreigner in this strange new land. Now, after ten years of living and working here, he was as much a son of Selah as any man.

But the certainty with which he knew he would be leaving also filled him with elation. Was God communicating with him at last?

He had never seen Canaan, trod its dry ground, smelled its air, or walked its hills. He had never learned so much as a word of its language until he had come here. Even now, when he rejoined his people, he would speak their language with a pronounced Edomite accent, as did his wife and her kin.

As he climbed still higher, he could see across the deep vale to one of Jethro's many herds grazing. Remembering the sacrifice he had intended to make, he squinted into the distance and surveyed the animals, settling upon a half-grown lamb. Yes, that would do. If he could find his way to the pastures . . .

He slipped and almost turned his ankle. *I shouldn't have come on a hike without a staff.*

As he turned to retrace his steps, a strange feeling overcame him. Nothing seemed quite real. Everything looked strange, distorted, and there was buzzing in his ears. The wind stopped.

He looked at his feet. There lay a long, slender shepherd's staff of fine-grained, polished oak.

How could I not have seen this before? he wondered.

He stooped to pick it up, and as his fingers closed around it, he could feel a strange surge of power flowing into him through his hands. He stood, shivering.

Have I gone mad?

He found his feet leaving the path, going behind a ridge, and bringing him to a level area flanked by granite walls. He had been here before.

But where was the altar that Esau had placed here and sacrificed upon?

There was a flash of blinding, white light. He shielded his eyes and almost dared not look again. But he peeked timidly and blinked at what he saw: Where the altar had once been now stood a blossoming thornbush unlike any ever seen. It blazed with an uncanny fire that emitted no heat. It burned, yet the bush was not consumed. The flames danced but did not wither or char the twisted branches, the sharp thorns, the bright-green leaves, the white flowers.

The staff shook in his hand. He felt faint. His heart was pounding.

Without warning a Voice sounded: "You stand on holy ground. Take off your sandals."

Moses did so immediately without moving his eyes from the white light that played over the thornbush.

"Moses," the Voice said.

"Yes? I am here," he croaked.

"I am the God of your fathers, of Abraham and Isaac and Jacob. I hear the cries of My people in Egypt, and I know their suffering. I have chosen you to lead them out of oppression to a land rich and broad, a land of milk and honey. I shall take land from the present inhabitants and give it to them. And you are the instrument I have chosen to accomplish this."

Moses trembled. "Me, Lord? Who am I, that I should be able to do such things?"

And the Voice said: "I will be with you. My hand will guide yours."

"But Lord! How can I speak for You? I know nothing about You! What shall I say to the Habiru who question me?"

"Tell them you come in the name of Yahweh. Tell them that this is the name by which I shall be known among them henceforth. Tell them that He Who Is has sent you."

"Yahweh," Moses echoed. "He Who Is."

The man felt a wondrous sense of peace that he had never known before. His confidence returned. He felt strong, capable. "Speak, Lord, and I will obey."

"Hear Me, then. This is what you must do."

VI

Bata met his father at the well. "How did the bargaining go?" he asked.

Sekhti shrugged. "One does not conclude a deal quite so quickly. Jethro is a shrewd businessman."

"The bargaining does not go smoothly?"

"It does not. I need somehow to shift the balance in my favor."

"I met Moses and his wife. I made friends with Zipporah and gave her some Egyptian garlic for her garden."

Sekhti nodded approvingly. "The more you can ingratiate yourself, the better things will go for me. I keep asking myself, 'How can I get Jethro in my debt? How can I get him to need something in my possession?' "

Bata considered a moment. "Moses' wife is very beautiful. Do all the Kenite women look like her?"

"I don't know," Sekhti admitted. "Jethro's wife was quite pretty, and all his seven daughters are stunning. Imagine! Seven daughters! And no one to marry them off to! A pity— each would bring quite a sizable dowry."

"Was that one of his daughters who was bringing refreshments in the cave?"

"Yes. Lovely little thing. A real jewel for some lucky man, I'd say."

"Father, I have the solution for your problem."

Sekhti's eyes were veiled. "Oh, you have, have you? Then tell me, O wise one, I want an exclusive franchise on Jethro's woven goods without renegotiation for seven years."

"First, tell him that we're going to throw *him* a feast. We can do it: We've enough provender on the pack animals to invite his entire family and his closer relatives."

"Well, it's unusual, but it could be—"

"This would allow us to meet all six of Zipporah's unmarried younger sisters."

Sekhti's eyes widened.

"Then, when I have made my choice of a wife, you can start the bargaining again. Only this time he'll be dealing with the father of his future son-by-marriage." Bata grinned.

"Would he give the business to a stranger when he could keep it in the family?"

Sekhti's smile split his face. "Buy you a rich wife from Selah! Tell me more."

Moses hunkered down, feeding dry branches to the camp fire and watching the sunset. He had decided against going home tonight; he did not wish to risk injury hiking many leagues in rough terrain in the dark.

As he watched the red sun drop into the far horizon, he realized sleep would evade him. How could a man sleep after hearing what he had heard, seeing what he had seen? At last he had been told the exact nature of his destiny and the nature of the covenant between God and His chosen people.

He was to be not just a Deliverer but a spiritual leader as well—the intermediary through whom God would speak. He was to become a prophet of God.

It had been too much for him at first. He had been shown signs of the infinite might of the God he was to serve: the shepherd's staff becoming a wriggling snake, spitting venom, then changing back into a staff. His hand decayed from leprosy one moment, and cured the next.

He had protested that the means God had proposed for subduing the Egyptians were quite impossible. And of course they were.

"Trust in Me," the Unimaginable had said. "All things are consistent within Me. All is Order within Me."

He sighed, thinking about it. The burden was his. His! *Make me strong!* he prayed. *Make me worthy! Make me equal to the task!*

CHAPTER TWELVE

Nubia

I.

"Please have a seat, Captain," Seth invited, gesturing toward a long Babylonian-style couch. "I'll send for food and drink. My wife's just outside, in the garden."

"No, sir, please," the guardsman responded. "I . . . I'd love to stay to accept your hospitality—I've never seen a place quite like this—but . . ."

"Ah, now," Seth said, "you've touched one of my weaknesses: my pride in my house. I'm capable of conforming to society's rules on most occasions, but when I meet someone who hasn't seen my house before, I can't just let him go without showing him around. I never really had a home of my own before coming here to Kerma. I created the design, after—"

"Really, sir. A thousand pardons, but I can't stay, as much as I would love to. This is the middle of my workday, sir, and I have three more calls to make before lunch. By your leave, sir, the boy is outside. The men are holding him."

"For that you deserve my gratitude! May I ask what the charge is this time?"

"The same as before, sir. Petty theft. Nothing terribly serious—fruit stolen from a stand—but of course you realize that we can't show favoritism in these matters. If I catch him at it again, I'm going to have to take measures, sir, whether you and I like it or not. That is, sir, unless I get special instructions from your son, the king."

"No, no," Seth said quickly. "I quite understand. And my son wouldn't be king long if he allowed special people to break the law while others went to prison for the same offenses. If I can't talk the boy out of doing this sort of thing again, he'll simply have to pay the penalty. What would that be?"

"If he were fully grown, he'd lose a hand to the chopper. But a boy of ten? We'd have to take him away on a work detail for a month. He wouldn't like it, I assure you."

"I'll do my best to turn him around." He steered the captain gently toward the door. "Please accept my thanks."

The guards ushered the boy in. He kept his eyes downcast. Seth thanked the men and was showing them out just as Mai came in from the garden.

"Ah, Mai," Seth said, nodding at the boy. "We've got ourselves a little problem again, I'm afraid."

"Pepi!" she moaned, her face falling. "You haven't!"

The sullen boy said nothing. He looked at the wall between them.

"I'm afraid he has," Seth responded kindly. "Pepi, my boy, what are we going to do with you? You know what the penalty is for stealing when you come of age?"

The boy looked at him for the first time. "They have to catch me. By then I'll be impossible to catch. I've been doing the same thing for a week, and it took them this long to nab me."

Seth and Mai exchanged glances. "This is more serious than I thought. I think you'd better go to your room. I'll be up in a moment." He watched as the boy hesitated. "Go along now," he insisted gently but firmly. "I want to talk to Mai."

The boy looked up from hangdog eyes. "You're not going to tell Mother?"

Seth thought, then shook his head. "What good would

that do? Now go on up. We'll have to come to some sort of an understanding, you and I."

"Just don't use any of that stuff you do with your eyes."

Mai looked glumly after Pepi as he disappeared up the stairs. "So he's back to his old tricks."

Seth nodded, stroking his beard. "Do you have any idea where Neftis is?"

"No one ever seems to know where Neftis is at any time of the night or day. I don't think she came in last night, but I'll go upstairs and check her room if you want, my dear."

Seth reached out and caressed her face. "No, I'll look in her room after I've talked to Pepi." He sighed. "I'm not sure what I can do with him."

"Can't you do something with that little mind-control trick?"

"It would only be a superficial change. He has a strong will. I could do more if I were better at it. But, as we all learned to our sorrow, I'm no Apedemek."

Mai put her arms around him. "You're not going to start in on that again, are you?"

Seth, in anguish, tried to move out of the circle of her arms but found out that he did not want to break away badly enough to succeed. "I'm sorry," he said, suddenly returning her embrace as if he were afraid of losing her forever. "Oh, Mai. What would I do without you? I had no idea that my old age was going to bring me a gift as lovely as you."

"There, now," she said. "That's the kind of thing a woman likes to hear." She kissed him. "Now go up and talk to the boy. I hope you can get through to him. Underneath it all, he's a good child. If only his mother—"

"I know. I really wish I could do something for her. But she blames herself for everything. When she hears about Pepi, she's going to take the burden on her own back."

"Not entirely. She loads some of it on the boy, and he is too young to carry it. And that's the problem with him: Neftis has told him too often that he's the bastard son of the most evil man in the world. What child could deal with a thing like that? Pepi keeps searching for the evil he thinks is inside him, and as we all know, if you go looking for something, you'll find it."

"And he never hears anything about the goodness in his mother—not from her, anyway—so he says to himself, 'My father was bad, and my mother says *she's* bad, so *I* must be bad.' The next thing you know, he goes out to prove it, endangering his own innocence."

"Poor Pepi. But at least he's got a wise and understanding friend like you to reassure him. Go up and talk to him."

"I will," he said. "Then I think I'll look in on his mother, if she's come home without our knowing it." He sighed. "And if she hasn't . . . well, I'll ask around. Perhaps someone has seen her."

II

"You did right to come to me with this," commended the king. "I thank you."

The captain of the guard saluted, but there was apprehension in his eyes. "Sire, if I might be permitted to remind the king . . ."

"Yes, yes," Het said. "I know. You want to make sure Seth does not find out that you have betrayed his confidence. I won't let him know I know. I want to continue to be told everything that you think is of interest here in Kerma."

"Yes, Sire."

"That includes everything you know about the mother," Het added. "Is she in trouble again?"

"There's been no sign of her recently, Sire. But last week there was a recurrence of the public drunkenness. My men had to pick her up. She wasn't able to walk."

"You didn't put her in jail, did you?"

"Oh, no, Sire. I wouldn't put her in with the real riffraff. I took her to the detention hall. She was in pretty foul shape, stewing in her own vomit. I had the women wash her and her dress. She fought like a lioness but was too drunk to hurt anybody. We left her there to dry out for a couple of days, then let her go."

"Does my father know about this?"

"I'm not sure. He didn't mention it today, at any rate."

"Then perhaps he doesn't know. She may have gone right back out and hit the taverns again. The next time this happens, have the men see her home and make certain she goes in the house with either my father or Mai. I don't want this sort of thing to go on without their knowing about it. What was the exact day when she was seen last?"

"I'm not sure, Sire. The last time I saw her was a week ago."

Het frowned. "Something may have happened to her. She has a history of getting in over her head. Have the men keep an eye out for her. If they find her, have them bring her in. I want to have a talk with her myself."

"Yes, Sire. Consider it done."

Seth sat on the other end of the bed, looking at Pepi. "I suppose you think you're pretty bad. You get in trouble, and you embarrass me, your mother—"

"Me? Embarrass *her*? No fear about that."

"What do you mean?"

"She doesn't even know I'm around, except when she gets drunk and tells me what an evil man my father is." The boy's lip trembled as he spoke. "Are there people who don't have any good in them anywhere?"

"I doubt it. I knew the man who fathered you. There was good in him once, or he never would have been admitted to the order."

Pepi snorted. "'The order.' 'Children of the Lion.' A fine lot you are, to raise a man like that."

"Insult the order all you like; it can't be harmed. But when you insult the Children of the Lion, you insult yourself. You're one of us, whether you like it or not. That birthmark on your back—"

"That doesn't mean anything. That doesn't mean I'm a good person."

"Not necessarily," Seth conceded. "A number of us have come to grief. Pepi, do you think I'm a good man?"

"You? Sure. But you aren't the son of a bad man like I am."

"I wonder. My father suffered great disappointments in life, which led him into some pretty reprehensible behavior.

He ran away from home, became convinced that my mother had been unfaithful to him—"

The boy shot him a sharp glance. "Was it true?"

Seth frowned. "Yes. But he took this to mean that he wasn't my natural father, that I was a bastard—"

"Like me! And were you?"

"Well, no."

"Huh! How do you know?"

"I suppose that my birthmark, for all it looks nothing like a paw print, comes to me from my father. The man I assume to have been my father was Ben-Hadad, a Child of the Lion, even though my mother's lover was Baliniri, who came to be a hero of mine. Of course the Children of the Lion have produced a few heroes of their own over the years."

The boy said bitterly, "Has *my* branch of the family, or were they perhaps all bad people like my father and me?"

"You're not bad! Don't say that! I don't know anything about Apedemek's family, Pepi."

"Then how can you reassure me? You're just talking nonsense about things you know nothing about."

Seth smiled wryly. "You've got Apedemek's intelligence and caginess, I see, and these aren't bad qualities. It all depends on how you use them."

"Go on."

"My father was very bitter, and he would have nothing to do with me."

This attracted Pepi's attention. "How long did this go on?"

"Until he died. You know, I hardly even *talked* until I was your age. Let me tell you, I had every right to be mean and bitter."

"Huh!"

"As you have."

This came as such a surprise that Pepi had no answer for it.

"The trouble is," Seth continued, "bitterness doesn't accomplish much. It's a poor poultice for heartache. Haven't you found that to be the case? Be honest with me."

Pepi stared, unable to say anything.

"Ah," Seth said, "I see you know what I'm talking about.

I tried it, and it only made matters worse. I was so lonely you wouldn't believe it." He paused. "Or maybe you would."

"You were lonely?" Pepi said. "You had no one to talk to? Your mother didn't understand?"

"She was all sunk in her own hurts. She tried to find time for me, but she couldn't stop thinking of herself. She left the job to a stranger she hired. Sometimes it works out best that way, having someone who hasn't an ax to grind take care of you."

"What kind of person was this?"

Seth smiled fondly. "Oh, Kedar was wonderful. He reached inside me to where I was hiding, found me, and pulled me out. He was the first one to realize how smart I was. As I am the first to realize how smart *you* are." He grinned conspiratorially. "I *am* the first, am I not?"

"Well . . ."

"Come on. Give me credit. I don't get credit for much anymore, you know. I used to be such an important fellow. And who am I now? Just an old man with a beard gone gray and a disappearing hairline."

"You're the king's father."

"Let me tell you, that's nothing compared to being a king." Seth drew himself up proudly. "I was king of Babylon once—the greatest city—"

"I know. You told me."

Seth scowled. "I see. To you I'm just an old man who goes on and on about the good old days. Right?"

This drew a resentful glare, but Seth thought to himself: *Good! I'm getting through to him at last. At least I'm getting a reaction.*

There was a knock on the door. "Seth, it's Mai. Could I see you for a minute?"

Seth looked at Pepi. There was a different expression on his face. *I'll have to settle for that,* he acknowledged to himself. *Any change is better than none at all just now.* "Would you excuse me? Don't go away. I want to talk some more with you about this. I think you're helping me understand some things."

The eyes retreated into distrust and resentment. "You mean about me?" the boy asked. "You think you've found a way to make me do things your way."

"Oh, no," Seth denied blandly. "I mean about myself. I don't think I ever understood my childhood before. And I think that I'm beginning to, just a little."

III

Going out, the captain spotted his aide Ergamenes in the great hall, chatting with a subordinate. He locked eyes with the aide and nodded curtly; Ergamenes joined him, saluting smartly. "Stand easy. The king wants the woman Neftis brought in for questioning, and I could use some company."

"The king, sir? I'd no idea it had got that far."

"She isn't in any real trouble. Come along; I'll explain as we walk." The two set out at a brisk clip through the streets of the city toward its major marketplace.

"Begging your pardon, sir," the aide said, "but if she isn't in trouble now, she will be soon. She's been sleeping around. We don't think she's taking money for it yet—"

"Why should she be? She's quite well-to-do."

"Not really sir. Last time we picked her up, she was on the verge of getting kicked out of those rooms she'd rented, for nonpayment."

The captain's eyebrows lifted. "I thought she lived with Seth and Mai."

"Officially, yes. But she's been keeping a dingy little place near the market. She's been using it to keep from Seth and Mai the fact that she hasn't drawn a sober breath in months."

"Interesting. I wonder why no one has brought this to my attention."

"I'll see that you're personally informed of every new development. Neftis got pulled in some time back, and I had a talk with her. It's no use talking sense to her, sir. It's a great pity. She must have been a great beauty once, and she could be very nice looking again. But there's something in the eyes. Something that's died."

"Here's the market. Why don't you look in on her apartment while I ask the neighbors about her."

"Right you are, sir."

The aide took the steps two at a time and in a moment was rapping smartly on the wooden door. There was no answer. He drew his sword and knocked again, this time with the weighted handle of the weapon. Again, no answer. He checked the handle and, to his surprise, felt it swing open.

Gods! he thought, looking around. *It looks as if there's been a fight here.* A table and an unpainted chair were overturned on the floor. There was rotting food just beyond them. The bedclothes, filthy and foul smelling, were on the floor next to the chair.

His eyes wandered to a bronze mirror—expensive from the look of it—on the wall. He could see that someone had taken a sharp instrument and defaced the gleaming surface, scoring it deeply. *Ah,* he thought. *Just about where her face would be if she were standing in front of it . . .*

A voice called out behind him. "What are you doing in here? This is private prop—"

The aide wheeled and saw the building's owner. But then the man recognized Ergamenes' uniform. "Oh, pardon me, sir," he said in a changed voice. "Can I help you, sir?"

"Where is the woman who rents this place from you?" the aide asked.

"She's gone. A bad lot, that one. I got rid of her the day before yesterday, sir. I can't have trash like her giving people the wrong impression about my hostelry, sir."

"I suppose she created this mess."

The owner nodded in disgust. "Imagine someone defacing my beautiful mirror like that."

"Don't try to tell me it was yours. Why, that's Theban work. The cartouche says Iri of Thebes."

"Sir, I swear to you, that was my mother's, and that wicked woman—"

"Is the *sister* of Iri of Thebes and a lot more likely to own a piece of quality than you are. Don't lie to me, my friend. People who lie to me get surprise visits from the health inspectors."

The landlord's face paled. "I may have been mistaken, sir."

"I think you were. I'll just take it along for evidence."

"Oh, please. Don't bring charges, sir. I was only—"

"Thinking of stealing the woman's mirror, eh?"

"But she owed me a great deal of rent! It may be the only way to recoup a fraction of my losses. She's gone. Left Nubia. Skipping out on her debts. She'll be on the way downriver by now, sir. Perhaps even past the border at Kerma."

"Pardon me," the aide said. "She's left the country altogether?"

Pepi put his ear to the door, straining to hear, but Seth and Mai were too far away for him to make out the words. He scowled, cursed under his breath, and opened the door to peer down the hall.

Good: Their backs were to him. He slipped out and crept down the corridor to hide behind a couch. He flattened himself against the floor and listened.

". . . suppose she's really done it?" This was Mai's voice, soft, concerned.

"You know Neftis. She means what she says. I don't like this. I don't like it at all. She's in no condition to confront him again. I'm not sure she will ever be."

"Oh, Seth!" Her voice was full of pain. "I'd held such high hopes for her. I kept thinking that if you could only get through to her, reach down to that level where he hurt her so badly—"

"I don't know what will ever cure poor Neftis. She thinks that if she can only find him and kill him, she'll be whole again." His voice changed, became soberly reflective. "The strange thing is, my dear, I'm not sure she's wrong. If he could be killed, and by her—"

"Oh, *Seth!*"

"I know. It would only create new problems. Even if she could do it and get away with it . . ."

He paused for a long moment, and Pepi, behind the couch, wished he had got here earlier to hear the whole conversation. Had his mother gone to Egypt to try to kill his father? She had been threatening to do that for as long as he could remember. But he had never taken much notice of it; usually she would also berate him for being the evil spawn of his horrible father.

Was he bad? Did it come in the blood? Were all his bad impulses deep in him and unalterable? Was it foreordained that he would be a rotten, mean person who liked to do people harm?

That would make hash of everything Seth had been trying to tell him. Seth had been trying to say that he himself had had a bad father, but he had changed his nature to become a useful person in the community. But if being a useful person was so wonderful, why had it not brought Seth more happiness? There was a lot of buried anger in Seth, and he was not at peace with himself deep inside.

And then the heretical thought leapt to the forefront of his mind: What if his *father* was the happy one? What if being bad had made him not only rich and powerful but happy, fulfilled, and at peace? If this was true, was there not a useful lesson to be found in the fact? Was there not something important to be learned? Was there not an example to be followed?

IV

The aide met the captain of the guard in front of Neftis's erstwhile apartment. The captain's expression told Ergamenes that his findings would come as no surprise. "She appears to be gone, sir."

The captain nodded grimly. "A neighbor says he saw her at the docks, taking passage downriver. What's under your arm?"

The aide tilted the bronze mirror so the ruined section showed.

The captain shuddered. "Hates herself, doesn't she? That's pretty sad. It's also pretty frightening."

"The landlord says she's skipping out on her debts, sir."

"There's more to it than that. She has a son. If she's

really gone, she's abandoned him. I wonder what that's going to do to the boy; he's already getting in trouble."

Ergamenes stepped up his pace to match the captain's long strides. "Where are we going?"

"To the waterfront. We'll see if we can get corroboration of the report that she's taken off downriver. Then we're going to go talk to Seth of Thebes."

"And then the king?"

The captain sighed. "I'm afraid so. I'm not happy about having to report that she's already gone. I wonder what her real reason is for going. Seth will likely have something vital to tell us. Come on! You're dawdling!"

When Seth and Mai went out to the garden, Pepi slipped back to his room and threw himself across his bed, his mind a messy aggregation of conflicting ideas. The only thing that was certain was that his mother was gone. What this meant for him was not clear. He would probably become Seth's ward, formally under his supervision. That meant he would have to do what Seth said. He would have to go to scribes' school, as Seth wanted him to do. But why should a rich kid, who did not have to work, learn a trade?

If only he could get his hands on the money Seth had deposited for his mother! He knew quite a bit had accumulated, because his mother never touched it. Then he would not have to undergo a rigidly strict apprenticeship, which demanded an enormous amount of work and memorization.

He grasped more of the problem: Society forced people, in a thousand little ways, to capitulate, to accept idiotic points of view, and to waste their time with irrelevancies. He was sure his father had discovered this, too. And his father had rebelled, as he was beginning to do.

Now, thinking about the matter, he came to a decision that seemed infinitely attractive: He would meet his father and talk with him. He had to learn if being evil made a man happier. He had to learn whether his father was, as Seth and his mother had always told him, a terrible person. Most of all he had to find out whether he was like his father.

Otherwise, who was there to take after? His mother, a drunkard? No, that was unthinkable!

He felt better for having made the decision. *Yes! I've got to find him,* he thought. *And I can warn him about Mother. If she gets to him before I do, and kills him, I'll miss the answer to the great mystery of good and evil, of which one is the more attractive. . . .*

The captain and his aide separated at the docks and moved in opposite directions down the long line of boats, questioning the boatmen. After half an hour they rejoined.

"Well," the captain said, "I found one fellow who saw her buy passage. She paid cash, too."

"I've also got a positive identification," Ergamenes reported. "I talked to a man from whom she tried to buy a one-way passage. She offered a good deal of money, more than I earn in six months. But where's she going? Why? I understand her brother is in the delta now, probably Avaris."

"I don't think she's going looking for her brother. The man I talked to said that she was very hostile. He said he wouldn't want to be the one who had wronged her."

Ergamenes' brow furrowed in thought. "Wronged her, eh? Who might that be?"

"I don't know," the captain admitted, "but that might explain why she hasn't taken control of her life. Somebody's out there that she blames her unhappiness on."

"So she's probably going downriver bent on revenge."

"Yes, that's my guess, too. But we'll get more information when we talk to Seth. I have the feeling he has the answer to all of this."

Seth stood in his rear garden, looking down the long row of ornamental shrubs and flowering trees. "No, Mai. I don't have the answer. All I know is that she's my responsibility."

Mai put a gentle hand on his arm. "Are you sure? She was my own mistress; for many years it was my job to look after her. But there comes a time when an adult has to take control of her own life. She's over thirty, Seth. She's going into terrible danger, but it's a thing of her own choosing. In her note she asked you not to come looking for her. The least you can do for her is to honor her request."

"It's just that—"

"Seth! *I* am your responsibility now. The boy and I.

Didn't you tell me you had just got finished making a real breakthrough with him?"

Seth took her hands. "Yes, my darling. Your point is very well-taken. I agree with everything you say. But if I let her go to what *has* to be her death, I'll never be able to look myself in the face again. It concerns my honor!"

Mai closed her eyes. Feeling that all hope had flown, she buried her face in his chest. He was leaving her.

V

The little man's name was Teritekas of Napata, and he had as bad a reputation as any man in the marketplace. Pepi did not trust him. The situation was delicate, however, requiring an adult partner, and beggars could not be choosers. He watched Teritekas warily. "Well? What do you think?"

The little man squinted down at the booty the boy had dumped out of the bag, then looked around furtively. "I don't like this. Somebody could come down the alley right now and—"

"Nobody ever comes down this alley," Pepi said. "That's why I picked it."

"And you're sure nobody is going to miss this stuff?"

"Not a chance. The person who owned it has left town forever. Look, do you want to be rich, or do you want to haggle like a fishwife all day?"

"I'll tell you what I don't want, boy," the man growled. "I don't want my fist on the chopping block for thievery."

"Nothing's going to happen. Trust me."

"Huh. Trust a smart-ass kid who's probably stealing the stuff from his old lady?"

This struck uncomfortably close to home, so Pepi quickly changed the subject. "What do you think we could get for this stuff?"

Teritekas looked over it again: combs, brooches, bracelets, anklets, necklaces—everything that was left of Neftis's jewelry. "This cartouche says . . ." He squinted, pretending to be able to read it. "My eyes are bad. What does it say?"

"Iri of Thebes. That's a pretty important name in jewelry these days."

"I've heard of this Iri. He's supposed to be the ugliest son of a bitch in the world. This is pretty good stuff." He bent over the goods, totaling in his mind. When he looked up, there was a crafty look in his eyes. "Maybe a hundred. No more."

"You're crazy! I could get a hundred and fifty myself, without going through you."

"But I'd be taking all the risk. If we're caught, they won't be chopping your hand off, they'll be chopping mine." He snorted. "We'll split the money sixty-forty, with me on the long side. Or no deal."

The boy started putting the jewelry back in the bag. "I can see we're not getting anywhere."

Teritekas put a staying hand on Pepi's arm. "Wait a minute. How much do you really need, boy? If I know that, I can figure out how hard I've got to bargain. If I can make a decent profit on top of that, maybe we can both come out as winners."

"I've got to have at least a hundred." Pepi glanced at Teritekas and wished he had picked a higher sum. The thief had a look of relief on his face.

But surely a hundred would get him where he was going and still leave him with money to live on. He decided to stick with the figure.

"A hundred," he repeated. "Take it or leave it."

Teritekas eyed him, weighing the risk, the danger, the chance that he might not be able to make the sort of deal he had in mind. "Let's see what I can get from my receiver. If he thinks this stuff's worth enough for me to give you that, maybe we have a deal."

"Yes or no," Pepi insisted. "You're not the only person in town I could go to with this."

Watching the play of emotions on the little man's ferret face, the boy was amazed at his own audacity. *I'll bet my father would be proud of me.* "Well?"

Teritekas took a deep breath. "All right. A hundred it is. We've got a deal."

*   *   *

"I'm afraid we've got bad news for you, sir," the captain said to Seth. "The woman seems to have gone downriver. She seems to have quite a lot of cash on her."

"I'm not surprised," Seth said sadly. "All her jewelry is gone." He turned to Mai. "I'll go to the bankers and find out whether she withdrew her savings as well."

"I already sent one of the servants down to the bankers. He returned with a note saying that she hasn't been seen there in over three years."

"Then she'll have some money left if she comes back," Seth said. "And if she doesn't"—he sighed long and deeply— "Pepi will have an inheritance. Mai, you haven't seen the boy around, have you?"

"Not since you had your talk with him. I assumed he was in his room."

"He isn't. If he's gone to town without asking me—"

"Sir," the aide said, "I think I saw the boy in the streets. If it was he, he was keeping bad company."

The captain turned to look at him. "Who?"

"That scurvy little cutpurse from Napata," the aide replied.

"Teritekas?" the captain snarled. "One of these days I'm going to get the goods on him."

"They were headed for the market area, sir, and Teritekas had a parcel under his arm, wrapped in patterned cloth." The aide stopped to watch one of the servants coming through the room, carrying a basket of laundry. "It was that pattern there!"

Seth stopped the servant girl. "One moment, my dear." He plucked the cloth from the top of her pile. "It's a bed sheet. One we keep in the guest room, isn't it, my dear?"

"No," Mai said, a strange expression on her face. "They're the sheets from Neftis's room. And Pepi's. Oh, no. He wouldn't. Seth, you don't really think—?"

"I don't know what I think. I just know that Pepi is terribly confused." He pounded his fist into his palm. "Curse it, this is my fault. If I'd been paying attention to him, he wouldn't have gone this far down the road to—"

"Seth! You mustn't blame yourself! We don't know for a fact that he's taken his mother's jewelry. Surely when we find him and talk to him . . ." The words trailed off. The same thought that had occurred to her was written all over Seth's face.

"*If* we find him . . ." he said.

VI

"Well, here you are, boy," Teritekas said. "One hundred in certified coin, just as we agreed upon. Count it before you go, so we don't have any disagreements later."

Pepi took the purse and sat down on the stoop. He glanced at Teritekas as he counted, in case the little thief should decide to run off. Finally he threw the last coin into the purse. "One hundred. All right. Now you've never heard of me, and I've never heard of you."

"You're catching on, boy. You're going to be some fellow when you're older. It would be best for us to take off in opposite directions. Which way are you going?"

"That's none of your business," he said warily. "I'll ignore you as you go away, and then I'll take off."

Teritekas felt panicky from the boy's self-assurance. What if the little snip were to report him to the guards? He nodded at Pepi. But after he turned and went around the corner, he doubled back to spy on the boy.

He let the child get to the end of the block, then followed him swiftly and stealthily. The boy was three quarters of the way down the road and moving into the tree-lined esplanade that lay between the city and the docks.

Why, the little bastard! He's going to skip town! Teritekas stepped up his pace to keep up with the rapidly vanishing figure. He fell into a slow jog all the way to the corner, where a large, sturdy-looking city guard stepped out of a side street and blocked the way.

"Excuse me, your honor," Teritekas said in a fawning voice. "If I could just—"

"Well!" the guardsman drawled. "If it isn't Teritekas! How very convenient! How could you have known that only this afternoon I'd get orders from my captain to bring you in? Now come along. I'd better pat you down, hadn't I? There's no knowing what sort of weapon you may have hidden in your sleeve."

Teritekas backed away. "I haven't done anything. I'm clean. I don't have any weapons on me."

But a hand twice the size of Teritekas's own grabbed him by the front of his robe. "We'll see about that. A sneak like you usually has some sort of blade on him, and I'm going to find it."

Teritekas was terrified. His hands flew to cover the bulge in his robe. "No," he begged. "I'll give you money. Just don't—" In a panic, Teritekas pulled himself loose and made a break for freedom. His skinny legs pumped. If he could only get to the end of the street before—

But as he rounded the corner he happened to look back just as the rock left the guardsman's hand. He ducked—right into the missile, which caught him on the temple. He fell to the ground, dazed. He tried to lift his head but dizziness overwhelmed him.

The guardsman came ambling up to him. "You should know better than to run from a dead shot like me," he chided. "Now come along. I've got to get you back to the guard station."

The boatman scowled down at him. "Take *you* somewhere? Don't make me laugh."

"How much to take me to the border?" Pepi asked. "I'll pay it."

"You? You don't have any money. You'd have to ask your papa for it. 'Daddy dear, could you please loan your little boy enough money to run away from home?' "

"Name a price within reason, and it's yours. I have the money on me."

The boatman seemed to be wavering. "Still . . . yesterday, when that woman wanted to go all the way to the delta, I didn't believe her. And that foul-smelling, toothless boatman from Semna got the job instead. Tell you what, son. If you had the cash—"

Pepi leapt into the breach. "How's forty?"

"Forty? You?"

"Look." The boy held out an open purse and jingled the coins inside.

"I don't know, son. What if you're some rich man's brat, and he blames me for your taking off?"

"You know whose brat I am? The woman you didn't give a ride to yesterday, that's whose."

"Huh. The guards were asking about her earlier today. What if they—"

"They don't need to know. No one's watching. If I board this minute and put forty copper pieces in your fist, and you pull anchor immediately—"

"You're crazy, boy!"

"Sure I am," Pepi agreed. "But not half as crazy as you'd be if you turned down the second fat purse in two days."

The boatman pondered this. "You're a persuasive little bastard."

"Who's about to make you forty pieces richer."

The boatman grinned crookedly. "You're right, this is too good to pass up. But the moment you're on board, get below. I don't want anybody to see you."

Grinning, Pepi leapt on board and headed for the open door of the deckhouse. He felt wonderful. He was sailing away! To a new world! To his father! To a new life!

"Captain," the aide said, "we've got Teritekas. He had three hundred fifty copper pieces on him."

"Wonderful! Bring him in." The captain turned to Seth. "My men do good work when they set their mind to it."

"Uh . . . Captain," Ergamenes said, "there's a problem. The guard who caught him had to throw a rock at him. It caught him right on the temple. There's a fracture. We can't seem to wake him up."

"Gods!" the captain hissed. "Don't tell me we've killed the first lead we've had!"

"He's not dead, sir. But the outlook isn't too good." He brightened. "I was also bringing you a report from another of the men. The home of one of the principal receivers of stolen goods was raided a few minutes ago. They found the missing jewelry."

Seth snorted. "Did he identify Teritekas as the one who sold it to him?"

The aide grinned. "Better than that. He discreetly followed Teritekas down the street and saw him dividing the loot with the boy."

"Well, isn't that wonderful?" the captain grumbled. "We've got everyone but the boy and his mother, and they're the only ones who really matter in this whole thing."

Seth patted the captain's shoulder. "Don't be too hard on yourself. We think we know where the boy is."

"You do, sir? Where?"

"Probably on his way downriver, following his mother." He shuddered. "What an unpleasant surprise he has ahead of him!"

The captain looked at Seth's face. The late afternoon sun fell on it sharply, and the light was not kind to him. He looked old, very old. "What are you going to do?"

Seth stared wordlessly at him with eyes that held no hope.

The hour was very late. Mai reached to pat Seth's side of the bed and found it empty. She rose, put on her robe, and padded to the door. In the hall she took down a candle, lit it from an overhead torch, and walked softly down to the great central hall.

Seth sat before a guttering fire, staring glumly at the flames. As she entered, he looked up at her.

Mai frowned with extreme annoyance. In one stroke, Neftis and her son had rendered Seth an uncertain, prematurely old man, as he had been when she had brought him south a decade before.

"Come to bed, darling."

"Ten years," he moaned. "I've let ten years go by, and I've done nothing for either of them."

"Seth, don't start that," she said tersely.

"Iri placed Neftis in my care. It hardly matters that he didn't know she was expecting a child at the time. I've been derelict in my duty."

"You haven't! I won't let you say a thing like that about yourself!"

"Mai, Apedemek will kill her, as if she were an insect."

"Seth, you can't—"

"But the boy's in greater danger. He goes to his father,

looking for a hero to worship. Apedemek will slowly, painstakingly mold him into a copy of the worst man in the world!"

"Seth, what are you going to do?"

"I have no choice. This time I'll kill Apedemek, or die myself."

CHAPTER THIRTEEN

The Nile Delta

I

"I don't understand," Dathan protested peevishly. "Do you know what they'll do if you leave now? It's bad enough when you're here, but when you're not around to handle the overseers . . ."

Aaron sighed. Dathan had a way of always testing a man's patience. Everyone had hoped he would mellow as he grew older, but ten years had passed, and he was still angry, high-strung, and fidgety. "It's not something I can discuss. Don't worry, I'll be back soon."

"Huh! 'Don't worry,' he says. Easy enough to say! But when the overseers start in again about—"

"I know, I know. I'll talk to them when I get back. But an emergency has arisen, and—"

"An emergency! Every day is an emergency around here! Aaron, ever since the order came down from Kamose, the pressure has been building. Ever since you appointed me foreman of my crew, I've had a daily tongue-lashing from the overseers. Yesterday they told me that if I couldn't keep my unit up to quota, they were going to beat me."

Aaron frowned. Appointing Dathan to a position of responsibility had been a bad idea, which he had regretted from the first. Yet he could not revoke the appointment; it would be a matter of losing face with the Egyptians. "I'm sorry, but I can't do anything about that until I get back. You'll just have to get on as well as you can without me until then."

"Because you can't be bothered to do your duty?"

"That's enough, Dathan."

Dathan did not perceive the change in Aaron's tone. He was about to continue in the same harrying vein, but then he saw the glint in Aaron's eye. "All right," he conceded in a surly voice. "But if someone hits me, I won't be answerable for what I—"

"You *will* be answerable for everything you do, or I will replace you as foreman of your unit." His eyes fixed Dathan in his place. "If you are not up to this job, I will find someone who is. I promise you that."

"But—"

"I cannot afford to have anyone in a position of authority who is not capable of standing between our people and the overseers, which includes taking the blows and the burdens off their backs. Tell me now: Are you up to the job or not?"

Dathan cringed under his steady gaze. "I . . . I suppose."

"There isn't any 'suppose' about it. Either you can or you cannot."

Dathan snorted, but he bent his head. "All right. But you'd better be back soon, or—"

"Or what? Are you threatening me?"

"No, no. It's all right. Just come back soon."

Aaron looked Dathan hard in the eyes, fearing he was going to cause real trouble someday. Perhaps it would be better to get rid of him now, before he folded under pressure at a crucial time when nothing but strength would do. But then he remembered the overriding importance of his errand. He sighed and gave in. "I'll be back as soon as I can."

"What do we tell the overseers if they ask about you?"

"Tell them I'm trying to find a good source of straw. That ought to satisfy them, considering the fuss they've been making over that business."

"All right. I'll try." Dathan nodded and went away.

Aaron watched him go. He pursed his lips and blew out violently. *What a trial he is,* he thought. *If God were to offer me the choice of keeping him or trading him for a foreigner, an unbeliever—what would I say?*

Kamose's most recent order had made things more difficult for the Habiru. The king had decided that the Egyptians no longer needed to provide straw for the Habiru brickmakers and had ordered the Habiru to provide their own. Aaron had futilely pointed out that the Habiru could not gather straw and maintain the same punishing daily quotas of bricks. His protest had earned him threats of violence, to himself and to every man who failed to maintain his production quota.

It was admittedly a bad time to go away, but the order had come in his sleep, from the God of his people: *I am Yahweh—He Who Is. Go into the wilderness to meet your brother. The time has come.*

"The time has come!" At first he had not fully understood the implications. After he had awakened, sat up, and thought for many minutes about the Voice, there was no doubt in his mind what God—Yahweh—had meant: It was the time of the deliverance of the Habiru from bondage, from their long exile in a hateful foreign land. And he and his brother, Moses, were among the instruments of this miracle.

He wondered what Moses was like now. There had been no contact at all between them for ten years. Aaron felt a tug at his heart. His brother had turned out to be such a delightful surprise, and yet he had no sooner met Moses than lost him. It would be good to see him. Aaron smiled, thinking of it.

From the moment he had known his brother was alive, he had known that it was not to be his own fate to lead his people back to Canaan. Last night's dream had confirmed this. God had told him to go into the wilderness and meet his brother, who would be the promised Deliverer. Aaron found this easy to accept. He knew his own gifts—those of the speaker and the second in command. He could organize things well on a short-term basis, but the long line tended to evade him.

In truth, he did not really wish to lead. He had only been forced to act as liaison between the Egyptians and Habiru by the lack of a better man. When the time came to lay down this increasingly irksome burden, he would be glad to do so and would pity the man forced to assume it.

Life had become increasingly cruel for his people since Kamose had come to the delta. The reason had not been hard to find: Apedemek had come with the king.

Aaron shuddered, thinking of Apedemek. Other men were led astray by evil; Apedemek embraced it, indeed created it where there had been none.

He had only met the man once, and that had been enough to frighten him. The knowledge that Apedemek could control other men's minds, forcing them to do his bidding, saved Aaron from coming under that control himself. He had for a heartbeat looked into those amazing eyes, and he had immediately forced himself to look away.

Now the thought struck him, and his heart skipped a beat: Had Moses ever looked into Apedemek's eyes?

And if he had, had he been able to withstand them?

II

After Amasis had been allowed to cool his heels in the anteroom for a full two hours, Neb-mertef gave the order to have him shown in. But even as the servant went out to invite the ex-regent inside, Neb-mertef took pains to receive Amasis in a fashion that asserted his present superiority aggressively and demeaningly.

Thus, when Amasis was ushered brusquely through the door, Neb-mertef greeted his former employer from a high dais, like the one the king used for his morning divans. He sat behind a long table, his legs hidden by drapery; he allowed himself to be seen fiddling with a spread-out papyrus, pretending to read the document intently. He made Amasis stand before him for two minutes, fidgeting uncomfortably, before he looked up.

"Oh, it's you," he said. "Do you have the figures for me on the fig harvest?"

"No, I don't," Amasis said irritably. "That isn't why I'm

here, and you know it. I left instructions with your servant to tell you I was coming in today to—"

"You don't have the fig-harvest statistics?" Neb-mertef asked with mock incredulity. "I left orders that you were to have them in my hands by today! Can't I trust you with anything?"

"Don't start in on that!" Amasis shot back. "You know good and well no such message was delivered. I'm on to your little games. You know why I'm here, but you don't want to talk about it."

"I'll thank you," Neb-mertef said frostily, "to remember to whom you're talking. I won't put up with it. Unless you can abide by the rules of court courtesy, you can go right back out that door and make another appointment for when your temper's under control."

Amasis' eyes were mere slits. "You've grown very mighty in recent years, but I can remember when you were no more than a cringing, fawning—"

"You try my patience too far!"

"You may have Kamose fooled, but I see through everything you do. For instance, he thinks that you can foretell the future—you had me bamboozled that way for a time too, I'll admit—"

"Silence!"

This time, however, Amasis could not be stopped. "I have incontrovertible proof that while I was regent, you were employing the services of an astrologer named Set-Nakht and passing off his predictions as your own."

This was startling enough to make Neb-mertef drop the papyrus in his hands; it rolled itself up and fell on the floor. "Set-Nakht?" He sounded less confident, less arrogant. "Do you know where he is?"

"Hah!" Amasis sneered triumphantly. "You still haven't found him, have you? He got away the day of the fire, and you've never been able to replace him to your satisfaction—or to the king's either, have you?" He knew he had struck a vulnerability. The bribe he had paid for this had been worth every *outnou*. "The king is beginning to doubt you because the new man isn't anywhere as accurate as Set-Nakht was. You've had a succession of seers, haven't you? How many? Three? Four?"

All color drained from Neb-mertef's face, and no words would come.

"When Kamose decided to degrade me," Amasis pressed on, "you took my place by convincing him that you could predict the future. But you'd need help predicting the direction the sun will travel across the sky tomorrow." A mean smile twisted his face. "The male whores you were buying . . . they weren't for you, were they? They were for your pet magus."

He could see how accurate his sallies had been from the look on Neb-mertef's face. "It all falls into place," he said in a voice mellow with deep satisfaction. "I wonder what Kamose would say if he was to know what a fake you are."

"You won't tell him!" Neb-mertef said. "He won't listen to you. He hasn't listened to you in years."

"That's true," Amasis admitted. "I acted very stupidly with regard to Kamose. I kept putting off killing him, when I should have done it as soon as he returned from Canaan and Syria."

"You dare speak of this openly, here in my own chamber?"

"Of course," Amasis said mildly. His smile was reptilian. "No one's listening to us. Tell me now about your magus. How are you getting him to cooperate? Such people usually prefer to get the credit for their predictions."

"N-none of your business!" Neb-mertef fumed. "Now get out before I have you thrown out!"

"Whatever you say," Amasis said with exquisite mock politeness. "But aren't you afraid of where I'll go? Of what I'll do? Of to whom I may speak? I may not be able to speak directly to the king anymore, but there are any number of people in the court who still speak to me and who have the king's ear."

"Now wait a minute—"

"There are dozens of people who would jump at the chance to expose you for a fraud."

Neb-mertef scowled. "What is it that you want?"

"I'm not sure what I want to do just now. But we can agree, can't we, that our relationship has suddenly improved?"

Neb-mertef's expression wavered between worry and resentment. "I . . . I think we can come to some sort of accommodation. In the meantime, I ask you to avoid doing anything hasty."

"Hasty?" Amasis echoed in a silky voice. "Nothing could be farther from my mind, I assure you. I was thinking of moving slowly, deliberately. I was hasty before, and I have learned my lesson. It took me quite a while to come up with today's revelations, and I intend to use them to my best advantage."

Neb-mertef's face was slowly beginning to assume a crafty expression. "I think that deliberation would suit both our purposes. After all"—he looked right and left nervously—"we do have a few things in common, among them a certain number of enemies."

"To be precise, one particular enemy," Amasis said. "And he is more than one man can handle. If there ever was a perfect time to discuss our common problem concerning him, it's now, while he's away on business."

"I don't like this," Neb-mertef quavered, stepping down from the dais. "He could be right here right now, and we wouldn't know."

"*You* wouldn't know, perhaps," Amasis said, "but I would. That trick with the eyes—it doesn't work on me. He tried it, and he failed, and he knows it. They taught us about that sort of thing back in the North, when I first came to serve the Great Goddess."

"You withstood him? When Seth of Thebes couldn't?"

Amasis nodded. "I did. There's a certain kind of mind that cannot be controlled. To be among the most vulnerable, one must have an active imagination. Seth of Thebes, like other brilliant men, is surprisingly defenseless against superstition if approached in the right way."

"There is some sense in what you say," Neb-mertef allowed. "I have a certain imaginative tendency, and the one time he tried it on me—" He shuddered.

"Exactly. But what if I offered to teach you how to withstand his assaults?"

"That would be extraordinarily useful. Could we hide from him the fact that we were not under his control?"

"I'm not sure. I don't know how I could test it, either. I don't move in Apedemek's circles anymore."

"I could change that."

Amasis locked eyes with Neb-mertef. "I am gratified by your willingness to cooperate."

"Allow me to be frank: better no partnership than one in which we cannot trust each other. In order to work with you, I would have to feel that you would not suddenly betray me to the king."

Amasis nodded agreement. "I can see that that would be important in such a relationship."

Neb-mertef continued. "I could get you into places that are now barred to you. I could lift restrictions that the king has imposed on you. But this would all have to be handled very discreetly. Kamose must not know."

"Surely not. Then we are partners against Apedemek? Against the king if need be?"

Neb-mertef hesitated, but only for a moment. "Done," he said, and they clasped hands to seal the bargain.

III

All the way home Neb-mertef struggled with mixed emotions. *What have I done?* he asked himself again and again. Had he made a pact with a monster who would betray him?

Neb-mertef knew there was no use having any illusions about Amasis, having served him for years before the tables had been turned. Amasis was concerned only for himself, for self-aggrandizement at the expense of everyone with whom he came into contact.

Then why had he committed himself to a partnership with the man? He stopped in the middle of the street, thinking about it, and pedestrians had to move around him. *I need him,* he admitted. *As he needs me. We can benefit from working against Apedemek, in particular.*

Yes, that made sense. Apedemek was a wild animal loose among the flocks. You never knew what he was going to do next, and the people he had in thrall might well include those closest to you. They might be reporting to him, and you would never know.

Gods! What if he knows about Agha of Chaldea? Why, *that would mean—* A wave of fear washed over him, and he felt an urgent need to see Agha, to reassure himself.

He turned and hurried down the side street, toward the apartment where Agha lived.

As he walked, he looked at the construction work, which had raised Avaris from the ashes of the devastating fire a decade before. Everywhere there were Habiru, mixing mud bricks here, stacking them there; raising high walls; framing windows; dressing wood for the half-timbered residential buildings.

Cattle, he thought. *Less than human.* How glad he would be when the restoration was completed and the Habiru could be done away with!

He knew that there were too many of them to kill, for all Kamose's threats. Besides, the Egyptians had gotten used to having a slave caste do all the dirty work. The citizens of the delta were not about to assume the messy, backbreaking jobs.

He scowled, watching the Habiru. *Dirty foreigners!* When the work was done, they might all be dispersed into the country nomes, to do the hard labor for the yokels. At least then he would not have to put up with their alienness, their *differentness.*

He had to step out of the way as a slave, burdened down with a heavy load of bricks, staggered and almost ran into him. He cursed at the man as he passed. If he had had a staff with him, he would have struck the fellow a blow. *Damned rabble!*

"Wake up!" the servant urged.

Agha of Chaldea raised his head off his folded arms and blinked. "Wh-what do you want?"

The servant shook him. "One of the boys spotted the boss heading this way. If he finds you in this condition—"

Agha groaned. "I'm sick."

The servant snorted. "If I were you, I'd try to improve my appearance before he gets here. You look like you've been sleeping in a pigsty, and you smell like the bunghole of a palm-wine barrel." He sneered. "At least comb the hair out of your eyes."

Agha did so, using his fingers. "I feel awful."

"Here's a basin of water. Wash your face."

"All right. But bring me a drink. I've got to have a drink."

"You don't need a drink; you need a bath. If there were time, I'd dunk you in the river and—"

"If you did, Neb-mertef would have you decorating a spit before nightfall."

The servant made the sign against the evil eye.

"Think about that while you're scouting me up some thing to drink."

"If you get to work, maybe I'll think about it. Isn't there something you promised to have for him by—"

"Oh, eternal gods, I forgot! The horoscope! The horoscope on the cataclysm. And on the two upcoming feast days. I haven't even begun. For the love of Bast, man, get me a scroll! Where are my brushes? They were right here yesterday!"

"You haven't picked up a brush in a week. And as for charting the stars, you're too bleary-eyed to see that far. I'll bet you can't even tell me how many flies there are on the ceiling right now."

"You smart-mouthed son of a dog, get me a drink. I'll throw something together. If I can find a clean scroll . . . here, this ought to do. Get me water for making ink. I can use this brush. Gods! Filthy thing! Now, there, let me see: the sun here, the moon there, the evening star over—"

"Come on. Wash up, then you can get to work. He'll be along before you know it, and if he finds you looking like this, you're in trouble, and probably I am too."

"Oh, all right," Agha said in a phlegmy, alcoholic voice. He weaved to the table and looked in the bronze mirror above the basin. *Do I really look like that?* He winced. Bleary-eyed, gray hair and beard streaked with dirt, sallow skin sick looking and slack, a general look of puffiness. *Nobody would believe how young I am. I wouldn't believe it myself if I didn't know.*

He splashed his face with the water, then splashed it again, shook his head, and took down a comb, attacking his matted hair and beard.

I should stop drinking. Perhaps I could get away somewhere and straighten up. It wouldn't take long. Get on a healthy diet, start taking care of myself.

He closed his eyes, knowing in his heart of hearts that it was not going to happen. He had tried once or twice. The days were not so bad, usually. He could get through the days if he kept working steadily. But the nights! The nights!

Lying awake and discarding every fantasy he had harbored during the day—illusions of how brilliant he was, how he was going to make something of himself, how he would find a beautiful wife with a fat dowry and family connections.

When the moon was full and bright, he was prey to every known madness, and he would not be able to last out the night without a drink.

The horoscopes, he thought. *I have to do something about them, and quickly. But what?*

The answer was the same as it had been the last six times: Fake it. Fake up something quick and shabby and sleazy and put him off with that. Neb-mertef wanted to hear only good news anyway, as reassurance against his insecurities— Kamose apparently never looked at the charts and surely did not know any more about the Chaldean system than Neb-mertef did. *But what if another Chaldean shows up at court?*

That thought led to the worst of all: What if Apedemek were to look at those fake charts? Surely Apedemek would know the real from the bogus. What if Apedemek knew already? What if he was on to Neb-mertef and his imposture and was simply playing with him?

He bent over the basin to splash his burning face again. *You've got to do a real chart this time. And you've got to teach Neb-mertef how to make the exposition of the chart look authentic, because if Neb-mertef falls, you fall. You haven't the resiliency you once had, and this time the failure may spell the end for you.*

He wrung his hands. His fingers were like brittle sticks. His throat was dry. His hands shook. He searched his mind for the knowledge—was it still there? Did he remember how to cast the charts? Did he still have a magus's skills? Or had he simply faked it too long?

He put his hands over his face. "Where's that drink you promised me?" he shouted. "Damn you! Get me something to drink!"

IV

Aaron had ridden all day on his borrowed horse along the track Moses had taken ten years before when he had gone into exile. First the track had pointed due east; then, as the land became level, the route had curved to the south, toward the Red Sea.

Now, at day's end, Aaron's pony began to limp slightly, so he dismounted to examine the animal's hoof. "Ah, I see that both of us could use a good night's rest. We will stop here, my little friend." He hobbled the animal and set about making camp.

The desert nightfall was dramatic. The sun would dive into the western horizon; there would be a moment or two of afterglow; then all would be eternal night, and he would be alone with the million stars.

I must be outside Egypt altogether now. It would be the first time he had ever been outside the alien country where he had been born; it was a strange, unsettling feeling. Yet soon he would help Moses lead their people across hundreds—perhaps thousands—of leagues of forbidding desert to the land God had promised them. They would probably be met with hostility from the people who had taken over the land and would encounter the savage Ishmaelites, the blood enemies of his people. Fierce Bedouin warriors from the desert lands of Edom, the Ishmaelites were the descendants of Abraham, like the Habiru. But the Ishmaelites' descent came through the patriarch's concubine, not his lawful wife.

Aaron fanned a tiny flame into a larger one and added fuel he had brought in his saddlebag. He shuddered. Alone in the desert! *What am I doing here? I have none of the traveler's skills.* He looked toward the south.

Across the expanse of alkali flat he could make out a lone figure on horseback moving slowly toward him. Aaron stood, squinting. The figure's shoulders were broad, and although the face could not be made out under the hooded robe he wore, there was something about the stature, the stance, the posture . . .

"Moses!" he cried out, and rushed forward to greet him, just as the last rays of the sun died.

*   *   *

Agha's hands shook as he looked down at the nearly illegible squiggles his unsteady fist had made. *I must have committed a major miscalculation somewhere.* But where? He had checked and rechecked his charts.

He licked his lips. *I need a drink. Oh, how I need a drink.* But of course that was impossible. All the servants had heard Neb-mertef's temper tantrum that afternoon.

Having completed the first chart, he almost wished he had been doing the work properly all along. Something of paramount importance had slipped by him, and it was imperative that he cast and recast horoscopes over the last year to see if he could pinpoint the event. He would have to project horoscopes of individual days in the future, to see if he could accurately assess the time the cataclysmic events would occur. He peered at his calculations in the light of the flickering lamp. They were difficult to read—the blunted brush did not even approximate the clean meeting of stylus and clay—but the meaning was nonetheless clear. The reassurances he had given Neb-mertef all this time had been bald-faced lies. The great upheaval, which would cause whole civilizations to die in one stroke—was at last at hand. It could happen tomorrow.

Gods! he thought desperately. *I need a drink. I need a drink* now!

Aaron looked across the wind-whipped flames of the camp fire into his brother's calm eyes, reveling in his company. "There is no doubt, then? This is the time, at last?"

"Most of my adult life has been spent in a condition of doubt," Moses said in a peaceful voice that Aaron did not remember from before. "But at last I am totally sure because God has spoken to you too."

Aaron hesitated. "I'm used to being an earnest plodder, steady and earthbound. All of a sudden I'm expected to walk with you on the heights. I think I am more afraid of this than of any danger involved in the thing we are told to do."

"I understand," Moses said. "I find myself thinking, '*Me,* Lord?' But if He has chosen me, then I must be up to the task. The same should be true of you."

"Tell me everything you know."

"We are to meet with the great king." He said this in all

humility, as if he himself had not been groomed for the throne Kamose now occupied. "We are to tell him the words of Yahweh, that 'Israel is My firstborn son, and I order you to let him go, to offer Me worship. If you refuse to let him go, I shall put your own firstborn to death.'"

"Kamose has no children," Aaron pointed out.

"I think God means the firstborn of the Egyptians."

Aaron's eyes widened. "Do you remember those stories about Kamose's youth? His father ordered that all the ten-year-old boys be put to death."

"I know. He'll be infuriated by that threat, but we must make it anyway. We are not speaking for ourselves; we are passing along what God will do if Kamose does not agree to let our people come here to the wilderness for three days to worship Him."

"Kamose is stupid and vicious enough to kill the bearers of evil tidings."

"If we obey the will of God, nothing will happen to us."

Aaron was deeply moved. "I will obey without question and hope that my faith may come to equal yours."

"It will," Moses assured him. He sat cross-legged on his blanket, his arms folded over his broad chest. "We have spent our entire lives in an unnatural state, depending on our own will to get us through bad times. The work of our wills is never stronger than a house built on sand; the smallest tremor can destroy it. The things God wishes us to do, in which we give up our own will and abandon ourselves to His, are built to last forever. Only your return to the precarious self-willed state can bring them down."

Aaron bowed his head. "Think of me as a tablet upon which no stylus has written," he said fervently. "Teach me, my brother."

CHAPTER FOURTEEN

Thebes

I

The boatman dropped anchor halfway across the river. "All right. Nobody will hear us. You understand the need for precaution: Seth was well liked around here, and if word got around that I'd told you where he'd gone—"

"I understand," Apedemek cut in. "Get on with it."

But the boatman chose this moment to misjudge the man he was speaking to. "It seems to me that the information is worth more money than we talked about. I'm a poor man. I have people to support. The tax bills alone up here are—"

Apedemek's eyes narrowed. "Look at me!" he commanded.

Startled, the boatman obeyed, locking eyes with Apedemek and finding himself unable to look away.

"There, now," Apedemek said. "You can't move a muscle. You can't refuse me anything. Whatever I tell you to do, you will obey."

The boatman's eyes reflected his terror. He could not move.

"There's a good boy," Apedemek continued in a patronizing voice. "Now, you rat's whelp, where is Seth of Thebes? How recent is your news? Who told you?"

The boatman found himself blabbing everything. "Seth was in Nubia as recently as two months ago, living in great state as the father of King Het. This, from a trader—a reliable man."

"How did he elude the men I had watching the river?"

"He went overland to the Second Cataract. This I heard from a caravan driver who calls on El-Kharga. Someone smuggled Seth out to the oasis along the desert path. Some say the man who took him there was the soldier who had escaped to the oasis with Queen Mara."

"Ah. That makes sense. That probably means that the women of the oasis still send spies into Deir el Bahari."

"Yes. Little happens in Egypt that Weret does not soon learn about."

Apedemek looked the wretched puppet up and down. "Nubia, eh? And that via the land route? That's not much information to be paying you all that money for, you chiseling bastard. I don't think I'll pay you anything. And you'll thank me for the privilege of swindling you."

"Yes, my lord. I am eternally grateful. A thousand pardons for my earlier behavior."

"I tire of you. You will step to the gunwale and jump overboard when I next say the word *yes*. When you enter the water, your arms and legs will not move, and you will inhale the water as if it were air. As you go overboard, you will silently thank me." He smiled nastily. "That's all." He paused. "Yes!"

Bracing his feet against the redistribution of weight in the boat, he watched as the boatman leapt overboard, bobbed to the surface, as stiff as a board, then was carried downriver by the current, rolling over and over like a log in a torrent.

Apedemek snorted as he reached over for the anchor line. Looking up, he noticed another boatman watching him from upstream. He shrugged in mock helplessness. "There wasn't a thing I could do," he said in a voice not meant to carry.

At the docks he was recognized, so the people on shore who had come to protest what they had seen—one man drowning, another making no move to save him—took one look at those terrible eyes and backed away. He stepped ashore and secured the boat as if someone were going to come and make use of it, then strode past the timid souls, daring them to disapprove.

He was glad he was widely recognized; he did not want people to come too close—not unless they were prey, and then he wanted to initiate the meeting. Control of every situation was all-important.

He walked up the slope toward the city, looking directly at no one, savoring the crowd's fear from his peripheral vision. He was further satisfied that, as the day came to an end, he had gleaned information about the fate of his old nemesis, Seth of Thebes. That was, after all, the purpose of his return to the city, although he was not certain just why Seth had taken on such importance in his life.

He had twice defeated Seth; he should have killed the man. Seth had escaped physical destruction in both meetings, and there was the chance that he might strike back.

Perhaps his desire to find Seth was based on the fact that the man he had killed ten years ago—Hieron, of the Order of Chalybia—had told him the order was closing in on him. If there had been any truth to this threat, then Seth presented a clear and present danger. He had witnessed Apedemek's defeat at Hieron's hands, and if Seth ever managed to make direct contact with the Grand Council . . .

He cringed. That was a distinct and frightening possibility. He had known from the first that in a contest with Seth, he, Apedemek, would always be the winner. But Hieron had been only the advance man for an even more powerful member of the order—one capable of snapping him like a dry twig. Would Demetrios send another agent to confront him, or would he come himself? .

Apedemek entered the city's all-but-deserted streets. Thebes was little more than a ghost town, now that the court had been gone for ten years. The few people he passed were miserable, defeated nonentities who had not been able to afford relocation to the delta.

He headed through the back alleys, seeking a shortcut to the old palace quarter. A movement, quick and furtive, shot out from deep shadow, and his preoccupation blunted his response. He put up one hand to ward off the blow, but the assailant lunged under his arm, and the knife slid into his chest.

Apedemek staggered back against the building, then looked down. The knife protruded from his body halfway down his rib cage. The shock of it hit him then, and he put a hand on the handle, trying to ease it out. When it came loose and clattered to the ground, a rush of blood stained his robe's front.

He slid slowly down the wall, the rough brick clawing at his back. At last he sat in the dirt alley, glassy-eyed, clutching his side, focusing on the tattered scarecrow who had stabbed him.

"W-who are you?" he asked in a voice grown suddenly weak. "Why did you attack me?"

The figure raised one frail arm, and Apedemek threw up a hand to ward off a blow. "No!" he begged. "Don't! Leave me alone. . . ."

He let the words trail off as the emaciated form made no new move toward him. He looked at the shaking hands, the unsteady posture, the thin, bare feet, and the haggard face, ravaged by dissipation and near madness. The eyes betrayed the identity at last. He had seen them before. "I know you," he said.

"Of course you do," she hissed. "Monster! Rapist! Murderer! Torturer!"

She had aged twenty years in the last ten—but he knew her.

"Neftis," he whispered. "You!"

II

Instead of responding, Neftis reached down and in one lightning-swift movement retrieved the blood-smeared knife. He waved one ineffectual hand but could not stop her. She moved back and crouched, full of tension, glaring at him.

"I hope you die slowly, painfully. I wish there were

some way of showing you how you've made me feel all these years."

He pressed one hand to his chest, stanching the flow of blood, and used the other hand to lever himself to his knees. The pain was not extreme, and he wondered if this was a good sign or a bad one. He put one foot on the ground and tensed himself for the rise to his feet.

"You get up and I'll stab you again," she threatened. "Maybe I'll cut your throat this time."

He looked up at her, remembering. "I didn't do anything to you. Everything that happened, you did to yourself."

"I know." Her voice was full of self-loathing. "But it wouldn't have happened if it weren't for—"

"Ah," he said through clenched teeth. "Do I have to listen to the sad, sad story about the wicked man bending the poor virgin to his will? How the nasty old lecher stole her precious innocence?" He gathered his strength and stood. She shrank back, and the setting sun, slanting in a golden shaft of light between two buildings, glinted on the red-stained knife blade.

"Is that it?" he demanded. "It's all black and white, isn't it? I'm all bad, and you were pure, unspoiled. You can load the blame on me, thus easing the conscience that's been troubling you all these years, right?"

She clutched the knife with both hands. He kept a nervous eye on the blade tip. "I can live with what I did to myself," she retorted. "It's not pleasant, but I could deal with it except that—"

She seemed to be getting at something new. "Except what?" he wanted to know.

Her dark eyes flashed with hatred. "I'm not the whole story. My life is ruined, and it's true that I did it to myself. I accept that. But you! You poison the lives of innocent people, just as you poisoned the blood of your son—"

The revelation shocked Apedemek as much as her indiscretion now jolted her. She shrank back, and the knife almost fell from her hands.

"Son?" he erupted with a triumphant smile. "A son of my own blood, and by you?" He straightened, still clutching his side. He looked down; little new blood was coming through.

He was not as badly wounded as he had feared. He looked back at her with renewed interest.

"My son!" he said. "I hadn't known!"

"I didn't mean to tell you," she confessed. "B-besides, he died a long time ago."

"You're lying. He's alive—and he knows about me." He sneered. "He's getting curious, isn't he? He wants to know what his father is like, doesn't he? If I'm as bad as I'm said to be?"

He threw back his head and laughed. She could withhold nothing from him. "He has the birthmark, doesn't he? A Child of the Lion, and from both sides of the family! Well, I'm going to find him! I'll raise him my way!" The jubilation died suddenly as he demanded, "Where is he?"

She edged back, grasping the knife tightly, trying to avoid his eyes. "I'm not going to tell you. Far away, where you'll never get your filthy hands on him."

Apedemek moved toward her but was stopped by a sudden stab of pain. "Where are you keeping him?" His tension honed his voice to a sharp edge.

"You stay away from me!"

He kept one hand on his wound and reached out toward her with the other. "Come on," he said softly. "I'll get it out of you sooner or later." He knew better than to threaten her. He fought to remain calm. "You don't want to oppose me. Think of all I can do for the boy. I'm very powerful now, the power behind the king—and that's just the beginning. By the time I'm done, there'll be a single authority in charge of the whole Crescent, everything from the Libyan border to the Hittite marches. I will be the man behind it."

The knife waved in her trembling hand, and her feet did not move away from him.

"There, now," he said soothingly. "Just give me the knife, Neftis. He's my son too, and I have a responsibility to him. We have to think about his future. He has to be well provided for. He has to be well educated. I can see that he is apprenticed to the best masters, in any discipline you prefer. I wouldn't think of doing anything without consulting you, but we have to talk this over."

It was the tone that did it. She looked up at him just

once, and he had her. She tried to tear herself away. "Oh, no!" she moaned. "Please . . ."

"It's quite true, of course, I do have responsibility to the boy—to make certain he isn't raised according to the kind of mindless, smarmy banalities he's likely to hear around Seth of Thebes—" He understood at last. A dark light glittered in his eyes. "Of course! You went to Nubia with Seth. You've all been living under the protection of Het and Tharbis, haven't you? Answer me! Answer me, you little bitch!"

She managed somehow to stagger back a step or two.

"I can just imagine the sort of pious balderdash Seth has been filling the boy's head with. *My* boy, curse him! Well, those days are over. I'll teach him that the only things that matter are will and power. Ambition! I'll teach him ambition!"

"Leave him alone," she said miserably. "He's just a little boy. He's confused. He doesn't know who he is."

He could still feel the pain, but a feeling of excitement grew within him. He was bursting with insane energy. "Doesn't know who he is, does he? I'll teach him! He's the son of Apedemek! The one to carry on in my footsteps and take up the burden when I lay it down!" He laughed, but the laugh turned into a cough. He looked down at his hand; there was more blood seeping from the wound, and he was feeling dizzy.

"To find him you'll have to enter Nubia," she taunted, "where there's a price on your head."

"Empty threats," he said. "No Nubian can stop me from doing anything I want to." He let out a nasty laugh. "Ask the queen. I've had *her*, just as I had you."

There was such malice in his voice that Neftis's fingers tightened on the handle of the knife and she moved as if to lunge at him. Instead she made a valiant effort to turn the knife on herself; but he kicked out viciously, knocking the knife away.

"There now," he said. "Do you know what we're going to do? We're going to send a message to Seth of Thebes, telling him to release the boy to your custody. We'll say that you've found a good, safe situation in Thebes, far from such dangers as I represent, and that you want the boy to join you."

"I'll never do it!"

"You most certainly will. You defied me once, but you can't do it again. There's no Hieron to defend you. We're here alone, just the two of us."

Beads of sweat covered her forehead. Her mouth moved, her skin taut with the effort, but no words came out. Her hands became carved claws.

Then, to Apedemek's amazement, the light went out of Neftis's eyes. One moment her expression had been desperate, yes, but intelligent and full of purpose. The next, there was nothing there at all. Her lower lip gaped. The dark eyes opened wide but saw nothing. Her face registered no emotions, no reactions, no understanding.

"Gods!" he exploded. "The little bitch has escaped me! She's retreated into madness!"

The eyes left him to follow a butterfly passing nearby. She made the cooing sounds of an idiot deprived of speech. She squatted, her hands trailing in the dust as she relieved herself.

Aware again of the pain from his wound, he pressed his hand more tightly to his chest. Where was the Street of Physicians? Surely someone must remain in Thebes to minister to the sparse population. With a curse he staggered down the street, wincing with every step, leaving the madwoman wretched in the dirt, uttering meaningless sounds. His heart was leaping wildly, and he was shivering uncontrollably. The Street of Physicians! Where was it?

III

The morning had come and gone, and part of the afternoon with it, but not a single customer had come to the pottery stall that Khem and his wife, Mut, continued to maintain in the main market of Thebes. Khem had been frustrated by the matter for an hour, and now, looking around at the nearly empty square in the baking sun, he pulled the barrow from under the stand and began to stack his pots neatly in the top of it.

"What *are* you doing, Khem?" his old woman asked. "The sun is still high. A customer may yet come our way."

"It is my considered opinion, my dear Mut, after prolonged ratiocination, that there is a blight upon this day. The chance of our seeing the smallest financial profit by sundown is nil."

Mut stared at him. When Khem began speaking this formally there was little use in arguing with him. She cast her eyes heavenward with a great sigh. "Gods defend me! Who will take me in when my husband has, in his folly, got me evicted into the street with my few possessions?"

"I am impressed by your performance, my dear Mut," her husband commended. "I am sure that the mountebanks of the quays would be appreciative to the point of adoration, if indeed they ever bothered to make a stop in Thebes anymore. Nevertheless, the day is one of great beauty, and there is a most delicious breeze coming up from the river. The pleasures of commerce, even on a profitable day, must occasionally give way to the simpler enjoyment of walking along the shore and taking one's ease in the satisfying company of one's spouse."

"My," Mut said, "we *are* possessed by eloquence today, aren't we?"

"Indeed, my dear. Surely if a thing is worth saying, it is worth saying in a fashion fit to gladden the ear and exercise the mind."

Khem made a flourish worthy of an ambassador calling on a queen. "Come, let us close the shop and derive the maximum enjoyment from existence."

"But how do you expect me to put bread upon our table?"

"The gods will provide, my dear Mut. If we had more money, there would be no one to spend it on. Our grandchildren took all their babies away, and with no young ones to squander it on, what do we need more money for?" He smiled, and there was, once again, the trace of the devastating, irresistibly youthful smile that had made him such a handsome man so many years before. "Are you going to help me load the cart?"

"Oh, you," she protested lovingly. "Why do I let you get

around me like that?" Her hands were already on the pots, stacking them neatly in the barrow.

Just as the old couple were leaving the square at one end, Apedemek lurched unsteadily into the marketplace at the other. His knees wobbled, and he was suffering from cold sweats and chills in the middle of a hot afternoon. Bleary-eyed, he looked around him and spotted a city guardsman, one of the tiny token force left behind.

"You!" he said. "Come here!"

The guardsman was a new recruit brought up from the militia at El-Kab and did not recognize Apedemek. He turned away, thinking Apedemek was a beggar grown insolent.

"Damn you!" Apedemek sputtered, holding onto a green-grocer's stall for support. "I'm hurt. I need help."

The guard looked at him again, scowled, and came closer, one hand on his sword hilt. Apedemek, even bent over, was taller than the guardsman, who was taking no chances. "Here, what's this? Are you trying to cause a disruption? You've picked the wrong man's shift. Now, move along—"

"You son of a whore!" Apedemek erupted. "Do you know whom you're talking to? Somebody stabbed me, and I've lost a lot of blood. If you don't help me get to a physician soon, you will find yourself in a desperate situation."

"You're threatening me? You filthy scum, I've got half a mind to—"

"Get me to a doctor, you swine! And hurry about it!" Apedemek's hand closed on the guardsman's wrist with a hysterical strength. The guardsman's first impulse was to pull away, but he could not; his second was to reach around with the wrong hand and yank his sword from its scabbard. But as he did so, he looked Apedemek in the eye. The dominance was established instantly.

"There now," Apedemek said through clenched teeth. "Get me to a doctor. Let me lean on you. I'm getting weak. If you get me there in time, I may let you live a day or so longer. Now get a move on!"

"Wait a moment," Mut said, setting down the handles of the cart. "This street doesn't go to the quays. It's a dead end."

"I must reluctantly contradict you, my dear," Khem said. "The king ordered a block of buildings torn out to make room for a warehouse to store lamp oil. The restructuring left a clear path to the river."

"This wasn't the street they did that to. Khem, I hate to say it, but your memory's failing."

"It is a well-known and well-attested fact that people bring matters of record to me, asking me to settle disputes. Would they do that with a man whose memory was anything less than painstakingly accurate in the smallest detail?"

"People used to do that, Khem, but that was a long time ago. You think it was only last week, but what you're talking about happened years ago."

Her expression changed so precipitately, that Khem turned to let his eyes follow her gaze. "My word! Whatever could *that* possibly be?"

"I don't know," she replied. "It looks like a child, all huddled up against that doorway. Oh, I hope the poor thing isn't hurt! Khem, look at that knife on the ground!"

The elderly couple hurried to flank the filthy figure on the ground. Mut reached down to raise the haggard face by the chin. "Dear, we're here to help you. Can you understand me?" After a moment she recognized the futility in this and turned back to Khem. "As crazy as they come," she said, shaking her head. "And look at her thin little arms. I bet she hasn't eaten in a week."

Khem peered at the tattered figure. "A most pitiful sight," he agreed. "But look at the cloth of her robes. That was a very expensive garment."

"So it was. It's very old." Mut looked closely at the madwoman's face. "I've seen this woman before, but I can't say where or when. Why don't you put that famous memory of yours to work and see if you can dredge up something to help me identify her?"

"I have an even better suggestion, my dear. She could use a bath, clean clothes, food, and a bed. Let's take her home."

"You're right, of course," she agreed. "Help me pull her to her feet, will you? We'll dump the pots from the cart and load her in that."

Khem glanced at her with affection, then complied. The

same crotchety old woman who had complained about taking
the afternoon off was asking him to abandon four days' work
at the potter's wheel to save a starving waif. *For a copper
outnou I'd grab her and hug her as if we were still twenty*, he
thought. But the thought did not become father to any action;
instead he chuckled and began to unload the pots, one eye on
his wife, holding the madwoman close, cooing softly and
reassuringly in her dirty and uncomprehending ear, and looking fifty years younger a young mother cuddling a frightened child, once lost but now found.

CHAPTER FIFTEEN

Avaris

I

"Yes, I know," Kamose said irritably. "I've heard that one before—several times. The great cataclysm that is supposed to wipe out whole cities. People have been prattling about that for years. Tell me something new."

"It is true," Neb-mertef acknowledged, "that the great conflagration has been expected for some time. But we of the craft have now consolidated our computations by consulting with one another, and we can predict with confidence that the time is at hand. If you'd only take a look at this chart I have here—"

"Charts!" Kamose fumed contemptuously. "Mumbo jumbo!" He turned his back on his adviser and paced rapidly, impatiently, in the great hall of his half-finished palace.

Neb-mertef, watching his back, smiled. Just thinking of the king's imminent downfall amused him. "Permit me then, Sire, to summarize the latest charts."

"Spare me! I know what you're going to say. What do you expect me to do? If a thing is foreordained, I can't do a thing about it."

"Perhaps you can, Sire," Neb-mertef suggested. "The charts say that the level of the Great Sea will rise, and shore cities will drown. If the residents were to be evacuated to higher ground and levees built—"

"At fabulous expense, no doubt." Kamose sneered. "With the work to be contracted out to one of your own firms, I suppose?"

Neb-mertef scowled. Kamose had grown quite bald across the top of his head. This and the leathery skin from his twenty years in the northern lands had aged him terribly. He had balked at displaying a bald scalp and had begun wearing a wig, pitch-black and shiny. The effect added another ten years to his age and made him look ridiculous. "Surely Your Majesty jests. I have never taken a day's profit from our association."

"Oh?" Kamose turned and stared. "Is that a fact, now? Then why did you award the contract for the wall murals in the new temple to that subcontractor friend of yours? His bid was the highest."

"One pays for quality, Sire. Would you have me put upon the walls of the Temple of Amon the work of anyone but the best artist in the Black Lands?"

"I'm told there are better in Thebes, and they work cheaper."

"Undoubtedly, Majesty. But some of them refuse to leave Deir el-Bahari."

"*Refuse!* They dare to refuse a commission from their king?"

"Of course, Majesty, I could have them brought here in chains, like the Habiru stoneworkers, but the problem with work done under that kind of pressure—" He stopped in the middle of his thought.

Kamose looked up, sharp-eyed. "What were you going to say?"

"Oh, nothing, Sire. I forgot to tell you that there is a delegation from the Habiru waiting to speak with you. I suppose that if they've waited this long for an audience . . ."

Kamose scowled, lifted the wig off his head, and scratched his gleaming pate. As he replaced the wig he said, "I suppose I should hear them out. Who are they? That fellow Aaron ben whatever?"

"Yes, Majesty," Neb-mertef confirmed, then paused. "And his brother, once known as Prince Moses."

There was a long silence; then Kamose smiled. "The mouse comes to make demands upon the cat, eh? Has he forgotten there is a price on his head?"

"After a certain period, Sire, a proscription has to be renewed, or it loses its force. It is the custom. Of course, the king can abolish custom anytime he wishes."

"So he can." Kamose grinned. "But in the meantime, the spectacle of a 'prince of the blood' turned slave might afford us a bit of amusement. Send him in, will you? This could be a most pleasant diversion."

Neb-mertef turned to go but then had second thoughts. "Majesty, wouldn't it be better to receive him from the high dais in the great hall with an audience in attendance?"

"Whatever for?"

"The only purpose of granting him an audience—other than for your private amusement—would be to humiliate him. After all, he was the man who had been raised to be a pretender to your own throne."

Kamose laughed heartily. "That's true, isn't it? And now he's a slave. Why isn't he out there hauling bricks?"

"He's been away—escaped some years ago and has only recently returned with his family."

"Ah! Then he's still a slave. I could imprison him if I chose."

"I suppose, Sire, but he's harmless. The Habiru aren't the kind to revolt."

"Then you think I should go easy on him?"

"Do as you like, Sire. As always. But keep in mind that the rebuilding of Avaris is not finished. And while the Habiru remain held to the mark by Aaron, they are free labor."

Kamose nodded. "Have them shown into the great hall. I'll keep them waiting a bit."

"Indeed, Majesty. The power a superior exerts over an inferior is much enhanced by the amount of time the inferior is made to wait."

The long thoroughfare ended at the half-finished palace; Iri and his assistant Baufra could see it plainly as they made their way down the street. As always, Baufra winced at the ungainly design. "I'll bet Neb-mertef made a fortune from the bribes generated by the construction of this building."

"More likely it was Apedemek." Iri walked with his eyes fixed straight ahead, ignoring the stares of passersby. "The smaller bribes go to Neb-mertef, but in recent days Apedemek has been raking off the big ones for himself."

Baufra's face fell. "Does that mean I'm going to have to bribe *him* to get funds to purchase ore?" he asked.

"Oh, no," Iri said. "That's why I came along with you. We're going to Kamose. If he balks at putting up the funds, his new elite guard unit can wait for their weapons until the Nile freezes at Memphis."

"Iri," Baufra said, concerned, "the last time you took him on, I thought he was going to strike you. Do you think it's wise to push him?"

"Why not?" Iri asked carelessly. "He needs me more than I need him. If I was to shut down the forges tomorrow, I'd be able to pursue work I much prefer to armsmaking. My jewelry business has never been more profitable. The Cretan receipts alone would allow us to live in comfort. Besides, if Kamose struck me, I'd take his head off. I've already won a physical confrontation with him, some years ago. He was in much better physical shape then." He chuckled. "Well, here we are. Come along."

"But that's the main entrance."

"It's the one I always use. Don't tell me you've been using the service entrance?"

"Well, Neb-mertef said—"

"Don't be concerned about Neb-mertef. He has lasted longer than most, but functionaries like him, who live on the bounty of others, have lives like mayflies at a court as corrupt as Kamose's. I'll still be here when he's only a dim memory. If Neb-mertef bothers you, refer him to me."

"I will. Shall I do the same if Apedemek gets in my way?"

"He is quite another story," Iri said, ushering Baufra through the great doors. "But he's not invulnerable. Hieron faced him down, and I suspect there are others who could do as well."

Iri stopped suddenly in the center of the broad corridor to look at a pair of bearded, berobed foreigners sitting quietly on a bench by the door of the great hall. "Aaron ben Amram! Is that you? And Moses! As I live and breathe!"

II

As Baufra moved to one side, Moses stood and smiled broadly as he came forward to embrace Iri. Then he stood back and looked into the bright, intelligent eyes, basking in the essential warmth and decency of the man. Iri was self-assured and had the controlled strength that marked maturity.

"What a great pleasure," Moses said. "The first man I see other than my people, after ten years away, and I have the good fortune for it to be you."

After embracing Aaron, too, Iri turned back to Moses. "Isn't it dangerous for you to be here?"

Moses dismissed the danger with a gesture. "I have been told by the One God that there is something I must do here, and I have come to do it."

Iri blinked. This was a new Moses indeed: There was an immense calm in him, and it seemed to be contagious—Iri could feel it seeping into his own heart. "I wish there were something that I believed in so completely," he said, deeply moved. "So! You are the servant of El-Shaddai?"

"I am impressed that you, an unbeliever, remember the name we knew Him by. He has revealed His true name to me in a vision. He is Yahweh: He Who Is. Yes, His hand is upon me."

Iri did not say anything, so Moses went on: "As His hand is upon Aaron and many others who do not know it. His hand is upon you, my friend, and upon every righteous man."

"I do not know why that should move me so," Iri confessed, "but it does. Thank you for telling me. But surely your God must know that you come into great danger."

"I come to deliver a message, no more. Kamose stands at

the edge of a precipice, and disaster balances on the way he directs his footsteps. It is hardly a threat to point this out."

Iri frowned and looked at Aaron. "I think I'd better go in with you." He turned to his assistant. "Wait for me here."

"No, please," Aaron said. "He won't harm us. And you would only get yourself into trouble."

"I insist. Ah, here comes the herald. You there! I'm going in with these men."

"The king specified that they were to enter the hall alone, sir," the herald said.

"I'll take the responsibility." He looked the herald in the eyes, forcing him to look back, in spite of the man's obvious revulsion. "That's a direct order as armorer to the king and an officer of the court."

"Yes, sir," the herald said, looking away. "Right this way, if you please."

The great hall was empty but for the guards stiffly flanking the throne on the high dais. Iri scowled angrily. "What is this? He calls you inside, yet he's not here. He's deliberately making you wait."

"Indeed," Moses said softly. "Imagine a man being so insecure that he would go to such lengths to humiliate a pair of slaves."

Iri grinned. "You haven't lost your wit. Well, we'll give him a few minutes, then leave." He could feel the fury building within him. He raised his voice and spoke sarcastically. "Probably he's hiding behind an arras watching us through a hole."

"Hush!" Aaron said, stifling a smile.

Iri half turned, caught his eye, and winked. "Just getting his attention," he said innocently. "He'll be out presently."

The curtains parted behind the dais, and a herald announced, "His Highness, Kamose, Lord of Two Lands." He would have continued, but the king appeared behind him and tapped him on the shoulder. He turned and hastily made his way to safety behind the curtain.

Kamose looked from face to face. "Iri, I looked for you yesterday at the inspection of the forges."

"I was busy, Sire," Iri explained casually. "My assistant is qualified to deputize for me. He probably gives a better account of our current state of preparedness than I do these days."

"*Hmmmm.*" Kamose did not quite seem to know how to take Iri's tone, which was just short of insolent. "Well, enough of that. Whom have you brought me? These look like Habiru slaves. What are they doing calling on the king?"

"They have a petition for you, Sire," Iri explained. The word *sire* somehow managed to come out sounding like an insult. "It occurred to me that I ought to be present."

"If I did not know better," Kamose fumed, "I would think you are suggesting that, without your presence, I might not give these two fair treatment."

"No doubt, Sire. Let me present Aaron ben Amram, leader of the Habiru. And, oh yes—Prince Moses, son of Princess Thermutis and—"

This was too much. "Son of whom?" Kamose exploded. "Son of a slave, you mean! You came here to tell me something. Get it out."

"Very well, Sire," Moses said. "I come as the voice of Yahweh, the One God. Yahweh asks you to let my people go into the wilderness for three days to observe a festival in His honor."

Kamose gaped at him. "I am amazed at your effrontery. I know nothing of any 'One God.' The gods are as numerous as the grains of sand. Who is this Yahweh, that I should let my slaves frolic in the desert? If I listened to petitions from indolent nonentities who don't want to do an honest day's work, nothing would ever get done. The answer is no. I know nothing of your Yahweh, but I know something of His followers. They did me an ill turn in my youth, and I've never forgotten it, Prince Mutton, lord of the sheep. Tell your phantom with the funny name that it is my pleasure that the Habiru shall not only stay at their work, the daily quota will be raised."

Moses offered a minuscule bow. "Yahweh told me you would need to be persuaded. He knew that both you and your people would require evidence of His power. Very well. Yahweh said for me to tell you: Israel is My firstborn son. I have ordered you to let My son go, that he may offer Me worship. You refuse. So be it! I shall put the firstborn of your own land to death."

Under Kamose's incredulous expression, one could see the anger building. All three men remembered how Kamose's father, Apophis, had murdered Kamose's mother and tried to kill him as well.

Moses went on. "You know, deep inside, that if you obey your impulse to have Aaron and me put to death, it will be the end of you."

Kamose's face was a study in hatred.

"We will take our leave now," Moses concluded, "but if you send guards after us, you will learn what happens to mortals who challenge the power of God. In the end you will beg us to leave, to remove the fearsome hand of God from your blighted nation. You will offer us rich bribes to quit your country. Remember what I tell you; it will all come to pass just as I have said."

Iri, flabbergasted, watched as Moses and Aaron turned and left the great hall, unrestrained. Then, his mind reeling, he stumbled after them. *This isn't just a confrontation,* he was thinking. *This is a duel to the death.*

CHAPTER SIXTEEN

Thebes

I

Not daring to look Apedemek directly in the eyes, the assistant stood by the door, ready to bolt out into the hall. "I beg to report, Your Worship, that—"

"Get out!" Apedemek shouted from the bed.

The assistant hovered uneasily. "I'm to tell you that your, uh, case has been transferred to a new physician, a man who—"

"New? What do I need with a new one?" Apedemek screamed in a voice tight with pain. "The old ones are bad enough! Get the chief physician for me!"

"I was trying to tell you, my lord," the frightened assistant continued, "the old physician has been, uh, taken ill. He has sent the new man in his place."

"I am surrounded by incompetents!" Apedemek reached toward the bedside table for something to throw at the assistant but succeeded only in knocking over a cup of watered wine. This inspired a fit of cursing, great stabbing pains, and violent thrashing about, which threatened to reopen Apedemek's wound. "You!" he said in a weaker voice. "Get me some *shepenn* for the pain! Now!"

The assistant disappeared as Apedemek continued to curse. But when a figure again appeared at the door, it was not the assistant's; instead it was a portly man dressed in the stately robes of a master magus. His beard was styled in the fashion common to the valley of the Tigris a generation before.

"I understand you have hurt yourself," he said. "Let me give you something to ease your pain."

Apedemek glared at him. "Who are you? Get out! Bring me the chief physician!"

The Assyrian bowed. "I am the new chief physician. The old one is indisposed. That is a fancy Egyptian way to say that the man is so drunk he can't sit up. I prefer straight talk, don't you? You must be in considerable pain. Let me prepare you something."

Apedemek looked at him with new respect, taking in the sharp eyes, the no-nonsense competence, the quick hands that produced a tiny jar of *shepenn* from inside his garment. The voice was most interesting. Although the accent was thick, the physician spoke Egyptian fluently and with admirable correctness. A good linguist himself, Apedemek had never taken seriously anyone who had no skill at languages.

Now the doctor offered the *shepenn*, which he mixed with other ingredients in a little bowl, on a sliver of bamboo. "Swallow this," he said. "Besides the *shepenn* there are other substances that may help to set your mind at rest."

Apedemek thought to protest, then changed his mind and accepted the potion. He lay back on the pillow afterward. "That's strange," he mused. "I fancy it's already beginning to help. Whatever that is, it works faster than pure *shepenn*. What is it?"

"That's my secret—for now," said the Assyrian. "Introductions first. I am told you are Apedemek, a magus of high rank. I am Rapsag of Nineveh. At your service, sir."

Apedemek particularly liked that there was neither fear nor servility in the fellow's manner. "You have your facts right," he said. His mind was beginning to reel, and the sensations of peace and relaxation were spreading to his limbs. "They apparently still teach doctoring in the valley of the Tigris on quite a high level. You'll have to give me the formula for that. I'd guess you have added a derivative from a certain mushroom, which, as I recall, grows—"

"There, now," the magus said with a tiny smile. "We don't want to discuss secrets, do we?"

Ordinarily this kind of conspiratorial tone would have sent Apedemek into a fury. But a glorious feeling was permeating his whole body, mellowing his wary mind. A spirit of highly unusual bonhomie animated his tongue. He *liked* this man! "I quite agree," he found himself saying. "You can tell me whenever you want."

"Perhaps there is something you might be able to impart to me in exchange," Rapsag offered. "Within the Great Circle of the Arcana, knowledge is the soundest currency."

"Indeed," Apedemek responded. The more he heard, the more he found to like. Suddenly, without warning, he spoke in the language of Shinar: "You are, then, an adept of the craft?"

"A mere beginner," Rapsag said, but immediately added three words in the ancient tongue that made a liar of him.

"Close the door," Apedemek requested. "But first tell the guards outside to move back ten paces."

After Rapsag did Apedemek's bidding, he advanced to the patient's side to offer, then receive, a secret handshake—known, perhaps, to no one else in Egypt. "We are not of the same blood," he said. "My inebriated colleague has told me that you are a Child of the Lion. I am not. I trust you do not share the, uh, conventional ethics of the Sons of the Lion?"

"Pah! What sort of fool do you think me?" Apedemek flared up for a moment, but his tone was calmer when he spoke again. "Your path to the Arcana was different from mine, but I would not be surprised if we once had the same master at a lower stage of learning."

"We will compare notes anon," Rapsag said. "For now I must ask you to rest and let your body heal. You have miraculously escaped death. Only quiet and calm will restore you now. You must abandon all thoughts of travel for a time."

"I understand," Apedemek said with uncharacteristic docility. "I am in your hands. Meanwhile, please tell me what a magus of Assyria is doing in the backwater that Thebes has become."

"A long story, my friend. I have taken pains to remain in obscurity until I could have a look around Egypt. I did spend some time translating diplomatic documents for the court and learning whatever secrets I could. I felt too exposed while living in Avaris."

"You were wise to be circumspect," Apedemek said. "But you now have a friend in high places. Tell me, what have you learned about the government that I might not know?"

Rapsag thought for a moment. "Did you know that the king's ranking assistant, Neb-mertef, is a fake? His astrological predictions are nothing but lies."

"I suspected as much," Apedemek said. "He had Amasis fooled for years, and Amasis isn't easily fooled."

"A different man was faking his charts for him under Amasis. He's currently using a lout named Agha, who has been too inebriated or too lazy to cast real charts for years. I got hold of two of these bogus charts and picked my way through them. If the king knew what garbage Neb-mertef has been fobbing off on him, he would go into a rage. This could offer valuable leverage. Of course, I have no doubt that you could destroy Neb-mertef easily without any such help—"

"In the blink of an eye."

"But instead of destroying him, it might prove more useful to threaten him with destruction, thus enlisting him in your service."

Apedemek was feeling splendid, absolutely splendid. "I am in your debt. How may I repay you?"

"It would be enough to be in your confidence. If we remained in regular contact, here or in the delta, I could continue to be useful. And of course the perquisites of merely being associated with such a person as you would—"

Apedemek nodded. "At this time there is no magus or physician of stature associated with the court. I could see that you get the appointment."

"I would be much obliged."

"Meanwhile, there is something you could do for me."

"Name it."

"I was stabbed by a young woman who came at me from the shadows before I could bring her under mental control." His speech was becoming slurred. His tongue seemed thick, dry. "Afterward, she retreated into madness."

"I take it that you want her for questioning?"

Apedemek nodded. "I want the city scoured. I want the

person who brings her in—untouched and alive—rewarded handsomely. I want the city guard to know that if she escapes, it will go very badly for them."

"I have no authority to command this."

"Show them my signet ring. Keep it with you at all times as proof of your new authority. When I am recovered, I will find you a sinecure with a bit of power behind it."

"I am honored. I will give the order. The woman is to be delivered unharmed."

"And unquestioned."

"To make sure no one enriches his own store of knowledge at her expense, perhaps I should hear what they should not know."

Apedemek ordinarily would have treated this as the effrontery it was, but the drug had moved him to too exalted a plane. "She was a plaything of mine once. And she is the only person in Thebes who knows how to find the son she bore me ten years ago." He lay back and sighed, thinking about it. "I had no idea. Imagine! A son to raise as I will!"

II

The day was warm and sunny, but a cool breeze had stirred up from the river behind her. Mai sat atop the bundles of Seth's and her belongings and listened to the musical murmur of the Nile. As Seth came toward her on the quay, she smiled up at him. "Do we have a place to sleep tonight?"

"We do," he told her. "I kept Kedar's lodgings near the city market when Mother and he died. I sold her house. I'm sure Kedar's place is dirty and thick with dust, but we won't be there long."

"This assuredly isn't the Thebes of old," she said. "The streets are empty, and no one has volunteered to carry our bags. In the old days you would have been besieged by every strong back in the quarter by now."

"I'll find someone to help, if you'll wait a moment or two," Seth offered. "I'll send him along to you—"

"You're going somewhere without me?"

"Yes, but nothing dangerous. I do want to verify something I overheard: Two guards were discussing a boy of Pepi's age they're trying to apprehend. He's been stealing from the stalls in the city market. There aren't many children left in town, so it is well worth checking whether or not it's our boy."

"You do that," she encouraged. "Learn what you can, but don't take any chances."

He smiled and pressed her hand. "I had thought to leave you home, you know. But you've spoiled me terribly. I don't think I could have come this far without you."

"Find us a servant to carry our things. Tell me how to find Kedar's place. I'll wait for you there. Perhaps I'll even try to clean it up a bit."

He bent to kiss her brow. "Fine. I'll use the time to ask around."

The madwoman had yet to speak to them. She had dispiritedly accepted food from Mut, and she had slept a bit, but she had little control over other functions. Mut was cleaning up after the woman as she might for a backward child.

Yet this was no child; her age? Perhaps not yet forty.

Now, on the following morning, Mut looked at Khem over breakfast. "We've got to find out who she is. I believe she will turn out to be related to someone we've known. There's something about her face. . . ."

"It is highly unlikely that this poor woman has anyone in the city who would be much interested in hearing of her present discomfiture. If anyone had cared about the poor dear, they wouldn't have let her deteriorate into this deplorable condition."

"There's truth to what you say," Mut allowed, "but that face haunts me."

Khem reached to a nearby shelf and pulled down the bloody knife they had found beside her. "The questions *this* brings to mind are many, and few are reassuring."

Mut, having forgotten the knife altogether, stared at him.

"The possibilities are few, and all are unpleasant. I doubt that anyone tried unsuccessfully to stab her."

Mut frowned. "Go on."

"The woman may have been a witness to a crime in which one unknown person assaulted another. Thus, we may assume that the attacker, who presumably removed the body, may be aware that there was a witness—albeit an impaired one. Let us assume that he left her and the knife in place, while he removed the corpse. If this is true, then he might have returned to the scene and found us there, packing her up to bring her home."

He took note of the horrified look on Mut's face and raised one eyebrow. "I am thinking, my dear Mut, that we may well have barely escaped something terminally unpleasant when we brought this stranger back with us."

"The gods forbid!" she responded. "Tell me another possibility. I don't like that one at all."

"Very well, you may not be any more fond of this one." His eyes were somber in his mild old face. "The woman herself, under attack, fought back and stabbed her attacker. She harmed him, but he got away and found medical help."

"How could anyone in her condition stab anyone?"

"Remember the extensive scuff marks in the dust where we found her? What if, up to this point, she was unstable but rather more competent than she now appears? People have dissolved into madness under extreme stress."

"What would happen if the fellow she stabbed survived the attack and brought charges?"

"Or hired thugs to avenge him? They might be scouring the streets at this very moment, in search of her."

Mut blanched. "Have we made a mistake by taking her in?"

"I would never regret a decision soundly and firmly based on altruism. If we ascertain that she is being sought by anyone hoping to hold her responsible, we should do everything in our power to keep the pursuer from finding her."

"A simple no might have sufficed, Khem."

"It might behoove us if I were to open our stall and spend the day keeping my eyes and ears open. If our guest is wanted by the city guards, I don't want to draw undue attention by acting in ways out of the ordinary. That's also why I retrieved the pots we unloaded from the barrow to bring her here."

"It would be best not to take chances. Yes, go in, and I'll stay here and mind her."

Khem stood, stretched, and yawned, showing a missing tooth. "Try getting her to talk. Already she seems less afraid, and who knows—she may wake from this walking sleep."

Mut looked skeptically at the woman. "I wish I felt optimistic about that. But it's worth a try."

Khem smiled, standing at the door. "I feel like a father again. Caring for her has taken years off my age. Yours too, my dear Mut."

"Oh, you! You're just saying that!"

The pair of tall, hulking guards strode past, their sword scabbards slapping their hard thighs. Pepi watched them from cover, his back pressed against the warehouse wall. Curiosity possessed him; this was the fourth such pair to pass through this mostly deserted quarter in the past hour. He pondered for a moment, then scurried to the top of the wall and cut across the back alleys, hoping to get ahead of the guards and find a place from which to listen in on their conversation.

It was almost a fatal mistake; coming over another wall, he came within a heartbeat of being spotted by yet another guardsman. Pepi froze, and when the guardsman had managed to look right past him without seeing him, Pepi slipped to the ground and crawled on his hands and knees out of sight, behind an abandoned dwelling.

This was no good; he would surely get caught. Waiting until the guardsman turned the corner at the end of the alley, Pepi emerged and climbed to the building's flat roof. There he waited another long moment, then took a deep breath and peeped over the top.

The guards he had wanted to intercept were confronting an elderly man pushing a vendor's cart. Pepi settled down, hoping to hear what was said.

So far Pepi had done well enough in Thebes. One city's back streets were much like any other's. He had no trouble finding a place to sleep, or food and drink to steal. But now, with the streets full of soldiers, survival was more problematic. If Thebes was in the middle of some sort of crackdown, it was not worth staying. He would have to get back on the river, then to the delta, to find his father.

He had hoped to learn about Avaris before actually going there, but the one thing he had not been able to do yet was talk to anyone. He was prepared to be flexible; finding his father was what he had come for, after all.

There! The guards were talking to the vendor! He crawled closer to the edge, leaned over, and looked down.

III

The captain of the tiny Theban garrison looked at the black-bearded Assyrian standing at the foot of Apedemek's bed. *I don't like this man or trust him.*

He did not like Assyrians, for one thing; to date, all his experiences with foreigners had been bad. Assyrians in particular had been unpleasant, arrogant bastards, and he had had his run-ins with them.

It was more than that, though. This one had become so thick with Apedemek so quickly! The captain had learned not to trust the likes of Apedemek, and anyone accepted on short notice by the tall magus had to have something dead wrong with him. He listened to Apedemek's description with one ear, eyeing Rapsag coldly.

"Sir," he said, "it sounds as if you're describing the sister of Iri the armorer. He made a sword for me. She came by the forge once, and he introduced her."

"That's the one," Apedemek said gleefully. "Rapsag! Give me some more of that painkiller, will you? And send in an orderly to change this bandage. I'm bleeding again."

The captain respectfully waited while the Assyrian prepared and administered a dose of the potent drug. Only when Apedemek's head had sunk back upon the pillows did he dare to speak once more.

"Sir," he continued, "I think I spotted someone else

connected to these two. It was this morning, down on the quays."

"Who?" Apedemek asked.

"Iri and the girl had a servant woman who used to bring Iri food at the forge. She had apparently been acting as a mother to them for quite a long—"

"Yes!" Apedemek said. "I remember now!"

"If she's turned up in Thebes again after ten years' absence, it might mean—"

Apedemek looked sharply at the captain. "Now you're thinking." He stopped and thought. "Wait. She was there when I had that terrible meeting with Hieron! I remember her bending over to help Seth." He looked at Rapsag. "What if Seth of Thebes was back in the city, looking for Neftis and the boy?" He turned back to the captain. "Did you have the servant followed?"

"No, sir. There didn't seem to be reason. But perhaps my assistant took the initiative to have her followed."

"Find out!" Apedemek said, gripping the coverlet. He turned to Rapsag. "If I could nab all of them at one time . . ."

"A wonderful coup," the Assyrian agreed. "Was Seth of Thebes the one who married the daughter of Samsi-ditana of Babylon, just before the city fell? The one the king had designated as his heir?"

"Yes. Do you know him?"

"I met him once, many years ago, in Babylon. He wouldn't remember me: I was among a delegation of visitors from my country. That may be an advantage. We could track him down, and through him find Neftis."

"Yes! Seek him out, worm your way into his confidence, and—"

"My thoughts exactly." Rapsag turned to the captain. "You're quite sure about the servant woman?"

"Not absolutely sure, no, but worth following up. Not that it should be easy for them to hide—the city's too sparsely populated for that. If I was to close the city and send patrols from house to house—"

"No!" Apedemek said. "Not on the first attempt. If she should come to her senses, she's quite capable of committing suicide to keep from betraying the boy." He nodded dismissal.

The captain saluted smartly. "I'll get to work immediately, sir."

The vendor was old, bald, and a bit bent from many years of hard work. His rickety little cart was loaded with utilitarian pots, barely fit for use in the poorer neighborhoods.

Pepi watched him. He spoke in an elaborate, formal manner, with much fancy decoration to his words. The gestures of his twisted old hands were overdone.

". . . telling my wife the other day that it's no good blaming the guards for all the crime in the streets. People have to decide to do something about the shocking dishonesty around us. People have to take the responsibility themselves. Don't you think so, officers?"

"I'm sure that's all very true, sir," said the junior guardsman. "But what we're trying to find out is whether anyone has seen—"

"Seen crime? Of course I have. Why, only last year there was a man who came to our market stall, and I told my wife that I didn't like the look in that fellow's eyes. But she wouldn't listen to me; she never does, you know, not until it's too late, and then—"

"Sir," the elder guardsman said, "we're looking for two people. One is a boy who has been stealing food in the market. He's about ten, this tall, and dressed in—"

"How tall? Pardon me, but it does seem important to get these things right, just in case I should run into someone who answers the description. Would you say he stood this tall on you? Or that tall?"

"I've never seen him myself. I'm just going on the description given me by—"

"Ah, now, that's a great pity, sir. If we really knew these things from direct experience, well, then I might be able to give you some sort of positive identification. Otherwise, sir, I might be talking utter nonsense, and that wouldn't be much help to you at all."

"Wait. Are you saying that you've seen such a boy? And you're afraid to make a positive identification because—"

"Oh, no, sir, not at all. How could I say I've seen such and such a boy when we haven't even established how tall he is? Oh, no, sir, that would be quite wrong, wouldn't it? I wouldn't begin to take the responsibility of saying—"

"For the love of the gods, can't you just give a simple yes or no? Every time I ask you a question, you go off on another one of these wild, rambling—"

"Well, sir, I don't really think that every question can be answered with a simple yes or no, do you?" The old man turned to the other officer. "Or you, sir? Take, for instance, what would happen if I was to ask you, 'Haven't you stopped drinking to excess lately?' If you say yes, it implies—"

The guardsmen exchanged disgusted looks. The senior officer took his colleague's arm. "Come on, let's go. We're never going to get a straight answer. The people in the marketplace all think he's a bit gone in the head."

"There, now, sir! I really must protest. Anyone who impugns my peerless memory has robbed me of my good name!"

The soldiers made hasty salutes and retreated.

Pepi chuckled to himself. It was obvious to him that the old man was less of a dotard than he appeared. He watched as the elderly fellow gripped the handles of his cart and prepared to continue his progress down the street. *It was a close call,* Pepi thought. *The guards were talking about me.*

Just then the old man craned his neck and looked up, right into Pepi's eyes. "They were talking about you, weren't they, son?" he asked, smiling. "I'd be very careful if I were you. Try your luck across the river in Deir el-Bahari. Someone here seems to have turned you in."

"How did you—?" Pepi asked, blinking down at him.

But the man waved and turned back to the street. Pushing his rickety cart, he began to make his slow way down the dirt street.

IV

"Wait!" Pepi called out. He stood, dashed to the far edge of the roof, leapt down to the roof of the one-story building next door, then jumped from there to the street. "How did you know I was up there?" he asked, keeping pace with the slow progress of the cart. "I never saw you look up!"

The elderly potter continued to push the cart slowly. His smile was merry and conspiratorial. "You young fellows always think you're the first to discover something. But when you've reached my age, you'll know that nothing in the world is new."

"What do you mean?" Pepi asked. "All I know is that those guardsmen never got to ask their question."

The man turned a solemn face his way. "Unfortunately they asked half their question—the part about you. That was you that they were talking about, wasn't it?"

Pepi examined the wrinkled face, trying to decide how far to trust the man. "I suppose so," he admitted after a pause. "I guess you're not the kind to betray me."

"I'm not the kind to betray anybody," the man responded. "Not to guardsmen, anyway. When I was your age I had been surviving in the streets for three or four years. But you're new to this, aren't you?"

Pepi frowned. "How'd you know?"

"You've been stealing from the wrong people," the potter answered. "Don't steal from the city market if it's the only one in town. Vendors in the marketplace haven't a thing to do all day but watch faces. There probably isn't a person there who can't identify you to the guards."

The boy reached for the cart's handles. "Here, let me help you. You'll never get the cart over that bump."

"Right you are! How kind of you."

Pepi helped roll the cart around the big bump in the road. "Tell me who I should be stealing from, then."

"There's a big warehouse three blocks back, owned by the government. The first shift after dark is manned by a fellow who can't leave the palm wine alone. By midnight he's dead asleep. A quick-witted fellow like you ought to be able to steal enough food for a week while the guard sleeps off his potations."

" 'Potations.' Huh! You have a funny way of talking. You're worse than Seth. He—"

"Did you say Seth? There are very few people of that name in Egypt—"

"Oh, he's in Nubia. But he used to come from here, like my mother did. Why?"

"I used to know a bright young man who haunted the bazaars right here in Thebes and would answer people's questions. There was never a question he couldn't answer. My wife and I used to press food on him. He turned out not to be as poor as we thought; actually, he was quite well-to-do, although he never touched an *outnou* of it. His father was a rich armorer."

"That's Seth of Thebes!" The boy smiled, then sighed. "I—I ran away from him to come here. All the way from Nubia. I have to admit that there have been times when I wished he were here. The boatman cheated me, and—"

"I'm sure you have a fascinating story to tell, and I can't wait to hear it," the old man interrupted, looking around cautiously. "But if the guardsmen are looking for you, this is not the place to tell it."

The boy looked at him with wide eyes. "You know the city. What should I do?"

"Do you have a good place to hide?"

"Uh . . . yes. Why?"

"Go there and stay put until nightfall. Then go to the Street of the Well, past the fountain, heading toward the old palace. You do know how to find that, I hope."

"Yes. Then what?"

"Go to the fourth house on the right. Knock twice, pause, then knock twice again. It'll be my house. I'm Khem the potter, and I live there with my wife. Make sure nobody sees you. We can put you up, but you'll have to be very discreet. The only thing that makes my house a safe one is the fact that everybody thinks I'm a dotty old fool."

Pepi grinned. "You're not, are you?" he said appreciatively. "Not at all."

"Shhhh!" Khem warned with a smile. "Don't give me away!"

Only halfway in the front door of Kedar's abandoned house, Seth knew something was wrong. He tried to stop, but his forward momentum carried him into the room. He froze, looking around in the dimming light. "Mai?" he called, cautiously.

When his eyes adjusted to the light, he was horrified to find that she was bound and gagged in the chair before Kedar's old desk. Beside her stood a tall, competent-looking garrison captain, who swiftly outflanked Seth and pushed the door shut behind him.

The captain fingered the bronze sword at his belt. "I wouldn't try anything if I were you."

"I wouldn't dream of it," he said. "Was it necessary to tie my wife like that?"

"I'll loosen the restraints," the captain offered, "if you'll agree to talk."

"Release her and ask me any question you like. But first I'd like to know why you have broken into my house and why you are holding an innocent woman hostage."

The captain released Mai's hands and cut the cloth that gagged her. "I'm sorry, ma'am. I couldn't take any chances." He looked at her husband now. "If you are Seth of Thebes, you're wanted for questioning. A crime has been committed, and it may concern someone close to you."

"How can that be?" Seth asked. "We came here alone, and every friend we've ever had in the city has long since gone away to the delta."

"A high official of the government has been attacked and is in serious condition. A young woman is wanted in connection with the crime. It's our understanding that she is well-known to both of you."

Seth and Mai exchanged glances. "We may be looking for the same person," Seth said cagily. "She has a history of mental instability, and she's quite capable of doing something like—"

"Seth!" Mai cried out indignantly. "How can you—"

"I'm sorry, my dear," he replied. "There's nothing to be gained by dissembling. We have to tell the good captain everything he needs to know. It's the only way we can get any information out of him. I'm sure that he'll be only too glad to help us. Isn't that so, Captain?"

The soldier shot him an incredulous glance; this was coming all too easily. "I . . . I suppose so. If you're willing to cooperate . . ." But his eyes locked with Seth's, and he found himself immobilized.

"This has gone far enough," Seth said forcefully. "Now

I'll ask the questions. The girl you're looking for: Is her name Neftis?"

"Yes, Neftis, the sister of Iri, the armorer to the king," the captain replied in a monotone.

"Seth!" Mai said.

Seth waved her to silence. "We have to get it out of him as quickly as possible. Captain, what do you know about the girl?"

"She's considered dangerous. There was also a report against an old couple who live in the Street of the Well, a potter and his wife. Apparently they were seen helping a woman into their cart and trundling her down the street. Apedemek's man was sent to their house."

"A potter?" Seth said, his eyes narrowing. "Was he a talkative sort? An eccentric?"

"Yes."

Seth turned to Mai. "Khem and Mut! I remember them from my youth." He turned back to the captain. "What's to be done about them?"

"If they have the woman, they'll be brought in with her and be impaled for sheltering a dangerous fugitive."

Seth looked at Mai again. "They'd be just the type to take her in if they found her wandering the streets. They must be ancient! Quick, Mai. We've got to find them! Captain! Where exactly on the Street of the Well do they live?"

"Fourth house on the south side, right after you pass the fountain. My superior ought to be there right now."

"Thank you, Captain," Seth said. "You've been very helpful. For all your hard work, you deserve a rest. You may sleep now."

The captain's head suddenly slumped forward, and he slid easily to the floor to lie in a snoring heap.

"Come, Mai," Seth urged. "They've got her!"

"Seth! How did you do that?"

"I've been studying. And our sleeping friend here has a strong back but a weak mind. Let's hope everyone we run into fits that description!" Taking her hand, he hurried out the door into the darkening streets of the half-deserted city.

V

Only habit saved Khem from blundering in the front door of his house and being captured. Fifty years of work experience had taught him never to leave his cart in the street unattended—not for even a few minutes—so he took the time now to park the cart in the alley behind the house, cover it with cloth, and stack the pots in a cubbyhole well out of sight behind it.

As he did, he heard the voices inside and crept to a side window to listen. After a few minutes he had learned most of what he needed to know and shrank back against the building, to sort things out.

It was obvious that the interrogator was waiting for him, Khem. Thankful there was only one of them, Khem wondered why the man spoke with an Assyrian accent. It was clear that he had not yet searched the house but had come for the madwoman; if this chap was to be believed, the woman had tried to kill a high-ranking government official.

More power to her, he thought wryly.

But what to do? He was old and weak. He looked at the dusky sky. *The boy! He'll be showing up at the front door any moment—and he'll walk right into a trap.*

When the knock came on the front door, bold and strong, Mut started.

"Answer it," the black-bearded man told her, moving to stand behind her.

She closed her eyes, breathed a hasty prayer aimed at every god in the pantheon, and opened the door. She found herself looking into the clear, calm eyes of a man beyond his middle years. Behind him stood a gentle-faced woman. The man smiled, then let his gaze go to the Assyrian man.

Unhurried, unruffled, he said, "Hello. My name is Seth of Thebes. I knew you and your husband a number of years ago. May I come in, please?"

She could not hide her panic. It was an awkward moment. Mut, her hand on her heart, stepped back as Seth came in, bringing Mai with him. "Excuse me," Mut faltered. "I don't think—"

Seth of Thebes smiled and took her hands. "It's all right. The Assyrian gentleman knows who I am. He is here looking for the woman. But I've come for her."

"All right," the black-bearded man grated. "Just stop right there."

But Seth raised his eyes and engaged the Assyrian's, and the Assyrian's forward rush stopped as abruptly as if he had run into a wall. Seth chuckled. "You've had some training in the mystical arts, haven't you? But not enough to test wills with a Child of the Lion. Quick: your name?"

"Rapsag."

"Who sent you, and why?"

"Apedemek. The woman stabbed him. He wants her because she knows where his son is."

Seth looked at Mai, his eyes wide. "We didn't arrive a moment too soon. The boy mustn't know anything of this—particularly that Apedemek is here. We've got to get Neftis and him out of Thebes, and fast." He spoke to Rapsag. "Does Apedemek know about these two?"

"Yes. They're to be brought in."

Seth turned to Mut. "Mut, you and Khem were very kind to me when I was young. I won't leave you here to be mistreated by these swine. Mai, please bring Khem and Pepi in from outside. I told them to hide in the shadow of the building across the street. Then fetch Neftis from the other room." He took Mut to the far corner of the room and let her look at him in the light of the lantern.

She smiled. "You're the raggedy boy who used to answer everyone's questions?"

"The very one," Seth said affectionately. "We're all in terrible danger, my dear old friend. Would you come downriver with us to safety?"

"This is all so sudden. How will we live? We barely get by as it is, Seth."

"Now don't you go worrying about that. Khem's future is assured."

"But I don't understand," she said. "Khem hasn't an *outnou* to his name."

"It'll be all right, I promise you. But we've got to get down to the quay and leave tonight."

"But boats don't leave at night."

"I'll pay a boatman so much money, he won't be able to refuse me. I'm very rich, Mut. Rich enough to take care of both of you, and that's what I've decided to do."

"Seth! This is all going too fast for me."

"Trust me. If I can get all of us to safety now, I intend to buy you and Khem a nice house in Athribis, down by the waterfront, with an assured income and servants to look after you."

"Oh, Seth! It's like a dream come true!"

The door opened, and Khem preceded Pepi inside. Then Mai led-Neftis from the bedroom.

Seth looked at the boy, the old man, the gentle-faced older women, and the blank-faced young one. "I don't think it's a dream," he said grimly. "Dreams are simpler than this."

"Seth!" Pepi said. "I don't understand about Mother. How did this happen? Will she ever come out of it?"

"I hope so, son. As for the rest, it's a long and confusing story. I'll tell you when we're on the boat. But right now there's a price on your head and your mother's, and before morning there'll be a price on the rest of us as well."

He turned to the immobile Assyrian. "You will go back to the man who sent you and tell him that you came across our trail and we all took off upriver, heading for El-Kab."

"I understand," said the Assyrian. There was rebellion in his eyes, however.

"You'd like to lock minds with me, wouldn't you?" Seth challenged in a hard voice. "Well, let's test you on an even more formidable opponent: when you get done reporting to the man who employs you, I want you to look in his eyes and try to control his mind."

"I will do this," vowed the Assyrian, his dark eyes blazing. "I will match my mind with his!"

"Good," Seth approved, then turned to the others. "We'll leave our belongings at Kedar's house, Mai. Pepi, help your mother, would you, please? Do you know a good, dark way to the waterfront? One that won't lead us past too many guardsmen?"

"Sure I do," Pepi said, putting a protective arm around Neftis's back. "Just follow me! I'll get you there!"

VI

Rapsag the Assyrian stumbled through the streets of Thebes, his steps the clumsy ones of a drunkard. But he had taken no strong drink. Intent upon the mission Seth had given him, he paid no heed to the irregular surface of the ill-maintained street or to the puddles of filth he stepped in with every third step.

At the end of the thoroughfare he passed under an overhanging lantern, and his face became clearly visible to the foreign visitor Yahadu of Mari, lieutenant of Demetrios the Magnificent. Yahadu, noting the blank stare and clumsy movements, guessed that the man's mind was being controlled. Could he provide information on Apedemek's whereabouts? The visitor ran ahead to await Rapsag's blundering approach.

When both men were encircled by the light of the lantern, Yahadu said, "Halt!"

Rapsag looked at the stranger. "Yes?"

"Where are you going?" Yahadu asked.

"To destroy Apedemek. I will control his mind. I will best him and take his place."

"Well, now," Yahadu said startled, "that's a big order. Where are you coming from?"

The Assyrian spoke in a flat voice. "I captured Seth of Thebes—"

"What? Seth of Thebes?"

"Yes. With him were Neftis, sister to Iri the armorer, and her son, and—"

"Wait a moment," the visitor said. "Go over the whole thing from the first. I want to know all of it."

On the waterfront Seth haggled with a boatman while the others huddled in the lee of a spread sail, which served as a windbreak for the dock workers sleeping on the quay.

"I don't care what the custom is," Seth was saying. "We're leaving tonight. And we'll pay more money than you've earned since you were a boy."

The boatman snorted. "I'm not risking my boat on the say-so of some drifter with no proof of having money."

Seth opened his half-closed lantern a crack farther, then

withdrew a purse from his garment. "Take this," he urged. "The bag's full of gold coins."

"Gold?" said the boatman.

"I've got your attention now, so let's get down to some serious bargaining. For a start, what would it take to set you up for life?"

In the street under the lamplight, Yahadu of Mari listened with mounting excitement to the last of Rapsag's incredible tale. What luck! He had not been in Thebes for six hours, but he already had a line into the whereabouts of everyone he had been sent to find except Iri. Seth of Thebes, Neftis, and for a bonus, the son he had not known she had!

"And Seth told you to go back to Apedemek and try his mettle?" This was the most preposterous thing of all, but it spoke volumes about Seth's witty mind, that villain should be pitted against villain this way.

"Yes," the Assyrian continued, "I may be able to best him. He is ill. Neftis stabbed him and incapacitated him."

Yahadu's eyebrow rose. "Go on."

"Seth was taking the others to the quays, to find night passage to the delta."

Ah! There wasn't much time. "Very well," Yahadu concluded. "You will forget having met and spoken with me. But you will not forget the commands to test and to lie to Apedemek. When you do so, you will spit in his face and call him the sort of amateur magician who swallows baby chicks on festival days and pulls ribbons from his ears."

"I will remember."

"Then go," Yahadu commanded, turning his back on the Assyrian, to move rapidly toward the waterfront he had left only hours before.

The boat was loaded, and everyone but Seth was aboard. Mai leaned over the starboard rail. "Seth!" she whispered loudly. "The guards could happen along at any minute!"

"I've got to cut the other boats free," he replied. "Mai, if anything happens to me, I want you to get Neftis and the boy to Iri. They'll be safe with him. And deliver Khem and Mut to my banker in Athribis. Iri knows his whereabouts. Khem has a signed draft addressed to the banker."

"Come aboard, Seth!"

He stood, holding the rope he had been untying, and tossed it aboard. "Boatman, cast off!"

"No, Seth! No!"

But she could see him moving from boat to boat, grasping the razor-sharp knife he had taken from Rapsag and stooping to cut the mooring lines of vessel after vessel. After the third boat he stood, looked after her, and waved, a calm and confident smile gracing his face.

Yahadu found him there, sawing through the last boat's lines, then standing to watch the disorderly bobbing of ships, boats, and coracles wallowing unattended in the slow current of the Nile. Yahadu blinked and swallowed. This offense was punishable by impalement, if Seth was caught.

"Seth of Thebes?" he ventured, holding his torch high.

"Do I know you?" Seth asked.

"No," Yahadu said, dousing his torch. "I come from Demetrios, once called Khian of Thebes. Your kinsman. He sent me after you. We've got to get out of here."

Seth peered into Yahadu's eyes. "You *have* to be an apprentice of Demetrios's. Other than Apedemek, nobody in Thebes could look into my eyes like that and be unaffected. What does Demetrios want?"

"I'll tell while we're getting out of here," Yahadu said.

"All right," Seth agreed. "Where are we going?"

"I've a boat of my own a league downriver," Yahadu answered. "Demetrios sent me to take you away. The others have been sent to the delta?"

"Yes, to Iri in Athribis. I still don't have your name."

"Yahadu of Mari. I'm not a Child of the Lion, but I'm close to Demetrios. I'm in charge of Home."

"Of home?" Seth asked. They had fallen into step, heading north. Yahadu's gait was confident, purposeful. "I don't understand."

"Home—that's our name for Demetrios's secret headquarters on an island in the Great Sea. The island's about to blow up. The eruption should blot out the sun for thousands of leagues and shower ash over the civilizations beside the Great Sea. I'm to take all of you away—the others to a safe harbor of Demetrios's choosing, and you to the new Home."

"Why am I being singled out?"

"Demetrios has had his eye on you for many years. He has wanted to bring you to the new Home, to design it, as you designed the Babylon you never got the chance to build."

"How does he know all this about me?"

"At his high level in the Order of Chalybia, one keeps up with the exploits of those who, at the lower levels, show promise. He once owned your library, the one from Babylon. It was saved from the fire when the city was under siege, and found its way into his hands. Your designs were magnificent. He decided that, if you still lived, you were the only man in the world to build the new Home."

Seth whistled and picked up the pace. "How far away did you say your boat was? Step lively there!"

VII

When the captain had awakened from the nap Seth had inflicted upon him at Kedar's house, he hurried to Apedemek's bedside to make his report.

"Curse it!" Apedemek roared after hearing the captain out. He sat up on the bed, albeit with some difficulty, and reached for the little vial of the *shepenn* mixture Rapsag had left for him. He smeared some on his tongue. "I'm getting up. I can't leave anything to subordinates! Where's Rapsag? Get me Rapsag!"

Rapsag's aide nervously hovered, afraid equally to let Apedemek out of bed in violation of the doctor's orders and to try to restrain him. He knew he could expect no help from the soldiers who flanked Apedemek's bed. He looked anxiously at the bandage over Apedemek's wound. "Rapsag said he'd be back by nightfall. I can't imagine what could be keeping him."

"The rotten bastard is probably drunk in a ditch. Serves me right for trusting an Assyrian. The whole lot of them are worthless." The medicine he had just taken began to work, and Apedemek's long face took on a thoughtful cast. "The

Assyrians can teach doctoring, though. If the son of a bitch would stop wasting time on vain ambitions, he might make a decent apothecary. Mixing the mushroom with this stuff wasn't a bad idea." He suddenly looked at the aide with angry eyes. "You! Has he taught you the formula for this? Mix me a big jar of it. I'm getting out of here."

"Sir, I must protest! I'm under strict orders to keep you quiet and calm. That's the only way that wound is going to heal."

"Don't argue with me! Make up a huge pot of this! Get busy, curse you!"

The aide, hands trembling, signaled to a lesser functionary standing by the door. "Stand by my lord's bedside, will you? I've got to get to the laboratory."

Apedemek swung his long legs around and put his feet on the floor. "And take that ex-captain out of here!" he bellowed at the soldiers. "Take him to the dungeons for immediate execution! Imagine! Having Seth of Thebes right in his hands and letting him go!"

The lesser aide came toward the bed. "Please, sir, let me help you if you insist on getting up."

"Get me my traveling robes. I'm going out. And send for the captain of the night watch!"

"Y-yes, sir," the aide said, gesturing to another functionary standing by the door. That man left the room. "Where are you going at this time of night?"

"I'm going after Seth! He may still be in Thebes, waiting for the morning tide. You can be sure that he'll be getting out of Thebes as fast as he can. Let's see. If he went across the river to Deir el-Bahari, he could be taking them all to the oasis—then he'd be safely out of our hands. We'll never get past Weret's women."

As he spoke there was a noise in the hall, and the guards at the door parted to allow Kapsag entrance. His urbane self-possession had deserted him, and his movements were jerky.

"Where have you been?" Apedemek seethed. "You'd better have quite an excuse, you—"

The two looked into each other's eyes, and the tension in the room was palpable as they both stood immobile. After what seemed like a long, long time, the witnesses gasped as

Rapsag wilted. All his power seemed to flow into Apedemek, who, wounded or not, seemed to grow a head taller in the blink of an eye.

"You'd try your hand against me, would you?" Apedemek screamed. "You insect! You eater of offal!" His eyes narrowed. "You wouldn't have done this of your own volition—you'd have known better." His face twisted into a crazed mask of hatred. "Seth! You ran into him, didn't you? Answer me, you slime!"

"I . . . met Seth of Thebes," said Rapsag.

"What did you learn from him?"

"Seth knows about the woman. Your son is here in the city. Seth has him. Seth and his wife and the two old potters were heading for the quays to try to arrange night passage to the delta. He told me to tell you that he was going to El-Kab."

The captain of the night watch came through the door. "I got your message, sir. There's a crisis down by the waterfront; someone cut all the boats loose from their anchors and—"

"*What?*" Apedemek screamed.

"Yes, sir. Fortunately a few boats ran ashore a bit downriver, so we managed to retrieve them."

"Seth!" Apedemek moaned. "Seth did this! He's taking them all to the delta, and—" He suddenly turned back to the captain of the night watch. "You! You said some boats were salvaged. Are they ready to sail?"

"Yes, sir. But we've missed the favorable tide. We'll have to wait until morning."

"It can't wait that long!" Apedemek screeched.

"We have no choice, sir," the captain said, "but we can make up the lost time. On the beach half a league upstream, where we repair government vessels, we beached a war galley. You could order the repairmen to get it into the water with all haste and bring it to the docks, sir. Meanwhile, I could put together a crew by raiding the city guards. That would give us a fighting force when we catch the escapees, sir. Nothing can beat a war galley for speed, sir!"

"Yes!" Apedemek was gleeful. "How long would it take to get us out on the water in pursuit?"

"Around dawn, sir."

"Very well, give the orders."

"I'll get on it right now, sir." The officer saluted and turned on one heel. Three steps down the hall he was barking orders to the soldiers who had accompanied him.

Only then did Apedemek turn back to Rapsag. "And now to deal with *you*, scum," he said with chilling malice. "I have until dawn to come up with the worst death I can think of for the likes of you. What shall it be?"

The aides standing by the bed closed their eyes and shuddered.

VIII

The moon was a sliver short of being full, and the river was adequately visible in its light. The boatman steered the vessel by taking note of the tug of the current and bearing down on the tall steering oars. Seth stood in the bow with Yahadu.

"What's the matter, Seth? We're making good time."

"I'm worried about our pursuers."

"Pursuers?"

The older man nodded. "Apedemek won't let us get away like this. He'll know Rapsag was under my control. He'll doubt that El-Kab is our true destination and will send boats both north and south after us. Unless something drastic happens, they ought to catch up with us by sunset tomorrow."

Yahadu groaned.

"The solution," Seth concluded, "is to make something drastic happen."

"But what?"

"You've been on the river recently; did you notice any places downstream from Thebes where the channel narrows a great deal? Where the current is really fast and the water shallow?"

"Well . . . yes. There's a place coming up where the river flows around an island. There's shoal water all around the island. One side is blocked by reefs, and nothing of deeper draft than a one-man coracle could make it through. The other side of the island is almost as bad. While the leadsman called out the depths, the steersman had to cut very close to the right bank. Even so, I could feel the bottom brushing sand."

"Well," Seth said, "it sounds as though we have an excellent opportunity to stop our pursuers' progress. You're an observant man. How long before we're there?"

"By dawn. The river will begin to narrow as the island approaches on our left."

"Well, we've got to figure out some way of making that strait impassable. How much water is in it at the deepest point?"

"A fathom at most."

"Unfortunately that's enough to get through—unless a boat were sunk in the channel just below the waterline, where it can't be seen."

"So you propose that we create a snag where there was none before!"

"Exactly. My guess is that Apedemek will follow us in a war galley that was being repaired in a boatyard outside Thebes. We're going to insert an obstacle that a war galley can't avoid."

"But where are we going to find—"

"You're standing on the deck of it, my dear fellow."

"This boat! Then how will we get to the delta?"

"We'll walk overland to Hut-Sekhem and hire another boat—or steal one, if necessary."

Yahadu laughed. "Demetrios is right! You do belong at Home! The two of you will swap sharp deals and stratagems like a couple of Damascene horse traders." He laughed again.

"After we sink this boat, I figure it'll take them two days to clear the strait out enough to pass the galley through. They'll be fighting the current as they work, and it'll slow them down terribly."

"All the better! But what of our boatman?"

"He'll awaken in Hut-Sekhem a rich man with no memory of us or how he got there."

"All right." Yahadu grinned appreciatively. "We're to meet Demetrios in Athribis. He's going there as soon as the evacuation of the old Home is complete. He'll pick up Iri—

and it appears Iri has an assistant who may want to come with him."

"Yes. A chap named Baufra."

"Then we'll go to the new Home."

"I may have to postpone that," Seth warned. "Apedemek must be destroyed. I had thought to stay in Thebes to carry that out, but the more pressing thing was getting the others to safety. If Apedemek finds them, he will kill Neftis, my wife, and the two old potters. But even more I fear what he will do to his son."

"Ah, a bad situation!"

"Yes. Now you tell me that I'll be meeting Demetrios in Athribis?"

"Yes."

"I expect that Apedemek will also be coming to Athribis. Would Demetrios stand with me and confront Apedemek?"

Yahadu pondered. "I honestly can't say. The Grand Council of the Order expects its adepts to control or destroy the members who have gone astray. But like you, he would consider the saving of his kin as the higher priority."

"But if they were saved—what then? Without Demetrios, frankly, I'm not sure I'm up to the job. I have come up against him again and again, and each time I have failed."

"I cannot commit Demetrios. Nobody can answer for him but himself."

"Then I'll bank on my persuasive powers when at last we meet." Seth smiled. "How strange to have my life opening up again, after so many years. I had thought that I would spend the rest of my days in quiet contemplation of the past. I was happy in Nubia. I found the kind of woman I wish I had found when I was twenty. How much easier my life would have been!"

"Perhaps life is not meant to be easy," Yahadu ventured. "Things happen as they are destined to."

"Perhaps you're right," Seth said doubtfully. "Look, why don't you get some sleep? We'll need you at dawn to point out the island you mentioned and to show us where the channel runs and the location of the reefs below the surface."

"All right," Yahadu said. "Wake me when it's time."

*   *   *

Despite the best intentions, Yahadu lay awake thinking of Home and of how it was doomed to destruction. Like Seth, he had found a place where he had been happy, although he had neither wife nor family there. And like Seth, he had had to leave it. Would the life that followed bring him more happiness or something of the same disquiet that plagued Seth? Would his face ultimately show signs of inner peace, or would it bear the heavy furrows and wrinkles of worry and pain and guilt—and, yes, fear—that marked Seth's face?

He was still pondering this when Seth came in and exchanged places with him on the rough pallet. There was a chill in Yahadu's heart as well as in his bones when the first streaks of pink at last appeared in the sky, and he shivered, unable to keep his eyes on the channel before him.

He could see the great, black, glowering clouds to the north. There was a darkness over the far north that did not presage rain; it was like the great darkness that might foretell the end of the world. And it seemed to be slowly spreading, spreading. . . .

The horror had arrived at last! The terrible moment had come!

CHAPTER
SEVENTEEN

In the Greek Waters

I

Demetrios, aboard his unmarked flagship, saw the great cloud from the high prow of his boat. Immediately he realized that the volcanic eruption, the cataclysm foretold by astrologers in many countries, had finally occurred. He called down from his high perch to the sunburnt, naked sailors struggling with the folded sail on the deck. "Cover up! That cloud can burn you terribly."

The sailors looked at the cloud, then exchanged puzzled glances. Demetrios jumped to the main deck and spoke loudly, to carry his voice over the sounds of the sea and the distant rumble of the multiple explosions.

"When that hot ash hits, it's going to blister your skin wherever it touches you. It's going to get so dark here soon that you won't be able to see your hand in front of your face. Hold damp cloths over your mouths and noses, and wet a rag and wear it as a hood. This is the big explosion we've been waiting for. That's Home destroying itself."

"But sir," a sailor called out, "where can we go to escape this?"

"We won't be escaping; we have a mission, to pick up my kin, and your friend Yahadu of Mari. We're going to Egypt, right in the path of the cloud, if I'm any judge. Some of you men have wives and children aboard the boats that will remain out of the path of danger. Any man who wishes to change ships and join them may do so. Say so now, because everyone who's with me after the first cut will accompany me to Egypt." He paused. "*And* earn a bonus equal to his entire salary."

The men exchanged glances. This was a regal sum for a single trip, but several sailors known to have personal responsibilities opted to leave. The rest, donning rough robes, stood by Demetrios.

"Well, sir," said a self-appointed spokesman, "we're for it, whatever happens. Might as well die in Egypt earning money as anywhere else. Just tell us where to sail, and we'll go there."

Demetrios smiled with appreciation. "It'll be a long, difficult voyage ahead, and some of it is going to be frightening. When the cloud catches up with us, we'll have to lay at anchor, no matter where we are."

"How long will that go on, sir?"

"I'm not sure," Demetrios confessed.

"Sir," said a young sailor, "will we ever be able to go back to Home? I mean to the old one, sir?"

Demetrios nodded gravely, thinking with terrible regret of the island he had loved for so long. "You probably will, but by the time you can, you won't want to. You were born there, weren't you?"

The boy nodded.

"Well, son, by the time it's cooled down and the mountain has stopped blowing off, what's left of the island will be buried under a pile of ash as high as or higher than your head. And there's no guarantee that it won't erupt again."

"Pardon, sir. You say, what's left of it?"

"Yes," Demetrios said. "From the reports I've heard of eruptions, the center of the island will collapse, and the sea will rush in. Much of what you know will be buried underwater, the rest under ash. It'll have harbors where there were none."

"That's enough for me, sir," the boy said. "We're in your hands. Lead on!"

II

From the epicenter of the volcanic activity, a gigantic seismic wave raced out in all directions at terrifying speed across the Great Sea. As Demetrios had predicted, ships far out in the water did not feel the effects, but there was great and terrible destruction wherever a shoreline was in the wave's path. On nearby islands, the wave appeared out of nowhere, towering to tremendous heights and dwarfing every building in the shore communities. It rose over the ports and smashed down with unbelievable force, crushing houses and storerooms and palaces and killing entire populations. Tiryns, Amnisios on Crete, and the budding seaport of Piraeus on the Greek mainland were wiped clean, as if a giant hand had reached down and removed them.

The great shock spread across the sea faster than any bird could fly. The wave fell on the Phrygian coast, obliterating seaports and fishing settlements with one mighty blow and depopulating whole islands, leaving nothing alive. The Libyan and Cypriot ports were devastated, and even on the far coast of Canaan, many days' sail away, waves over four times the height of a tall man battered the shorelines, smashing the walls of fortified settlements. Sidon disappeared in five minutes' time; Ashkelon was pounded flat; and rocky Tyre became an island again as the artificially constructed isthmus was wiped out, cutting off the city from the mainland and wrecking both the northern Sidonian and the southern Egyptian ports in the same stroke.

While the sea was rearranging the shorelines around all the known world, the great outpouring of ash spread darkness overhead. A steady storm of pumice settled on the waters and silted up the coast of the Greek mainland and clogged the rivers' openings to the sea.

The pumice cloud drifted inexorably toward the Great Crescent, choking birds, which fell to their death from the polluted skies. Fish died by the millions in waters now poisoned, and land animals went mad, stampeding in staggering numbers until the panic-stricken beasts plunged into the ash-choked waters to drown or succumbed to the choking pollution in the poisoned air.

At length the wave came to the shore cities of the Egyptian delta, far in advance of the slower-moving cloud of darkness that loomed in the northwestern skies like the terrible finger of some malevolent god pointing accusingly toward the earth. At each of the many mouths of the Nile, the wave, building an immense head in the shallow coastal shelf, rose over the tiny port towns, lifting ships at sea far over the tops of the highest buildings and tossing them well inland to crash and shatter on the land beyond. Plowing up the continental shelf, the water redistributed the underwater sandbars, silting up some mouths of the Nile while creating new ones elsewhere.

And always, slowly, steadily, behind the fast-moving and brutal fist of the sea came the gathering darkness. . . .

Demetrios's flagship lay at anchor well out to sea, and the sailors had furled the sails and shipped the mast in anticipation of turbulence. Thus far, the rough weather had been quite normal except for the gathering darkness and light rain of pumice. As the cloud slowly enveloped the ship, though, thunder could be heard, and lightning bolts began to burst whitely around them.

After a time, the darkness grew increasingly thick, and the lightning bolts faded until they were dim flickers seen through thick fog—only the fog was ash, which clogged the nose and mouth, burned the eyes, and accumulated on the deck like drifted snow.

"Hang onto something!" Demetrios cried out, his eyes running with hot tears as the light slowly faded and his companions became less visible. They had brought up sturdy bronze lanterns, lit them, and positioned them around the deck, but now their light was visible from no farther than three steps away.

The men hunkered down against the rails, grasping anything that would provide secure purchase. Demetrios sat with his back to the stanchion that held the mast and watched the light of his lantern die.

If the world was to come to an end, he thought, *it would look like this.* He reached down and probed the deepening layer of ash on the pitched deck; his hand sank to the full length of his fingers before touching the deck, and the ash was still warm. His fears of scalding-hot ash had not materialized, and for this he was thankful.

The men must be frightened, he thought. In a voice both confident and strong he called out over the sound of the thunder in the distance. "Can everyone hear me?"

There was a general assent, if some of the voices seemed weak and tremulous. Demetrios spoke up. "There's nothing to fear now! All we have to do is stay calm and wait it out! The worst is over for us!"

It was a brave enough thought; the blackness surrounding them was total. He swallowed and began again. "We'll just wait here for the darkness to pass! We're only on the fringe of the cloud, so it'll pass over us quickly."

They're still afraid, he thought. *I'd better do something.* He remembered a prayer from his childhood in Thebes, called Hymn to the Sun. That seemed like an appropriate invocation in this darkness. He began:

Hail to you, Ra, at your tremendous dawning!
You rise! You shine! The heavens are rolled aside!
You are the king of gods, the golden morning;
From you we come, in you we're deified.

Halfway through the last line a single voice joined in. Then another chimed in, louder, stronger. Demetrios continued powerfully:

Your priests divert their hearts at dawn with mirth;
The winds of music touch your golden strings.
At sunset you transfigure sky and earth
With flames of blazing color from your wings.

More were praying now.

Hail to you, Ra, who wake our lives from slumber!
You rise! You shine! Your radiant face appears!
The years that pass—we cannot count their number.
You heed them not; you are beyond the years!

After much elapsed time—and many prayers with multiple verses, some in a number of different tongues—the darkness began slowly to lift, the fall of ash decrease, and what had been utter blackness assumed a reddish color. At length the crew became visible through the gloom. Demetrios grinned at his nearest neighbor, a sailor from Libya. "You're covered with ash. If I look as silly as you do, don't laugh. I feel enough like an idiot already."

The sailor scowled. "The ship's fouled with this stuff!"

Demetrios nodded. "Let's clean it up. Volunteers! Let's have some volunteers!"

Half a dozen sailors quickly came forward, and soon they were sweeping the ash overboard. Demetrios, observing it all in the dim light, smiled. He had averted panic. Having survived the first crisis, the crew might be able to weather the next one with more equanimity—he had no illusions; there would be other emergencies. He believed that Home would continue to explode over a period of days, the resulting black ash would continue to pour forth.

CHAPTER EIGHTEEN

In the Delta

I

Standing by the lee rail Pepi watched the elderly couple care for his mother. Mut was preparing food for Neftis, and beside her Khem tied a bib around Neftis's neck. "It's like watching parents fussing over a baby," he said, visibly upset. "She can't do anything for herself."

Mai put an arm around Pepi's shoulders and gave him a squeeze. "When Seth is able to sit down with her, this will change, I'm sure of it. Think about good things, like the new life you're going to enjoy in the delta. You've never met your uncle Iri, and I know you'll like him. He's a remarkable man."

"Seth says that it'll take time to get used to looking at him."

"When you've been around him a bit, you'll see him quite differently."

"He's an armorer, then? A Child of the Lion?"

"Yes. And you're a Child of the Lion yourself, even if you know relatively little about the family and its traditions."

"King Het told me about Ahuni and how Ahuni's father,

333

Belsunu, helped arm the Habiru when they left Egypt the first time to move into Canaan."

"That's right. And Seth says that the present-day Habiru hope to return to Canaan once more."

"I don't know," Pepi said skeptically. "From what King Het told me, the Habiru will have to fight their way."

Mai nodded. "Since the Habiru have been in Egypt, many new people have carved Canaan up: Hittites, Hivites, Ammonites, and Moabites, Amorites, Kivites, Amalekites. And there's been a new migration: the Philistines. They supposedly have the secret of ironmongery. If that's true, the Habiru are going to have double problems."

"They'll need their own armorer," Pepi suggested. "But isn't Seth the only living Child of the Lion who knows the process of making iron weapons?"

"Your uncle Khian knows it," Mai said, thinking that Apedemek, corrupt or no, was a Child of the Lion, and Seth had said Apedemek knew the process; all Chalybians of high rank did.

"But Iri doesn't?" Pepi asked.

"He knows, but he's no expert. To keep his abilities secret from Amasis and Kamose, Iri has never practiced the procedure."

"Seth says that Iri is a friend of Prince Moses and that the prince is a great fighter but refuses to take up arms."

"That's true, dear."

"If things are so hostile up in Canaan, how is Prince Moses going to bring his people there without fighting?"

"I don't know. Perhaps you'll have a chance to ask him." She watched as the channel took them into an ever-widening stretch of the Nile. They had passed the pyramids a day ago. Now they were leaving the Red Lands and moving into the rich delta Black Lands.

She excused herself and went to speak with the boatman. "How far to Athribis?" she asked.

"We'll dock there before evening," he answered. "At least, I think we will. That huge cloud up ahead . . . I hope that isn't a storm. I wouldn't like having to navigate strange waters in a storm."

"Before evening!" Mai enthused. "How wonderful!" She returned to Pepi amidships. "The boatman says we'll arrive today," she told him and the others. "We'll dock in Athribis this afternoon."

"Athribis!" Khem said. "Who would ever have thought we'd be coming to live downriver? A dream beyond my imagining appears to be coming true. I hope nothing happens to ruin it."

But as he said it, he looked at the ominous cloud on the northern horizon. Mai and Pepi looked too. There was something strangely wrong about it.

Darkness, Mai thought, signing against the evil eye. *Darkness coming to cover all the world.*

When the war galley had foundered on the unseen snag, a fuming Apedemek escaped to shore in a goatskin coracle. He had ordered four of his stoutest men to retrieve a litter from the stricken boat and had thereby made his way into Kaine, with the rest of his command marching doggedly behind. At the little port he had commandeered a squat and sturdy fishing vessel, and loaded down to the waterline with its unaccustomed burden of soldiers, the borrowed boat had moved downriver.

At Memphis he had hauled a new galley out of dry dock, staffed it with a recently augmented complement of warriors, and then continued to overtake Seth and the stranger, but except for the usual fishing vessels and traders' boats, the river was devoid of traffic.

At one point, near Ausim, his boat was stopped by a government inspection vessel, and an officer came aboard. When the guardsman recognized Apedemek, he saluted smartly. "Beg to report, sir. You may appreciate hearing information just here from Avaris."

Apedemek shifted in his seat and winced; his injury was painful, and he was almost completely out of the preparation Rapsag had devised. "Get it out," he demanded impatiently.

"Very well, sir. Prince Moses is back in Avaris, and—"

Apedemek sat bolt upright and all but cried out with pain. "Moses back? I presume Kamose has him in prison."

"No, sir. It would appear that the prince—"

"Don't honor him," Apedemek snarled. "He's the son of a foreign slave."

"Yes, sir. The king is being cautious about jailing him. In

the ten years Moses has been away, he has become a magus himself, with considerable power."

"Nonsense!" Apedemek snorted. "Go on."

"Very well, sir. Moses demands that his people be allowed to return to Canaan as free men. He's apparently made a number of threats—I mean, if the king doesn't let them go."

"Threats! A slave makes threats!"

"The threats were made before a huge gathering—" The soldier stopped abruptly, peering ahead. The sky seemed to be dotted with pinkish flecks, which fell lightly to the land. He held up a hand, caught a fleck, and rubbed it with his finger. "That's very curious. What do you suppose this stuff could be?"

Apedemek scowled, holding up his own hand, captured two or three of the little flecks, and examined them carefully. "They could be volcanic ash, but that's absurd. There are no volcanoes for a thousand leagues around." He looked up as the tiny flakes continued to float down. "There has to be some explanation for this."

A thin film of perspiration beaded the soldier's upper lip. "That cloud has been growing, sir. And there are reports of giant waves crashing on the cities at the Nile mouths, sir."

"Giant waves?" Apedemek echoed.

"The trouble is, sir, these phenomena are consistent with the threats Moses has been making."

"What are you talking about?"

"Well, sir, Moses said that if the king wouldn't let the Habiru go, a succession of plagues would cripple Egypt, each worse than the one before. And he said that if Kamose continued to hold his people hostage—"

"Hostage! They're slaves!"

"I'm just reporting, sir. He said the rivers would run red as if with blood, and small animals—frogs and the like—would crawl onto the land and would choke the roads—"

"That's not uncommon with volcanic activity!"

"Yes, sir. But flies and mosquitoes and other stinging creatures would supposedly beset us. To tell the truth, sir, this apparently is happening near Avaris. The boat that came up from there yesterday—"

"Yes, yes. Animals and insects tend to go mad in such circumstances, but—"

"The problem, sir, is that everything happened in the sequence he predicted—including the livestock dying. The fellow from Avaris said that the rivers turned red, and whatever is in the river is killing the fish."

"And the people credit his prophecy?" Apedemek asked.

"They think these things are happening because he threatened to make them happen, sir."

"I'd better get to Avaris quickly. You stay on board. Captain! Draw anchor! Hortator! Battle stroke!"

As he turned away, his glance went to the water. The pink flakes were falling on the waters of the Nile, slowly turning the waves red.

II

Seth had disembarked from the boat just below Memphis, and Yahadu had to make his own way to the appointment with Demetrios. Seth made his way on horseback overland toward Avaris, riding day and night. Now, just outside Bast, he realized that the dawn was, by his reckoning, long overdue. But the huge cloud that had darkened the northern horizon for a day appeared to be upon them, and ash fell around him, like the pinkish petals of some poisonous flower. There was a sickly reddish glow in the east, but the full flare of an Egyptian dawn was nowhere to be seen.

I hope I'm not too late, he thought, worried. But if anyone had asked him, "Late for what?" he was not sure he could have answered. He knew that a terrible confrontation was under way, and Moses, who had been his protégé, needed his help, his advice, his presence.

He knew he would miss his wife, his friends, and Demetrios at Athribis. Nevertheless, from the first he had felt a special desire to be in Avaris when Moses finally locked horns with Kamose.

Now, grim-faced, he urged his mount forward. "Go!

Give it everything you've got! We've an appointment with destiny!"

When Neb-mertef returned to his rebuilt, palatial town house in Avaris, he found Amasis waiting in the outer hall. Amasis saw the light dusting of ash on Neb-mertef's head and shoulders and moved forward to brush it off. "This stuff makes us look like bums who have been picking through garbage."

Neb-mertef looked worn out. "I suppose I don't have to tell you that I've been with the king."

"I suspected as much. I can almost imagine the dialogue: Given the public mood, you counseled moderation and compromise; he told you to soak your head in the Nile."

"Very close," Neb-mertef admitted. " 'If they think I'm going to let some slave's grubby offshoot dictate Egypt's official policy, they have another think coming.' "

Amasis resumed his seat on the stone bench. "Perhaps we've been going about this in the wrong way. We've been trying to talk him out of his preconceived position."

Neb-mertef, kicking off his ash-covered sandals, joined him. "So?"

"He's very frustrated by Apedemek's absence. He believes that to vanquish Moses, he needs only to unleash Apedemek. I think Kamose is just trying to hold out until Apedemek gets back. Meanwhile, his own people are frightened by these plagues—not that I blame them—and want Kamose to do whatever is necessary to return things to normal."

Neb-mertef looked puzzled.

Amasis' eyes glittered. "Why don't you start agreeing with him? No matter what he says, tell him he's absolutely right."

"But he's being a fool."

"And so may he cause his own downfall. That would benefit us."

Neb-mertef raised first one brow, then the other. He smiled, understanding. "Have you had breakfast? No? Be my guest. And while we eat, you can elaborate on your plan."

"Thank you. Incidentally, whatever happened to that Chaldean astrologer of yours?"

"He lives across town. He's done some decent charts,

and it might interest you to know that the present troubles are quite clearly delineated in his papyruses."

He stood, and Amasis joined him. "Good. If his predictions present an accurate picture, you can show them to the important people—the people who count, the people whose support we'll need when the time comes—and tell them that you warned Kamose, but he wouldn't pay attention."

"Ah, yes," Neb-mertef said, stopping before the dining hall and clapping his hands. Three servants appeared at three different doors. "Breakfast, please, for two." The servants disappeared. "Thus making me look like a man with Egypt's best interests at heart."

"And," Amasis added, "making him look like an irresponsible monster who risks the life of every man, woman, and child just to maintain his bloated ego."

Neb-mertef stopped to think. "Still . . . this strange weather we're having . . . you know the astrologers have been predicting the end of the world for years. You don't suppose . . . ?"

Amasis snorted. "People who are paid for predicting events thrive on disaster. I've been near a volcanic eruption before. They're not all this bad or this large, but they follow a certain pattern."

"And everything will be all right again after a while?"

"All right for *us*. Not all right for Kamose and that hard head of his."

Neb-mertef settled into a chair. "I'll stop worrying. I'll convince him that he's a fountain of wisdom."

"And in the end we'll share a kingdom," Amasis said. "One from which the king has miraculously been removed."

As they spoke, the astrologer Agha of Chaldea was keeping a morning appointment with a sensitive named Nabu of Akkad. The sage sat cross-legged on a cushion, looking starved and ascetic.

"Well?" Agha asked timidly. "Have I diagnosed the situation properly?"

Nabu looked disconsolately at him. "Sit down, please. I can't concentrate with you pacing."

Agha obeyed. "I'm sorry. I realize you need tranquillity to do what you do."

"It is your Chaldean blood," Nabu said. "Chaldeans never know how to relax. All that turmoil! All that strife!"

"My apologies," Agha said meekly.

"You need a drink," Nabu knew somehow. "You feel as though if you don't get strong drink in a moment, you'll fly apart. You'll scream your head off." This was not said judgmentally; Nabu's face remained mournful. "You cannot handle your dependency on strong waters. You need one last drink at the end of the day to get off to sleep and another in the morning to wake up."

Agha bristled, but he knew it would do no good to get Nabu angry. "You were going to tell me about my charts."

"Worthless. You cannot do a proper chart anymore. Even if you could, you would be totally helpless before the task of interpreting them properly."

"That's not fair."

"I merely state facts," Nabu reminded him. "You stole your material from the old charts left behind by Set-Nakht. But you missed the thing that Set-Nakht would have caught."

"And that is—"

"That when the cataclysm appears to be done, it will, in fact, not be done. When everyone thinks it is over, there will be more. The ash comes from a mountain far away, one that is blowing itself to pieces. When the present cloud is dispersed and everything seems calm again, the island will finish the job of destroying itself."

"How could I indicate that on my charts?"

"*You* will not be able to, although Set-Nakht, who dwells far west of here, has correctly predicted it. But he would never share his predictions with any member of the court."

"Can't I . . . well, fake something? Predicting a second cataclysm on the heels of the first would seal my fame." The man looked desperate. "It would get me out of the predicament I'm in now."

"You will never extricate yourself from your current problems. The only way you will escape will be through death."

"Oh, gods."

"I speak only facts. Are you sure you want to hear more?" There was compassion in the sad voice.

"Tell me my future. Tell me whether I will survive this terrible time."

"You will not. You will not live to see the end of it." Nabu rose lightly. "The interview is over. Try to find some peace in the time that remains."

Agha clutched at Nabu's garment as he passed, but the sensitive broke free and disappeared behind a beaded curtain. Agha started to say something, but his lips would not form words. He walked unsteadily out the door, heading for the apartment Neb-mertef had appointed for him in the commercial quarter.

Neb-mertef's runner found him there an hour later, hanging from a rafter, reeking of palm wine—the cheapest and most powerful kind.

III

Mai sat with Khem on one of the long stone benches in the great hall of the Athribis home of Siamon, the city's most powerful banker. She put a reassuring hand on Khem's and felt it tremble. "Now don't worry," she said. "Everything's going to be just wonderful."

"I'm afraid I can't help it, Mai," the old potter replied. "I'm a fish out of water here. I'd feel better if Mut was here. She has a steadying influence on me."

"Well, I'll try to be a good substitute," Mai promised. "I'm sure you understand that someone has to be with Neftis at all times. And I don't want the boy loose in the streets. For all we know, Apedemek may be right behind us. If Pepi should meet his father now . . ."

"I know." Khem looked down. "I'll try to control myself."

As he said this, a distinguished-looking young man seated on one of the other benches, his beard cut in the manner of the Greeks, got up, walked toward them, and came to a stop directly in front of them. "Pardon me," he said. "Would you perhaps be Mai, the wife of Seth of Thebes?"

"Why, yes," Mai said cautiously. "But who wants to know?"

"A thousand pardons," the young man said. "Yahadu of Mari, at your service. I left your husband two days ago; we came downriver together from Thebes. He asked me to look you up here. He's gone ahead to Avaris."

"Oh!" Mai said, rising to greet him. "This is Khem of Thebes, who helped me bring Neftis and the boy to Athribis."

Yahadu bowed courteously. "I am honored. My thanks, and those of Demetrios the Magnificent, to both of you."

"Demetrios?" Mai said.

"Yes. I am here to meet him. Seth's banker has been Demetrios's representative in Athribis for many years. I am Demetrios's assistant, and I would be honored by any service you would allow me to do for either of you. From what Seth tells me, you, sir, have been of great service to Demetrios's sister and nephew. You will find that Demetrios's gratitude stretches a very long way."

This was almost too much for Khem. "Demetrios! Even I have heard that name."

"Count him among your friends now." Yahadu turned back to Mai. "The boy is here? And Neftis?"

"Yes. With Khem's wife. They are settled at an inn."

"Good. Once we've got these good people taken care of, Mai, you and I must make our way to Iri in Avaris. We'll go overland; I don't trust the river. For all I know, Apedemek may already be here in the delta."

"Here?"

"Yes." He explained what he and Seth had done to impede Apedemek's progress. "We slowed him, but we haven't stopped him. He'll be right behind us. And he mustn't get to either Neftis or the boy."

"Of course not! Just tell me what to do."

Pepi had slipped out of the inn, and now he roamed the Athribis streets. He wandered through the riverside market, fascinated by everything and everybody. And as he watched, a boy his age purloined a ripe pomegranate from one of the stalls and slipped it under his robe. Pepi smiled in admiration and followed the boy.

After a number of twists and turns up this alley and

down that street, the boy, thinking himself unobserved, sat on someone's back stoop and began to peel the fruit.

Pepi stepped from behind the corner of the building. "For half the pomegranate, I won't tell anyone I saw you steal it."

The boy was instantly on his feet. "Who are you? What do you want?"

"Oh, nothing," Pepi replied with a conspiratorial grin. "But you've got a thing to learn about stealing."

The boy's eyes narrowed. "So you're not going to turn me in. What do you want?"

"Not much. I'm new in town, and you could give me an idea of what's happening." He reached up and brushed the ash out of his hair. "Ugh! Filthy stuff! I wish it'd all pass and be over with."

The boy snorted as he handed over half the fruit. "Here. My name's Joshua. What makes you so sure it's going to be over with?"

"I'm Pepi. It's ash from a faraway volcano. People who know about these things have told me all about it."

"That's your story. People here know it's magic, done by the magus Moses, who used to be a prince."

Pepi sat next to the other boy. "I don't know anything about that. Tell me."

"I only know that Moses came back after having lived many years in the desert and started threatening the king."

"How?"

"Moses told Kamose that if he didn't let the Habiru go back to Canaan, all sorts of horrible things were going to happen—locusts, frogs, skin disease. . . . My uncle told me about it. He was there."

Pepi spat out a couple of seeds. "And the king hasn't given in?"

"Not yet. There are a lot of people who think the king ought to let some of the Habiru go. But Moses says it's got to be every man, woman, and child, or it's no deal. I admire him. Imagine facing down the king! But Kamose is waiting for Apedemek to return."

"Wait," Pepi said. "Apedemek isn't here."

"I heard he was up in Thebes."

"Thebes!" Pepi's eyes were wide. An ash drifted into one of them, and he rubbed it. "I was just there!"

He stopped and reflected: They had left Thebes in a

terrible hurry because someone Seth feared was chasing them. Then there was that business about what had happened to his mother. No doubt his father had had a hand in that. He had been in Thebes at the same time as his father! And they had conspired to keep it from him. Anger and indignation surged in his heart. How dare they? How dare they keep him from meeting his father?

"Do the people in Avaris think that Apedemek is more powerful than Moses?" Pepi asked.

"I don't know. Apedemek's very powerful, and everyone's afraid of him, even the king. My uncle says that everyone in Avaris knows that Apedemek is the real power here in Egypt. *He'd* take this spell off the country and stop all these crazy things from happening. I wish Apedemek were here."

"Me too," said Pepi in a low voice, as if speaking to himself.

Siamon's house was majestic, its stone courtyard leading down to the river, where goods could be unloaded on his private quays directly from the trade ships that docked in Athribis. Mai came out of the great door smiling. "I'm so glad," she said to Yahadu and Khem. "Khem, your worries are over. Siamon will have a house for you within a day or two. You can stay with Siamon until—"

But now Yahadu took hold of their arms and steered them quickly behind a stone kiosk. He peered out from behind the structure and looked out on the river. "Mai," he whispered, "we'd better step up our schedule. That's a war galley passing, and standing in the bow, looking as if there were nothing wrong with him—"

"Apedemek!" she breathed.

IV

"So the king needs me home," Apedemek said smugly. "I gather he has problems he can't handle?"

The captain of the Athribis garrison stood at attention

before Apedemek's chair. "Not to disparage the king, sir, but there are dilemmas only a magus of your rank can solve."

"Call in your aide," Apedemek ordered. Immediately another soldier stood before him in the same stiff posture. "Take this papyrus ashore to the chief physician. There's a formula on it for a preparation for pain. Tell him that he'll be richly rewarded if he follows the formula precisely. Speed is of the essence." His nod was a dismissal, and the aide hurried out. "Now, Captain, tell me about the king's problem."

The captain tersely sketched in the confrontation between Moses and Kamose.

At the end Apedemek chuckled humorlessly. "Well! For once I approve of something the king has done. If he hadn't stood his ground, I'd have felt great contempt for him."

"You and I may applaud the king's stand, sir, but the citizens of Avaris look on the matter differently. The dissidents' number include the richest people in Avaris, the priesthood of Amon, the—"

"Let them carp," Apedemek interrupted. "When I'm done with the impostor, they'll be talking out of the other side of their mouth. I'll explain that there's a natural cause for all this, and everyone's mind will be set at ease."

"I agree, sir. It's good to have you back."

Apedemek glared at him. The flattery irritated him. "Captain, put your command in the hands of a subordinate and come with me to Avaris. I may have need of a man like you."

The captain beamed, and the military posture grew even more stiff and pompous. "Yes, sir! I'll have the message sent ashore. Do you want to cast off, sir?"

Apedemek looked at him, his half-closed eyes veiling contempt and malice. *Somewhere between here and Avaris, I'll break you as a man breaks a horse.* "Yes, as soon as I have the prescription." He stood, not without difficulty, to look out over the Nile.

Pepi walked along the waterfront, thinking. The urchin boy's talk of Apedemek's power and prowess had stirred strange, forbidden feelings. To this street boy, Apedemek was not a villain; he was a hero in a nation of weaklings.

Of course everyone seemed also to fear Apedemek. But

this was a further sign of the man's importance. Seth, for example, was granted respect, but that was because he was the rich father of a man who had become king of Nubia. Riches bought a certain respect; so did family.

But although he, Pepi, would be well off when his mother had passed on or he had come into his manhood, he enjoyed none of the respect people granted Seth. This, of course, was because he was a bastard. People had always known that he had no father. So everyone had looked at him askance, and the boys of his age would not admit him to their circles. This was one reason he had gravitated to the slums. People in the lower-class quarters were mostly bastards themselves.

The past had taught him that it might be better to be feared than liked. Publicly deplored characteristics were secretly admired. Power, success, strength—these were the qualities to have. He firmed his jaw and hardened his heart.

A great war galley, stately and powerful, glided past. The hortator's stroke had shifted from slow to fast, and the great vessel, with its long ranks of rowers, was picking up speed. A lone man standing in the prow, tall and impressive, caught Pepi's eye. As his sharp, magnetic eyes scanned the shoreline, his craggy face was impassive, but his posture was strong and powerful. He was easily the most impressive man Pepi had ever seen. For a moment he looked Pepi's way, noticing him, and their eyes met.

Then the ship moved past a line of merchantmen with half-furled sails, and Pepi could see no more. But someone on the quay near him spoke up: "Did you see? Standing in the prow of that war galley, as big as you please."

"Who?" asked his neighbor, whose back was turned to the water.

"Why, Apedemek, that's who! And headed for Avaris, unless I miss my guess."

Pepi's heart lurched. Apedemek! His father! Here in the delta!

Mai and Yahadu found him standing there, still lost in thought, his eyes focused on an empty space far downriver. "Pepi!" Mai called out. "We've been looking all over for you! Come along, now. We've got to leave."

"But we just got here," he protested. "And who's he?"

"This is Yahadu, a friend of Seth's. He's going to take us to Avaris—"

"Avaris!" His face lit up.

"Yes, dear. Yahadu thinks—and I agree with him—that we have no choice but to go to Avaris now and find your uncle Iri. He'll arrange for a safe place for us. Now come along, darling, and we'll get ready."

"You'll like the trip," Yahadu said. "Have you ever ridden in a chariot?"

Pepi's eyes widened. "A war chariot? Like the soldiers use in battle?"

"Yes. It's the fastest way there. You can ride with me. Perhaps I can teach you a bit about driving."

"A chariot!" Pepi said, genuinely excited.

But his enthusiasm was not limited to this. Even more exciting than the thought of a fast ride in a war chariot was that they were not escaping Apedemek; they were, instead, riding to meet him.

Mai and Yahadu did not know that, and he was not going to be the one to tell them!

Apedemek, perplexed, stood by the rail for a long time. As the powerful rowers drew the great vessel steadily and briskly downriver, the captain approached him.

"Have you ever had a child, Captain?" he asked in a flat voice.

"No sir. The service is my life. I've never thought much about settling down. I thought it might interfere with my being able to take a promising assignment if one was offered to me, sir."

Apedemek felt revolted by the man's blatant pitch. Yet once again the magus chose not to destroy him. He felt an unfamiliar need to discuss his inner turmoil.

"Just now," Apedemek said, "I spotted a half-grown boy on the Athribis quays. There was something about him that was oddly intriguing. If I had a son, I would want him to look something like that: sharp-eyed, clean-featured, bright, and fearless. I could see that the boy admired me, looked up to me."

"And why should he not, sir? After all, you're the most

powerful man in Egypt. I'd wager that everyone in the delta can recognize you by now."

Apedemek silently put another black mark by his name, then went on. "If I had a son to raise, I'd teach him to look at the world through my eyes. He'd learn immediately that self-interest is the first law. A man must have an iron will coupled with a strong sense of self."

"Yes, sir. I couldn't agree more."

Apedemek scowled, but the soldier missed it. The soldier did not matter; only the vision that he, Apedemek, had now mattered.

My son! Mine, to mold as I wish!

V

Iri glared at the gate guard. "Everyone in Avaris knows who I am. Nobody in Egypt looks like I do."

The guard looked embarrassed. "I'm sorry, sir. It's just that the king is getting upset at the, well, all this trouble with the Habiru. Anyone entering through the north gate—which *they* use—well, the feeling is that he's already suspect."

"Bosh!" Iri said, then turned to Baufra. "Have you ever heard such drivel? Suspect of what? I'm the royal armorer." He turned back to the guard. "Look, my friend, for your information—and for the king's too—the problem isn't with the Habiru; it's with the king. If he weren't so stubborn—"

"Sir, I . . . I am not permitted to agree, sir, if you understand me, but—"

"I understand all too well. Look, I'm bringing these carts of provender to the Habiru. If this makes me an enemy of the government, so be it. Under the laws of Egypt I am your superior officer, and I'm losing my patience. Let me and my carts through right now, or I'll have you up on charges for disobeying a direct order."

"Yes, sir. Pass!"

Iri steered his horse forward. "Baufra," he said, "the more time I spend with Egyptians, the more I enjoy the company of the Habiru. And the more I think of what's been going on, the less I feel like an Egyptian."

"That puts you in a peculiar position, sir," Baufra pointed out. "You can't very well become a Habiru."

"No," Iri agreed with a sigh. "But I'm beginning to think like one. They and I have a lot in common: I'm as stiff-backed proud as they . . . although I can't imagine you wouldn't have noticed by now," he added with a wry smile.

"That would be hard to miss."

Iri brushed the ubiquitous ash away. "I hate this stuff. I *dream* of it. One of the apprentices at the forge told me that when I was catching a nap the other day, I was wiping away ash in my sleep."

"I know. I thought I'd get used to it, but I haven't."

"Well, brace yourself. If Kamose doesn't budge, there'll be more, and worse, plagues. And I don't blame the Habiru a bit! These people, through no fault of their own, are outcasts in a strange land, rejected by all. In this way, I understand them, for I have always been a man apart. Yet they haven't let their bondage defeat their spirit. I admire that."

"I *have* noticed the friendship you have developed among them, sir."

"I'm sure you have. Aaron and Moses have become like brothers to me."

They were in the Habiru quarter now. People on all sides waved at Iri and called out to him.

He responded in the Habiru tongue. "I'm becoming fairly proficient," he said proudly.

"There's Dathan," Baufra said.

Iri beckoned the one-time rebel.

"Iri! You're always a welcome sight."

"Even more so, I'll wager, when you see what I've brought." He nodded at the carts of food. "Enjoy!"

"Thank you!" Dathan said. "I'll help to distribute it. It will be most appreciated; Moses warns that we must prepare ourselves for privation. He's gone to Kamose for another confrontation—Aaron and he together."

Iri's face fell. "I asked him not to go without me!"

"I know," Dathan acknowledged. "But he says there's a higher authority whose orders he has to follow. He should be there any minute now."

Iri looked at Baufra. "I was afraid of something like this. Would you help Dathan with the food? I've got to get to the palace before the king does anything rash."

"Go!" Baufra urged. "We'll take care of everything here!"

Kamose looked down from the rooftop garden of the unfinished palace. "Look," he said, his voice fairly crackling with tension. "They're out there again, demanding to be heard."

Neb-mertef's voice was calm. "It is an outrage, Sire. You would be justified in taking any form of retaliation."

Kamose turned to his adviser. "You've come around, eh? I thought you were promoting leniency for these foreign bastards."

Neb-mertef inclined his head slightly. "May I never grow too set in my ways, Sire, to acknowledge when I am wrong. I was blinded by stubbornness and could not see the rightness of your views."

"Well, it's about time. I wish the rest of my court would come around."

"How true, Sire. The sooner your ministers and counselors come to realize they are in error, the better. Are you going to respond to these arrogant swine? I could save you the trouble and tell them—"

"No!" Kamose said. "In this no one can speak for the king but the king himself."

Neb-mertef smiled secretly. "As you prefer, Sire. I was just thinking of your nerves."

Kamose held up his hand. "It's all right. I'll stay calm. I promised the royal physicians that I'd not let these upstarts excite me." He looked toward the gray skies, with the great beetling black cloud still in the distance. "Wait for me here. This won't take long. I'll just tell them no, and that's all."

"As you prefer, Sire." He offered a gesture of polite submission, which, he had found, soothed the king. He watched Kamose go to the stairs and heard him stomping down the steps. And only now did Neb-mertef permit himself a smile of victory.

In the courtyard the crowd had grown to fifty people. Kamose came roaring through the great double doors, trailing the guards he had accumulated in his hasty passage through the halls of his palace. "Here!" he shouted angrily. "What do you want—as if I didn't already know?"

Moses gave a tiny bow. "We come only to reiterate the same request. Let the sons and daughters of Jacob go, in the name of Yahweh."

"You're wasting your breath!" Kamose said. "Never!"

Moses held up his palms. "Then I can only tell you what the alternative is, as told to me by God. We stand upon the richest soil in the world. If you let my people go, the harvest will make you richer than any king of Egypt has been since the days of the last Sesostris. Your people will prosper and multiply. Fortune will attend your every action."

Kamose grinned sourly.

"If you refuse," Moses continued, "a famine as great as that of the last days of Salitis will fall upon Egypt. Famine brought on by a series of calamities the likes of which Egypt has never seen: the heavens will go mad; thunder and lightning will strike fear into the hearts of all; hailstones the size of a large man's fists will fall from the sky and kill whatever livestock still survives. Only the livestock of the Habiru, outside the walls of Avaris, will be spared."

Kamose hooted with laughter. "There's been no hail here since—"

Moses went on calmly: "The stones will destroy the barley and flax crops. Only the wheat crops will be untouched—"

"Ah! Your God is unable to destroy wheat, then?"

Moses went on unperturbed. "If you still refuse to let us go, the locusts will blacken the skies and will clog your roads and your houses and your fields and your storerooms. There will be no place where a man can walk that he will not step on their massed bodies. They will eat everything left uncovered. And they will make short work of the wheat crop. How, then, will the Egyptians feed their children? How will the Egyptians live? And whom will they blame for the great calamity that will fall upon them?"

"Curse you, you misbegotten—"

"And when they have cursed you and all your works, the hand of Yahweh will strike again. He will call off the plague of the locusts, but at midday He will cause the sun to disappear. So deep a darkness will cloak the land, that a man will not be able to see his hand before his face and fear will strike the hearts of young and old. People will curse you, but though you will cry out for light, none will come—until Yahweh causes the sun to shine."

Kamose stood speechless. Then his voice, raw and hoarse and constricted, could be heard: "No! No! Slave you are, and slave you shall remain!"

"So be it," Moses said quietly. He extended his arm as if signaling.

Lightning flashed, and a deafening clap of thunder split the air. Through the light shower of ash, a chill rain began to fall, which then turned to hail.

"Damn you!" Kamose shrieked. "Do your worst!"

The white balls bounced on the ground before him, growing larger with every minute. Someone in the crowd began to scream, again and again.

CHAPTER
NINETEEN

On the Great Sea

I

The new storm caught up with Demetrios just off the great spit that marked the Rosetta Mouth of the Nile. With the sky looking dark, low, and gloomy for the last three days, and with an unaccustomed chill in the air, it was reasonable to expect bad weather. But nothing had prepared him for the intensity of the sudden fury of the storm.

"Shorten sail!" he bellowed above the powerful, vicious winds. There seemed to be a problem, though, and Demetrios came down off the high poop of the boat to join his men at the cleat. "What's the matter?" he screamed as the great, cold raindrops battered his face.

"Stuck!" the young sailor nearest him howled. Demetrios rushed past the mast and looked up. The brails on the starboard side of the yard were fouled, and the men yanking on them from the cleat could not shorten sail, no matter how hard they pulled. As he watched, a gust of wind beat at the starboard brace and nearly pulled the two sailors holding it into the sea.

"Sir," an old salt shouted in his ear in a rough voice, "it's

353

got to come down, or we're done for. Maybe we could cut the lines—"

"No!" Demetrios threw his head back again and looked up the stout mast at where the wind was trying to pull the sail apart. "I'm going aloft!"

"No, sir!" the grizzled sailor said, clutching his elbow. "Let me! The crew can do without me if something goes wrong!"

But the wind carried away half his words—not that they would have changed Demetrios's mind. "Man the brace!" he yelled. "Don't let go of it!"

He had approached the mast, wondering how to get purchase on its slickened surface in this freezing rain, when lightning split the sky. He winced; it had struck dangerously close. Again he looked up at the tall mast and whipping sail, wondering how long they would last. Already the yard was bending.

"Don't go up, sir!" cried the old salt. "The lightning! The lightning!"

Demetrios shielded his eyes and peered upward through the driving rain. A gust of wind seized him and nearly lifted him off his feet. The starboard brace pulled taut, and one of the young sailors manning it was hurled over the side and into the sea with a strangled cry.

"Man overboard!" Demetrios cried, and saw one of the men toss a spar attached to a long line after the stricken man. The boy surfaced, spewed water, and fought his way in the roiling waves toward the spar.

Demetrios looked up again at the wildly flapping sail. Something had to be done.

"Hold her steady!" He began to climb the slender spire. But the moment he did, the wind shifted and blew the sail back against him, slamming him off the mast and down onto the deck. He fell flat on his back, the air knocked out of his lungs, and slid helplessly toward the rail as the ship suddenly pitched. At the last possible moment his hand, flailing wildly, caught hold of a deck cleat and halted his sideways roll; after a moment, puffing, buffeted by the wind, he got to his feet and staggered toward the mast.

"No, sir!" the graying sailor cried out. "Don't try it again! We'll cut the lines!"

But Demetrios shook his head doggedly and once more approached the mast. Gritting his teeth, he shinnied up the pole a full body-length before the wind once again seized him. He hung on for dear life as the ship was wildly tossed about by the wind in her sail. When she righted herself, he continued his precarious way up the mast.

Finally, he reached the splice and stood atop it, grasping for the fouled brails, tearing at them with fingers numbed by the cold and the wind. Finally he managed to tear one free, and the sailors on the deck succeeded in hauling the sail in a couple of hand spans. His bleeding hands tore at another rope, and he cursed at the rain-soaked hemp.

As he pulled at it, he looked up to see a giant waterspout heading his way. His heart almost stopped at the sight. He cursed and reached up to liberate one more fouled brail and felt, rather than saw, the sail shorten.

The ship pitched suddenly. *I'd better get down from here.* But there was still one brail stuck, and until it was freed, the men could not bring the sail down. He could not quite lay his hand on it and still stand atop the splice.

He cursed through clenched teeth, feeling the storm nearly pull him down. The wind howled, and the twister rose from the water, then dipped down again, spinning the water it touched. The waves towered high above the boat, and Demetrios could no longer see the horizon.

He bit his lip, then threw his legs up and over the yard, pulling and wrestling until he was straddling it. He looked down and saw the sailors, steadying the port brace and looking up at him with frightened faces. *They think I'm going to die. And perhaps I am. . . .*

The trench they were in was so deep that he could no longer see the twister. He hoped it had gone in another direction. As the boat rode up the crest of the wave, however, he could see it again—so close that he shuddered in terror as he inched along the yard, hooking his bare feet under the taut brails for purchase.

As he did, the waterspout caught the ship and tossed it over almost onto its side; it would have capsized had an opposing wind not suddenly righted it with a violence that threatened to destroy the vessel. His own hold was precarious, he felt himself slipping.

He slid off the careening yard and tumbled down, end over end. A lightning bolt, followed by a deafening blast of thunder, rent the sky, striking the mast a second after his fingers left the wood. The mast burst into flames, and the sail caught fire as the men fell to the deck, their hands burned by the lightning. Just as Demetrios hit the water, the tornado struck the boat and tore it to pieces. The spout lifted him from the water, bringing him high above the wreckage in the sea below.   .

Unable to catch his breath, unable to move, he was tossed far from the wooden scraps that were all that was left of his flagship. He hit the water, his numbed arms and legs windmilling crazily; he went down, swallowing water, and came up on the tall wave again, helplessly carried to the crest and down again, bobbing like a cork. The rain turned to hail, which slammed into his unprotected head. As the wind howled, Demetrios looked frantically about for survivors. But he found none, none anywhere. . . .

After a time, bone tired and quite sure that he would drown, Demetrios felt a hard object slam into the back of his head, dazing him and sending him under for a moment before he struggled to the surface.

He turned and picked it out: It was a section of tough oak planking from his destroyed ship. Locking his numbed fingers around it, he struggled atop it, clinging to its sides. The waves tried to dislodge him, but he managed to hold tight. Exhausted and delirious, he lay atop the planking and let it go wherever it might.

Hours later the sun peeked through the layers of powerful-looking clouds of ash. Demetrios raised his head and looked around. The sea was calm. He was slowly drifting toward a sandy beach.

Beyond the beach was a wrecked town, devastated by the great seismic wave. He blinked at the sight: buildings mashed flat; sailing ships leaning against crushed houses; everything lifeless and dead.

He seemed to be deaf. He tilted his head and pounded his ear; water rushed out, and sound rushed in.

He rolled off the planking, and his numbed feet touched a shallow sandbar.

He staggered through the surf and fell forward onto the beach.

He was in Egypt again—naked, battered, exhausted. And weaponless in a land run by a homicidal madman.

CHAPTER TWENTY

In the Delta

I

The storm had continued for a day. When at last it broke, the locusts came, as Moses had predicted—millions upon millions of them. Everywhere the eye looked, they covered everything, loudly buzzing. Seventeen years had come and gone since their last appearance.

And they ate! When the farmers ventured out to estimate the devastation wrought by the hailstorm, the men found that the flax was quickly going the way of the barley. The Egyptians cursed and cried out against the king.

The people of the delta had been so brutally victimized by the inexorable chain of disasters, their patience and resilience had been exhausted. Tempers flared; spouse struck spouse; fights broke out in the streets, taverns, and wherever men and women gathered to escape the hateful ubiquity of the locusts. A sword fight erupted in the city-guard barracks of Avaris and quickly turned into a riot. By the time order could be restored, six men had been killed and twenty more injured, half of them critically.

Through it all Kamose remained indoors, brooding. He

could no longer go out among his people. One morning, a delegation of wealthy landowners and speculators in grain futures chose a spokesman to encourage Kamose to consider compromise with the wizard from the desert. This provoked a tantrum the likes of which had not been seen since the terrible days of mad Salitis, and the landowners went away questioning the king's sanity. Their spokesman immediately called for a conference with representatives from the priesthood of Amon.

On this day, as people in the streets beat the locusts away from their faces, Seth arrived in Avaris, unannounced, unknown, and weary.

His horse had been injured during the fierce hailstorm, and Seth had been unable to find anyone willing to loan, sell, or rent him another. The last two days' travel had been on foot, as he cursed the locusts like everyone else and very much felt his age.

Now he trudged down the principal street of Avaris. He felt like a stranger in a strange land, a man among creatures that might be of a different species. Right and left he looked, and nowhere did he like anything he saw.

Pausing before an unfinished work project, he stopped a passing slave and asked, "Pardon me, friend. Where might I find Iri of Thebes?"

The slave shot a wary glance at him but indicated the north gate. "He'll be in the Habiru quarter."

"Thank you." Before Seth turned to go, he noted the calm on the Habiru's face, which sharply contrasted with the desperation he had noticed on the Egyptians' faces. He pondered this as he started out, unavoidably crushing five or six locusts with each step.

The source of that calm perplexed him. Egypt had just lost its grain crop. Did the fellow not realize that the slaves always starved first?

He carried this concern all the way into the Habiru quarter. He beckoned another passerby and was about to ask the same question as before when he spotted a familiar face. "Iri!" he called out. "Over here!"

The man he sought hurried toward him, smiling and swatting away the locusts that hung from his robe. "Seth!" He embraced the older man. "Is it really you? I can't believe it."

"You'd better believe it," Seth said, beaming. "Have I beaten Apedemek here?"

"No sign of him yet."

"Good. What's been happening? Fill me in."

Yet another delegation from the moneyed classes had come and gone, and Kamose was a bundle of nerves. Neb-mertef hovered close by, offering soothing words, agreeing with whatever the king chose to do.

"What did they say this time?" he asked unctuously.

"Insolent bastards!" Kamose snarled. "It was all I could do to keep from throwing them out."

"This group is perhaps too powerful to risk offending, Sire?"

Kamose nodded glumly. "I told them that there ought to be enough food to feed everyone in the delta but—"

"But there's no evidence of that?" Neb-mertef suggested.

"No, and they wouldn't take it on faith."

"They're all upset, Sire."

"Just between us, I'm stretched thin myself. I could use a week of respite from all this. You don't suppose . . ."

"What, Sire?"

"Oh, I thought I might send for Moses. To order him to stop. Neb-mertef, don't you think a compromise might be worked out? Let them have a few days in the desert?"

"It might have worked a week or so ago, Sire, but now I think they want to leave Egypt forever."

"But what if I told them just to get these damned locusts out of our hair—"

"Sire! You're not beginning to believe them?"

Kamose glared. "Moses is a sorcerer! I mean, one minute there was nothing happening, and the next cows, sheep, and horses were being killed by hail!"

"It was awful, Sire, but it is my understanding that there has been a major volcanic—"

"Ridiculous! How could something so far away have an effect on our lives? No, the man's a sorcerer, plain and simple. If I could fool him and get a few days of peace until Apedemek arrives."

"Sire, I really think—"

"Send for Moses right now!"

When Moses arrived, not only was Aaron at his side, but Iri the armorer and a balding graybeard.

"Seth of Thebes!" Kamose said, incredulous. "What are you doing here with these rabble?"

"Visiting my friends," Seth said mildly.

Kamose shot him a disgusted glance, then turned to Moses. "I've decided to let you and your people take a few days off to worship this God of yours. As long as you're back by the first of the week and work twice as hard—"

Moses turned as if to leave.

Kamose stood on the high dais and shouted at him. "Where are you going? How dare you turn your back on me? *Guards!*"

Two heavily armed soldiers moved toward the Habiru.

Moses slowly turned and faced the king again. "You waste my time. The patience of Yahweh comes to an end. You know the demands of the One God. You must—"

"Who are you to tell me what I must do? I am the king!"

"I convey what God has told me to say and no more."

"Curse you!" Kamose screamed. "You're stalling! You can't stop the locusts now that they've started! Once the seventeen-year cycle has come around, it runs its course. You've been taking advantage of existing conditions and claiming credit for things no man can control!"

"I didn't say I could control anything," Moses corrected calmly. "It is not I who does these things."

"You're right it isn't!" Kamose said, exulting. "Just wait until Apedemek gets here! He'll destroy you—as he destroyed Seth!"

Now his eyes bore into Seth's. "Tell him what happened when *you* faced Apedemek!" Kamose screamed. "Everyone thought you were so wise, so powerful! He wrecked you! Tell him! Tell him, curse you!"

But it was Moses who spoke. "Hear me. The locusts will go away. The wind will rise and blow them out of Egypt. But beware of what comes in their wake. You may wish the locusts back, and the hail, and the other plagues."

He looked at the two guards and, unmolested, led his companions from the room.

As Moses opened the door, Kamose could hear the wind rising in the street.

II

Outside, Seth said to Moses, "Would you pardon us? I have to talk to Iri."

"Don't be long," Moses warned as the wind whistled down the long avenue, stirring the ashes at their feet. He left with Aaron and the others.

Seth hitched his tattered robe around him. "I need a change of clothes. It's getting chilly."

Iri steered him to the shelter of a wall of the Temple of Amon. "Well, you've seen the new Moses in action. What think you?"

Seth shivered. "I think I need a warm fire, a bowl of wine, and something to eat. Let me buy you dinner."

"If we have time," Iri cautioned. "Remember what Moses said. He always means what he says."

"So I gather." They stopped at the door of an inn, and Seth ushered him inside. The innkeeper showed them to a table under a lamp. "Wine, please," Seth requested. "Olives, bread, lentil stew, whatever you have ready."

He turned back to Iri as they sat down. "I'm eager to talk with Moses at length. I'm mightily impressed. He's every bit as substantial as I had expected him to become, but in such a different way."

"Yes," Iri said, taking the wine jug from the innkeeper and pouring it into bowls. "He's a man of his people. He has added their strengths to his own."

"He acts as though he believes what he's saying to Kamose."

This did not produce the result Seth had expected. Iri sat back, eyes wide, bowl in hand. "But, Seth," he said seriously, "that's the whole point: He believes every word of it."

Now Seth registered surprise. "I thought this whole campaign was intended to frighten Kamose. But you're saying that he's *not* just fooling the king? He has himself fooled as well?"

"No, that isn't the way I'd put it. This isn't a ruse. Everything that has happened since Kamose's first refusal has been Yahweh's direct response to the king's stubborn behavior. I wish you had seen how immediate the consequences were. Moses' predictions were completely accurate; he'd stretch out his arm, and the thing was done!"

"No! Not you, too!"

Iri leaned forward and spoke fervently. "Seth, don't take my word for it. Stick around and you'll see what I'm talking about."

"But, Iri! These phenomena normally accompany a large volcanic eruption. Some of us who have traveled and talked to people know about such things, and—"

"Seth! Do you think that *you* could do as Moses is doing, armed with your own knowledge of that fixed cycle of events?"

"Probably not. He's most impressive. He's playing the king like a fish on the end of a line. But really, my friend—"

"Moses knows nothing about volcanic eruptions. If you speak to him about this, you'll find that he doesn't understand what you're talking about."

"But he must!"

"You'll see." Iri put a hand on Seth's wrist and changed the subject. "Tell me about my sister and Pepi."

Seth sketched in the events that had led to his return to Avaris. "So there you are. I asked Yahadu to stay with Mai, Neftis, and your nephew in Athribis. Apedemek should be on the way here."

"Yes, I know. Ach! If only she'd killed him!"

"You wouldn't say that if you'd seen her. She has enough guilt to shoulder without adding murder. I hope she never lays eyes on him again. It's going to be hard enough nursing her back to health as it is."

Iri's brows knitted. "It's that bad, then?"

"You'll see." Seth tilted his head. "Is that the wind out there?"

"It's the wind. I guarantee it'll get worse."

"I suppose it will." He paused. "Funny, it does almost seem as if it happened on command."

"That's what I've been trying to tell you," Iri said. "Tell me more about Pepi."

"He's the one I'm really worried about," Seth confessed. "What happens in the next little while will make or break him. I don't think I can keep him away from Apedemek unless I can get to Apedemek and destroy him."

"How?" Iri asked.

Seth saw the doubt in Iri's eyes. "Ah, you don't believe in me either," he said sadly.

"No, Seth! I didn't mean—"

"But of course you did, dear fellow. And why not? I'm not sure *I* believe in my ability to face Apedemek. Unfortunately, unless Demetrios comes to the delta in time, as Yahadu hopes he will, I may be the only hope we have to get the job done."

Iri looked at his kinsman with despair. Once more Seth was willing to lay his life on the line, and this time he knew with a terrible certainty that it was no use, that his life would be sacrificed in vain. It was almost as if he could look into Seth's heart and see there the fearful knowledge of his own expendability.

"The only hope?" Iri pondered. "Maybe not. Perhaps there's another." But his words came out so softly that they were buried by the sound of the rising wind outside.

And at that moment the four battered travelers, tired in every bone and muscle, entered Avaris by the southern gate. Pepi had one arm around Mai's back, helping to brace her against the terrible wind that buffeted them mercilessly. Yahadu carried Neftis.

They had left the chariots outside the city and set the horses free, the better to escape notice. The trip had been a nightmare, arduous and painful, but they had made it, if at the expense of their final reserves of strength.

The guard at the gate, shielding his eyes against the windblown debris, made a feeble effort to detain them, but as he began to conduct the customary interrogation—name, place of residence, and so on—he locked eyes with Yahadu.

"You don't need to ask us any questions," Yahadu suggested gently.

"I don't need to ask you any questions," the guard echoed, and was about to say "Pass!" when Yahadu spoke again.

"Direct me to the home of Iri the armorer."

"Yes, sir," the guard said. "Continue northward on this street until you come to the Habiru quarter. . . ."

*   *   *

The wind howled like the voices of a million tormented souls and tore at the treetops, bending supple palms double and sending the fronds to fly willy-nilly through the air.

Standing on the bank, Apedemek watched the captain and crew of his boat wrestle with the cumbersome task of anchoring the vessel well out into the current, to keep it from being slammed against the docks, the way it had been earlier, forcing them to stop upriver for repairs.

They had docked in Avaris only moments before, and he had been put ashore, handed onto the dock by the captain of the port.

Apedemek glowered up at the huge, black cloud, which seemed to move closer to the city with every passing moment. He turned to the captain. "Just before the weather changed, Moses prophesied that the winds would be followed by a terrible storm in which the sun would be blotted out and total darkness would descend upon Avaris. Right?"

"Why, yes, sir," sputtered the official. "But how did you know?"

Apedemek, surveying the sky, ignored the question. "I'll say this for him: He's learned his lessons well, and he has a sense of drama. Well, I'm not going to be drawn into his little trap." He looked at the captain again. "Where's the nearest lodging outside the city's walls?"

"The closest inn of any consequence is half a day's ride, even in good weather. Surely you can't mean to traipse about in a bad blow like this!"

"Hmmm," Apedemek said. "There's merit in what you say, but I can't be seen or recognized going inside the city. He'll be able to show me up as an inferior magus who can't stop the darkness he's brought about."

"Perhaps no one would take note of you if you were accompanied by only a couple of men. After all, everyone expects you to travel with a sizable retinue. And if you entered through the northern gate, where the slaves and people of low caste live . . ."

"Good idea," Apedemek said, shivering. "I'll cover up so no one can recognize my face. The soldiers who accompany me will wear the cloaks of civilians. Let's get on with it. This wind is wretched. I'm chilled to the bone."

Above, the blackness drew nearer and nearer.

III

And then there came a morning when the wind was gone and the sun did not rise; and the darkness that blanketed the land struck terror in the hearts of the Egyptians. The men could not go out into the streets to their occupations. The women were trembling so violently, they could not prepare food for their family. The children huddled beside their beds, wondering if the end of the world had come.

Only in the camp of the Habiru was there peace of mind. The families had been warned about this occurrence by Moses and Aaron, who had visited every household. The slaves had sung and prayed through the night, and when the morning came with no sun to mark it, no one panicked.

Moses and Aaron had commandeered an abandoned warehouse on the fringe of the Habiru quarter and sealed the doors; within this windowless structure the leaders of the children of Jacob, their numbers augmented by Iri and the newly arrived visitors from Nubia and Thebes, held council to discuss the coming days.

"The king will not let us go yet," Moses announced. "Soon the darkness will end, and I fear that sterner measures will be needed to change Kamose's mind."

"Sterner than this?" Dathan asked from the rear. "Already Egyptians have tried to bribe us with rich gifts to get us to leave. As if we had any choice in the matter! How long can Kamose defy his people?"

"Until they protest strongly enough to him," Moses replied. "They will do so shortly. The angel of God will strike at the firstborn of all creatures. I have explained to you the precautions we must follow, we and all those"—he nodded toward Seth, Iri, and their companions—"under our protection, to exempt us." Moses inclined his head slightly—a bow to the will of God—and drew apart. Instantly voices that had remained silent burst in animated conversation.

Seth, Yahadu, Iri, and Aaron joined Moses in a far corner.

"There's a problem," Seth reported. "A party, composed of high Egyptian officials, entered your quarter just before nightfall yesterday. One member was unmistakably Apedemek."

Aaron raised a brow and turned to Moses. "He will harden the heart of the king and is capable of creating a mass illusion to influence the citizens against us."

Seth nodded. "That's true. I'd been thinking primarily of his effect on Neftis and Pepi."

Moses remained unperturbed. "Don't worry. Apedemek can do nothing."

Yahadu bit his lip. "If only Demetrios were here! I left a message for him in Athribis. I'm sure he was held up by the darkness."

"Yes," Seth agreed. "But whatever Apedemek chooses to do, it'll probably happen before Demetrios can get here."

"If Pepi sees what powerful magic his father can perform," Iri added, "we'll lose him."

Moses raised his hand. "Apedemek is about to meet a far greater foe than any he's ever encountered—the angel of God. When the hand of God strikes down the Egyptians and passes by the houses of the righteous, it will be a great and holy day, which our people will remember forever."

During the night Neb-mertef, sleepless from the tension that surrounded Kamose, slipped out of his palace suite for some air. There was a vague, blurred outline of a full moon.

The implications struck him immediately: The darkness, which had lasted throughout the day, was lifting! By morning there would be a real dawn.

He laughed softly. How best to use this information? He would not tell Amasis or Kamose. No, he would benefit most by alerting the most powerful man in the delta. He returned to his suite and dressed.

A few hours later, Apedemek, flanked by a squad of towering spearmen, moved into the open area between the Egyptian and Habiru quarters. He stood in the dim light, smiled humorlessly, and nodded to the guards.

From their number stepped two men with trumpets of bronze.

"Now," Apedemek ordered.

The trumpets blared.

Apedemek took a spear from the nearest guardsman and held it high. His huge voice roared. "Hear, O ye gods of the

Netherworld! I command you to lift the darkness that lies on Egypt! I command the day to dawn!"

And the morning dawned.

Habiru and Egyptian alike in their nightclothes stepped outside, yawning and blinking, to see that the darkness was gone.

Apedemek looked at them, his eyes flinty and malevolent. "Let all bear witness," he bellowed, "that the works of the charlatan Moses are confounded and undone at my hand! Let all remember that where the feeble mountebank brought darkness, I, Apedemek, bring light!"

The crowd was shocked to silence as Apedemek continued. "I challenge Moses! I command him to come forth and test his weak powers against me! I defy his false and powerless desert god! Let him destroy me if he can! Let us settle once and for all whose power shall reign in Egypt!"

Mai came back inside to find Seth still sleeping. She shook him gently. "Seth. Wake up, please."

He blinked, then sat up as she swiftly told him of the startling scene in the street.

"Go to Moses!" he said. "Tell him not to answer the challenge till I get there!"

Her shoulders drooped. "It's too late. He's already gone."

IV

Aaron stayed in step with Moses all the way from the warehouse in which they had spent the night. "Now remember," he advised, "you're not dealing with Kamose anymore. This fellow is a master of illusion, and he can control a crowd as no other man can."

Moses shrugged. "Don't be afraid. Stay beside me. Keep the staff I gave you close at hand."

"You don't think there's going to be violence, do you?" Aaron asked, gripping the staff.

"No, only trickery. Apedemek makes people believe in him, but Yahweh is on our side."

They pushed their way through the crowd; the Habiru stepped back to make room for them.

"Look," Aaron whispered. "There's Pepi, next to his friend, young Joshua. And Neftis over there. Yahadu is trying to pull her away."

The brothers approached the clearing, where Apedemek stood opposite them. "Ah, there's Kamose. I knew he wouldn't want to miss this."

Aaron looked worried.

"Faith," Moses said. "Have faith."

"Just look at him!" Pepi breathed. "He's as tall as a Dinka." Hero worship lit his eyes, and his heart was pounding hard.

"Oh, come on," Joshua said. "Moses will take him down a peg or two."

"Watch your tongue!" Pepi warned. "That's my father you're talking about!"

"Well, I'm sorry to hear that," the young Habiru retorted. "Just don't get your hopes up. You'd be counting on the wrong man winning."

Mai, overjoyed that Neftis was showing some awareness at last, had joined Yahadu in his efforts to budge the young woman. "Come away, dear, please. You'll just upset yourself." Then she saw the gleam, halfway between madness and sanity, in the young woman's eyes and felt the trembling in her arm. "Neftis, darling. Let me take you inside."

"Mai," Yahadu said, "if things get bad, Seth and I will intercede on Moses' behalf, although we promised not to."

"Yes," she said bitterly. "And afterward Zipporah and I will pick up the pieces." She turned back to Neftis. "Please, dear, come on."

To her amazement, Neftis wrenched away. "No! I want to see!"

It was the first coherent sentence she had spoken since the madness had come upon her, and her eyes held a clear but smoldering fire.

Moses, with Aaron at his side, halted ten paces from Apedemek.

Apedemek's voice rang out with power and authority. "Are you the charlatan who claims to have caused the plagues?"

"Lower your voice," Moses said. "Everyone can hear you. And yes, you know very well who I am: You were impersonating a half-witted tinker when we met in Nubia."

This was not the way Apedemek wanted the interview to go. His eyes blazed. "Do you deny that you have tricked the people into thinking that your magic brought the darkness that I have driven away?"

"I have warned the king of how Yahweh would respond if he continued to hold my people against their will," Moses answered. "And just as I did not cause the plagues, you did not cause them to go away. You can create illusions; you cannot change reality."

His manner was so unassuming, it successfully broke the spell of Apedemek's dramatics.

Apedemek raised his trembling hands high; lightning flashed, with jagged bolts exploding toward the earth, and caused the crowd to cower. Immediately a deafening blast of thunder split the air.

"See the master of the elements at work!" Apedemek screamed. "The very sky obeys! Beware, lest the ground swallow you whole!"

Moses did not seem fearful. "Beware yourself," he warned, reaching for Aaron's staff. He threw it on the ground before him.

As the crowd looked on in horror, the staff became a huge snake, hissing viciously, its triangular head darting, its forked tongue probing the air! It was a poisonous viper of the desert, but it was many times larger than any such serpent ever seen in Egypt. The onlookers gasped and drew back.

Apedemek, too, drew back, and there was fear in his eyes. "Guards! To me!"

Moses smiled, sensing hope in the crowd.

When the guards gathered protectively around him, Apedemek pointed at the great serpent. "Kill it! Now!"

Shrinking from the viper, they nonetheless thrust down with their spears.

There was a great blinding flash, and when the crowd, rubbing their eyes, looked again, there was, between the two men, where the spears had fallen, a writhing nest of serpents!

Neftis screamed and ran into Mai's arms.

Nearby, Pepi craned his neck to see. His eyes were wide, and his heart was beating fast. Could his father be doing these things? This was a man to admire!

Suddenly a strange light emanated from the clearing in which the snakes writhed. Then there was a blinding flash.

When the onlookers blinked away the glare, the snakes were gone and the staff was back in Moses' hand, but the spears were no more. In their place were the bronze spearheads, attached to splintered wooden fragments. The hafts had been mysteriously destroyed.

The crowd buzzed.

Apedemek, his face white, drew back uncertainly. Something in Moses' calm demeanor made him wince.

"How did you—?" he began, but his voice, weaker now, broke. His hands shook.

"I am finished with you," Moses said calmly. "These people before us are finished with you. Egypt is finished with you. But the God of Israel is not finished with you."

Apedemek blanched. Two soldiers had to hold him up. His hands clutched at the tender area in his side, where he had been stabbed.

"N-no," he said in a voice gone weak. "Let me go. Please."

V

As part of the king's party at the clearing's edge, Neb-mertef and Amasis watched the tense scene. "Look at the king's expression!" Neb-mertef said. "Wouldn't you love to know what he's thinking?"

Amasis snorted. "He's wagered on Apedemek, but Apedemek has failed him. He looks ill." He made another contemptuous noise.

"I'm a bit surprised," Neb-mertef admitted. "After all, he defeated Seth of Thebes twice."

"Huh," Amasis said. "Seth defeated himself. He lost his confidence."

Neb-mertef turned back to the window. "But I always thought Moses to be a rather ordinary young man when he was at court."

"It wasn't Moses who brought Apedemek down. I ran across El-Shaddai's path some years ago in Canaan. There's more to him than the usual lot of hot air." He pursed his lips in thought. "As a matter of fact, Kamose was with me. I'm surprised he's been so defiant."

Neb-mertef spun to look at him. "I can hardly believe what I'm hearing. You give the credit to this deity of theirs? *You?*"

"He's dangerous. I felt safe in treating the Habiru harshly because they fell from El-Shaddai's good graces. Moses must have got them refocused on their religion."

"If Kamose is ignoring how dangerous El-Shaddai is—"

"—he'll bring about his own downfall. Look at him. He knows he's licked."

"Would you have fared better than Apedemek?"

Amasis shook his head. "I would never have challenged Moses publicly in the first place. No, I'm content to watch Apedemek, then Kamose, fall apart before our eyes. And, with you, sweep up the pieces."

Apedemek tried unsuccessfully to avoid Moses' unruffled gaze.

"You have used your power," the Habiru leader said, "to hurt the innocent and to destroy the woman who bore your child. Now your intentions are aimed at the boy, and you would bend his blameless mind to your will."

"No," Apedemek denied miserably. "I only thought—"

Moses pressed on. "You have felt the power leave you. At last you are aware of your own ordinariness."

"No!"

"Aware of your own conscience."

"No!"

"You realize who you are and what you have done."

"*No!*"

"Until now you have prided yourself upon your fancied uniqueness, your imagined superiority. You considered yourself to be above the common man, simply because you could manipulate him."

"Please, if—"

"You have been wearing blinders, sauntering arrogantly and irresponsibly through life. Now the one God has removed the blinders. From this moment you will see the suffering around you with a cold and terrible clarity, and it will touch your heart as it should have done for so many years. You will feel a kinship with the whole of mankind, rich or poor, whatever race or nation. When those around you suffer, you will suffer. If their suffering has come about at your hands, you will feel it to an extent that they do not, and the empathy will be a white-hot pain in your heart."

"Please! No!"

Moses held out his hands in an eloquent gesture of finality. "The rest is between you and Yahweh, now and forever." He turned to go.

"Wait!"

The voice was Kamose's. The king strode into the clearing. He shot a look of withering contempt at Apedemek, being led away by his own retinue. Then the king faced Moses and, in a voice quaking with rage, said, "I have not given you leave to go!"

Moses bowed to acknowledge the king's rank. "I should have known you would learn nothing. So be it. This is Yahweh's message to you, then: 'Toward midnight every Egyptian firstborn shall die, from the highest to the lowest—'"

Kamose's eyes bulged. "Threats!"

" '—and there will go up a loud cry in all the land. Then your courtiers will come before Me and bow down and tell My people to go away. And only then will I lead them from here.' "

Again Moses turned to go. This time no one stopped him.

Seth grabbed Iri's arm. "Have you seen Pepi?"

"I saw him with Joshua earlier this morning. I'll try to find him."

"Please. He saw what happened to his father, and I'm concerned about him." Seth watched Iri go, then he turned back to Mai and the girl. "Neftis, he'll never be able to hurt you or anybody else again, dear."

The young woman looked up at him, her eyes clear and

untroubled. "Thank heaven I was able to witness that. He's finished. Moses knew where to hit him so that it'd hurt him most. If he has to think of himself as merely another human being, one who can be hurt just like the rest . . ."

"Yes," Seth agreed. "We made ourselves vulnerable and let him outsmart us. You had no experience with men like him, but I should have known better."

"No, Seth," she said. "Don't blame yourself. We were both at a disadvantage. We considered the consequences, while Apedemek didn't. We were fighting with one hand tied behind our back."

"Perhaps you're right," Seth conceded. "Whatever the problem, Apedemek will never be able to harm anyone again. Now come, both of you," he said, slipping his arms around Mai and Neftis. "We have to prepare for tonight."

Iri found Joshua, then the two hurried into the palace, where Apedemek and his bodyguards had gone. They were stopped by a guardsman wearing Kamose's private livery, who questioned Joshua's right to enter; but after a furious reprimand by Iri, the guard backed off.

"That's better," Iri said. "Now which way did Apedemek go?"

"Upstairs, sir," the guard said. "But I still don't think it would be wise to take the boy—"

"I'll take the boy wherever I please. Have you seen another boy about this one's age?"

"No, sir."

Iri scowled. "Come along, Joshua."

Pepi crept up the side of the wall, fingers and toes curling around the creeper vines. At the top he poked his head over the ledge. Their backs were to him. Silently he lowered his legs over the top, swung his feet to the floor, and slipped behind a wall hanging.

Apedemek moaned. "Put me on the bed. You're hurting me!"

"Here, sir," a voice chimed in, deep and dignified. "Here's some of that compound against pain that you had made up. Try to calm yourself, sir."

"Calm myself!" Apedemek said in a voice stretched tight.

Pepi heard footfalls from the stairs.

"Look here! Where do you think you're going?" a guard challenged.

"Lower your voice," Iri said.

Iri! What was he doing here? Pepi peeked out from his hiding place, and Iri and Joshua caught his eye. Iri made a discreet motion with his hand before turning to Apedemek.

"Just try to relax, Apedemek," he advised.

"How can I? That accursed Moses put a spell on me! My mind's all full of crazy drivel and sentimental nonsense!"

"That's just the normal baggage everyone else has to carry around," Iri said. "Compassion, fear, worry, conscience—"

"Conscience! *Aaaaiiii!*"

"Take my word for it," Iri continued. "It'd be a lot easier for you if you could accept the change. It's not really that bad, being human."

"Get out! Get out, curse you!"

Iri caught Pepi's eye again, and he signaled: *Go back over the wall. I'll see you downstairs.*

As Pepi eased down the creeper, he could hear Apedemek's curses—and Iri's merry laugh.

VI

"It couldn't have worked out better," Iri confided to Joshua as they went downstairs. "I knew your God would prevail over him, but I expected Apedemek would be destroyed. I'd never have imagined this. He's been given a conscience!"

"I wonder how Pepi will take it," Joshua said. "He was very impressed when his father was so powerful."

"I guess that you and I are going to have to watch out for him. Will you help me?"

"Sure," the boy said, grinning. "For a price."

They were in the sunlight now, and Iri got a good look at the boy. His eyes were clear, and his back was straight; he looked as tough as nails. "You little scamp! What kind of price?"

"Make me a sword, the kind a soldier would carry."

"What would you be wanting with a sword?"

"Moses says we're going to have to fight our way into Canaan, and when we do, we won't have a lot of weapons. There will be enough for the men, but a kid like me will have to make his own arrangements."

Iri laughed low in his throat. "You're my kind of boy, you know that? All right, I'll make you a sword."

"And teach me how to use it."

Iri's mouth made an O. "How can I teach you how to fight when you can hardly lift a sword?"

"Hand me that one in your belt."

Iri chuckled, handing over his sword. He was not sure what to expect; the boy's arms were as thin as reeds. But to Iri's considerable surprise, Joshua took the weapon in both hands and performed a surprisingly good imitation of the Egyptian army's small-arms drill, parrying, hacking, and thrusting. How old was the boy? Ten? Eleven?

Joshua finished with a salute and a grin. "There," he said, his voice showing only a trace of strain. "How did I do?"

"Very well," Iri commended. "Now hide the sword. You don't want anyone taking it away from you."

Joshua blinked. "This? You're giving me this one? But I thought you said—"

"Count your blessings, my young friend. You don't realize what a prize I'm giving you. You could sell that sword and buy a comfortable house in the country with acreage."

"This looks old and beat-up."

"It is. But it has a tradition behind it. This was one of the swords Belsunu, my ancestor, made for the army of your ancestor Abraham, when he, too, fought his way into Canaan." He clapped the boy on the shoulder. "Now hide it under your robe, and let's get Pepi and go home."

Back in the Habiru quarter, Moses called a council of the elders. "Does everyone know what he has to do tonight? Follow the rituals exactly, and nothing will go wrong for us."

"But won't the Egyptians be so angry, they'll want our blood for revenge?"

Moses shook his head. "Go to your homes, all, and pray to God that He spares us, now and in the days to come."

* * *

Mai and Neftis had found shelter with Elisheba and Aaron and their four sons. For years Neftis had paid no attention to grooming; now she sat happily in Aaron's wretched home while Mai combed her hair for her.

Elisheba came in. "Well, look at you! How pretty you are!"

Neftis turned to look at her. "All of you make me feel so good, and here I am, about to lose you."

"I appreciate your sentiments," Elisheba said. "But we've dreamed of going home for so long! None of my generation has seen it—not even Moses."

"I envy you," Neftis said. "If only . . ."

"If only what, dear?" Mai asked.

Mai locked eyes with Elisheba over Neftis's head, and a strange, surprised expression was exchanged. "Elisheba, are you thinking what I'm thinking?"

As darkness fell on Avaris, the aromas of dinner cooking were in the air. Mothers stepped outside to call their children in—but with no more than the usual urgency. Only in the Habiru camp was there a feeling that something monumental was about to happen.

While the Egyptians rejoiced that the unnatural darkness had lifted, the Habiru prepared a sacrificial feast. Animals without blemish, either sheep or goats, would be consecrated to the will of God, and then roasted. The blood of the animals, slaughtered according to strict ritual, would be used to mark the Habiru doorposts and lintels. These marks, Moses had explained, were signals to the angel of God to pass by the house in peace.

Despite Moses' reassurances, husbands and wives looked at each other apprehensively as the time came near. Something mysterious and final was about to befall them, and although they had been assured of ultimate victory, the worry remained. Night was coming on. Death was close by. What would the morning bring?

VII

As the last rays of the sun were sinking below the western horizon, Demetrios, riding a horse purchased two days before with funds from one of his representatives, entered Avaris just as the guards were closing the great city gates.

At a stable he gave the horse up to an ostler. "I'm looking for a man. I wonder if you might know where I could find him."

"Yes, sir?"

"Moses of Thebes."

The ostler laughed. "I thought you were going to ask me something difficult. Everyone in town knows where to find *him*. Right down this street, take a hard turn to the left at the crossroad. Then ask anyone."

"Thank you," Demetrios said. "But now my curiosity is aroused. Why would Moses be so well-known?"

The ostler quickly sketched in the events that had brought Moses to prominence.

As Demetrios listened, his mind raced. Obviously Moses had learned of the eruptions at Home and had managed to predict accurately the sequence of extraordinary events that had followed. Apedemek had tried to play the same game, only to fall victim to a superior magus. Where had Moses learned his craft? What cult had spawned so eminent a master?

Demetrios walked toward the crossroad. He wanted a bed and a bath more than anything, but it was important that he make contact with Moses immediately. By finding Moses, he was sure he would find Seth and Yahadu, whom he had missed in Athribis. He would locate his kin too: The banker in Athribis had told him of Yahadu's decision to take Neftis and Pepi to Iri in Avaris.

Seth. Neftis. Iri. Pepi. He wanted them at the new Home, where he could look after them.

Drawing his dusty cloak about him, he walked strongly and purposefully down the deserted street.

The physicians had given Apedemek his medication, but it had had no effect. Even the strongest preparation of *shepenn* could do nothing to alleviate his mental agony; even in sleep—

perhaps most of all in sleep—the ghosts of all those he had harmed now haunted him.

After a time the physicians had gone away, leaving the servant Hetep at his side. A man with medical knowledge and great strength, Hetep had been able to restrain Apedemek's violent outbursts.

Now, morose and sleepless, his eyes red from hysterical weeping, Apedemek slumped in a chair, staring into a tall bronze mirror on the far wall. He saw not only his own haunted and haggard visage, but the faces of his victims as well—tortured visages he did not want to see.

The faces in the reflection seemed to loom behind him in the poorly lit room, but when he swiveled to look at the ghosts, they were not to be seen. "You!" he cried in a hollow voice to the servant. "Get that mirror out of here!"

"Do it yourself," Hetep responded indifferently.

"C-curse you!" Apedemek fumed, and tried to get up; but the hasty movement pulled at the wound in his side, and he moaned with pain. "Go away. I've got to think. I've got to work things out."

The servant snorted. "You don't understand yet, do you? You're *yesterday's* sensation. You ought to hear the way the king talks about you now. It's all over for you."

The fires of hatred in Apedemek's eyes were damped. It was as if all the passion had drained from him, and with it all his strength. "J-just go away."

"I'm supposed to stay with you."

"Then get me some dinner."

Hetep shrugged. "As you like."

As the servant went out, Apedemek sat back, and his eyes fell once more on the mirror.

A face appeared, suspended in the darkness on the metallic surface, behind and above his own mirrored image.

"Y-you," he whispered.

The face was Neftis's, as she looked a decade before: young, trusting, and innocent, a delicate and beautiful face, one that deserved gentle treatment.

"Leave me alone," he moaned. "I . . . I didn't mean to hurt you."

But he knew that was not true; because of reasons he could not fathom, falsehoods did not work for him anymore.

The moment a lie formed itself on his lips, pain erupted in his body. And now he uttered one of the worst lies of all.

"I . . . I mean, yes, I did, but I hadn't any idea what the result would be."

The pain stabbed inside his head in a throbbing, hateful rhythm.

"How was I to know that you would be so devastated?" he asked in anguish.

But you did know underneath it all, didn't you? You had trained yourself not to care about it, to think only of the perverse pleasure it gave you, how it made you feel strong.

"No! No!" he whimpered.

But the inner voice of his newfound conscience bored in deeper. *The most loathsome thing was to convince her that her corruption had always existed within her—that you did not put it there.*

"No! I didn't mean it!" he screamed in a strangled voice.

But he had. It had given him as much pleasure then as it pained him now.

The face faded . . . another replaced it, and another. The faces of all the people he had hurt in his life, tortured, and corrupted, and killed. . . .

Now came a single face that accused him silently.

"Karkara of Sado!" he breathed. "My master! My teacher!"

No, the voice in his head said. *Your victim, whom you murdered, making a mockery of your oath to the Chalybian Order, of the honor that you might have accepted. This man taught you much, but you turned on him and sank to the level of the most savage animal.*

The face changed again, intimidating him and torturing him with incomparable pain. It was the face of his son, whom he had planned to corrupt as he had corrupted the mother. . . .

He screamed and screamed again. He pressed his palms to his temples, trying to stop the pain. He wrenched himself to his feet, feeling the stab of pain in his side. He staggered headlong into the upright column that stood before his chair, opening a gash on his forehead. Blood ran into his eyes. The pain! The pain!

He turned to confront the face in the mirror, but there was only darkness. Thankful, he closed his eyes in relief. But behind his eyelids the faces stared silently at him, and he could feel the despair he had inflicted upon each of them, and that despair was magnified fifty times in his throbbing head.

"Please! Let me redeem myself!"

But he was trapped in the prison of Self and would never be able to escape. He screamed in horror, and screamed again.

Neb-mertef cautiously skirted the subject. "On the other hand, Sire, we could have some contingency plan in case anything happens tonight that could be mistaken for a confirmation of Moses' prediction."

Kamose scowled. "What are you talking about? When the morning dawns and nothing has happened, that'll be the last of his bluster." His lip curled with disdain. "And as soon as Apedemek is physically able, it's out the door with him."

"I'll leave the orders, Sire. The moment he can travel."

"I should have known all along this was coming. Where were you, my faithful counselor, then? Why did none of this show up in your Chaldean star charts?"

Neb-mertef blinked. "Sire, I've been warning you of a great cataclysm for years."

"Yes, but I depended upon you for specific advice. You've let me down almost as badly as Apedemek has. A couple more such disappointments and—"

"Sire, I'll be more careful."

"See that you are." The curt phrase was itself a dismissal, and Neb-mertef bowed to Kamose's back and crept out of the room, wondering, *How am I going to write new astrological charts when my astrologer has killed himself? There isn't another Chaldean within two hundred leagues!*

An angry voice called to him. "Well," Amasis said, "there you are. Worried, aren't you? Your man Apedemek let you down. *Now* what are you going to do?"

Neb-mertef grabbed his arm and propelled him well down the hall. "Quiet!" he hissed. "What are you talking about?"

"You thought you'd double-cross me. You gave Apedemek the information that the ash cloud was lifting, so that he could claim credit for it."

Neb-mertef's mind raced madly. Someone on his staff

was spying for Amasis. "You've got it all wrong. There was no time to consult with you. I saw an opportunity and took it."

"Cutting me totally out of the picture as you did."

"You don't understand," Neb-mertef babbled, improvising wildly. "I set him up. I knew he wasn't up to a confrontation with Moses. It was inevitable that if I put him under pressure, he'd come apart."

Amasis scrutinized his face. "You're lying."

"Think it out." Neb-mertef looked both ways down the hall. "And count your blessings. I've struck a blow for both of us, and here you are, insulting me just because there was no time to consult with you before doing it."

Amasis ruminated. "It has worked out to our mutual advantage," he admitted. "But if I find out you've been playing with me—"

"Look at it another way: With Apedemek out of the way, we've only one obstacle left." He smiled. "Who is about to remove himself."

"What do you mean?"

"People in the city have been having serious problems breathing since that volcanic ash settled. Let a half-dozen children die, and mobs of parents will demand that Kamose step down."

Amasis' eyes narrowed. "You may have something there."

"Of course I do. Trust me."

En route down the hall, Geb, in the uniform of a general of the Egyptian army, paused, lost in thought.

It was as if he had been blinded, under some strange enchantment for a long time. But suddenly the mist had lifted from his eyes.

Ten years he had served Kamose, promoted from underofficer to general before Apedemek and Kamose had accused his mentor, Khafre, of treason and ordered his execution.

Why had he not questioned the order then? He had known that Khafre was the most upright officer Egypt could hope to find. Why had he chosen to follow a fool like Kamose, a villain like Apedemek?

It was a spell, he realized. *I was under Apedemek's spell, just as the king was.*

All that had ended for him today. The fall of Apedemek had meant the end of his power over anyone. Now Geb was free to seek employment elsewhere in the region and perhaps redeem his decade of folly through honorable service. There would always be work somewhere for a soldier of his quality. He would resign his commission in the morning. It would require facing Kamose down, but he would do it. First, however, he would tell Apedemek what he thought of him. His jaw firmed and his eyes narrowed as he strode swiftly down the hall to Apedemek's rooms.

Geb was astonished to find no guardsman on duty. He knocked. No answer. Perplexed, he turned the handle, and the door swung open. He looked inside—then drew back in horror, breathing hard.

He forced himself to enter the room. Apedemek, Geb realized, had cut his wrists. Blood was on the marble floor, the walls, and the furniture.

Geb averted his gaze as his gorge rose. Hastily he stepped back and vomited on the tiles of the blood-smeared and defiled room.

VIII

Demetrios looked around. The windows in the Habiru quarter's wretched houses had all been covered over so that no light filtered out from any of them. *Where to start?* he wondered.

Almost as if in answer to his unspoken question, a calm voice spoke up. "Pardon me, sir. Could I help?"

Demetrios whirled. The man facing him, holding a lantern high, was taller than the average, with powerful shoulders and sturdy forearms.

"Thank you," he said. "I seek Moses of Thebes."

"Your pardon, sir, but many who seek Moses do not wish him well. May I know your business?"

"My name is Demetrios. I want to locate Seth of Thebes, my other kinsmen, and a man named Yahadu. I understand they have found shelter here."

"Indeed they have," the big man said with a smile. "My name is Aaron ben Amram. I am Moses' brother. If you'd come with me . . . ?"

Kamose was deep in thought as he stood on his balcony overlooking the quiet city streets. *There'll be no sleep again tonight. If only I could get some rest, I might organize my strategy!*

Again Moses had emerged triumphant. Moses had utterly defeated Apedemek and made him, Kamose, look foolish. The slave's support now extended from the Habiru themselves and the lower classes, to the landowners, merchants, and traders, even the priesthood of Amon. The priests remembered Moses as a supporter of their own interests when he was still thought to be a prince.

With Apedemek gone, there was no reliable second in command with whom to discuss problems. Neb-mertef was more a liability than an asset. But a sufficiently humbled Amasis might well have good advice. *What a fraud you are! You just want private access to* shepenn, *and Amasis is the only magus at court who will keep his mouth shut about the nostrums you need to sleep.*

He rubbed his eyes miserably. He would call for Amasis and give him another chance. He would establish the relationship with himself firmly in charge. Anything for a night's sleep!

The reunion with his kinsmen had been heartwarming and satisfying. Now, a lavish meal of roasted lamb in his belly, Demetrios sat in a circle with Iri, Seth, and Yahadu on the floor of the big warehouse. "Seth," he said, "I want a great city built in my new headquarters. And as the work progresses, I want to complete your initiation in the higher degrees of the craft."

"I am in your hands, kinsman."

"And you, my brother?" Demetrios said. "Can I count on having you and Neftis and the boy by my side when we go to the new Home?"

Iri looked at him, undecided. "I am still disoriented by your arrival. May we talk of this later?"

*   *   *

Amasis mixed the ingredients of the potion vigorously. "Mind you, Sire, this isn't the same preparation I gave you before. There was a flaw in the old substance, which is why you became addicted."

"Just get it right this time," Kamose snarled.

"Yes, Sire," Amasis said unctuously. "A little honey for a binder, and it's ready."

"You're sure this is safe?" the king asked. "If there's anything wrong with it, you'll pay with your life."

"I deserve your reproach," Amasis admitted. "But if you take this spoonful, you will quickly find rest, then awaken in the morning refreshed and ready to face the new day."

"Good," Kamose said, taking the little bowl.

Amasis went to the door and bowed deeply. "Happy dreams, Sire."

When he had left the king's wing, Amasis let out his breath. He had been perfecting this mixture in anticipation of the king's call. It was obvious that Kamose suffered from insomnia that had plagued him over the years. *Did I fool him? And is the formula correct?*

This was indeed a different formula, with a different purpose: Kamose's fall depended upon the continuation of his erratic behavior. Ideally he would be kept in a state of agitation and would make all the wrong decisions about the conflict with Moses. If the new formula worked, it would intensify his spiky, unpredictable aggressiveness.

King Amasis! It had a good ring to it. . . .

IX

As the moon rose, Moses walked to the center of the big room and raised his hands for silence. "My friends, it is time for us to go to our homes and await the passing of the angel of God."

"What would happen if we were to look out as the angel passed?"

"Let us not put the matter to the test. We have grown

stronger every time we present a united front to the enemy
and at the same time remain obedient to God. Now go home,
all, and may God spare us from the terrible fate of the
Egyptians during the night."

"Show me the sword again," Pepi asked.

Joshua grinned and handed the wrapped parcel over. He
watched with pride as the boy unwrapped the weapon and
held it up. "Beautiful, isn't it? It was made by an ancestor of
yours."

Pepi looked up quickly. "I didn't know that."

Obviously he was impressed. Joshua, coached by Iri an
hour before, pressed on. He was trying to steer the boy away
from Apedemek and toward more positive models. "Oh, yes.
Belsunu. Don't you know your own family history? Some of
the most famous people in the world came from your line."

"I guess I heard some of this when I was younger, but I
never paid attention." Pepi hefted the sword, then handed it
back to Joshua hilt first. "You said the destinies of your
people and mine are linked?"

"Yes. Ask Moses or Seth about it."

Pepi smiled. "Thank you. I'll see you in the morning."

As Pepi went away, Joshua looked after him thoughtfully.
He's taking his father's downfall well. He's got a lot of guts.

On the way back to his own small room, Amasis ran into
Neb-mertef. "Well!" Neb-mertef said. "What are you doing
in this part of the palace?"

Amasis' mind raced. He was not going to discuss the
evening's events with Neb-mertef. "I was asked to deliver
something. Why?"

"Oh, no reason. But have you heard the news? Apedemek
committed suicide."

Amasis scowled with disdain. "A coward's way out."

"I'm on my way to tell the king."

Amasis was on the verge of saying: *No use—he's out like
a light.* But he held his tongue. "Well, have a good evening.
I'll see you tomorrow."

In the Habiru quarters no one stirred out of doors.
Families huddled together to pray and offer comfort.

Aaron had taken in Mai, Neftis, Iri, and Pepi. Seth, Yahadu, and Demetrios had accepted shelter with Moses' family.

"What is it that will pass the door when the time comes?" Demetrios asked Moses.

"I don't know, frankly. An angel visiting the earth may or may not be in human form. I'm not that curious; once I stood in the physical presence of Yahweh, and the experience still shakes me down to my bones whenever I think about it."

Demetrios looked at Seth. "I cannot even imagine being so near one of the great mysteries without wanting to know more."

"I had a normal man's curiosity ten years ago, didn't I, Seth?" He smiled.

"Perhaps a little more than the normal," Seth said. "On the way to Nubia you were all questions. You—"

Moses held his hand up for silence. "It is here. I can feel it."

All eyes flew to the door. There was a strange feeling in the air—a tingling, a sensitivity of the skin. From the silence came a sound: far away at first, then coming slowly, steadily nearer, like the sighing of a faraway wind in the palms.

Zipporah and Gershom exchanged excited, fearful glances, then they looked at Moses. His eyes placidly returned the gaze of his wife and son. His lips were relaxed.

The sound came closer, closer . . . then under the door, a shaft of intense light blazed through the narrow slit into the room. It was a light such as none except Moses had ever seen.

It paused for an instant, as if probing, inspecting, and then it slid away. Under the door was darkness again. The sound of the sighing wind faded.

Demetrios leapt to his feet, threw open the door, and went into the street. Above the buildings of the Egyptian quarter, he could see the unearthly glow moving down the thoroughfare. He stood for a long moment, then reentered the room.

But just as he closed the door, he could hear the first of the faraway screams, high and piercing—shrieks of horror, despair, and loss!

As Moses rose to bar the door, he looked at Demetrios in the dim light of an oil lamp. Seth rose to join him, aghast.

"What's the matter?" Demetrios asked, frightened.

"Demetrios," Seth began. "Your hair . . ."

"What about it?"

"It's turned white. Stark white! Are you all right? What did you see? What did you hear?"

And in the palace, in the royal apartments where the window stood wide open, the light and sound passed unnoticed. Kamose, deep in his drugged sleep, slumbered on, unaware.

X

In all of Avaris only the king slept soundly that night. In the slaves' quarter the Habiru's guests tossed and fretted, trying to make sense of the day's events.

Seth put a hand gently on Demetrios's arm. "Are you asleep?"

"No," Demetrios answered in a low whisper. He raised himself on an elbow and faced Seth. "I'm still trying to figure out what happened last night."

"We don't really know what's happened," Seth said. "We won't until we find out whether the Egyptians' firstborn have died in the night."

"You believe it, though, don't you?"

"I know Moses. He's not the type to fake something. You couldn't ask for a more straightforward person. It is possible that he has, in the years since I knew him, become a true prophet, a man who can see into the future. What if Moses' God is not a phantom but a fact?"

"Seth! You, a believer in the gods?"

"Not 'the gods.' Not the Egyptian pantheon, or the Greek one. I couldn't give credence to a god with all the negative human attributes: jealousy, spite, pettiness. . . . This one has none of these. He is not of this world. He is outside it. As Moses has described his Yahweh to me, He is vast, limitless, unimaginable, faceless, and unknowable. If I was to conceptualize a believable Power beyond all things, He would have to be a virtual copy of the one Moses says he speaks to."

Demetrios sat up and faced him. "And your point is?"

"I'm not sure. This thing you saw last night . . . ?"

"*Almost* saw."

"Well, we'll know in a bit. Either the Egyptian firstborn are alive and well, or . . ."

Demetrios's eyes narrowed. He looked hard at Seth but did not say anything.

The Egyptian firstborn were not alive and well. The angel of God had struck with a terrible finality, and the city was in chaos. The guards at Kamose's palace had to bar the doors against a growing crowd of grief-stricken parents, many cradling their dead children in their arms. All were cursing Kamose for bringing destruction to their families.

Neb-mertef, roused early by the din, went down to the great hall of the palace to investigate and found Geb conferring with several officers. After Geb sent his men back to their posts, Neb-mertef approached him.

"General," he said. "How bad is it?"

Geb frowned. "I expect a full-scale riot. I've sent messengers to other units in the region for reinforcements."

"The people blame the king for this and not Moses?"

"They consider the king's stubbornness to be behind the disaster."

"And you, General?"

Geb shot a cautious glance at him. "It's not my job to make a judgment, sir. It's my job to deal with the reaction." His impersonal mask cracked for just a moment. "It doesn't help that Apedemek's body is displayed, impaled, in the public square."

"I wonder who could have ordered that?" In fact he, Neb-mertef, had given the order. "It does serve as a warning to potential traitors—"

"The mob perceives it as an attempt to shift the blame for last night's tragedy to a subordinate. And they know otherwise."

"Your words approach treason, General. I would advise you not to let them get to the king's ear."

"I appreciate your tender solicitude, sir," Geb said in a

voice barely short of insolence. "I was on my way to resign
my position when I discovered Apedemek's body. I had
planned to be on the road by now. But with a riot on our
hands, I can't leave until order has been restored."

"I'm sure the king will appreciate your loyalty."

"I'm equally sure the king won't appreciate any such thing.
You have his ear. Can't you wake him up? The political future of
the country is at stake, and key decisions have to be made by the
king—in full possession of his faculties, if you get my meaning."

"I do," Neb-mertef said sourly. "Are you accusing the
king of being drunk last night?"

"He hadn't been drinking. But everyone knows about
the king's weakness for drugs." There was bitterness in his
voice. "Although I'm not sure how he got hold of any."

Neb-mertef frowned. How indeed? And then, in one
blinding flash, he knew.

XI

No one was to disturb Moses at his prayers, but the
events were so extraordinary that Dathan tried to push his
way past Aaron to reach the Habiru leader.

"Aaron, you have to let me talk with him. The most
amazing thing has happened. The people of the city! They're
outside! Thousands of them! The poor! The rich!"

"That's hardly reason to—"

"Aaron! They want to talk to Moses!"

"Nothing takes precedence over offering up praise to
Yahweh."

Aaron put a firm, strong hand under Dathan's elbow and
propelled him to the door. "Now, run along, please, and tell
them that Moses is praying. Tell them that the obstacle to
our leaving is the king's will. Perhaps this will stir them to
get rid of him. Tell them that only a fool defies Yahweh."

Dathan shrugged and nodded. "I'll tell them that Moses
will be out in a while."

"Yes, Dathan. And tell them what I told you."

* * *

Neb-mertef looked down at the sleeping body of the king, sprawled across the broad bed, and made a disgusted face. *It's true then. He's back on drugs.*

"Hello, Counselor," a voice said from behind him.

Neb-mertef whirled to see Amasis silhouetted before the open window. He wore the richly decorated, expensive clothing of a highly placed courtier.

"*You* did this." Neb-mertef's hand indicated the king.

Amasis smiled nastily and took his arm to steer him into the next room.

"You betrayed me," Neb-mertef said, wrenching his arm free.

"Perhaps, perhaps not."

"Why incapacitate him at a time like this?"

"You and I could not bring him down; perhaps the good people of Egypt can do what we have failed to do."

"But the government could fall—not just the king!"

"Well, you and I wouldn't let *that* sort of thing happen, now, would we?" Amasis' smile was bitter. "We wouldn't allow anarchy. We'd make sure there was an orderly transfer of power."

There was a noise from the king's room. Amasis froze, listening.

"What is this?" the king bellowed in a slurred voice. "What's that crowd doing down there? Why isn't someone out there breaking some heads? Can't I trust anyone around here to be doing his job? *Guards!*"

Amasis' eyes locked with Neb-mertef's. "See what I mean?" he said in a soft, silky voice that dripped malice. "He won't rule much longer. And when he falls . . ."

Half-dressed, his wig a tangled mess, Kamose came barging down the stairs toward the great hall. His retainers trailed behind him, with Amasis and Neb-mertef bringing up the rear. His dresser caught up with them.

"Sire," he ventured, "let me outfit you before you go out to meet them. Your wig, Sire. Just let me do your wig and help you put on this robe."

"Your sandals, Sire," said his assistant. "If you'll just stop for a moment—"

"What? Dress up for the rabble?"

Neb-mertef caught up with him now. "That's the problem, Sire: They're not rabble. They're the cream of the city. Merchants, traders—" Neb-mertef looked around, trying to find Amasis; but somehow Amasis had contrived to hide himself. "Sire, do you remember Moses' threat yesterday?"

"That nonsense?"

Neb-mertef, his heart in his mouth, took a deep breath and told of the night's tragedy.

"Don't talk to me of sorcery! The man's a fake! I had guards patrolling the neighborhoods—"

"Sire, we found the guards. They're blind and quite mad."

"Nonsense!"

"Sire, you haven't seen them. Their eyes are covered with a white film. You can't see the pupil or the iris. Their hands tremble uncontrollably."

Kamose frowned. "Here, get out of my way. I'll go out and tell the rabble a thing or two."

At the foot of the stairs Geb looked at Neb-mertef.

"Shouldn't a detachment of guards be with him?" the adviser asked.

They watched the king open the door and lurch out. "Do as you wish," Geb said, disgusted. "I don't care what happens to him. Let the wolves have him."

Geb's aide, at his elbow, looked at him. "Sir, should you be saying that out loud?"

Geb sighed. "I have precious little to protect or salvage."

"In all due respect, sir, you couldn't help yourself."

"Couldn't I? In my heart I wanted to be a general, and when the job was offered to me, I didn't give a thought to Khafre, whom I'd served for so many years."

"Sir," the aide said. "Something's happening. I'd better get some guards into the hall."

The noise grew. Geb, not moving, merely watched the aide gather up three guardsmen and rush to the door. It was time to get away from here, before he was soiled forever. Perhaps it was too late to make up for what he had done, but he need not live in continuing dishonor, supporting folly and wickedness.

XII

The shouts of the angry confrontation between Kamose and his subjects carried down the great lateral artery of the city to the Habiru quarter, and after listening to the din, Iri motioned to Joshua and Pepi. "How would you two like to go for a walk to the palace with me?"

The boys' eyes brightened. "Sure!" Joshua said. "But won't we get into trouble? I'm not supposed to be in that part of town."

Iri laughed. "Don't worry. You're with me, and Pepi is a free citizen of Nubia and a friend of King Het's. Isn't that right, son?"

"Well, yes," Pepi confirmed. "He declared himself Mother's protector when she arrived in Nubia. I guess that makes me—"

"A person of substance in your own right. Besides, without me and my forges Kamose would be in trouble, and he knows it."

"Let's go!" Pepi said with a smile.

As they approached the palace Iri could pick out the king's voice. ". . . think you are, talking to me that way, you insolent scum?"

Iri and the boys exchanged surprised glances. "That's no lower-class mob," Iri said. "There's Zoser—gods, how he's aged!—and Khenzer the wine merchant. Unless I'm mistaken that's Sekhti of Bast, whose caravans go as far as Damascus. And look, there's Menkhuhor, the tycoon who first bought my jewelry for export. These are men of substance! Has Kamose taken leave of his senses?"

"Look," Pepi said. "Here come the guards from both sides, hemming the people in."

"The madman!" Iri fumed. "Come with me. If we climb to the top of that wall, we should be able to see and hear well enough."

They clambered atop and sat, dangling their legs, while the king, surrounded by guardsmen, insulted the crowd: "This desert fake, stinking of sheep, makes a couple of threats, and you take him to heart."

"It's your fault!" a woman screamed, offering up in her

arms the limp body of her toddler. "You killed my child! You and your arrogant defiance!"

Other women joined the chorus, hoarse from weeping. "Murderer! Traitor! Child killer!"

"*Shut up!*" Kamose shrieked. "Guards! Seize her!"

The guard nearest him hesitated, looking to his immediate commander for confirmation.

"Do as I say!" Kamose ordered. "Guards! Break this up! These people are gathering illegally!"

But before anyone could move, a single figure, bent with age but dressed in expensive robes, moved to face Kamose. "You know me, Sire," he said. "Zoser of Thebes. I have served my city and my king for over sixty years. I have in all that time been the last man in Egypt to question the wisdom of the Crown."

Kamose fumed. "Get to the point."

Zoser shrugged. "Very well. I simply want to caution you against impugning the loyalty, integrity, or honesty of any of these good people gathered here."

"This is insurrection!"

Zoser calmly persisted. "Sire, I doubt that you could find three people in all of Egypt who would agree with your actions."

"I don't have to have anyone agree with me. I'm the king! My word is law!" He snarled at the captain of guards. "What are you waiting for? Arrest him for sedition!"

The captain hesitated. "Sire, if I might have a word with you . . ."

But Zoser spoke again. There was still power in his old voice. "Sire, you may have me thrown in prison or executed. But word will get around about how you treat a humble and loyal band of petitioners. And, perhaps, about how you deal with a faithful servant who asks only that you reconsider an ill-advised decision made in haste." He paused. "Soldiers, you can arrest me now. I will not willingly live a day longer in a nation where such things can happen."

"Don't lay a hand on him!" warned a citizen. "You'll have to kill me first."

Iri whispered, "That's Khenzer the wine importer. Zoser is the most respected businessman in Avaris, but Khenzer is the most powerful. His wife's relatives own half of the Fayum.

In his family are over a dozen highly placed priests. To antagonize him would be colossal folly."

Kamose's eyes were blazing. He stepped toward Khenzer and seemed on the verge of violence. His hand reached for the missing sword at his belt.

But a burly, no-nonsense officer, wearing the uniform of a general, drew close to Kamose and whispered in his ear. Then, miraculously, the king withdrew, back inside the palace.

"Who's that?" Pepi asked.

"Geb. Kamose's top general. Listen now. What's he saying?"

". . . king will hear your complaints later today. If you would appoint a spokesman or two, perhaps? You, Zoser? And you, Khenzer? Good. I'll send a messenger to your homes when he's ready. Now go along, my friends. You will be able to present your grievances and suggestions in a more moderate atmosphere."

Iri smirked. "I doubt *that*. But he did an amazing job cooling things down. Can you boys find the way home? I want to find out what is going on here and bring the news back to Moses. He has the responsibility for all of you, so he must be informed immediately of any changes."

Joshua looked at his friend. "All right. Come on, Pepi. I'll race you home."

Kamose's face was a mask of mad rage, and his voice quivered. "How *dare* you interrupt me?"

Geb, fists on hips, ignored his bluster. "Sire, I suggest an immediate conference with the military leaders to plan a course of action."

"I already have a course of action! I'm going to have the leaders of this insurrection impaled, and—"

"I think not, Sire. Reports coming in from the other nomes say that the deaths of the firstborn appear to have been universal—"

"Nonsense!"

"—just as Moses predicted they would be. You are risking a revolution, Sire, a bloody uprising in which the entire country rises to kill the king. The country needs a firm but calm and judicious hand. Have I your authorization for calling a meeting of the generals?"

"Well . . . yes."

"Good, Sire. Meanwhile we need more troops in the city."

"Yes! In that we're in agreement! More troops to put down these rebellious, seditious—"

"No, Sire! Just to maintain order!"

"—and to deal with Moses! Yes! Now!"

After further venting of temper, Kamose finally allowed himself to be led upstairs by his retainers. Geb lingered, looking after him.

Yes! he thought. *The generals will come, but I'll talk with them privately, before they've seen Kamose. I'll explain that Kamose is beyond help and beyond control and must be deposed and replaced as quickly as possible, before the whole framework of the government comes apart!*

XIII

Zoser returned in deep disgust to his litter, where his respectful servants stood awaiting him.

"Shall we take you home, sir?"

"No, take me to the Habiru quarter. I want to see if I can talk with their leader. It might make better sense than talking to the king."

"But sir," the lead bearer said. "He's said to be a sorcerer who can cause death by waving his staff."

"No, no, no," the old man said, chuckling. "I've known Moses for years, and he'll do me no harm. Come my friends, there's much to be done."

Iri strode past the guards arrogantly, looked around, and spotted Geb. "Just the man I wanted to talk to. Geb! Over here!"

The general turned, scowling. But when he recognized Iri, his manner grew more relaxed. "Ah, Iri! Come with me. We have things to talk about that require privacy."

Iri looked at him skeptically. "That's odd. I can't visualize your awaiting my arrival with eager anticipation."

Geb put a hand on the armorer's rock-hard bicep and steered him down the hall to the officers' conference room. "I don't blame you for thinking ill of me. I hope you'll forgive me."

Iri looked at him hard as they reached the destination and went inside. "You do remind me a bit more of your old self, before Nubia. What happened?"

"Iri, I should have stayed an adjutant. Any man who can be dominated for ten years by Apedemek hasn't got it in him to be at the top."

"Huh," Iri said. "Maybe you have changed, after all. But what are you planning to do?"

"Some of this is my fault. I helped return Kamose to the throne. I must do what I can to make things a little better. Kamose plans, I think, to strike out against the people who defied him today and against your friend Moses. I've already called the troops in from neighboring nomes, and I'm counting on you to tell Moses to arm himself."

"Wait. *You* called the troops in? Why?"

"Reasons of my own."

"Either you tell me everything, or you can count me out." He rose and started to go.

"All right, but keep it quiet. You could not only cost me my life but risk all of us surviving this mess."

Iri looked at him, then smiled broadly. "You're thinking of a takeover."

"Not so loud! Damn it."

"You trust the generals enough to tell them of your plans?"

"At the moment I can't think of a better strategy. But meanwhile, whatever happens, Kamose is going to blame all his troubles on Moses. Your Habiru friends have not so much as a half-dozen swords among them. Don't go telling me how adept they are with the slingshot; no matter how good they are, they won't have a chance against the weaponry you outfitted the army with."

Iri nodded thoughtfully. "True. But how are they going to arm themselves before Kamose can strike at them?"

"A Greek ship, laden with weapons bound for the markets in Tyre, got itself stove in a few months ago. The cargo was salvaged, but the boat wasn't fixable. The Greek left his

representatives in port, with instructions to sell the cargo if
they possibly can."

"Greek weapons aren't bad. Their best stuff isn't up to
mine, though."

"Spoken like a true armorer. If you can raise the money,
you've got the weapons."

Iri frowned. "Where are a bunch of slaves going to get
enough coin to buy it?" He shook his head and blew out
hard. "Give me directions to the building where the weapons
are being stored, will you?"

The bearers put Zoser down, and the old man looked
around. "Pardon me, sir," he said to a broad-backed, muscular man. "I'm looking for the leader of the Habiru."

The man turned, looked at him, and smiled broadly.
"Zoser! How nice to see you!"

The old man looked at him quizzically. "Moses? Young
Prince Moses?"

The younger man grasped the merchant's arm warmly.
"I'll bet I wasn't more than thirteen or fourteen when I last
saw you. You showed me how to use the throwing stick on a
hunting party on the river, near Thebes! Come. Let me have
my wife, Zipporah, get you food and drink."

"Thank you, but no. You might give my servants something to drink; they've been out in the sun waiting for me,
listening to Kamose scream."

Moses called out his request to a subordinate, then he
took Zoser aside and found a seat for him. "Now, what did
you want to talk to me about?"

The old man sheepishly smiled up at him. "Quite honestly, I was going to ask you to name a price for leaving
Egypt and never returning."

"Kamose keeps us from going. It's what we want. We'd
do it for nothing. You aren't the first to broach this with me.
Quite a number of citizens have brought us valuable bribes in
the last few days, trying to get us to go. The truth is, their
money would have come in handy. But I can't in good conscience accept it. We'll be arriving in Canaan without money,
weaponless—"

"I can't let that happen to my old friend," Zoser said.

"How much would it take to assure you of . . . oh, a rather better arrival in your homeland than that?"

Taken aback, Moses said, "I—I don't know."

"Name a figure, my friend," Zoser said. "Name it and— when Kamose allows you to leave—it's yours."

XIV

"I don't understand what you're proposing," Moses said.

"I've called a meeting for this afternoon of influential citizens," Zoser explained. "Something must be done about Kamose, and that can be accomplished only by first removing the source of Kamose's irrational behavior—meaning, of course, yourselves."

"Well, yes."

"The men I've called together control a very large portion of the available wealth of the delta and, in some cases, of the rest of Egypt as well. They've absorbed tremendous losses recently—property damage and loss of crops and live-stock. They realize that further chaos here will prove ruinous."

"So?"

"I'm going to suggest that we take whatever action is necessary to get you and your people out of Egypt."

"I'm overwhelmed, sir."

"Keep your wits about you, now. You're very vulnerable. Kamose still controls the army."

"And you think that even if he lets us go—"

"Exactly. What route do you intend to take to Canaan?"

"There's a straight track that my people used to come here, when Joseph was vizier. It's called the Way of Shur—"

"Ah!"

"Although it's by far the shortest route there, it leads directly to Kadesh-barnea and to Beersheba, and both places are dangerous—Kadesh-barnea for the Egyptian garrison there, and Beersheba because of the Canaanites." He made an eloquent gesture of resignation. "The way I understand it, the first Canaanite tribe we'll run into is the most entrenched.

We'll have quite a fight on our hands. Before we face them, my people need to be trained in the use of arms."

"I forgot you were originally trained as a soldier."

"Trained by the best, although I will never pick up a sword again. I wish I had the aid of someone like Geb."

"That may not be the impossibility you think it. Geb broke up the confrontation this morning."

"That would be wonderful. To get back to your question about our route, sir, every path could prove dangerous. I've been living at a trading post for ten years, talking with caravan leaders, so I have an accurate set of maps, with estimated distances between oases. And of course I have an additional secret weapon."

"And what might that be, my young friend?"

"The one true God, omniscient and omnipotent, Who will not let His people be destroyed."

Zoser hesitated a moment, then he said, "I admire your faith, even if I do not share it. Take care that you do not lose it. A most formidable secret weapon it is indeed. Now I must go. I will confer with my peers. Geb is supposed to send a messenger to set up yet another meeting, so there is a chance that he does not represent Kamose in this. I will keep you informed by reliable messengers. Rest assured that we will help you with your financial needs, even if I have to hold my associates upside down until the money pouches fall out of their garments."

Iri and Baufra set out on horseback for the waterfront, which lay some distance from the city proper. On the way they met the port's army detachment marching in to defend the city. Iri and Baufra steered the horses aside from the paved high road and kept to the shoulder, looking at the long files of soldiers, whose spears were held diagonally across the body.

"That's what Moses is up against," Iri said. "Three days from now Avaris will look like the jumping-off point for an invasion of Canaan."

"That's what it might wind up being, isn't it?" Baufra asked. "If Moses gets away and they pursue him—"

Iri nodded grimly. The last of the troops passed, and the two men moved their horses back onto the paved road.

"Baufra, if something should happen to me, what would you do?"

"Iri!"

"No, seriously. I've left orders with my representatives that the forge business will belong to you. I don't think you've any personal interest in the jewelry-making aspect of it."

"No interest because I have no talent for it. But what does this mean?"

"Anything can happen, my friend. These are perilous times, and I wanted to make certain that you were taken care of."

"I'm touched and flattered."

"I've taken these steps without consulting you. What would you do if you decided not to continue as armorer to Kamose?"

"I don't know. What are you planning for yourself? It sounds as though you are thinking of leaving."

"My brother, Khian, wants me to come with him. I'd be brought into the Chalybian Order and be part of a rich and powerful enterprise. I'd have a wonderful future."

"Oh, sir! If only I could go with you!"

Iri looked at him. "You'd give up the chance to become first armorer to the king to come along with me?" he asked, incredulous.

"I'm basically a follower. I've been happy following you."

Iri blinked, much moved by this. "What if my path led into danger?"

"Even then."

"I may find myself in opposition to official Egypt. I would hate to find myself in opposition to you, old friend."

"That will never happen, whatever the circumstances."

"Your reassurance makes my choice an infinitely simpler one."

Neb-mertef took Amasis aside, to a private room. "I've been keeping an eye on Geb. I don't trust him."

Amasis frowned. "I've noticed a difference in him in the last couple of days, but I haven't connected it with—" He stopped. "But of course! He came to his senses when

Apedemek lost his power. You're right! Free of Apedemek's control, he'd be very dangerous."

"I think he's cooking something up—something we ought to know more about. Today he met with Iri for a rather long time."

Amasis nodded. "I've half a mind to hire someone to put a knife in Iri."

"I think Geb's about to take a more personal hand in all this intrigue. He sent off the messages: one from Kamose, one from Geb himself. Both were for the general staff. The message from Kamose proposed a meeting. So did Geb's, but scheduled four hours earlier than the king's meeting."

"Ah! This *is* interesting! Go on."

"Geb also sent a missive to Zoser," Neb-mertef continued, "to be shared with the other merchants: They are to meet with Geb to discuss the present situation. He referred to it as dangerous."

"And this meeting would also exclude the king?"

"Right. Now you see why I'm concerned?"

"I do indeed," Amasis said. "Now how do we plant a spy at both Geb's meetings?"

"That'll be difficult. I could infiltrate the merchants' meeting, but the meeting with the generals . . . I haven't got anyone in the general staff on my payroll."

"*Hmmmm* . . . perhaps I do. There's Ketu. But I'll have to work fast."

"Do that," Neb-mertef urged. "Ketu is our only hope there. There's no time to lose!"

XV

Within an hour Iri had struck a deal, making a substantial down payment on the Greek arms by using funds from his own account and arranging for the rest to be paid upon delivery of the weapons to Moses. He then rejoined Baufra, who was waiting outside.

"I hope I haven't just done something foolish," he said. He named a sum that, to Baufra, seemed staggering.

"Can you afford it?"

"Oh, I'm not worried about that. After all, I didn't have any money invested in livestock or grain. All my money is invested in precious metals. I just hope Moses won't mind that I've made the arrangements without his knowledge. I expect he'll view this as a kindness, though. Come on, let's go tell him."

The riders Geb had sent to the outlying nomes had reached their destinations, and from all sides the hastily assembled units of the Egyptian army took to the high roads, marching toward Avaris. Meanwhile, Moses had sent messages to all Habiru settlements in far-flung locations throughout Egypt. These summons had similarly reached their destinations, and much more slowly the Habiru, bearing everything they owned, began converging on Avaris.

The Habiru prudently avoided the main arteries, so as not to come into contact with the soldiers. The deaths of the Egyptian firstborn had befallen all the areas they walked through, however, and the reactions of the superstitious, frightened locals varied from hatred—this was restricted to curses from afar, since the Egyptians were now terrified of the God of the Habiru—to fearful respect.

The Habiru sang as they marched: ancient songs of Canaan, some dating back to the first trek their ancestors, under Abraham, had made from Egypt to the land their God had promised them. Among their present number there was not a person who had been born in Canaan, but they remembered the stories their fathers and grandfathers had told of it in their youth. The nostalgia was there. The songs were happy, full of hope. They were songs of home.

The merchants gathered at the home of Zoser. Geb stood near the door, watching them file in, his keen eyes searching the faces. When the last man invited had arrived, Zoser stood and said, "My friends, we have come together to listen to General Geb; but first I want to tell you of a conversation I had with Moses, the Habiru, today." He quickly told of the financial offer he had made.

"Whatever happens with regard to the king, we will benefit from giving Moses the money he needs to move his people from Egypt. Will you match my contribution?"

After a brief discussion, Zoser passed among them a scroll bearing their names, seeking their private seals to complete the deal.

"Along the same lines," Zoser continued, "General Geb, like us, is deeply concerned over the potential for a complete breakdown of law and order here." He moved aside to make room for the soldier. "Geb?"

At the end of the meeting the merchants and traders took their leave, each man grasping old Zoser by the hand.

The last to leave was Shu, a man who had purchased several taverns when he had moved downriver from Memphis. "Well, Zoser, there was good work done today. May we be on our way to better days."

"Thank you for coming," Zoser said. "Remember, we must keep our plans secret until we're ready to act."

Shu went outside. *Secret indeed,* he thought, smiling to himself. He had enough on all these men to have them strangled and hung on a hook in the public square.

He had agreed to turn the information over to Neb-mertef, but what use would a weakling like him make of it? What if, instead, he was to pass the information to the king? He would be rewarded richly, most likely. Very well. That was what he would do. The quicker, the better. He never cared for Neb-mertef anyway.

He turned and reversed his steps, walking briskly toward the palace.

Demetrios stood in shadow and watched. In the center of the public square, guarded by a lone guardsman, stood the tall, sharpened stake on which the body of Apedemek lay impaled. The crows were at work. The sight was not a pretty one. Before it stood Pepi, the ten-year-old son of the dead man.

Demetrios's eyes narrowed, and he tried to read the expression on the boy's face. It proved impossible. He sighed, then moved slowly to the boy's side. "May I join you?"

The boy nodded.

"May I ask what you are thinking?"

Pepi turned and looked up at him with eyes filled with anguish. "He was so strong! And then he became so weak!"

"Yes," Demetrios said, putting his arm around the boy's thin shoulders and leading him away, toward a bench. "You know, Pepi, life sometimes seems to be an endless series of forking paths. Every moment we make decisions that will affect the rest of our lives, decisions that move us toward the light or toward the darkness. Do you know what I mean?"

He sat next to his uncle. "Maybe I understand."

"If you do, you're smarter than I was at your age. Fortunately, we tend to know what kind of decision we're making when we make it."

"Yes," the boy agreed. "Why didn't Fath—why didn't Apedemek? Or did he know he was doing bad things all the time?"

"I'm not sure," Demetrios said. "Maybe he forced a negative turn of mind on himself, until he reversed the meaning of good and bad in his mind. You know: Take the bad thing and call it good, and vice versa."

"Yes. I used to do that. Stealing from the marketplace. I wanted to be tough, hard."

"But in the end you always paid for what you stole, didn't you?"

"Yes. I'd get cramps in my stomach from the fruit I'd stolen."

"That means you didn't follow your father very far down that road, doesn't it? Maybe you weren't meant to follow him."

"No." Pepi moved to look at the grim sight, then turned his tormented face away. "But he was the only father I had."

"I know. But if you need to talk, at any time, I'm here, and I'll always listen. There's Seth, too."

"But it's so hard to talk to Seth. Everything he says sounds like criticism of me. I get mad."

"Talk to Moses. He's a very wise man. And I'm sure he'll be glad to spend time with you once these current problems are resolved."

"Yes, he is. You know, he *really* has the kind of power I thought my father had. And Moses doesn't use it in a mean way."

"Keep that in mind. Meanwhile, don't forget you've got friends. All right?"

Pepi looked up at him, and while there was confusion in the boy's eyes, Demetrios felt confident. *Thank goodness! He's turning the corner. He's coming around.*

XVI

Contact with the king was made through a low-level aide; Shu's heart was in his mouth while he waited, for fear Neb-mertef or Geb would see him waiting in the anteroom. Finally, however, he was ushered into the king's apartments.

Shu bowed low. "Sire," he said, "I beg to report—"

"Come on, get it out," Kamose said irritably.

Shu's hands were shaking. The king seemed to be on the edge of a monumental tantrum, and the two guards flanking him also appeared tense. "S-Sire, there's a revolt afoot against your authority. One in which some of the biggest names in Egypt are involved."

"How do you know this, and how do I know you aren't lying?"

Shu, his voice trembling, managed a halting, bumbling description of the meeting he had just attended. "Moreover, Sire, I think the money they're giving Moses may be earmarked for weapons."

"You mean the general is arming my enemies? That's absurd. There are no arms for sale here."

"Sire," Shu said desperately, "I heard General Geb say that there was a warehouse full of arms, which were stranded in the port."

"Hah! Slaves, who don't know the arts of war, challenging the Egyptian army? They'd be chopped to pieces!"

"Perhaps, Sire, but such a battle within the city limits of Avaris, Sire? With the whole city looking on?"

"Ah, I see your point. I must make sure the arms never get to them. This must be headed off."

"Sire," Shu said, "that may be a problem. General Geb

said that arrangements were being made for the transfer of the weapons even as he spoke."

"Curse them!" Kamose sputtered. "Captain, make certain the gates to the Habiru quarter are double guarded. I want no major shipment coming through. And keep me posted on everything." He turned back to Shu. "This is good information. Now what else have you?"

"Why, Sire, the merchants."

"I can't do anything about them. They are too powerful for me to have them executed—unless, of course, they're caught in the middle of an actual uprising."

"Geb was on his way to a meeting of the generals. I think he means to turn them against you, to take over the army and depose you."

"Where and when is this meeting supposed to take place?"

Shu told him. "And, Sire, there's more. I was approached by a member of your own court and offered a rich bribe to report back to him instead of you. Of course, when I heard this I pretended to agree—"

"Hah! Did you take the money he offered?"

"W-why, yes, Sire. He would have known that I was going to betray him if I hadn't. It was a necessary step to gain his confidence."

"A likely story. And who might this conspirator-right-under-my-nose be?"

Shu was about to answer when a new voice broke in. "It was Neb-mertef, Sire," the newcomer said.

And Amasis walked out from the adjoining room to stand beside the king!

Shu's heart almost stopped. How to handle this? "Th-that's right, Sire," he said at last. "It was Neb-mertef."

"Very well," Kamose said, his face relaxing. "How fortunate that I had both of you looking out for my best interests. My good right hand here"—he indicated Amasis—"has also reported a plot involving General Geb. Well, we've got our own ideas about that, don't we, Amasis?"

"Indeed," Amasis said, his gimlet eyes on Shu. "And what shall we do to reward your faithful servant?"

Kamose looked hard at Shu. He did not speak for several seconds; then he turned to the guardsman. "Dispose of him.

He can't be trusted. If he'd betray his friends and the man who hired him, he'd betray me."

Shu gasped. "No, Sire! I—"

The garrote slipped over his neck and cut off his next word forever.

The meeting was held in an old barracks on the edge of the city, where the troops from the outlying districts had already begun to gather. Ketu, Amasis' spy in the meeting, looked around, where the fields outside Avaris were beginning to resemble a battlefield. The great muster of the military units had begun with the nearest garrisons, and now the soldiers from farther sites were beginning to arrive. They had encamped on three sides of Avaris, and the tent cities were going up quickly all around.

Gods! Ketu thought. *This is going to be a larger force than Kamose took along with him when he went north to wipe out the Shepherd Kings!*

This was not as odd as it first appeared; there was more danger of rebellion of once-loyal Egyptians than there was of an uprising of the Habiru chattels. Any rebellion would surely fall before the combined might of so many units—and, of course, there were more on the way. This made it more imperative than ever that Geb fail in his attempt to turn the army against Kamose.

Ketu nodded, thinking of this, as Geb, in his spotless uniform and riding a Moabite stallion, came trotting up. Ketu saluted as Geb pulled the animal up and dismounted.

"The gathering is almost complete, sir."

"Very good," Geb said, handing the reins to an under-officer. "Let's get this thing started. We don't have much time."

"Yes, sir," Ketu said. "Right this way."

He ushered Geb into the big barracks, taking care to stay two steps behind him. But when they entered the huge room where the generals stood assembled, Geb stopped just outside the door.

In front of the assembled officers Kamose stood facing him, looking like a demon from the Netherworld. Along the walls stood a detachment of bowmen.

As Geb watched, the bowmen moved as one to nock their arrows, raise their bows, and take aim.

"Have you anything to say for yourself?" Kamose demanded in a piercing voice.

Geb thought a moment. *I deserved this. Well, let it come.* He locked eyes with Kamose. "Do what you must."

When the arrows flew, Geb's eyes were wide open, and his chest was thrust out defiantly to receive the bronze-tipped shafts.

Iri and Baufra dismounted at Moses' headquarters. "I'll go talk to Moses," Iri said. "Would you take care of the horses, please, then find Pepi and bring him here?"

Baufra nodded, setting out in the direction of Aaron's house.

Once his destination was achieved and the horses tended, Baufra stood lost in thought for a moment. He knocked on the door, his mind still many leagues away.

When the door opened, neither Aaron nor Elisheba stood to welcome him. Instead it was a slender, darkly beautiful woman in her thirties. Her hair, pulled back neatly, was streaked with gray, and her large brown eyes seemed clouded with concern. There was something about the sweet curve of her lips, combined with the dark depths of the soft and vulnerable eyes, that reached deep inside and touched a part of him that no woman had ever touched before.

"Do I know you?" he asked. "I think I ought to, somehow."

"You used to, a little, long ago," she said in a soft voice that held the delicate minor key of immense sadness. "You're Baufra, aren't you?"

"W-why, yes," he said, entirely smitten. "And you?"

"I'm Neftis, Iri's sister. Won't you come in, please?"

XVII

By the time Aaron reached the north gate of Avaris, he was in a state of near panic. Everywhere were soldiers, foreign for the most part, vicious, fit, and armed with weapons from a dozen countries.

He had intended only to visit the Habiru whom Moses had called in from the outlying nomes, to make contact with them and invite their family leaders in to speak with Moses and learn the plans God had for their nation. But walking to their encampments in the far fields, he had passed through the ever-increasing numbers of soldiers Kamose and Geb had called home. Aaron had been the target for the soldiers' shouted insults and the rocks and clods thrown at him.

Kamose intends to kill us! He plans to wait until we've all arrived, and then he'll set these dogs on us.

How could the Habiru defend themselves against such numbers? It was impossible. They were doomed!

At the gate the guards stopped him and would not let him pass until someone was called to identify him. This was harassment. Seething, Aaron waited the whole process out. Then he hurried to Moses' headquarters.

There was a conference of the tribal elders in progress when he arrived. Moses turned and took note of him. "Ah, Aaron, did you talk to our brothers from the other nomes?"

"I did," Aaron replied in a voice that reflected his discomfort. "But have you seen the soldiers? Do you know how many are out there? At least as many again are expected to arrive by this time tomorrow."

"Have faith, my brother," Moses soothed. "It is nowhere near so bad as it looks. I was just telling the elders here—"

"You don't understand. Kamose means to have these people kill us!"

Moses shrugged. "Many people have tried to kill us before. None has succeeded."

"Moses," Aaron said, "you must take this threat seriously!"

"But I do," Moses assured him. "You forget Who is on our side."

"Moses—" Aaron threw up his hands, exasperated.

"Wait," his brother said. "Look who's come in! Iri! Where have you been? I've had people looking for you."

Iri carried a rolled scroll, and he waved it in the air on the way to the center of the crowd where Moses stood. "How do we stand in the way of money?"

Moses smiled mildly. "Zoser and his merchants have given us more than we need. Why, my friend? I agree Kamose can be bribed, but I don't think he will stay bribed."

The elders laughed. They liked Iri; he was fearless and loyal. He felt the warmth in their laughter. "I want to buy what will break his head, not bend his resolve. I've found us some arms. Not enough to outfit everyone, but enough to do some damage."

"Weapons?" Aaron asked. "Where?"

"They'll be delivered here just before the gates close for the night."

Iri sketched in the day's events; when he admitted to his paying for the arms out of his own pocket, there was a rousing cheer for him.

"Iri," Moses said. "That was most generous. But it will be repaid, dear friend, from Zoser's offer."

"Now if I could only locate more arms somewhere . . ." Iri said.

Moses stopped him. "My friends, do you think that we, uninstructed in weaponry, can stand up to the largest Egyptian war force ever assembled?"

"That's what I was trying to tell you!" Aaron pointed out. "Even with Iri's good news, we've no chance against them!"

"Friends! Kinsmen!" Moses said, quieting the virtual uproar. "You're still drawing the wrong conclusions! Do you think that a victory over the Egyptians is going to be managed by force of arms? Do you think that armed might will win us our freedom?"

"But, Moses!" someone called out from the rear. "Surely the hand of God is in this gift of Zoser's and in the cache of arms Iri has located."

"I agree. God's hand is in everything that happens to us. But I do not think that it is His will that we become instant masters of the sword."

"Then what . . . ?" the man began.

"Have faith," Moses urged. "God's hand is upon us. We

have His promise for that, so long as we keep the faith with Him. If we do not break the covenant, He will not break it either."

A moment of silence followed this. Then the door burst open. "Moses!" said Dathan, loud and strident. "Bad news! It's General Geb! He's been executed by Kamose—for treason!"

The news came like a physical blow to Iri. "Geb? But I just talked to him today. He told me about the arms for sale. He was going to try to convince the generals against following Kamose."

"That's where they caught him! Someone informed on him!" Dathan reported.

Iri frowned. "This is terrible. It wipes out whatever good news I brought."

Moses put a hand on his arm. "No, my friend. The arms will come in handy. We'll need them later, when we get to Canaan, to fight our way in."

A young man suddenly ran in. "Moses! Come along! There's a problem! Come quickly! All of you!"

The problem was at the north gate. The gate area swarmed with guardsmen who had intercepted a line of wagons bound inside. Before the wagons stood Kamose, his eyes blazing. "So!" he accused. "All the time you were talking peace to me, you were arming yourselves. Do you know what the law is regarding slaves owning weapons?"

"We are in God's hands," Moses said. "Say what you have to say."

Kamose spat in the dust by Moses' feet. "You think you're going to get away from here, past the armies, and across the desert to your precious Canaan. Well, let me disabuse you of that notion. Your friend Geb is dead!"

The moment of triumph was not quite what Kamose had expected it would be.

"We know," Moses said. "We mourn a brave man murdered by cowards."

"All right, then," Kamose said. "Did you know that I've infiltrated Zoser's cabal? I know exactly who joined him in pledging the money for these arms—which will now go to my own army."

Iri walked to one of the wagons and pulled out a sword.

"If you hand them to those mercenaries they'll laugh at you," he called out insolently. "They're the worst cheap Greek junk I ever saw in my life."

"Be that as it may," Kamose said, "I've got them now. And Zoser and the others are under constant surveillance. The first time one of them steps out of line, he's dead." His eyes narrowed. "Your own actions steer uncomfortably close to treason, Armsmaker. You think you can get by with this sort of thing, but you can be replaced easily enough. Keep up your present conduct, and you'll learn a lesson you won't like."

He turned and strode away, surrounded by foreign soldiers in Egyptian uniforms.

"Well," Moses said, "it was worth a try, Iri. You did your best. We'll think of something else."

There was savage and angry despair in Iri's expression. "We will, eh? What?"

XVIII

Night settled on Avaris: a night of doubts, a night of fears, a night of despairs. A night of testing . . .

Kamose pushed his untouched dinner aside and reached for the wine. He drank, but the wine tasted sour, and he spat it out. It was not a night for wine anyway. He reached for the vial of *shepenn* Amasis had given him. Then he stopped, holding the vial.

I should be feeling jubilant. I should be glowing with my victory over Geb. I've intercepted a shipment of arms destined for the Habiru. I've unmasked a conspiracy. I've got the goods on Neb-mertef at last.

Then why this disquiet? Why this feeling that things could still go disastrously wrong for him?

He started to open the vial of *shepenn* but once again stayed his hand. Something was wrong. He had to puzzle it out. What was missing? He had the pieces in his hands, and

all he had to do was put it all together. But some random
element kept the picture from being complete.

Ah, the human factor. That was always a problem. He
had closed an almost totally foolproof trap around his enemy,
cutting him off from all sources of help. Moses could be
expected to show some sign of fear.

But Moses was not afraid. And neither was Zoser. That
alone spoiled his victory, soured his stomach, and made it
impossible to eat.

Moses! Zoser! He gritted his teeth and, with a shudder
of frustration, opened the vial of *shepenn*.

The afternoon had been one of successive shocks for
Neb-mertef, but the night was far worse—a time of sitting in
his apartment waiting for the ax to fall.

He had heard of Shu's death at the same time he had
heard of the interception of the arms shipment to the Habiru
camp. Since then he had heard nothing.

How much had Shu revealed before he died? Had Shu
betrayed him? He knew he would not rest until he learned
the answer. Panic rippled through him. *There, now! Get hold
of yourself. If you'd been fingered as a conspirator against
the king, Kamose would have struck out at you by now.*

Kamose was not the type to exercise self-control. If he
had devised plans for Neb-mertef's slow and painful death,
would he not have done something about them by now?
Yes—unless he had left the matter to a subordinate.

Neb-mertef, pacing, wished for the morning. There would
be no sleep tonight; he knew that. Whatever came in the
morning, it could hardly be worse than the waiting.

Seth and his friends had joined the elders, Moses, and
Aaron in the big warehouse, as before, but this was the only
thing that remained the same. The mood of the Habiru
approached despair. Seth occupied his mind by quietly discussing his architectural plans for Home with Demetrios,
while Yahadu, listening in, took quick notes on scraps of
papyrus. Iri sat alone, thinking.

Moses sat on the floor in a circle of his friends and
advisers. Nobody had spoken for quite some time. Now,

however, Pepi approached him from one side. "Moses, would it be all right if I joined you?"

His young voice carried to all corners of the room. Moses turned, smiled, and made room beside him. "Certainly, Pepi. I was hoping you'd come sit beside me. I had some things to talk about with you. I assume you saw the impaled body in the public square."

Pepi was startled by the straightforward approach. He nodded.

"You wouldn't be normal if it didn't bother you. It's good to talk about it with a friend. Do you think you can?"

"Moses," the boy blurted out, "what does it mean? I mean, for me?"

Moses put an arm around his shoulder. "Maybe nothing. If you're worrying about having inherited something from your father, forget it. The things we inherit from our elders are tools: a strong back, a fine mind. Character is something we create ourselves by making right or wrong choices."

"Moses, about your own choices: Was it easier for you to make the right ones?"

"Easier? Why?"

"Joshua was telling me about your traditions. He says your God calls you His chosen people. Is this because you're especially good or smart?"

Moses chuckled. "Quite the opposite. He chose us in spite of being nothing special in either category. We believe He chose us for secret reasons of His own, which we will never learn."

"Then what is your duty to Him?"

"To praise Him at all times, obey Him, and glorify Him in everything we do."

"But if you're nobody special, how can you do that?"

"We make careful decisions, asking Him to tell us what His preference would be."

They had a larger circle of listeners now. Around the room all eyes were on them. Pepi pressed on: "But that means giving up control over your life. If you always let God control what you're going to do, isn't that like being a slave?" He blushed, realizing what he had said. "I never had a father. I don't know anything about having a father except what people tell me about theirs. But . . . would your relationship with God be anything like the relationship of a child to a good father who loves him and cares for him?"

"Ah, Pepi," Moses said, smiling. "How did anyone so young become so wise? Your questions come so close to stating the truth, they don't require answers." His voice was mellow and pleased. "Yes, it is very much like you say. The just and caring father wants to be acknowledged and respected. If he is, there is no limit to the love he will shower upon the child."

"Love?" Pepi said. "Then why are you slaves, at Kamose's mercy? How is it that your God lets you sit here, worrying over the danger you're in?"

"Do you see me worrying? I've never been more relaxed."

"Then how can you *not* worry? Here you are, surrounded by your enemies—"

"And they in turn are surrounded by my Friend, Who is so much larger and more powerful."

Pepi stared, wide-eyed. "You really *aren't* afraid, are you?"

"Of course not," Moses said. "I'm in God's hands. And, Pepi, the covenant doesn't say that He would make things easy for us. It just says that He will take care of us."

Pepi's face wore a confused smile. "I don't know if I understand, but I feel a bit better."

There was a moment of silence. Then several other voices spoke up at the same time, Seth's the loudest and most resolute. "I do, too," he said.

XIX

Zoser's servant met Khenzer and Menkhuhor at the door. "Oh, sirs," he said, nonplussed. "My master is preparing for bed. I know that if he'd had any idea that you were coming—"

A strong voice issued from another room. "What's that? Who calls on me at an hour like this?"

Zoser came out from behind a door into the room, already in the soft tunic he wore to bed. "Menkhuhor! And

you, too, Khenzer! What brings you here?" Without waiting
for the response, he turned to the servant. "Please! Bring
food and drink for my friends!"

"No, no," Khenzer said, waving the offer away. "This
isn't a social call. Did you know our meeting today was
infiltrated by a spy for the king?"

"Why, yes," Zoser answered. "I had my suspicions about
Shu from the first."

"Then why didn't you bar him from the meeting?"
Menkhuhor asked, dumbfounded.

"Why? There was the possibility that he could be won
over to our side by what we had to say." Zoser smiled and
gestured for the men to join him at the long benches before a
small reflecting pool. "You'd be surprised how many people,
given an opportunity, live up to your highest expectations. In
the present case, however, the fellow went right back to the
king to betray us and Neb-mertef, the fellow who had origi
nally hired him." He shook his head. "Well, our wicked acts
do have a way of catching up with us, don't they? After all the
people Neb-mertef has betrayed over the years . . ."

"This is the most amazing thing I've ever heard," Khenzer
said, sinking onto a bench. "You knew all this?"

Menkhuhor, equally stunned, joined Khenzer.

Zoser smiled blandly. "I have my own spies everywhere.
Tyre, Knossos, Byblos, Ugarit, Ashkelon." He chuckled. "Incidentally, guess who's sitting in the middle of the Habiru
camp right now."

"Seth of Thebes," Menkhuhor replied.

"Correct. But guess who else?" the old man asked with a
sly smile, full of amusement. "Demetrios the Magnificent! I
saw him. I don't think he recognized me; we haven't seen
each other since—well, since I looked a lot younger. I've had
a spy in his camp for quite some time. I even knew where his
secret headquarters were—before they blew up."

"*There?*" Khenzer was aghast. "No one has ever infiltrated his secret home."

"That's what he thinks. Please don't tell him if you see
him. My man can still do me a lot of good in the years I've
got left."

Menkhuhor regained control of himself. "Just how long

any of us has left to live is much in my thoughts tonight, Zoser. Now the king knows our minds."

"But dear fellow, we wanted him to know our minds, didn't we?"

Khenzer leaned forward. "But he knows who we are!"

Zoser's voice was patient. "We wanted him to know that, too."

"But, Zoser, dear friend, have you seen that monstrous army outside the city?"

"Why, yes. Should I be frightened of *them*? A bunch of mercenaries who have no particular loyalty to the king? If they were not paid, they would walk away, leaving the entire delta undefended."

Khenzer stared openmouthed.

"Who pays the king's bills but us?" he added mildly.

Khenzer spoke up. "How could I have failed to see what was right under my nose?"

Zoser gestured that Khenzer's oversight was perfectly understandable. "Not many people realize that Kamose is without funds. That the country is devastated. That the delta granaries have only a few days' food left. That by the time additional supplements of grain can be shipped from countries unaffected by the plagues, we'll have people dying of starvation. Kamose must concentrate his efforts on the food problem." He paused for effect. "Leaving, mind you, no time for such frippery as harassing Moses and the slaves."

"*Gods!*" Khenzer said.

"Yes," the old man agreed. "We must let the common people know all this. We merchants must spread the word in the marketplaces, beginning tomorrow morning. Why don't the two of you give me some assistance?"

Khenzer's face slowly broke into a broad smile.

Neb-mertef had thought the door was firmly bolted; but when he came back into his sitting room from the bedroom, unable to sleep, he found Amasis standing under the lamp, looking at him. "How did you get in here?"

Amasis offered a thin smile. "There are no walls, no doors, that can hold me back."

"Well—I'm glad you've come. Perhaps you will intercede for me, since *you* seem to be getting on so well with

Kamose now," he said sourly. "He's planning some move against me. But why? You and I were in this thing together, yet he goes after only me."

Amasis' lip curled. "Everyone thought I was permanently out of favor at court. They'll see. I'm going to be the only one here who survives this mess."

Neb-mertef looked at him, his lower jaw slack. "M-my present troubles," he whispered. "*You're* behind them!"

Amasis shrugged. "It was a matter of my betraying you before you could betray me, wasn't it? If I hadn't protected myself, I'd be decorating a sharpened stake right next to our friend Apedemek."

"You turned me in, you bastard!"

Amasis made a little mock bow.

"You reminded him that you and he have been friends for so many years, while you failed to bring up that you kept him a drugged prisoner. That you tried to kill his wife. That—"

"He didn't give a damn about his wife."

"—you were planning to kill him too. Now you're killing me, you treacherous swine!"

"Oh, no," Amasis drawled. "Not yet. I've just been given the job of seeing that it gets done before the king gets up tomorrow morning. For a time I played with the idea of bringing in a professional assassin and watching him work. But in light of our former partnership, I have decided to spare you that."

Neb-mertef's eyes burned with intensity. "Let me go, Amasis! Help me escape!"

Amasis' eyes were cold. "I have brought you a little flask. It will be quick and painless."

"Damn you!" Neb-mertef said with a sob. But he took the flask with a trembling hand.

XX

In the morning two more army units came in, having marched through the night. They set up camp just north of the city, facing the gate through which the Habiru would have to exit if they left Avaris. These units were dominated by tough, filthy Greek soldiers who wore no more than a sword belt, a helmet, and a coating of dust. They answered to no one but their own leaders, and they were unconcerned about the welfare of Egyptians and Habiru.

Beyond their tents, newly arrived members of the far-flung Habiru tribes encamped and were almost immediately subject to the coarse harassment from the foulmouthed Greeks. The Habiru representatives, going into the city to confer with Moses, endured taunts and insults.

Around noon, a rider came from Athribis, bearing a message intended for Demetrios. . . .

In the Habiru quarter Moses stood with Aaron and watched as Baufra and Neftis spoke and laughed in low whispers at the well. She had already drawn her jug of water, and he had taken it from her, eager to bear her burden.

Aaron grinned. "She seems totally recovered," he said. "Mai tells me this is the first interest she's shown in any man since her unfortunate affair with Apedemek."

"Baufra's a good man," Moses said, "fiercely devoted to her brother. The devotion, too, seems to have extended to her as well."

"Love at first sight is not that rare. Our ancestor Jacob fell in love with Rachel the first time he saw her."

"Yes. And Isaac and Rebekah. Well, I'm happy for them both."

Aaron nodded. "I'll miss all of them—Seth, Mai, Pepi, Iri—especially Iri."

"Yes, there is something unique about him. There seems to be a special affinity between our people and him. More than any outsider I have known, he fits in with us. May our people always have such friends outside the tribe."

"As we have in times past. Belsunu, Sneferu, Ahuni, Hadad."

Behind them a voice broke in. "Moses!" Demetrios was bearing down on them, a severe expression on his face.

Moses turned. "You look like the bearer of bad news."

"Unfortunately, you are right. I'd sent a message to my bankers in Athribis, asking if I could procure arms for you and have them delivered to Pithom, so you could pick them up there."

"That was clever."

"Clever or not, I've come up empty-handed. There's no way to have the weapons in under two weeks. All communications have been disrupted by the recent cataclysms, and river traffic is in a mess. The restructuring of the Nile's bottom from the great wave has left it unreliable."

"That is bad news," Aaron agreed.

"There's worse. The river and the overland high road between Athribis and here are clogged with the king's troops. I am at the end of any immediate resources I had for helping you."

"You do not need to help us," Moses consoled him. "We appreciate your generosity, but you must not take yourself to task."

"I can help with your finances," Demetrios offered. "I can have large sums transferred for your use so that when you arrive in Canaan, you'll have sizable deposits in your names in the northern markets and banks. Surely it would come in handy to arrive in Canaan well-to-do."

"I appreciate your offer of help, dear friend. Zoser and his associates have been generous, so I don't think we need to strain the resources of one man—not even a man of your immense wealth." He smiled. "Your own affairs need attention—you and Seth have headquarters to build. If you leave now, you will still carry with you our thanks and affection forever. Your friendship and loyalty have been beyond price."

Demetrios looked him in the eyes and, uncharacteristically, could think of nothing to say. "Bravely spoken," he replied at last. "I will never forget you."

Demetrios was vaguely disquieted when he approached Seth. He still felt weak and impotent—sensations he was not used to.

"Seth, I've talked to Moses, and he suggests that we gather up our party and leave." He paced furiously. "I still don't feel that I've done enough."

"Well, perhaps there is something you can do. Has the runner left for Athribis?"

"No. Why?"

"You've representatives in Sile, haven't you?"

"Yes. But there are no spare weapons there."

"What about spare grain? Livestock? Beasts of burden?"

"I don't know. My own stores could have suffered the same fate the local ones did during the plagues."

"If these items have not been destroyed or damaged, you could have them smuggled out of Sile in the guise of a caravan bound across the Sinai. Once out of sight of the garrison there, the caravan could change course and deliver the food and pack animals to Pithom."

"And have them waiting for Moses when he comes through!"

"It ought to work. What border guard would dare detain a caravan traveling under the auspices of Demetrios the Magnificent?"

"Particularly if Demetrios himself was there to supervise the departure of the caravan." He gripped Seth's arm. "You're as brilliant in small things as you are in the large ones. We'll leave tomorrow at dawn. There isn't much time."

Amasis entered the king's personal quarters just as Kamose was ending a conversation with Ketu, who had replaced Geb as commander of the delta armies.

The king's eyes gleamed with a mad light. "Amasis! You're just in time to hear my decision!" He turned to Ketu. "Go ahead, General. Carry out my orders."

Amasis' eyes narrowed. "Wait, Sire," he said quickly. "I've seen a couple of things in the city that you may want to know before you give any final orders." He looked at Ketu. "Perhaps you should hear this too, General."

As he spoke, he looked into Kamose's eyes. *He's abusing the drug I gave him. Within a week he'll be back up to the dosage he was on when he first returned to Egypt. He's addicted—and he's dangerous.*

"Well?" Kamose demanded. "Get it out. But don't think it's going to change my position. I want the Habiru all dead by nightfall."

"Sire," Amasis said, "you can't send the army in and murder thousands of slaves in cold blood."

"Why not?" Ketu challenged. "If His Majesty wants this, I don't see—"

"Sire," Amasis interrupted, "Zoser and other merchants spread word throughout the marketplaces, inciting the rabble. There was the distinct threat that if you didn't come to some accommodation with the city fathers, people would be sent out to the army units to notify the soldiers that you couldn't pay their salaries."

"*What?*" Kamose shrieked, livid. "And you didn't order the guardsmen to strike them down on the spot?"

"Sire, Zoser made a speech and I heard everything he had to say. Frankly, I'm glad I did. Now I know that sending the soldiers into the Habiru quarter would touch off a revolution. It would be a clear indication that you care nothing for the wishes of your people. They want peace; they want the Habiru out of here."

"Arrogance!"

"I agree, Sire. But I have a plan."

"Speak up, man!" Kamose's eyes blazed with a fierce, insane inner light.

XXI

The tribal elders from the local and the newly arrived groups had gathered at sundown at the warehouse that served as a meeting hall for the Habiru. The room was uncomfortably crowded as the people waited for Moses.

Seth poked around the fringes of the crowd, looking for someone. Demetrios caught sight of him and pushed his way through to his side. "What's the matter?"

"I haven't been able to locate your brother or the others all afternoon. If we're going to get on the road at dawn—"

"I'll help you look. Have you talked to Moses? Do you know what he's going to say?"

"I suppose he's going to mention that we're leaving, for one thing."

"There's more than that. He made attendance compulsory for the tribal elders."

"Well, we'll find out later. First, let's find our kin."

* * *

The place had been growing louder for many minutes, so that when Moses finally entered from a side door, it took a while for quiet to prevail. When all was silent, Moses, in the center of the room between Aaron and Dathan, looked out across the crowd.

"My friends and kinsmen, we have come a long way to this moment, but we cannot leave Egypt by our own efforts. We cannot fight our way through the army. Even if we had been allowed to receive the weapons Iri had obtained for us, we would have been doomed the moment we tried to oppose Kamose's legions."

"Then what—?" someone began.

"Only God can get us out of Egypt. Only God can save us. And if He chooses to do so, He can do it whether we are armed or not."

"Let us fight for you!" Dathan urged. "Find us the weapons, and we'll—"

"Ah, Dathan. If heart, and bravery, were all it took . . ." Moses shook his head. "Dathan, you've no training. Neither do any of our kinsmen. Somewhere along our march to Canaan I intend to stop and teach you the use of arms. I know that by that time Yahweh will somehow have found weapons for us."

A new voice broke in, vibrant and strong and angry. "If He doesn't, I'll make you some!" The man scrambling to his feet was Iri!

Moses was genuinely taken aback. "Iri, I don't understand—"

"Get me the ore, and I'll make you all the swords your people will ever need. As a matter of fact, if we go up the Arabah, we'll pass the Timna mines. There's enough good copper ore there for any number of . . ." He looked around him sheepishly. "I mean, if you'll have me. I am an outsider, but you'll need an armorer."

"Iri," Moses asked gently, "are you choosing to live among us, to share our dangers? If you are, I'm very happy. May God always send us such friends!"

"I am," Iri declared.

There was a pause. Then Baufra moved up from the

rear, his arm linked with Neftis's. "And I also," he proclaimed. "I'm Iri's man. He'll need an assistant."

"I don't know what I could contribute," Neftis said, "but without Moses and your God, I would still be under the spell of Apedemek. Where Baufra goes, I go."

"Pepi!" shouted young Joshua ecstatically. "You can go! Just like you've been wanting!"

And then there were fifty, a hundred voices, shouting approval!

Kamose had called old Zoser in for a conference. To the king's surprise, the old man had left his bodyguards at home. "Does this mean you don't fear coming here?"

"I'm too old for fear," Zoser answered. "The fewer people risking death by treachery, the better. I've settled my affairs. If you have it in mind to kill me, I'm ready."

"You wrong me," Kamose protested. "Why should I wish your death?"

Zoser snorted. "Or Neb-mertef's? Or Geb's? Or Shu's?" He looked at Amasis and General Ketu, who came to join them. "Ah, the survivors. Maggots always outlive the dead."

Ketu flushed, but Amasis' face remained unreadable.

"I had hoped this would be a peaceful and harmonious meeting." Kamose tried to sound reasonable.

"Let's get on with it," Zoser said. "I understand you have an offer for me."

"Why, yes," said Kamose. "I was given an account of your speech this morning in the marketplace."

"Indeed? What did you think of it?"

"Again you wrong me. It was quite accurate, particularly the part about the 'echoing emptiness in the royal granaries and the royal treasury.' It appears, my friend, that you and I need each other more than I need the blood of the Habiru slaves who have been such a trial to me in the past few days."

"I agree," Zoser said. "It's time to negotiate."

"Will you hear the terms I propose?" Kamose asked.

"I know what your terms are: My allies, who are the financial giants of Egypt, bail you out of the present mess. In return, you will allow Moses safely out of Egypt with all his people, chattels, and movables."

"*Done!*"

Zoser looked mildly surprised. He scrutinized Kamose's face. "If there's some trick—"

"No tricks," Kamose promised.

Zoser continued to stare. "Have you come to your senses at last?"

"The only thing for me to do, given the gravity of the present situation," Kamose said, "is to comply. Amasis! Summon a runner. I'll have him inform Moses that he may leave Egypt forever. He and his people are free. I wish him well and hope he prospers."

Amasis went out the door.

"Now," Kamose continued, "have you any other conditions? Just name it and you'll have it."

Zoser stared. He did not say anything.

"General," Kamose said to Ketu. "Draw up the order of the day: Moses and all his people are not to be touched, taunted, or tormented. Any soldier who disobeys is to be impaled without trial. The Habiru are to be aided in any way they require and treated with respect."

"Yes, sir!" Ketu said, standing and saluting. "I'll call the scribes!"

XXII

Kamose's runner reached the Habiru meeting just as Moses was preparing to adjourn. Moses went into the street to hear him out and then came back to share the developments quietly with Demetrios, Seth, and Aaron.

"What do you think?" Aaron asked.

"If it's legitimate," Demetrios said, "you and I, Seth, have to ride tonight to Pithom, to purchase provisions. We won't have time to go to Sile, but Pithom was out of the path of the destruction and should have some surplus food."

"Then we'll pass through Pithom on the way?" Aaron asked.

"Yes," Moses confirmed.

Seth looked uneasy. "I've known Kamose too long to trust his word."

"That has crossed my mind," Moses admitted. Then he shrugged as if Kamose's honesty were irrelevant. "It makes sense to stop in Pithom if there's any chance Demetrios can arrange for provisions and pack animals for the journey." He put a hand on Demetrios's shoulder. "We are grateful beyond measure."

"Thank me when I succeed," Demetrios said ruefully. "Come, Seth, let's get Mai and take to the road."

"One moment," Seth said. "Moses, my life is a series of increasingly sad good-byes."

Moses embraced the older man. "You will be always in our minds, our hearts, and our prayers."

Seth, his eyes wet, went to say farewell to Iri, Neftis, Pepi, and Yahadu. Moses watched him go. "He thinks himself a failure," he said to Demetrios. "I charge you with the task of changing his mind."

Demetrios nodded. "I'm giving him a chance to start over. Don't worry." He smiled. "And I charge *you* with the task of caring for my brother and sister and her son, but particularly Iri. He has never had friends. Let him give his love to you."

"I will. Go with God, Demetrios."

Demetrios went in search of Mai. "Come," he told her. "We have some serious riding to do. And when we're done with our errand, you and Seth are coming with me."

Concern shadowed her eyes. "I hope the change will be good for him."

Demetrios took her gently by the arms and looked into her eyes. "A man needs work; and the better the man, the more he needs it."

"As long as the work makes him stronger, I'll be happy."

But Seth was pushing his way through the crowd toward them now. Demetrios winked at Mai and turned to Seth. "Well, cousin? Are you ready to begin your new life?"

"I am," Seth said, putting an affectionate arm around Mai's waist. "Come! Let us proceed as if we were going to live forever!"

When Moses told the crowd the good news, their cheers rocked the warehouse. He allowed them long minutes of jubilation, then raised his two hands for silence. "My friends," he said, "it appears that the moment for which we have waited so long is here. But it would also be wise to remember that we have had promises before, which have been rescinded soon after the giving. Remember that it is Kamose with whom we have to deal."

"Do you think he's lying?" Dathan asked.

Moses thought for a moment. "I think that the moment it's safe to break his word, he'll do so. This is why we've got to move now."

"Very well. When do you want us ready to leave?" one of the elders asked.

"Tomorrow," Moses answered. "Before noon. Before he can change his mind, fall on us, and kill us, as he has already done so many times in his dreams."

The gathering was shocked to silence. And now, without further announcement, the crowd dispersed.

Yahadu, planning to travel directly to the new Home, had said good-bye to Pepi and had impulsively given him a parting gift. Now, as Joshua bore down on him, Pepi took it out and admired it. The bronze sword gleamed in the flickering oil light of the lamp above; the tooled leather scabbard was worn and supple. "Look what I've got!" Pepi said. "I wish I could put it on. But look, the belt needs a couple more holes punched in it, or it'll fall down around my ankles."

Joshua grinned, "It looks pretty good. Do you know who made it?"

"Another relative of mine," Pepi said. "Grandfather's sister, Teti. Look, here's a nick in the blade. I wonder how that came about? I mean, I wonder if somebody was trying to cut off someone's head, and—"

"What have you got there?" Iri asked, coming up and putting an arm around each boy's back. "Well, now! A sword! And a Child of the Lion sword, too!"

"Yahadu gave it to me."

"Let me see," Iri said affably. "Teti's! This is almost as rare as Belsunu's." He grinned. "You two may be something more than the only boys in the camp who own expensive weapons—you may be the only people among us who own weapons at all."

"Dathan has a sword he stole. And there are some others."

"Well, we'll have to do something about that," Iri said. "There's no Child of the Lion armorer for the next generation . . . unless I train you."

Pepi's eyes grew very wide. "Me?"

"Why, yes. Joshua's people are going to need arms for quite a long time. The Canaanites are not going to be easily conquered, you know."

"I hope not," Joshua said with a mildly bellicose edge. "I wouldn't want all the fighting over by the time I'm old enough to do any of it."

Iri laughed softly. "I see. You're going to be a soldier, eh?"

"I'm going to *lead* my people. I'm going to take them into battle and lead them to victory."

"An admirable profession, in such a cause," Iri said.

"Since Moses will never take up arms again," the boy continued proudly, "I'm going to be his sword arm. And when he doesn't want to lead our people anymore, there I'll be."

Iri clapped him on the shoulder. "Good for you! And if your friend Pepi could be making the swords that you used to smite your enemies?"

Joshua looked at Pepi with friendship and loyalty. "That'd make me really happy."

"Me too," Pepi agreed. "If Iri teaches me, I'll be the best armorer Canaan ever saw."

XXIII

That night Pepi could not sleep, and he did something he had not done since he was half his present age: He curled up close to his mother for comfort.

To his surprise she was awake too and reached out with a loving arm to pull him close. "Can't sleep?"

"No, I'm too excited."

"I understand, dear. My mind is racing. I can't believe what I've decided to do."

"You aren't changing your mind, are you?"

"No, dear."

"Are you and Baufra going to get married?"

"I think so. I can't imagine us not being together. Here I am, giving up all my money on deposit in Thebes and Nubia—and that's quite a large sum—and going into a new situation. Life is full of surprises."

Pepi sighed contentedly. "You were so sick for so long, and now look at you."

She hugged him hard. "Let's hope I'm well and strong! There could be hard times ahead. Fighting! But Iri and Baufra will make a lot of difference."

"And me too, Mother. Iri's going to teach me armsmaking."

"Well, I suppose it's time. Oh, Pepi! I should have told you about your family heritage long ago. I shouldn't have fought your destiny. It's the proper thing for the Children of the Lion. I should have listened to Seth . . . but I was so preoccupied with hatred."

"Don't worry, Mother. That hasn't hurt me. And I've been thinking about Apedemek. I wouldn't have followed him, even if he'd lived."

"No, you're a good boy." She sighed. "Oh, Pepi. I was such a fool. Baufra is a good, decent, gentle man, and Iri is, too. How could I ever have imagined that every man had an Apedemek hidden inside him? Now, Pepi, I know Apedemek was mad."

"Well, we'll learn new things together, won't we? I'm so glad I can talk to you again."

"I love you, dear. Come to me always, with any problem. I'll try to help you all I can."

"I will. Good night, Mother."

"Good night, darling."

Zoser was a creature of fixed habits: early to bed, early to rise. The next morning he rose bright and early and without breaking his fast went out into the city.

The marketplaces were empty; the great gates to the city were not yet opened. But as he approached the Habiru quarter, he could see and hear activity. He could see families out in the streets, choosing possessions to bring on the journey.

Good, he approved. *They're taking immediate advantage*

of the truce. He had hoped they would; who could trust the word of a man like Kamose?

As his litter passed the camp, he noticed that Moses had come out into the pale morning sunlight. Zoser called to his bearers to stop. "Now help me down," he said. Once on the ground again, he hailed Moses and drew near. "Well! You're not wasting any time!"

Moses grinned. "Our people have been dreaming of this day for so many years. I don't know what you did last night, but I could feel your influence in Kamose's announcement. Our thanks!"

"Go in peace! Do you need anything?"

"Well," Moses said with a smile, "if you have a map of all the wells in Sinai it might help."

Zoser laughed heartily. "I don't have a map, but here is the money pledged to you by the merchants' association."

Moses accepted the weighty pouches. "Our good friend and benefactor! Many thanks. We will use it to purchase provisions. Do you have a source of food and drink in the Arabah?"

"Ah, no, dear friend, I'm sorry. That trade route is in the hands of Sekhti of Bast and his son Bata."

"I'd forgotten all about them! Well, perhaps I'll run into Bata when we're up that way." Moses' face fell. "I didn't mean to tell anyone which way we intended to go."

"I had guessed you'd go that way. It wouldn't make any sense to tempt fate by going the northern coastal route. Kamose has that area jammed full of cutthroats who make this lot of mercenaries look like wet nurses." He frowned. "I'm distressed that you have no arms. I have racked my brains trying to think of a solution, but all I can think of is for you to stop at Timna. I'll extend my own line of credit to you there if you like."

"I appreciate that. We'll have our own armorers, and perhaps we can strike a deal there."

"Your own armorers! Iri?"

"The same. His sister and her son, and an assistant armorer are coming as well."

"Well! Give them my love. And tell Iri that I'll look after his interests here. If he needs anything, have him send a message to me. Without someone keeping an eye on things, his estate could get looted very badly."

"That won't be necessary. His brother is Demetrios the Magnificent, and he has his own men looking out for Iri's affairs and Neftis's."

"Demetrios? He's Iri's brother Khian? Wonder of wonders! Who would have thought it?" He shook his head, but his eyes twinkled. "Well, since I can't do anything for you, I'll just take a turn around the city walls and go back home. If I don't see you again, here's my hand in friendship, and may you have the best of fortune in times to come."

"And may God protect you and yours. Thanks for everything."

The bearers took him through the northern gate, through which Moses would pass when he left the city. Zoser wanted to have a look at the encampment of the late-arriving Habiru who had joined the great caravan as recently as the day before.

His route took him through the camp of the Greek mercenaries, whom he detested above all others. To his amazement the Greeks, who had a name for laxity, were up and about, taking sword practice and spear drill, grunting and sweating as they displayed their ferocity.

Barbarians! He curled his lip and called out to the bearers. "Let's get out of here!"

But as his litter moved slowly around the perimeter of the vast, sloping, Hai-built wall of Avaris, he could see other groups practicing the same warlike drills at this appallingly early hour. His eyes narrowed. What could be the reason for this? There was no war; the borders of Egypt were not being menaced. Why then had the soldiers not been dismissed by Kamose? The orders Kamose had sent along to his men the night before were a guarantee that the Habiru were safe from attack. He frowned. *Unless* . . .

But no! Kamose would surely have enough sense to realize— How could he fail to know that he would be found out immediately, and that the merchants and traders would abandon their commitment to bail him out of his financial bind? No, Kamose would hardly be that stupid.

*   *   *

Amasis stood over the king's bed as Kamose struggled to sit up. "I thought you would want to know, Sire, that the Habiru are already preparing for departure."

Kamose rubbed his eyes. "Good! The sooner the better. Filthy damned foreigners!"

"And," Amasis reminded him, "the sooner we can carry out the second half of our plan."

Kamose looked at him. "Yes. We honor the precise letter of our commitment to the merchants and at the same time eliminate our enemies." He yawned. "You've sent the message ahead to the border garrisons? To Sile and Pithom?"

"Yes, Sire. The moment the Habiru arrive in either jurisdiction, they're to be detained. And our informants stationed at the borders are ready to send runners back here to tell us when they have passed out of Egypt. We can strike then, without dishonoring the agreement we made with Zoser."

"Good. Make sure the Sile and Pithom garrisons understand that they're only to be detained. I don't want a drop of blood spilt until I've got there. I want Moses for myself. And that brother of his. And Iri! Traitor!"

"Yes, Sire. We'll take care that everyone understands. Your word is law, Sire. It shall be done!"

XXIV

To Moses' surprise, the announcement of the early departure of his people inspired a flow of gifts from the people of Avaris. From all classes they came, bearing gifts large and small, from money, gold, and jewels down to baked goods and bags of raisins.

Moses rode up and down the long queues of Habiru, each family bearing its own burden and ready for the order to move out. Once the lines had been inspected, Moses would surrender the horse and walk beside Aaron at the head of the column.

Dathan, similarly mounted, rode up from the rear, an angry look on his face. "Moses! The king is coming!"

Moses dismounted and handed the reins to an aide. "I wonder what he wants. Well, it does not matter much at this stage. We are moving out in a matter of moments, regardless."

Aaron joined them to watch the king approach, flanked by Amasis and Ketu.

"Greetings," Moses said. "We are honored."

"So you're leaving at last." Kamose sneered. "We might as well make the parting peaceful, free of angry words."

"You will hear none from me. I am intent only upon moving my people away from Avaris in peace and safety."

"You shall have both," Kamose said. "I exert little control over areas outside Egypt, but within its borders you will go in peace, and heaven help the man who hinders you. Good fortune to you." He turned away. But as he did, Amasis shot one last glance at Moses under hooded eyes, and Moses fancied that he could make out a small and enigmatic smile on the adviser's lips.

"Well," Aaron said. "What do you make of that?"

"Oh, he's up to something," Moses said flatly.

"If only we had weapons!" Dathan agonized. "He's going to pursue us, I know it!"

"So long as we remain true to this commission, God will watch over us." Moses took Aaron's elbow and steered him toward the front of the columns of people. Dathan followed.

Aaron smiled. "You make it all sound so simple."

"It is simple."

They stood at the front of the long lines now. Moses looked at them, and smiled at Iri, who had just joined them.

"Who knows the Song of Homecoming, which our ancestors sang on the road to Canaan in the days of Abraham and Sarah?" Aaron asked.

A strong young voice struck up the ancient tune, and a drum began to beat. The man with the ram's horn paused with the instrument to his lips, waiting for the signal. Other voices joined in one by one.

It was a song of joy in leaving the hated land in which they had all been born into bondage. Gone now would be the hateful servitude they had all known since childhood. They sang of the march, of the victories they hoped to know in Canaan, of the recapturing of the land that God had promised their ancestor Abraham so long ago.

The drum beat. The voices were augmented by others. The song became the single thought voiced by thousands of throats.

Moses nodded to the man with the ram's horn. "Let's go!" he said strongly, confidently, and when the horn blew, the first ranks stepped out onto the road.

"My heart is beating so fast I can hardly breathe," Aaron said. "I can't believe it. We're going home!"

Once in Pithom, the trio had split up: Mai went with Demetrios to look for his agents in the city, hoping to strike a deal for provisions, water, and beasts of burden. Seth headed for the thieves' quarter, hoping to find someone who might have a source of contraband arms.

He tried three different taverns without any luck before the innkeeper of a fourth, guessing accurately at his mission, suggested an address. But here, too, he found nothing but a dead end. There were no arms to be had in Pithom, it seemed.

Coming out of the house, however, he looked up to see a soldier in the uniform of Kamose's private guard entering the gate, leading a horse that had obviously been ridden many miles at all speed.

Seth was suspicious. *What sort of mission would he have in Pithom?*

Acting on pure instinct, he stepped into the man's way, blocking his path, and was recognized!

"You!" the soldier gasped. "Seth of Thebes!"

But when he looked squarely into Seth's eyes, the light went out of his own.

"Hello," Seth said sympathetically. He took the reins of the horse from the soldier and tied them to a post. "Come with me. We have some talking to do."

The soldier complied, his movements those of a sleepwalker.

Demetrios smiled at Mai over the table as his agent drew up the requisite documents for the transfer. "Well, so far so good. If Seth's done anywhere near as well, we've done good work."

"I doubt he will," Mai remarked. "This sort of deal is best done in a bigger city than Pithom."

"True, but you never know when a caravan is going to store some of its cargo while it visits an outlying post. Unless the caravan owner has a firm commitment on it, it's considered for sale to the best bidder. There is a chance we'll find something like that here."

His agent brought the document back and flourished the scroll. "Now, sir, if you'd give me your seal here . . ."

Demetrios pressed his ring into the hot wax. "I'd appreciate it if you didn't tell anyone to whom you sold the food and onagers. There's likely to be a bit of an uproar."

"Never fear, sir. A caravan's leaving town at about the same time as your friends. I'll tell the authorities that I sold the beasts and the provisions to the caravan owner. He won't betray you; he's retiring as soon as he gets home to Damascus."

He glanced out the open window. "Uh-oh. Trouble, perhaps. A soldier."

Demetrios spoke to Mai. "I'll handle him." He looked at the agent. "He's coming in?"

"It appears so, sir." He stood and faced the door as it opened. "Good morning, sir," he said to a person behind Demetrios. "May I help you?"

Demetrios slowly turned in his chair. "Excuse me," he said in a voice of command, "but we're doing business here—" He stopped, gawking. "Seth?"

Seth grinned and took off his Egyptian army helmet. "I didn't mean to startle you. I must look ridiculous. The fellow I took the uniform from won't, uh, be needing it for a few hours. I decided to relieve him of his identification, and then I hit on another idea."

"You grilled him?" Demetrios said.

"Yes. He's an aide to Ketu. Here on a mission, and thank heaven, I intercepted him before he was able to carry it out. He was supposed to tell the garrison leader to detain Moses and the Habiru. The moment Moses crosses the border, a spy here is apparently supposed to send back a message to Kamose, who will then march."

"And kill Moses' people?" Mai asked. "How horrible."

"Yes." He frowned. "That sounds like Amasis' thinking."

Demetrios scowled. "Surely Amasis knows how dangerous that would be! Zoser would foreclose on Kamose."

"Leaving Amasis the only viable candidate for the throne."

"So Amasis has outsmarted Kamose again!"

"So it would appear." Seth took off the military cloak. "Meanwhile, we've got to do something. Put this on. No one here knows you. I have an idea."

"What kind of idea?" Demetrios asked, taking the uniform.

"One that could get us some arms. From the Pithom garrison." He grinned.

Demetrios stared at him. "Why not?" he said at last. "It's worth a try, and we could cross up Kamose's plans to have them detained here." He paused. "Now if only we knew the identity of the spy who's supposed to send back the message to Kamose, we could delay the king's arrival long enough to let Moses' people get off into Sinai, where the king dare not follow."

"That's a problem. I haven't any idea who he is, and the messenger whose uniform you have there doesn't know. Unless we can find him in the next few hours, he'll get his message off."

"Then we'd better get busy."

Seth smiled. "Let's bring orders to the garrison commander to deliver all the spare arms to your agent here—"

Demetrios barked out a laugh.

"—and to send all available men to Sile, to defend the border post from attack by marauding Bedouin from the desert!"

"Ah, now you're thinking. I'll do it!"

XXV

An hour before sundown Dathan had decided to go back along the lines and see how his people, unused to long marches, were faring. Now he hurried to the front of the file to speak to Moses.

"Look here," he said brusquely. "You've got to give them a break. Many are exhausted from their journey to Avaris. If you keep this up all the way to Canaan, hundreds will die."

Moses maintained his steady pace. "Friend Dathan, I understand your concern. But surely you don't think all stretches of the road are to be taken at the same rate?"

"What do you mean?" Dathan asked.

"This first stretch is a very important one," Moses explained. "We will encounter nothing like it between here and our destination. For the good of our souls and our morale, we must traverse it quickly."

"Why?" Dathan challenged. "What's so different about—" Then he understood. "Wait. It's part of the road that still lies in the land of bondage. Right? You're counting on being out of Egypt for the first time in generations giving us strength and purpose. Right?"

"Correct," Moses verified with a smile. "Of course you could have figured that out by yourself, instead of giving me the benefit of your righteous disapproval."

"I'm sorry," Dathan said. "I can't help it. I operate on my feelings, and I feel things strongly."

"There are times for acting quickly, responding to a crisis. But there are many more times for thinking something out first, for planning ahead."

"But—you do intend to stop, don't you?"

Moses called to Aaron. "Let's stop here. Dinner stop."

Aaron raised a brow. "You mean we're going on afterward? At night?"

"Yes. Tell them that by dawn I'm counting on being at Pithom. I hope Demetrios will have been successful by then in finding us provisions and animals. I want to be off Egyptian soil before noon tomorrow."

"By marching all night?" Dathan protested.

"I know it's a lot to ask, but I have a plan."

Aaron called out the command, and slowly the long columns ground to a halt. Then he turned to Moses. "What kind of plan?"

"Keep this among us," Moses told Aaron and Dathan. "There's enough in our coffers now to buy our passage by sea to the borders of Midian. Normally there are a lot of boats stopping at the mouth of the Red Sea. If we can rent them, fine; failing that, we'll buy the boats. Then we'll enter Canaan from the vulnerable side."

"Ah! They'll never expect us to come by water!"

"Yes. But if it turns out not to be God's will, I will abandon my plan."

"On the surface it sounds like a splendid idea," Aaron said. "I'll keep quiet about it for now. Meanwhile I'll go back and supervise the dinner break; otherwise they'll start making camp."

Kamose and Amasis visited the Greek mercenary camp in Avaris. The evening camp fires had already been started, and the smell of seared lamb hung on the air.

The unit's commander, a much-scarred, hard-muscled man named Hipponax, came forward to greet them. "Well, Kamose?" he said, disdaining the royal honorific. "When are you going to unleash us? My boys are restless. We want some action. We want blood."

Kamose's ugly battle grin split his face. "That's the spirit," he said. "That's the way we were when we slaughtered the Hai."

"That was a long time ago," Hipponax complained. "Talking about past glories doesn't do a thing for us. You know how soldiers are: They get bored, and when they're bored, they're a nuisance. If you can't find anything for us to do, I'll be asking for our back pay and moving on." His eye narrowed. "You do have our back pay, don't you?"

"Certainly," Kamose said a little too quickly. "It'll be waiting for you the moment you return from slaughtering the foreign scum."

"And when will that be?"

Kamose put a hand on his broad, hairy back. "Come with me. The situation needs explaining. This business of letting the foreigners get away—that's just for show, you know. In actuality . . ."

Amasis watched the two walk away into the darkness. He looked around in the twilight and chuckled. He had taken no chances. First the Habiru had to go, then the king. Without Kamose's knowledge, he had already sent his own runners out in all directions to spread the news that the Habiru were coming. All Egyptian garrisons had been alerted to make sure the Habiru did not pass, in case they managed to elude Kamose.

But he had also sent a second round of messengers to tell

the soldiers of these distant garrisons that Kamose had bank-rupted the government—but that he, Amasis, was making arrangements to depose the king and to find new resources for the royal payrolls. He was openly wooing their support and seeking their personal loyalty.

Thus, even if Kamose lived long enough to destroy the Habiru, the garrisons of the far outposts would not obey him. They would, in fact, fall upon him and kill him—with the active assistance of the soldiers accompanying him in the present expedition. Amasis had done this by planting his own men with each of the major units that would accompany Kamose beyond the Egyptian borders. These men would, at the proper time, open their sealed orders and obey them, telling the unit commanders that Kamose had no money—that he intended to abandon them in the waterless desert and return to Egypt without them.

He smiled secretly. All he needed was time; then it would all be his.

Kamose and Hipponax came back from the shadows beyond the camp fire. "Amasis," Kamose said, "I've changed my mind. We're not going to wait to hear from our spies. We're leaving at dawn. Inform the cavalry and the chario-teers. Tell them to be ready to move out at first light!"

Amasis stared at Kamose's mad face, then at Hipponax's. He realized he had a new enemy to deal with, and a new rival. The man's face was malignant and amoral.

"Very good, Sire," Amasis said woodenly. "Right away."

Mai was just going around the office of Demetrios's agent, lighting the lamps against the growing darkness, when the knock came. Seth went to the door and admitted Demetrios, still dressed in the stolen army uniform.

"I gather you were successful," Seth said, locking the door behind him.

"I was," Demetrios said, smiling impishly. "The transfer will take place tonight. The arms will be at the same ware-house as the supplies and pack animals. Meanwhile, we'd be bloody fools to stay here. There's still a spy here, and if he comes from Avaris, he may recognize one of us."

"When is the Pithom garrison going off to rush to the defense of the Sile garrison?" Seth asked.

"Midnight," Demetrios answered. "They can't muster them before then."

"Then let's leave for Sile," Seth suggested. "On horseback we'll beat them there by hours."

"Sile? Why?"

"Keep your uniform on. We'll have a message for the Sile garrison as well. You'll barge in there and tell them you've a message for them from Kamose—that the Pithom garrison has mutinied and plans a predawn attack on Sile. Have Sile armed and ready so they can ambush the Pithom contingent when they pull into town. Tell them to wipe the rebels out for the dirty traitors they are."

"Ah, Seth, what a devious mind you have!"

"Enough flattery. Let's go. We've got to get to Sile with our secret message!"

But as the threesome rode out of the little town, Kamose's spy was standing in the shadow of a storehouse in the commercial quarter, watching soldiers leading pack onagers that were laden with shields, swords, and spears.

He frowned, wondering what sort of lunacy was afoot, as a well-known trader of the city emerged from the warehouse and directed the soldiers inside with the animals. The spy crept closer, hoping to peek inside the warehouse.

He flattened himself against the wall, and stopping just short of the window, he peered through and saw two dozen more pack animals, their backs bearing water skins and bulging sacks of grain.

What's going on here?

And then a scenario began to suggest itself: Someone in the local garrison had sold out the king! Someone had made a bargain to provision Moses' column and even to arm it! Kamose was walking into a trap and had to be warned!

There was no one but himself to do it if the garrison was in league with Moses. He had to leave now and get the word back to Avaris!

He disappeared into the darkness, heading for the stable where his fast, powerful horse was kept.

XXVI

As the Habiru marched through the night, Moses seemed withdrawn. When Aaron spoke to him, he gave no sign of having heard. After a time Aaron let him alone; but he would occasionally look over at his brother as he trudged doggedly along the track, wondering just where his mind was now.

What brought him back to himself, it seemed, was hoof-beats, which sounded halfway through the long night's trek. The horse, ridden at a steady clip along the track from Pithom toward Avaris, prompted Moses to issue quick orders, which were passed back: The Habiru should move over to the extreme shoulder of the road and continue to march.

The rider passed almost at the gallop. The hoofbeats faded before Moses spoke. "We'll be reported. Whoever the rider was, Kamose will hear from him."

"Then we'd better get into Pithom quickly," Aaron urged, "and get right back out again." He sighed. "If only the elderly and children didn't tire so quickly! They're going to require rest before we go on, but I don't like the idea of stopping in Pithom, where there's an Egyptian garrison."

"Your concern is well justified," Moses said. "If we were not protected by God Himself, our peril would be dire." He paused. "He has been speaking to me as I walked."

"I gathered as much," Aaron replied. "May I ask what He said?"

"I fear that there are those who will question what He has just told me. Like so much of what He says, the sense in it does not present itself immediately. One has to have faith because we cannot see the pattern He has planned for us."

"My faith would be so much greater, Moses, if He had spoken to me."

"The opposite is true, Aaron! The man who believes without hearing His voice is the man of greater faith."

"Perhaps," Aaron allowed. "Just ask Him, if you will, how we can get another six hours or so of walking out of the elderly and the little ones. My faith in them doesn't extend so far as understanding that."

*   *   *

As they walked toward Pithom, the spy galloped toward Avaris. When he arrived, he was hailed by the pickets, to whom he gave the password and was admitted to the advance-guard camp of the king, charioteers, and horsemen.

It was some minutes before aides could awaken the king, addled as he was by the heavy dose of *shepenn* that he had taken before going to sleep. At last he was alert enough to be told of the changed plans at Pithom.

"Treason!" Kamose screamed. "Bastards! They've sold arms to the Habiru!"

"But, Majesty," an aide ventured, "the Habiru haven't even arrived in Pithom yet. How can—"

"They've got representatives there! It's no secret that the locals have given gifts and money to Moses! Somehow he's sent money to Pithom and bribed the captain of the garrison! I'll have his heart cut out! I'll have the whole garrison flayed!"

"By the time this conversation is done," the spy said quietly, "the Habiru will be armed and provisioned, with onagers to carry weapons and supplies."

Amasis had been listening in silence. Now he said, "This is a disaster, Sire. With their burdens firmly on the backs of the animals, the Habiru's spirits will be high. By the time we arrive with the main force, they may already be well off into the wilderness, where we may not be able to follow."

"That settles it." Kamose's throat was tight with rage. "Amasis, you're in charge of the main force, the foot soldiers. Order them mobilized now. I'm going ahead with the mobile force."

"Ahead of us, Sire? But the Habiru are armed! Surely you'll want—"

"They're still no match for us. We've bowmen on every chariot. I'll stop them. If any mopping up needs to be done, you'll be right behind us. But I'm going out there at full speed, to stop them. Unit leaders! To me! We leave now!"

"And who are they?" the captain of the Sile garrison wanted to know. "They don't look like Habiru."

"They're not," Demetrios said. He looked at Seth and Mai. "They're good citizens, loyal to the king. If they hadn't tipped me off, I'd never have learned in time about this plot against the Crown or the attack expected against your own defenses. Thanks to their heroics, I was able to warn you in time against the traitors' attack."

"You've all done good work. I'll see that the king learns your name. He'll single you three out for special reward. Now if you'll excuse me, I have to arm the camp and deploy our men."

"May the gods give strength to your good right arm!" Demetrios said, leading Mai and Seth out the door to the waiting horses. It was all he could do to keep a straight face.

There was pink in the eastern sky when Moses and his people came within sight of Pithom. He brought the columns to a halt when he sighted a lone horseman heading their way from the city. "He doesn't look hostile," Moses said to Aaron, "but you never can tell."

The horseman, however, was Demetrios's agent in Pithom, who told of the purchases and of the deadly trick Seth and Demetrios had played upon the Pithom and Sile garrisons. "Now, sir," he said, "you'd better come pick up your bounty before someone catches on to what's happening."

"Moses! The gates to the town are wide open!" Dathan said.

"Yes," said Demetrios's man. "That cost Demetrios a pretty sum indeed. But you can't depend on anyone to stay bribed long in this volatile climate. Come along now."

The detail from Pithom was not even in fighting formation when the outriders first spotted Sile. No one had expected trouble from the local garrison, so the entire column from Pithom rode well inside the line of Sile bowmen in the hills before the Sile commander suddenly shouted, "Fire!"

The first volley felled a dozen men. Only then did the Pithom command regroup, draw weapons, and prepare for the forceful attack that followed. The fight was bloody and bitter, and the Pithomites were massacred. The Sile captain sent a triumphant message to Avaris, telling of the wholesale slaughter of the traitors. By that time Seth, Mai, and Demetrios—the latter now dressed as a civilian—were halfway to the Great Sea, bound for the distant destination Demetrios still insisted upon calling Home.

*   *   *

The pack animals bearing food and water had been merged into the two long columns pointing toward the Red Sea. Moses lingered now beside the pack animals that bore the weapons Demetrios had commandeered from the Sile garrison.

Dathan, grinning viciously, reached atop one of the onagers and pulled out a gleaming copper sword. "With these we can stand off Kamose and his cutthroats! We'll just lie in wait for them, and when they're in range we'll fall on them like wolves!"

Moses frowned and looked at Aaron. "Do you remember what I said about God's commands not being readily understandable in their logic?"

"Yes, but . . ." Aaron watched as Dathan swung the sword. "This is one of those occasions, then?"

"Yes. There will be vigorous dissent. Support me." As some of the other younger men drew swords out of the packs, Moses turned to Dathan and spoke his name.

"Yes?" the man asked, preoccupied with the sword. His back was straight, his shoulders thrown back. He looked like a soldier. "Let's get these distributed."

"Dathan," Moses said, "we're not taking the weapons."

Dathan stared, wide-eyed and incredulous. "Not taking the—? But, Moses! God has delivered them into our hands! How can we throw away a windfall He has given us?"

"This is not His work," Moses explained. "This is the work of man. God does not wish us to have these weapons."

"But that's absurd! Without them we're as weak as kittens. The Egyptians will slaughter us!"

"Nevertheless," Moses persisted patiently and firmly, "we're not going to take them along. We'll travel faster without them."

"Aaron!" Dathan pleaded. "Don't let him do this!"

Aaron put a hand on his arm. "Dathan, I realize it doesn't sound logical, but this is the voice of God speaking. We are not meant to have or use these arms. Help me unload them, now."

Tears of frustration welled in Dathan's eyes. "Please!" he begged. "Don't do this!" His voice rang with a heartfelt, anguished sincerity.

Moses put a hand on each of Dathan's shoulders. "Look

me in the eyes. Now, do you think me insane? Are these the
eyes of a madman?"

Dathan's nerves were taut. He looked as if he might
break.

"It has to be," Moses continued. "We have to travel
as quickly as we can. The king's soldiers are probably right
behind us, and our elderly and children are exhausted.
The only way we can push on is if they're riding these
animals. The animals—not the weapons—are the godsend.
And Dathan . . ."

"Yes?" His voice was that of a broken man.

"Consider these weapons as being cursed. If we are to
have weapons, these are not the ones."

"At least," Dathan sobbed, "let me keep this one."

"No. Not even one. Now help us get the elderly and the
little ones on the backs of these animals."

And so they rode on, defenseless but for the invisible
hand of Yahweh. And as they rode toward the sea, Kamose's
lightning-fast mounted legions gained Pithom.

XXVII

They rested at last. Moses had the Habiru hobble the
animals and told them they could sleep for two hours. Then
they would remount and continue onward.

But before the two hours had passed, they were awakened by the braying of the frightened onagers and a rolling
tremor within the earth.

Moses went among them. "This is the hand of God,
waking us and telling us that we are not safe yet. We will not
be safe while the Egyptians can still find us."

The elderly and children were remounted, while everyone felt torn between the fatigue that dragged at every bone
and muscle and the desperate urgency of the moment. Another tremor shook the earth; some riders were thrown to the
ground as the terrified animals shied. Prayers went up to God

as the long file started slowly down the mainland toward the Red Sea.

"You what?" Kamose gasped. His red-ringed eyes glittered with madness, forcing the officer in command two steps back.

"Sire, we did only as we were told. An officer in the uniform of your personal guard ordered us to march to the defense of Sile—"

"*What?*"

"—and to turn over all our surplus weapons and pack animals to this fellow."

"Who has disappeared, right?"

"Sire, who am I to question a direct order from your personal guard?"

"I smell Seth's hand in this!" Kamose fumed. He drew the sword at his belt and drove it to the hilt into the acting commander's gut.

The soldier sank to his knees, pulling the sword out of him, then let out a small, plaintive sound as he pitched forward.

"And so may all enemies of Egypt perish!" Kamose uttered in a strangled voice. "Leave orders for Amasis to execute the entire cadre here. Send a runner to Sile to find out what's happened! The rest of you, come with me! Let's see if the Habiru can use weapons."

But as Kamose's contingent galloped out of town, they saw where the Habiru had abandoned the swords. Kamose glared; what was the sorcerer up to?

"Forward! Full speed! A bonus to the first man who spots them!"

At last the Habiru stood at the top of a plateau, and looking out across the great sloping plain, they could see the Red Sea itself. But between the sea and them stood a deep, narrow inlet surrounded by steep, sloping hillsides, the path around it now obliterated by the rubble from the earth tremors.

Moses walked to the edge of the plateau and looked down. He knew that the track around the inlet had been passable before the tremors. Closing his eyes, he prayed:

Dear God, let the slope hold its shape until we're down the face of it.

But as he thought this, there was a new tremor, which racked the steep incline. Rocks, dust, and boulders plunged and rolled down around them into the water. Moses hung onto the rock face for balance. People screamed in fear, certain they would be propelled to their death below. "Steady!" he cried out.

But now, from the top of the steep slope where the rear guard stood, there came another cry: "Moses! I can see the dust cloud! Kamose is coming!"

A great and ancient rift in the earth stretched from far, far to the north all the way down into central Africa. All along this broad and unstable fault zone the earth moved now, in jerky and unpredictable lurches. And as the land moved, the sea moved. . . .

Moses stood still, eyes closed, withdrawn. Aaron, nearly panic-stricken, shook his arm violently. "Moses! Kamose is coming! We have to get down from here! But that long inlet at the bottom has cut off our path!"

Moses opened his eyes—eyes that had seen things so awesome that earthquakes and volcanic blasts were now petty matters, hardly worthy of mention. "We're going down," he said softly. "God has told me what to do."

"Look!" Kamose said from the lip of the plateau. "Up ahead—the sea! And there's the last of them, climbing down to the water! We've got them trapped now! Forward! Faster!"

They stood at the bottom of the steep slope where the waters of the bight spread wide before them. "Moses," Aaron moaned, "it's hopeless. We're trapped!"

"Don't worry," his brother said, just as another tremor shook them so hard it almost drove Moses to his knees. "Have our people gather with me here at the water's edge."

"What are you talking about?" Aaron demanded, his voice rising. "We'll be drowned! And the animals will be dragged to the bottom, with the people and the burdens on their backs!"

Far above and behind them, they heard the blast of Kamose's trumpets.

Moses looked out over the expanse of water to the other side, where the tall mountains of Sinai towered, secret and mysterious. He held up his rod in both hands, high over his head. As he did, the earth shook again. A whole section of the hillside shivered and went crashing into the water. The animals brayed with fright. People shrieked and clung to each other.

Then, suddenly, the bight before them emptied, as if some giant force were sucking the water out to sea. A great awestruck wail was loosed from the mouths of the thousands gathered at the bottom of the slope.

Aaron stared. "You don't mean to tell me God told you to—"

"To cross the bight on dry land," Moses finished, nodding. "Quickly, all of you! There's no time to lose!"

At the top, Kamose looked down. "What is going on down there? I've never seen anything like that! Don't tell me that the sorcerer is creating a mass illusion like the ones Apedemek and he did that day. . . ."

"Majesty," someone ventured, "if it's only an illusion, they're going to drown. There was a deep bay there only a moment ago."

"But look! It's dry! They're actually going out on it! And the bottom's solid enough for them to drive the pack animals onto it! That means it'll hold the chariots! Come on! We're going after them!"

"Sire, is that wise?"

"Anywhere they can go, we can go too! And out in the middle of that area, I've got them where I want them! Out there, we can move faster than they can! Come along! Now's our chance!"

The Egyptian advance guard, with Kamose in the lead, moved slowly but confidently down the slope.

"I don't believe this," Aaron marveled. "One moment the sea was here, and now we're walking across dry land, solid and even."

Moses glanced back quickly. "Tell the people they're not

bound by the order to maintain their columns anymore. Tell them to hurry! We're almost there!"

Far to their rear, Kamose reached what had been the nearer shore. He had carefully guided his horse down the slope, one hand on the brake of the chariot, and when he stood on dry land, he cried out in triumph. "It's solid! It's dry! It's real! Come on, men! They're trapped out there!"

Scarcely waiting for the others to catch up with him, he grasped the reins and urged his horse forward, blood lust in his eyes!

XXVIII

"Come on!" Moses cried. "We're almost there! Quickly now!"

He looked back. Zipporah and Gershom were faring well. But a young mother, holding a baby to her breast and a toddler in front of her, was feebly trying to quiet the onager on which they rode; the skittish animal refused to move, shaking its black head and braying with terror.

It isn't over, Moses realized. *The animals always know first.* "Here," he offered to the woman. "Let me help you." He took the reins and held them fast; with his free hand he stroked the little animal's nose as he guided it toward the shore. Looking around, Moses saw that the columns had disintegrated into a broad, disorganized mob. Some people had reached the shore and were leading the animals up the far slope; others were hurrying along, forcing the last measure of strength out of themselves and the onagers.

Again he looked back. Kamose's chariots were racing madly across the dried seabed, and behind them, the horsemen were pouring down the slope to join them. The bowmen on the chariots were nocking arrows on their longbows.

Moses urged the onagers forward. *Oh, God of Israel*, he prayed, eyes closed tightly, *help us in our time of need!*

He opened his eyes to see the chariots gaining on them.

Then there came a sound like none he had ever heard. And what he saw was so incredible, he could not believe his eyes.

When he looked out to where the Red Sea had inexplicably retreated, a huge wave was advancing upon them, growing in height with every beat of his heart!

"To the shore!" he bellowed. "Now! Faster! Faster!"

Behind them, Kamose and his chariots advanced at a full gallop, heedless of the suddenly irregular ground underfoot!

Moses looked again toward the sea. The wave was far, far over a man's head and was building!

"To shore!" he cried again, watching as, ahead of him, his people were climbing the slopes, desperately dragging the animals. Women helped their children gain toeholds on the steep hillside. The young frantically supported the old. Halfway up the slope he saw Dathan staggering upward under the weight of a young woman he was carrying. Behind him, Neftis pulled Pepi by the arm. He looked around for Aaron and Iri but could not see them.

Behind him only a few stragglers remained. "Quickly!" he urged. He gave the woman's donkey a sharp whack on the rear that propelled it a few steps up the slope, then he turned to help an elderly man guide his animal onto the path.

Moses looked out to sea, and what he saw struck panic into his heart. The wave, ten times the height of a tall man, towered over the charioteers in the middle of the bight. Like the fist of a vengeful god, it was poised over them.

Moses helped one last straggler onto the path and then lunged after him and scrambled up the slope, his heart pounding wildly. Only when he had crawled many steps up the rocky hillside did he dare to look back.

The wave entered the bight and grew to an even more enormous height. Then it crashed down on the chariots and horsemen with tremendous force, crushing them. The sound was deafening as the wave struck. The earth shook as if a tremor had rippled through it. The great convulsive shudder beneath Moses dislodged his grip, and he slid down several feet before a hand—Iri's—grabbed him tightly by the arm.

The water lashed out at them, and the wave crashed high on the slope, drenching them with its spray.

But then it withdrew; the waters pulled back as the earth rearranged itself after its moment of madness. The upheaval had stranded the little bay, and the great wave, having done its damage and left a path of destruction wherever it touched, receded.

The crowd on the hillside now exhaled a low moan, for scattered across the newly created dry land was the whole of Kamose's striking force. All dead—men, horses—and the chariots smashed. Nothing but devastation met the eyes as far as the Habiru could see.

Moses tilted his head. Up the slope Dathan cast a chastened eye on the scene below. His hands shook, and his eyes held immense sorrow at the sight of his enemies, scattered and broken against the floor of the bay.

Moses climbed to join him and put a hand on his arm. "Dathan," he said gently, "get your young men together. There's something you must do for me."

Dathan, stunned, could not answer.

"Go out and gather up their arms," Moses said in a low voice. "These, now, are the weapons God wishes us to have."

Dathan just stared at him.

Moses took his arm and assisted him down the hill. "Everything you said is still true: We will need weapons when we enter Canaan. Go and gather them up."

As if awaking from a nightmare, Dathan turned and beckoned to his men. Iri scrambled down the hill. "Moses, did you foresee this?" He swallowed hard.

Moses clapped him on the back reassuringly. "I knew that God would provide. Come. We will arm our people, Iri. Yours and mine. We are a family now!"

The look on Iri's ruddy face was enough reward for a thousand favors.

At the bottom of the slope they found a lone surviving Egyptian, who, galloping hard, had almost reached the shore when the wave struck. He had been lifted high by the water and dashed against the rocky hillside. His face was a mass of red, and he had many broken bones. When Dathan and Iri tried to move him, he cried out weakly in terrible pain.

Iri drew back, recognizing the man. "I know you! You're Merasar, aren't you? Merasar, of the Third Troop?"

"Iri," the man gasped. "B-beware!"

His voice hadn't much force behind it; his chest had been crushed by the wave. Iri leaned down, putting his ear close to the soldier's bleeding lips. "Yes, old friend?" he said in a voice of infinite gentleness and sympathy.

"Beware. T-tell Moses not to go . . . up the Arabah . . ."

"Moses!" Iri cried. "Come here!" He did not wait for Moses' arrival. "Why?" he asked, bending close to the fallen man.

"T-trap," Merasar whispered. "Everywhere. Amasis sent m-messengers. All routes to C-Canaan . . . guarded by Egyptians."

Iri looked up at Moses. "Did you hear that?"

Moses nodded.

Iri bent over the dying man again. "*All* routes? Or just the known ones?"

"Trade routes . . . wherever wells . . ."

Iri again exchanged glances with Moses. "The soldiers," he said to Merasar again. "They have orders to ambush us?"

"Yes. F-find new way . . ."

The words faded, and Merasar's life faded with them. The light died in his eyes, and then he was gone.

The columns were reassembling at the top of the plateau's far slope. Zipporah and Gershom stood by Moses. From this vantage they could see where the track circling the bight had once been; a rockfall, most likely precipitated by the series of quakes, had cut it in half. Beyond the washed-out portion, the road was narrow but serviceable.

Moses and Aaron stood looking at it. "We can't go that way," Aaron said. "There's no reason to doubt the word of a dying man." He sighed. "So now Amasis is undisputed king. Well, he can have it. I hope never to see Egypt again."

Moses was frowning down at the winding road. "There's only one thing to do. We're going to strike out through the wilderness." He pointed. "*That* way."

"Do you know where it goes?"

"More or less. To Canaan."

"But there's no road!"

"God will look out for us. Do you doubt that now?"

Aaron thought about the miracle he had just witnessed. "No, not at all." He embraced his brother, and when he drew back his eyes were wet. "Lead us where you will. We'll follow."

Moses looked up at the forbidding mountains, then at the cloudless sky. Hard days lay ahead, but they had successfully weathered the first of many storms. This day's events would mark the life of every Habiru man, woman, and child, and the tale would doubtless be told and retold for countless generations.

It had been a long road here, one that had led through many adventures, changes of direction, and even a change of identity. The road ahead was even longer and, no doubt, led to stranger experiences. But it had one advantage for Moses: Before, he had been struggling to gain knowledge of where he was going. Now he knew. And that made all the difference. It was not a journey through uncharted wilderness anymore; it was instead a journey through the vast and infinite mind of God, and along this unimaginable road, nothing could harm them but themselves. They had made a covenant for all time; only their failures could break it.

He smiled, then ruffled his son's hair. "Let's go home . . . wherever it turns out to be." Bold and confident, he took the first steps toward the mysterious North and the unknown homeland they had never seen.

Aaron stared after him. Then he became aware of Iri standing at his elbow. He shook his head. "For this he gave up a crown," Aaron mused. "Was there ever anyone like him?" His own shake of the head answered his question for him. "Come along, Armorer. We've a war to fight and a home to win!"

And the single walker became a file, and the file became a long line, and the long line became an army, and the army became a nation.

And an end became a beginning.

Epilogue

The wind had quieted, and the younger children, beyond the firelight, were asleep. The Teller of Tales looked out and counted the pairs of unblinking eyes in the darkness, watching him.

"Thus ended the exile of the children of Jacob in Egypt," he said. "Now begins the long story of their return to the Land of Promise.

"Tomorrow you shall hear of the days of wrath, when great upheavals shook the lands beside the Great Sea. Old empires fell before the onslaught of new invaders. War divided brother and brother. And the Sea Peoples, newcomers to the coast of Canaan, swept through the western lands as the sons of Jacob worked their way across the eastern and southern wastes and, armed by the Sons of the Lion, moved steadily toward an inevitable confrontation with the foreign invaders.

"As the great Moses grew old, there arose a stalwart young hero to take his place: a mighty warrior and wise general named Joshua, at whose hands the fledgling nation would become a mighty race of conquering heroes, whose tribes would sweep through the land and claim it for their own, even as the invaders gathered on their shores. Invaders," he said after a pause, "bearing weapons of iron . . ."

There was a last rush of interest, and the crowd leaned forward. But the old man raised his hand. "Tomorrow," he promised. "Tomorrow . . ."